Demon Princess

Volume 2

J. J. Pavlov

Academy Days

ISBN 978-3-9819877-3-7

To the many helpers and obstacles
that came and went along the way
all of which made me what I am today.

Chapter 24

Kongenssoevn

The Isdalen plains is a vast glacial valley that begins deeper in the Kongensgrad, somewhere to the south of The Maw. It reaches all the way down to the Gletsjersoen, the massive lake at the edge of which Kongenssoevn was built. There are no remains of the glacier to be seen, meaning that the lake most likely formed when it melted. Many rivers flow down from the mountains and feed it with fresh water.

The sheer size of the Gletjersoen has given rise to some people claiming that it's an inland sea, even though the water is fresh and various river fish are living in it. Due to its natural connection to the capital, many cities have been built around it, and a fleet of trade ships are sailing the gentle waters at all times.

We walk down the flank of the mountain, which leads down towards Kongenssoevn in an almost perfectly straight descent. The glacier has flattened the landscape, although it left behind many rocks and boulders that used to be trapped in the ice, scattering pieces of the mountains across the plains. Some have runic carvings on them, and others were sculpted into faces of prominent figures - according to the bard's explanations as we pass them.

The sun reaches its zenith when we're on the final stretch of our journey right before the city walls. And what magnificent walls they are. Even from a distance, I can tell that they are well-maintained and manned with attentive patrols. The east-facing main gate, which we're approaching right now, is open and guarded by a group of half a dozen soldiers on either side. They're watching the people entering and leaving, sometimes inspecting those that travel by carriage, have a lot of merchandise, or carry weapons.

The surrounding landscape has made way for fields, which lie barren due to the season; the harvest has already been completed, and the plain dwellers are waiting for winter to come down from the mountains, where it has already fully covered the summits in snow. The days have been growing noticeably shorter, too.

When we approach the gate, the guards obviously stop us to ask for our reason to enter the city. Rolan has a sword at his hip, and Gram's large shield can't be missed either. While Luna's staff is less conspicuous, the fact that it's a mage's catalyst is evident due to the gems embedded in its tip.

The biggest problem is Kamii. While her cursed arm hasn't barred us from any of the smaller cities and villages, the capital might have different rules regarding the handling of demonic corruption. And due to the still mild temperatures around here, she's not wearing her heavy cloak, which puts her right arm on full display.

When she steps forward from behind me, the guard who first sees her draws his breath sharply. The expression on his face is a mix of surprise and mild disgust, but since he doesn't look alarmed, he most likely won't refuse us entry. He comes over to check on Kamii's arm, puts a hand on the top of his helmet, as if to keep it from flying off, before waving at a bearded man surveying everything from a small elevated platform.

"Captain, you might wanna see this." He calls out to him. The captain wears the exact same suit of armor as all the other soldiers, except for a bronze embellishment on his right pauldron, which signifies his rank.

"What is- oh." When the captain sees Kamii, his words get stuck in his throat. An expression of pity fills his face as he looks into the little dark elf's eyes. "Poor thing."

"Is this going to be a problem?" Stepping between the man and Kamii, I ask in a defiant tone. I don't like the fact that he seems to be looking at her like one would regard a lame pet.

"Ah, no." My attitude actually intimidates him a little, as he averts his eyes in embarrassment. I guess he noticed that his show of pity was out of line, considering the little dark elf appears to be doing quite well.

"Can we pass then?" Taking a step forward and asking in a forceful tone, I try to cut this inspection short. "We're tired from our journey through the mountain and would like to rest."

"Through the mountain?" Raising an eyebrow, the guard captain gives me a skeptical look, before shifting his gaze towards my companions.

"That is right." The bard comes forward and speaks in a calming tone meant to ease the tension in the air. "We went through the former dwarven kingdom, and I need to inform you that the Bridge of Enleith has been destroyed."

"The Graebern did that?" The captain turns to the bard and scratches his rugged beard with a troubled expression. "We'll have to notify the other side, lest there are others who try to go through that route and find themselves at a dead end. Could I ask you to come with me to file a report?"

"Yes, if you let my friends pass, I'd be glad to accompany you right away." With a nod and a sly smile, the bard implies his compliance comes with the aforementioned cost. The guards exchange glances with each other, but ultimately it's their leader who decides.

"Alright, you may pass." He furrows his brows but judges that getting the information right now is more important than checking a group of obvious adventurers. Still, he turns to Daica, whom he most likely identifies as Kamii's mother due to her mature appearance - even though she's actually the little sister - and adds a condition. "But please make sure that the young lady doesn't wander off on her own. In the capital, cursed people without their guardians will be taken into custody."

I don't intend to leave Kamii alone in either case, but the fact that cursed people are being discriminated against like this doesn't sit well with me. But to expedite our entry into the city, I remain quiet about it and watch as Daica demonstratively puts an arm around the little dark elf's shoulder with a thoughtful gaze that tells me she understands the situation.

Thus, with the bard staying behind to report at the guard post, we enter the capital. The bustling main street is wide enough to accommodate six carriages at once and leads all the way through the city, across a large square, to the bridge connecting to the island on which the citadel stands tall.

At one glance I can tell that this place was built to last; all the houses are made of stone, unlike in the cities we passed on our journey. The streets are paved and clean, and most of all, I can see that they have a sewage system judging by grates covering holes in the ground. The only other city I've seen this in so far was Hovsgaerden - leaving aside the seemingly technologically superior

Dominion, that is.

Even though I thought that many things in this world were too much like in a fantasy story the architecture looks quite normal. Especially the palace, which I expected to have an obscene amount of impossibly tall towers that nobody would want to climb in real life, appears incredibly practical in design, with only one tower that juts out at more than twice the height of the second tallest one.

Our final destination for the day is the adventurer guild, to deliver the package from Ingrid and register our relocation from Hovsgaerden. I doubt we'll do anything else after that for today or just go to sleep after that marathon through the mountain.

As we walk down the main road, I notice that the people are staring at us unabashedly. We do make for a colorful procession, with Gram towering above most people by a head drawing the first looks. But after that, their eyes naturally stick onto Kamii and her right arm, as well as on the beautiful Daica. Some also notice Senka, whom I'm carrying in my arms, and give me unpleasant glances.

While she has gotten used to crowded places, the little dark elf is clinging to me and seems intimidated by the sheer number of people. Judging by the size of this city when viewed from afar, it should have several times Hovsgaerden's number of inhabitants.

"Kongenssoevn has a population of over eight hundred thousand people." Gram explains when I ask him. It's really little, compared to what I'm used to from my previous life, but for this world, it's a considerable number. Hovsgaerden is considered a capital on the other side of the mountains separating the Slaettermark and the Isdalen plains, but it only had one eight of that.

When I remember the report about the Alliance Army

losing six hundred thousand soldiers, I'm awed by how significant of a blow that must have been to the humans. It was a number close to this entire kingdom's capital city's population.

Also, the whole nation has about fourteen million inhabitants.

I don't know how big the kingdom is, but fourteen million is quite a small number when compared to Japan. Judging by the living standards outside of big cities and the fact that large-scale wars against the demons must happen frequently, I guess mortality rates are still pretty high. There don't seem to be that many old people, so the average age is much lower than that of modern-day nations.

Overall, they don't have a proper healthcare system even when there's magic that can heal many wounds almost instantly. The main reason must be that light affinity is rare, and the church is keeping a monopoly on it. Our party is quite privileged to have me, then.

The adventurer guild is located on the main city square just like the one in Hovsgaerden. It's much larger and looks much more impressive than any I've seen before, owing to the fact that this must be the central office of the entire guild network. The structure itself has all the makings of an official government building, with a set of marble stairs leading up to its two-winged mahogany door.

However, the most remarkable feature is that to the right of the guild stands a large mausoleum seemingly cut from granite itself. All the other buildings around it were constructed at a respectful distance from its overbearingly monolithic shape as if fearing that its contents may spill out at any moment. But the entrance is open, and I see people going in and out wearing adventurer gear.

"That must be the entrance to the Lost Tombs." Rolan comments in an awestruck tone. He mentioned it before when we were discussing our relocation to the capital, and it struck me as a name fitting for a dungeon. Now that I see it for myself, it's evident that it's exactly what it sounded like.

Somehow I feel like I could clear it all with a single Libera Animar.

"We are not going there right now. Come on." Luna nudges the leader with her elbow and walks ahead. He exchanges a glance with the big man and shrugs with a resigned smile.

The inside of the guild hall is more lavishly decorated than the one in Hovsgaerden, with a hotel-like reception area and a large crystal chandelier hanging from the ceiling. On the right-hand side stands a gallery of statues, most likely featuring famous people from both past and present. To our left is the actual gathering hall, where long dining tables and couches arranged in circles provide a communal space.

Rolan and Luna head over to the receptionist to fulfill Ingrid's request, while I follow Gram towards the dining hall. It's past lunchtime, so there aren't many people lounging around in there, but the smell of food still lingers.

"Let's get something to eat." I look at Daica and Kamii, and they both agree with nods of varying enthusiasm. The former, despite her appearance, eats as little as any normal dark elf. The latter is a prime adult specimen of her kind - except for the fact that she has a giant crab pincer in place of her right forearm - but she easily consumes as much as Gram does, if not more.

"Shouldn't we wait for Sigurd?" The big man scratches the back of his head and gestures behind himself in the general direction of the gate we just entered the city through. Then his stomach grumbles and he covers it with one hand while looking at me with surprised round eyes.

"He won't fault us for starting without him, especially since we only had a quite meager breakfast after we came out from The Maw." I grin at Gram and walk ahead. Since the path from the exit of the mountain to the capital takes only half a day, we decided to carry on so that we could rest in actual beds. That's why we ate a few dried rations on the move and skipped lunch to eat a proper big meal a couple of hours later.

Needless to say, everyone is incredibly tired and hungry at this point, and even with a tireless body, I'm feeling mental exhaustion from staying up so long without rest. But for now, the smell of grilled meat is making my mouth water, and all thoughts about sleep are blown away by the prospect of finally getting some good food again - not to discredit the big man's home cooking skills.

The two lovers join us shortly before the waitress brings the drinks and food we ordered. This establishment is on a different level compared to any we've been to before, featuring a large variety of dishes and quick service.

Not long after we begin, the bard enters the guild hall, and Gram waves him over. He filled an extra plate in case the big eaters - Kamii and I - didn't leave anything before he arrived, and pushes it over to him.

"Alright, it's official now." Rolan lifts his ale for a toast. "We're in Kongenssoevn, and we're here to stay!"

We clink jugs and take big thirsty gulps. As always, the dark elves don't drink any alcohol, and the same is true for the half-elf Luna. It must be a physiological thing for them after all.

In turn, I drink enough on my own to cover their share, even though I'm technically still three years from legal drinking age in Japan. I died and reincarnated into the body of a demon, so there's no point in worrying about conventions from my previous life anymore. After all, I've killed humans, too.

"So, when do you want to go to the academy?" Rolan asks during the meal, directed at either Luna or me.

"We still need to visit the Cathedral of Light and meet Arcelia Crux. I doubt that we will be able to enter the citadel without her written recommendation." Luna is the one who answers since I'm having a mouthful of the roast potato. I didn't know the academy was located within the citadel, but maybe the castle I saw was actually it. "But I believe we should rest for today and go tomorrow."

"I agree." Swallowing the food in my mouth, I quickly add with a glance at Daica and Kamii. The latter doesn't show it as she chows down on her food, but they're both exhausted after the forced march through the entire night. Everybody hasn't slept for over thirty hours now, and it's becoming visible in how sluggish they move despite their seemingly high spirits.

"Alright, we'll get rooms in the guild lodgings and take a good long rest today, before going to the Cathedral of Light first thing tomorrow." The leader makes the final decision on the matter.

After dinner, we get our room keys and quickly separate into our groups. As always, Kamii and Daica are staying with me, while the two lovebirds get one room and the two men get another. Tonight nobody is thinking about doing anything steamy, and after taking baths in turn - with the two sisters going in together and then me cleaning myself and Senka - everybody heads to bed immediately.

As I look up at the unfamiliar ceiling thinking about the events since the last time I slept, excitement wells up inside me. The encounter with the Graebern was quite dangerous for my companions, so I shouldn't look back at it as some light-hearted fun. But if I hadn't died and come to this world, I would have never experienced something like this.

Turning my head, I gaze upon Daica in the bed next to the one I share with Kamii. Both dark elves have fallen asleep already and are breathing rhythmically. I'm sure they both could have done without this excitement, but it'll be an event the bard can spin a legend around. And to me at least, being part of something like that does sound quite enticing.

I find myself drifting into sleep, as I stroke Kamii's hair and listen to her soft breaths.

The next morning we leave the room and go to the guild hall for breakfast. The two dark elves look well-rested, and the fatigue from the all-nighter marathon has disappeared after sleeping for more than half a day. But now Daica is complaining about sore muscles and back pains. I have an idea about where the latter is coming from when I glance at her chest, which can easily rival Maou-mama's.

"Do you want a massage?" I wiggle my fingers at the big dark elf suggestively and grin.

"N-no, it's alright." With a blush, she refuses my offer and quickly walks ahead of me. She's easily embarrassed and will make decisions unfavorable to her when pressed even slightly. From the tips of her ears, which are turning reddish-purple, I can tell that she actually wanted to receive a massage from me.

"I want one." Kamii tugs on my arm with her normal left hand and looks up at me with a straightforward gaze. She has been quite outspoken about receiving favors and coddling from me and is becoming increasingly proactive in bed as well.

"I'll give you one later then." Although I meant it as a joke when I offered it to Daica, now that her older sister has asked me for it I can only comply. I have a sweet spot for her after all.

When we arrive at the bottom of the stairs, the first person I notice is Rolan. He's standing at the notice board, already looking for jobs. I'm sure seeing the entrance to the Lost Tombs has ignited the adventurer flame in his heart.

"Hey leader, don't forget our goals for today." I say as I walk past him. He spins around in surprise and blinks at me.

"A-ah yeah." Scratching the back of his head, he follows me to the table where Gram and the bard are already sitting with Luna. It seems that they have already finished their meals and were waiting for me and the others.

We quickly begin with our breakfast, consisting of eggs sunny-side up, sweet bread and jam, and a guild special yogurt. I'm impressed at the quality and can't help but wonder just how much all this costs. The leader is taking care of the party funds after all.

Then it dawns on me: He was looking at the quest board because he understands that if we stay here without finding work, we'll run out of money quickly. I guess we do need to stock up a little before I can go off to the academy with Luna - this party would lose both their main damage dealer and their healer.

"After we get the letter of recommendation from Lady Crux, we can take a look into the Lost Tombs. I'm quite interested in it, too." I make sure not to show that I've seen through his troubles and casually remark while eating.

"Oh, that would be great!" But Rolan's almost desperate quickness in replying ruins my attempt at tact. Acting like I didn't notice it, I smile at him while thinking that Luna must have it pretty hard with his sometimes thickheaded behavior.

When we finish our meals and motion to depart the guild hall, I walk over to the quest board and take a look at the things posted there. There's one big list of items, most likely relics, that are confirmed to be in the dungeon, with some of them struck out. Most likely those have been found, while others are still missing in its depths.

I'm sure that if we find one of those named items, this party could be set for a while and won't have to worry about money. It's highly unlikely that things will go so smoothly though, and like any dungeon in games, there will be more difficult obstacles the deeper one goes. These relics should be somewhere really deep, or they would have been found already simply because there are so many adventurers going in and out all the time.

"Are you coming, Chloe?" Now it's the leader who calls me to move away from the quest board. When I walk over and join the party at the entrance door, he grins at me. "Found something interesting?"

"Yes, let's go for the Tomb King's Fortune." It was the relics at the very top of the list, which looked like it was arranged in order of difficulty rating. It sounds more like a treasure hoard than a single item, but that's what makes it so much more interesting.

"As expected of the missy." Gram raises his voice in laughter and pats me on the back hard. "Choosing the most difficult one from the get-go."

"Lady Marcott wishes to spread her name further, even before becoming known as the woman with all magic affinities." The bard strums his lute once and speaks with a charming smile. "I will make sure that your legend will be retold far and wide."

"Let us be more realistic." Luna doesn't look amused, thinking I was joking around.

"Yeah, even though the Tomb King's Fortune is on that

list due to historical evidence, at this point it has already faded into myth. How many people do you think have tried to find it and failed so far? Many paid with their lives, you know?" Rolan sighs in resignation.

Well, this matter can wait until after we return from the Cathedral of Light. I'll let them think I'm just joking for a while longer and then hit them over the head with acting on my words at the time. They'll have to follow up on my actions then since they definitely won't abandon me.

The Cathedral of Light is a towering monument on par with the castle on the island - sans the tallest tower. Even from The Maw, I could see the belfry jutting out from the surrounding houses which are all around four or five stories tall. Intricate figures carved from stone adorn the arch above the entrance, and the beautifully ornamented wooden doors look like they alone cost a fortune.

As with the church in Hovsgaerden, two honor guards in full armor and wielding halberds are standing guard on either side of the entrance. I already know that they won't let Kamii enter, so I ask Gram to stay outside with her; out of all the humans, she trusts him the most. At the same time, I suggest to Daica that she should take a look around the city for any locations where she might want to set up her new shop. This way, they won't have to wait in front of the cathedral for who knows how long our business might take.

With a worried expression, the little dark elf raises her hand as if fearing that we won't see each other again. We're inside the capital, so I'm sure nothing will happen. To take her mind off of waiting, she could go with her sister, though I'll leave that up to her.

"Don't worry. The big man will protect you while I'm away." I pet Kamii's hair and allay her fears. "We'll meet back out here at noon."

When the overly dramatic separation is complete, we finally walk up the stairs to the entrance of the cathedral and past the guards silently watching us. I suppress the urge to glare at them but remind myself that they're just doing their job.

Pushing open the doors, we're greeted by the smell of incense. The interior is just as grand as the exterior suggested. Delicate stained glass windows with iconographic motifs are let into the walls periodically, and the sunlight shining through them creates colorful images on the floor. The ceiling is so high up that one feels dwarfed by its sheer size, instilling a sense of awe that is only adequate for this sanctified place.

In the side aisles, both male and female clerics talk to each other in respectfully lowered voices. Citizens of noticeably different social standings sit as equals on the long benches praying, facing the larger-than-life female statue in the chancel. The woman is carved from marble and easily stands at four times my height. She has her eyes closed, and a gentle smile graces her lips. Her left hand rests on the center of her chest, and her right arm is outstretched at the height of her waist, the palm facing up as if sowing seeds. It's the religious gesture that Arcelia performed when she said her farewell blessings in Hovsgaerden back then.

"This feels a little oppressive." Rolan comments while looking around in awe. He has most likely never been in a building as spacious as this one before.

"Is it alright to just ask for Lady Crux?" With a hesitant glance at the clerics, Luna puts forward this question. I know what she means; it would feel weird to walk up to one of the monks or nuns and simply ask them to call Arcelia for us.

"Please leave that to me." The bard suddenly says with a reassuring smile, and a bad feeling wells up inside me. I hope he's not going to do what I think he's going to do.

Mirroring my exact fears, he walks over to the most beautiful nun and chats her up while putting up a charming expression. I can practically see the flowers blossom behind him as his perfectly white teeth seem to sparkle under no light in particular.

She actually blushes under his gentle pushiness and looks positively flustered, so he takes it as his cue to begin properly flirting with her. I think he's annoying, but it seems his ways work well with the women of this world. If it brings results, I'll close my eyes to his behavior, though I will never condone it.

"Sister Birthe has been incredibly cooperative and agreed to call Lady Crux for us." The bard returns to us and winks in mild triumph. "The Saint of Luminosity has some free time now, after being swamped with work due to the demon attack back then."

The demon attack in question occurred more than a month ago, and it wasn't even on this continent, so I wonder what kind of work she was swamped with. After all, it hit the Empire of Terminus, which is only in a loose alliance with the Kingdom of Lares. But I don't know the intricacies of the church, so it might just have been replying to letters from scared citizens and putting their concerns to rest.

"Miss Marcott! It is a pleasure to see you again." Arcelia's voice echoes through the cathedral, and I turn to see her approaching from a side chapel. She's dressed in a pure white robe just like the first time we met, but there's a white coif covering the golden hair she was showing off back then. As always, her eyes are closed, but it's obvious that she's somehow able to see us.

"The pleasure is all mine, Lady Crux." I greet her with a bow and reply truthfully. She's going to get me into the Royal Academy, so of course, I'm glad to meet her.

"How was your journey from Hovsgaerden?" She asks with a smile. I'm sure she was traveling safely over the King's Pass since she most likely didn't have a deadline for getting here.

"He can tell the story better than anybody else here." I gesture towards the bard, sidestepping the job while avoiding to give away the fact that I never really bothered to learn his name. What was it again? It rhymes with yogurt that much I know.

"My, your words are too kind, Lady Marcott." The yogurt in question steps forward and remarks with a bow. "Then let this simple bard recount the tale of our travels."

"You were really fortunate to have survived such perils." Arcelia leans back in her chair and comments when the bard finishes. We have relocated to her personal office, a neat space with a couch and tea table for guests.

Her expression has been neutral for the most part, but she showed deep concern towards the end when the story got to the Graebern attack and our escape.

"The magic I learned from the scriptures you gave me saved our lives." Without the shield, we wouldn't be here. At least nobody aside from me would be here since I'm immune to arrows. "You have my deepest gratitude, Lady Crux."

"It is only natural for a priestess of Belys to offer help to the virtuous, and bring salvation to the wicked." She waves her hand and speaks in a saintly tone. If her view on who's virtuous and who's wicked isn't twisted, she shouldn't be a bad person. If this religion has members like her and elevates them to such high posts, then maybe it isn't as bad as they usually are in these stories - even if they are the enemies of demonkind.

"Umm, excuse me if I'm rushing things since we have people waiting for us." I glance out the window to see where the sun stands. It has been at least an hour since we came in here since the bard started the story from when we attacked the illegal slave trade bastion and freed Kamii. "We came here to speak about the offer for us to attend the Royal Academy."

"No, do not worry. I can understand from Sigurd's tale that you really care about the cursed dark elves." Arcelia nods with a gentle smile. "Miss Marcott, your compassion is most commendable. I hope that your love, which can even reach the pariahs of society, will bring about great change in the rigid views of the people."

"... thank you." I don't really understand what she means, but it seems that she can accept cursed beings much more readily than others within her religion. Her sainthood isn't just for show.

"As for the recommendation to the Royal Academy, I will write them for you right away. Please wait a moment." With these words, the Saint of Luminosity takes a few sheets of papers and picks up a quill pen. Even though her eyes are closed, she begins to write without any issues.

I've seen several people use quills before; among others the guild master in Hovsgaerden, Ingrid. It seems to be reserved for people in higher positions though, as the receptionists at guild halls used dip pens with metal tips. The strokes created from quills look more elegant and refined, so maybe it's to differentiate letters by important people from common notes.

When Arcelia finishes writing, she gently sways one of the sheets of paper in her hand to dry the ink, before finally folding it up. Doing the same with the other, she puts each into a separate envelope, then closes them. Lighting a candle and bringing out a stick of red wax, she begins heating the tip of it until it starts to liquefy. Dripping the red wax onto the letter and pressing a seal into it, she makes it official.

I can't help but watch in silent admiration. The practiced motions remind me of calligraphy and tea ceremony, which both soothe my usually restless mind. Even though I'm the type that prefers an active lifestyle - otherwise I wouldn't have been in the track and field club - I do like to indulge in slow-paced disciplines that require more mind than matter sometimes.

"Here is an entry permit to the citadel. You will be able to meet the principal of the Royal Academy directly with this." Holding up a separate piece of paper, Arcelia explains the procedure for when we go to the citadel. "You may be required to undergo a test, but I am sure you will pass without any issues."

Even though she already checked my affinities, she directs this at me as much as she does it at Luna. After all, even if I have every magic affinity, I might not be able to use them properly. Still, I could use light magic without even practicing, so it should be no different in the case of the other elements.

"This is an opportunity few ever get. How can we repay you, Lady Crux?" The half-elf lowers her head and shows her sincere gratitude.

"Study and become strong, so that you can help those in need. Knowing that you will stay true to your convictions and lead a life you can be proud of is more than enough for me." Arcelia's radiant smile seems to cleanse the soul. She's expecting an unspoken promise, never to use what we may learn at the Royal Academy for evil purposes.

Unfortunately, I won't be able to keep that promise. My existence itself is evil in the eyes of humanity. If she knew that she's helping me - a demon - get more powerful, her faith would most likely be shaken.

Chapter 25

The Royal Academy

When we come out of the Cathedral of Light, the sun suggests that it's already past noon. I spot Gram and Kamii sitting on a bench next to the fountain; the latter is eating something reminiscent of a crêpe, and her legs are dangling playfully. Next to her is a small pile of empty paper bags, and the big man is looking at her with an expression of baffled resignation. It seems he bought her a lot of snacks to keep her mind off of the fact that I'm not here.

"There you are!" Gram notices us and calls out to me in a relieved tone while waving. Kamii must have begun to eat into his funds, so now that I'm back, he doesn't need to keep on doing it anymore. The little dark elf turns towards us and her eyes widen.

"Mahkotoh!" She immediately puts down her food and runs over to me, jumping into my arms.

"Sorry to make you wait." I mutter as she nuzzles into my chest. "Thanks for keeping her company, big man."

"Don't worry about it. So, how'd it go?" Bringing over the crêpe Kamii so carelessly left on the bench, Gram twirls his magnificent mustache.

"We got the letters of recommendation and could go to the citadel right away." Showing him the sealed letter, I reply. Then I turn to Rolan with a mischievous grin. "Or do you want to try exploring the Lost Tombs while we're still with you?"

"H-huh? Ah, no, that's alright." Taken by surprise, the leader stutters to find an answer. "Strike the iron while it's hot, as they say."

"Are you sure? You might not have us for a while after this." I put an arm around Luna's shoulder and pull her in demonstratively. I'm quite interested to know how they're going to fare without their mage since before I joined she was their only real damage output. Rolan will have to do it then, as the big man is a shield-bearer, and I don't ever see the bard filling that role.

"We came here so that you can attend the academy. Don't worry about us; we'll find a way." He crosses his arms and speaks in a confident tone.

"If you say so." I shrug and pet Kamii's hair. "Hm, where's Daica?"

"She took your advice and is going around town looking for any place where she might be able to set up her new store." The big man answers my question and scratches his chin. "I've noticed that prices here are quite a bit higher than in Hovsgaerden and I'm sure rent won't be an exception."

"We'll see what she has found out later then." I reply with a shrug. If she can't handle it alone, I might be able to help her out with my stipend from the academy. But that's for when I know the numbers. "Is she going to return to the guild hall on her own?"

"Yes, she told us not to wait for her and have lunch on our own. She'll be back before sundown."

"That reminds me, I do feel hungry." At these words,

all but Kamii freeze up. They know my legendary appetite, so they must be fearing for their funds again. But I still have my own money, and if we run out, we can always go for a quest before my enrolment. "Let's go have lunch!"

Gram is staring at Kamii with his fork stopped halfway to his open mouth. The little dark elf ate so many sweet pastries and snacks while waiting for us that he thought she wouldn't be hungry anymore, but she has finished her second plate before finally showing that she's full.

Everybody else is worried about the fact that she has a much smaller body than me, but seems to be eating as much as I do. They wonder where she's storing all the matter. It makes me think that she may also have a bottomless stomach, even though I'm sure she's not a Crawling Chaos. Maybe it's part of her curse.

We quickly finish our meals and head out towards the Royal Academy, so that we can get it done before sundown. Otherwise, Daica might return to the guild hall and find nobody there, and I can already imagine her flustered expression when that happens.

I've been neglecting Senka in our room for the whole day now, but she can take care of herself. If I bring her, it may cause some troubles because people in this world seem to think that she's in bad taste. My personality might be deemed questionable, and it could become an obstacle to my smooth enrolment.

I will bring her into the academy though, and nothing will stop me from doing so.

The path to the citadel is simple: The city is built in a half-circle around the large open plaza before the bridge that connects the island to the mainland. We walk down the road that connects the gate we entered through yesterday to that plaza. The stores on either side look venerable and are most likely very expensive; this is the city's main street after all.

Even though we can easily see the castle on the island, it still takes us a while of walking to get there. That just goes to show the sheer size of the city as well as the height of the tower. I'm beginning to learn the benefits of modern transportation networks, which I took for granted in my previous life. And I thought Hovsgaerden was big when I had to walk through it all the time.

There's a gatehouse before the bridge, and four soldiers are standing guard in front of it. Unlike the honor guards in front of the cathedral, these don't wear ornamental armor and wield regular spears. Atop the gate, I spot several other men with bows. I'm sure that there are even more inside, in case of an emergency. The portcullis is up, and the wings of the gate are kept open since it's peaceful and the citizens know not to try and enter without permits.

"Halt!" One of the guards calls out to us when we step across an invisible threshold. He's a man in his early thirties with a clean-shaven face and inquisitive brown eyes, the typical appearance of a nameless soldier. "State your business."

"We are here with a recommendation to the Royal Academy." Luna is the one who steps forward, of all people. Usually, the leader would do it, but she's showing some unexpected authority when holding the permit Arcelia gave us in her hand.

"Oh? Please let me see that." The guard takes the permit and skims it, stopping at the bottom where the Saint of Luminosity's seal is placed. He then returns it to Luna and gestures at another guard. "Frodi, guide the guests inside."

"Understood, sir." A young soldier steps up with an eager salute. He's still a fledgling, just around Rolan's age, and is taking everything incredibly seriously. With time, he'll ease into the job and become more cynical for sure.

"Please follow me."

With one hand on the hilt of his sword, Frodi leads the way and walks through the open gate onto the bridge. I finally notice that it has a pretty steep incline, which covers the height difference between the gatehouse at the bottom and the one at the top. It's obviously built with potential sieges in mind, with the steepness rendering battering rams less effective.

The gatehouse at the top of the bridge looks larger than even the ones let into the city walls. This is a real fortress, meant to weather any assault. Half a dozen guards are standing watch here, looking attentive even though the likelihood of something happening up here is incredibly slim.

We're guided through the second gate without even stopping, as the guards see Frodi and assume we have permission. They still keep their eyes on us just in case there's something suspicious. Everybody left their weapons in the guild - although Luna is carrying her staff - so we don't look like we pose a threat.

But there's one suspicious thing that they haven't paid attention yet; while Kamii is wearing a cloak that covers her huge cursed arm completely, that side is still bulging due to the large spikes growing from it. They could have pointed it out and conducted a search on everybody, and we would get a typical human reaction again.

Luckily, that doesn't happen, and we pass through unhindered. The inside of the citadel is a masterpiece of planning, even when compared to the almost perfectly symmetrical city itself. The extensive open grounds are separated into three parts, with the royal palace in the center and a forest-like garden which most likely features a hedge maze to the right.

The Royal Academy is a four-story building with two wings and a central tower that stands at more than twice the height as the surrounding building, which reminds me of pictures of old Western universities. It's easily dwarfed by the palace's tower keep but still reaches an impressive height. The entire building exudes the feeling of a long history.

There's a large grassy field in front of it, where students are relaxing in the shade of a few large trees. Most of them are wearing uniform white shirts, long plaid skirts for girls and trousers for boys, and cloaks or capes held together in the front by a circular brooch that features a crest of a diamond centered above two crossed feathers, which is also displayed above the entrance of the academy.

I spot a few people who are slightly older, wearing cloaks in various colors. They're sitting on the benches along the dirt path and reading books while taking notes. Each one of them has a staff next to them. Corresponding with the colors of the crystals, their clothing sense reveals their affinities. Earthen shades most likely stand for earth magic, deep blue for water, red and brown for fire, and bright shades that go all the way up to white for wind.

"Hello there. May I help you?" A woman with graying red hair wearing a brown cloak approaches us. She appears to be in her early fifties and has the presence of a mage, even though she carries a cane rather than a staff.

"Ah, yes, milady. These guests have a permit from the Saint of Luminosity." Frodi stands at attention before the woman, showing respect that borders on awe. She must be someone important at the academy.

"Is that so? I shall take it from here, thank you." With a friendly smile at the young soldier, the woman turns her attention to us. Her eyes fall on Luna's staff, and she addresses her first. "My name is Astrid Hagen. What do you seek from the Royal Academy?"

"I am Runa Sigint, and this is Chloe Marcott. We come here with a recommendation from Lady Crux, and wish to enroll at the Royal Academy." Luna steps forward and answers with a slightly shaky voice. She must be thinking that Astrid is a powerful mage, considering her more advanced age and the air of confidence surrounding her.

"My, a recommendation from the Saint of Luminosity!" She looks genuinely surprised and glances at me. I'm not carrying anything she can identify as a mage's catalyst, which is why she must have thought that only Luna has business here. "Please follow me."

Thus, we're led towards the main building, where the two-winged wooden doors are kept open at this time of the day. Along the way, we see people of various ages, though it's clear that Astrid is a teacher here. Nobody else is near her age, though there are some who look too old to be regular students.

I think this may be more akin to a university than a school. There are some children around middle school age though, so that theory might not hold true either. Let's observe a little longer before coming to a conclusion. In either case, the atmosphere feels quite relaxed, though an air of academics can be felt throughout the building.

We walk through long hallways and climb several flights of stairs which all look like they were built centuries ago. This academy is ripe with history, and I feel a hint of pride at the thought that I'm going to add my legacy to it.

"If the gentlemen would please wait here. We do not want to crowd the principal's office now, do we?" Astrid opens the door to a waiting room and gestures for Rolan, Gram, and the bard to enter. I'm sure she wanted to ask Kamii to join them, but because the little dark elf is defiantly clinging onto me with seemingly desperate determination, she keeps quiet about her.

We're then led towards a spiral stair in the center of the hallway, just two doors away from where we left the others. It leads up the tower above the main entrance, and when we pass a window, I look out to see the city beyond the citadel walls. The view all the way up there must be incredible.

At the end of the stairs, we reach a richly ornamented wooden door. Astrid knocks, and a man's muffled voice answers, upon which she pushes down the handle, opens the door and gestures for us to enter.

"Grand Master Eklundstrom, I have brought you students with recommendations from the Saint of Luminosity herself." With a nod, our guide explains the occasion. I look into the room and spot a man sitting behind a large wooden desk.

I have to suppress my laughter when I see him. He has long white hair, an extremely long beard that reaches down to his sash, and a wizened face that radiates wisdom. The dark purple robes he wears have bright dots sprinkled onto them like the stars in the sky, and a brimless flattop cap sits atop his head. When he stands up, I can see that he's pretty tall; while not on the level of Gram, he still towers almost a head above me. Inquisitive blue eyes examine Luna and me through square glasses - a first in this world.

If you were to look up the word 'wizard' in a dictionary, you'd see a photo of this guy.

"Thank you, Astrid. You may leave us." His deep voice, tinted with age, is soothing to the ears. He gestures at the couch before us while our guide walks out of the room and closes the door behind herself quietly. "Please, sit."

As Luna and I walk to the couch, we each look around the room. It's much cleaner than that of guild master Ingrid's, but there are still many signs of his line of work lying about. Stacks of documents and scrolls are strewn across his table, and there are many heavy books buried under handwritten notes. There's a bookshelf filled with what must be old magic tomes on one side, and a wall covered with portrait paintings on the other. Each one of the faces looks wise and knowledgeable; they must be all the previous heads of this academy.

"My name is Thorvald Eklundstrom, and I am the fifty-first Grand Master of the Royal Academy." He introduces himself while rounding his desk and waving his bony hand at the paintings. There aren't even twenty portraits here, but it's possible that many of the older ones didn't have one made for them, or they hang elsewhere.

As we sit down, Kamii's coat is flipped open, and her cursed arm becomes fully visible. The principal glances over it, but there's not even a hint of surprise or disgust in his expression. There isn't even self-serving sympathy in his gaze, and instead, he just takes note of it as if it were just an accessory.

He sits down on the couch across from us and crosses his legs while folding his hands on his knee, expecting one of us to begin talking.

"I am Runa Sigint. These are Chloe Marcott and Kamii." Luna introduces the three of us with a respectful nod. "We met Lady Crux in Hovsgaerden, where she noticed Miss Chloe's talent-"

"Ah, I hear that Lady Crux has written letters of recommendation for you?" Thorvald interrupts Luna to preempt a potentially prolonged account of everything that led up to this moment. He must be a busy man, so cutting story time short is understandable.

"Y-yes." Taken by surprise, Luna produces her letter from within her cloak, and I do the same with mine. Thorvald grasps them delicately with his long and thin fingers.

"What about Miss Kamii?" Raising a bushy white eyebrow at the little dark elf, the principal asks for her purpose here.

"She's just accompanying me." I put my arm around her shoulder demonstratively, to show that she's important to me and has all the reason to be here.

"I see." His eyebrow drops again in understanding, as he shows us both a warm smile. Is he suspecting our relationship or just appreciating the closeness between two good friends?

Then his eyes move down to the letters and the seals on them. Opening them carefully, he takes out Luna's first and begins to read what Arcelia has to say about the half-elf mage's talents.

"An affinity for fire, water, and wind, I see. The combination of water and fire is quite rare, even among those with three affinities." He looks into Luna's eyes with an inquisitive gaze, until she averts hers under the invisible pressure. "And a half-elf, I presume."

Luna stares at the principal with her eyes widened in surprise. He could tell at a glance even though her ears are hidden by her hair. There must be some other indicators that I'm missing, which he spotted.

Thorvald then proceeds to read the letter about me, and I keep close attention to his expression. As he gets to the passage I presumed would elicit a response from him, one of his eyebrows shoots up in slight bafflement. It's followed by the other as genuine surprise fills his face.

"All elements?" He looks up from the letter, and we make eye contact. I realize why Luna averted her eyes now because his piercing blue irises makes me feel like he could be reading all my thoughts. But I remain steadfast and return his gaze without blinking.

"I would like to ascertain your affinities right away, Miss Marcott." Thorvald stands up and rounds the tea table between us. I do the same, and we meet about halfway. Since I already know the procedure, I stretch out a hand towards him, and he takes hold of it lightly with his almost skeletal fingers. Moments later, he has gained the insight he needed and sighs as if in resignation. "Indeed... you do have every affinity. In the long history of magic, there has not been a single case like yours, Miss Marcott."

Why does the way he puts it sound like a disease rather than something awesome? Arcelia was awed by the discovery and showed it openly, but this old man is cautious about this news.

"This is an irreplaceable talent that has to be fostered well. You have the potential to become the greatest mage in history." When he puts his earlier phrasing into perspective, I start to feel much better about it.

"Thank you, Grand Master Eklundstrom." I bow to his assessment of my hidden talents. So this is what it feels like to be considered a genius, huh? He then turns to Luna and ascertains her affinities, as if hoping that she might be the same.

"Indeed, fire, water, and wind. Lady Crux mentions in the letter that you are experienced in magic so I would like you to take a practical test." When Luna's expression changes to one of worry, Thorvald quickly adds something to ease her mind. "Do not worry, you will be enrolled without a problem, it is solely to see the extent of the abilities you already possess."

He then turns to look at me again, the eyes behind the glasses filled with the gaze of an academic who has discovered a worthy student who could make history.

"As for you, Miss Marcott, I read that you are learning light magic, but have no training in any other element."

"That's right. The only spell from another element that I can cast is this here. Ignis." I raise a finger and create a small flame from the tip.

Then I remember that not using a catalyst is a big deal

and that I wanted to keep it a secret from the academy for the time being - even though Rolan and the others already know. I slipped up right away.

Thorvald's eyes are fixed on the finger below the flame, to discern if I have a catalyst embedded inside my nail. When he realizes that that's not the case, his eyes widen, and he begins to stroke his long beard. Just like Luna said, being able to cast magic other than that of the light attribute without a catalyst must be something unheard of.

"We will have to devise a lesson plan tailored to your needs." But he doesn't praise me for it and maintains a professional attitude towards a would-be student. "For the time being, you shall join the beginner classes of the nature elements."

He means fire, water, wind and earth magic, as opposed to light, dark and space, which are spiritual elements. But the one I'm most interested in is the space affinity. If my assumption is correct, it should be the domain of transportation magic. That way I can teleport into the demon castle instead of traveling across half the planet when the deadline draws closer.

Then again, Arcelia said there was only one known human with the space affinity, so maybe they're not even at this academy.

"Miss Sigint, if you prove to be at an advanced level, you will be granted a stipend to further your studies. Of course, you will also be exempt from paying any tuition fees." Thorvald turns to Luna and begins to explain the conditions of her enrolment. "There are accommodations within the academy dormitories you can make use of if you so choose."

Oh, so the practical test is to see whether she can wield her elements at an advanced level, so that she may skip classes and go straight to improving herself at an individual level. I'd like to get that as well, but I'm still a beginner in both theory and the number of spells I know.

"Miss Chloe, due to your unique status as a holder of all affinities, you will have to live in the dormitories. Please understand that we cannot risk losing someone as valuable to the study of magic as you." The principal shows me a warm smile that gives me the feeling that he's a genuinely nice person. There's just something about old men and their ways to put people's minds at ease.

That also makes it easier for me to bring up an important issue.

"Grand Master Eklundstrom, I would like to attach a condition to my enrolment." I find that the time is right for me to do it. I gesture at Kamii. "Please assess my companion here."

"A cursed child." He simply comments, most likely grasping my intention without needing to hear more. "It is exceedingly rare for the corrupted to retain their original affinities."

Kamii shirks away as the principal rounds the table and stretches out a hand towards her slowly. I give her a reassuring squeeze, and she turns to look at me.

"Don't worry; it's alright. He's just going to hold your hand for a moment." Smiling, I lift her left hand for her, and Thorvald looks into the little dark elf's eyes to ask for her permission. When she finally nods reluctantly, he lightly touches her palm.

"... an affinity for the dark element, nothing else..." Within a few seconds, he finishes his assessment of her affinities. "While those who possess the dark element rarely come to our doors, we prefer not to accept those without any further merits than that element alone. I am afraid I cannot enroll her."

Kamii stares at the principal for a second, then looks up at me with upturned eyes. She knows full well what he means and fears that we'll be separated.

"So she cannot stay in the academy dormitories with me?" I ask just to be sure, but the answer to that is quite evident.

"Outsiders not enrolled at the academy are not allowed to remain within the citadel grounds."

"Then I shall not enroll either." I state with a straight face. There's no way I'm letting Kamii get separated from me, even if it's for this academy. Luna's eyes are round like saucers as she stares at me with her mouth open. I'm sure she wants to scream at me that I'm stupid for refusing this once in a lifetime opportunity. "This child is precious to me; she will not leave my side."

I pull Kamii close to me, and she nuzzles into my side. But Thorvald seems to have anticipated my reply and doesn't seem taken aback at all. After all, the fact that the little dark elf is important to me is obvious to anybody at a simple glance.

"... but in light of the circumstances, we can make an exception. I can see that she is very important to you, Miss Marcott. If her absence is a hindrance to your studies, then we have to grant you this much leeway." He speaks as if continuing his earlier sentence, showing both the little dark elf and me a warm smile.

I must be an exceptional existence in his eyes, but at the same time, he has to maintain a professional attitude and pride as the principal of this prestigious academy. Groveling just to keep me here is not an option, and he easily navigated around it. What a cunning old man.

But I don't dislike that. I would have been disgusted if a person of his standing had acted like a starved businessman and changed his attitude in an instant just to get what he wants. This way, he successfully kept up the image of a wise man in my eyes.

"Thank you." I nod my head and show gratitude, even

though I know very well that he just navigated the situation cunningly. In a way, it would appear that I owe him for that favor.

"I am glad that we could come to an understanding." Thorvald says as he walks behind his desk. Picking up a bell, he lets its crisp sound ring through the room. The second the tone fades, there's a knock on the door and Astrid enters without waiting for an answer. She must have been waiting outside the room all this time.

"Would you please be so kind as to guide Miss Sigint to the training arena? She shall undergo a test to assess her magic mastery. I still have a little matter to discuss with Miss Marcott here." The principal's attitude towards the female teacher is on a far more professional basis than the friendly facade he put up for his would-be students.

Luna leaves with Astrid, looking back at me one with a hint of worry. She may be thinking that I could still mess up this situation and end up getting expelled before I even enroll - leaving her alone in this unfamiliar academy. I nod at her with a reassuring expression, although I can't guarantee that nothing bad will happen.

The door closes behind the half-elf, and Thorvald takes his time to walk back to his seat across the tea table while examining me with his inquisitive blue eyes, which are slightly enlarged behind the convex glasses.

"Miss Marcott, I have reason to believe that you are not from this kingdom, is that right?" He brings up the one thing I didn't want to be asked. Nobody has questioned me about my origins, and even when Rolan and the others did, they supplied more explanations on their own than I gave them.

I don't know much about this world and its nations, and the only foreign country mentioned to me at the time was the Mineva Republic, where my name seems to come from - according to Rolan. I didn't go out of my way to read up about that nation after I considered my position in the party secured, but I completely forgot that the academy could be another issue.

"While we do admit foreign talents to the academy, we have to know your plans. If you wish to return to your country right after finishing your studies, it would be a great loss to us." Thorvald provides an out for me right there. This way, I don't need to explain too much about where I'm from and just tell him the sob story that my party knows me by.

"You're right; I'm not from this kingdom. I came here with my family, but they were killed by bandits, and now I have no home to return to. I joined the group Miss Luna is part of; they saved me in my time of need, so I'm indebted to them." It means that I won't be returning to whatever country I'm from, and I don't even have to tell him which it is in the first place. "Our dream is to eventually kill the demon queen and bring peace to the world."

"Kill the demon queen?" Thorvald raises an eyebrow, then his features soften as he smiles. "Oh, youth is a beautiful thing."

He looks out the window and seems to reminisce about a time when he was as young and foolish as we are now. I think my explanation was enough to make him stop asking any more questions. With this, everything should-

"But do tell, what is your real goal, demon?" With the smile still lingering on his face, his blue eyes grow cold, as his gaze seems to pierce into my soul.

My heart stops, and I stare at him blankly.

Chapter 26

Like A Rat

"Excuse me?" I blink and tilt my head with a questioning expression. I must have misheard what he just said.

"You heard me, *demon*." Thorvald's expression and tone still don't change, but he puts an emphasis on the last word.

How does he know? Good thing I had myself under control enough and didn't stupidly blurt out that question. Still, I want to know how. Even the saint wasn't able to tell when she assessed my affinities, and they both had about the same amount of physical contact with me.

Can I play dumb? No, he said it as if he knows for a fact that I'm a demon. Did my transformation get undone somewhere? I hold myself back from looking down at myself and keep my eyes on the principal's face without backing away.

Was it something I said? I'm sure that there wasn't a single indicator in our conversation that could have hinted at me being a demon; I even said that my goal was to take down the demon queen in the same tone that Rolan employed. Could it be that he saw through my acting, or was able to tell that I didn't put all my heart into it?

What should I do now? Thorvald undoubtedly stands at the apex of this nation's mages. I'm sure he'll be able to fire some high-level spells very quickly. Luna's spells already look like they could kill me, unlike physical attacks from human weapons, so what would happen if I got blasted by one of those almost instantly? I don't want to face someone like that without any knowledge about magic combat. I have the light magic shield, but I don't know whether it only blocks physical attacks or is able to repel magic, too.

If I fought here, I would drag Kamii into it, too. Even if she has some fighting capabilities, this is without a doubt beyond her skills. Of all people, she's the one I want to see hurt the least. I could swallow her whole and keep her safe from collateral damage inside me. But I still don't know how powerful this old man is. What if he can obliterate my body in one shot? Then she would be killed, too.

Even if I was able to beat him somehow, what then? If I kill him here, I'd still have to get out of the citadel. While he may be the greatest mage of the kingdom, this is a magic academy, undoubtedly filled with a lot of talented mages. They would all come to stand in my way, and in that case, quantity is a quality in itself. Just ten mages on Luna's level would be enough to kill me if they spread out and chant at the same time.

Wait. If the principal hated demons as much as normal humans do, he wouldn't have given away the fact that he knows I'm one. He should have blasted me away with a spell before I could react. There must be a reason for him to go out of his way to call me out on it. Is this a bluff and he's doing this with all students, to judge from their reactions whether they're demons or not?

He didn't do it with Luna, so that seems unlikely. One the one hand, if I let him know that I'm a demon, he might just instantly kill me. But on the other hand, if I play dumb while he actually knows, he might do the same.

Damn, I feel like my head will start to overheat if this continues.

What do I do? I turn to look at Kamii, whose expression doesn't betray anything. She's fully aware of the tense situation because she knows I'm a demon and that humans hate my kind. I'm grateful for her unexpected maturity because, despite her almost childlike appearance, she's more than ten years older than me. Her gaze tells me that she's waiting for my decision.

My course of actions will decide not only my own fate but hers as well. If I make a mistake, we might both die, but the only thing I can do is gamble on the principal not being a xenophobe who wants to kill all demons on sight. He seems tolerant enough of Kamii's cursed arm at least.

But if things go wrong, I will have to give it my all to fight my way out of this situation, break out of the citadel, escape from the city and leave this continent. Protecting the little dark elf, picking up Daica and retrieving Senka from the guild hall will be impossibly hard, but I won't just leave them. No, I won't let things end here!

"My personal goal is to lead a peaceful life and give this child a warm home." After what felt like an eternity in thoughts, but was really just a few seconds, I finally respond while putting an arm around Kamii's shoulder. I confirmed that I'm a demon with this, and I anxiously await his response.

"Ah, a truly relatable goal. It appears to be true; you care deeply about her." Thorvald takes a moment before responding while stroking his beard and giving off a typical old man's laugh. He must enjoy watching me struggle like a fish on the hook. "Your compassion for her is commendable, especially coming from a demon."

He doesn't seem fazed by my admittance, so that means he somehow knew that I'm a demon. While he didn't just attack me, his behavior also isn't giving me any reason to relax. I can't tell what he's thinking at all.

"Knowing that I'm a demon, what do you intend to do with me?" While I don't show it on the outside, my body is ready to transform, in case I have to fight. I'll take Kamii inside my body, and then turn on Hedgehog Mode to instantly end this. If at that time he's still alive, I'll transform into a vularen and break through the window to run away as quickly as possible.

"No need to be so tense, Miss Marcott. You are scaring her." The principal sees right through me as he points at Kamii, who's glancing at me with a worried expression. "As I said before, the academy accept foreign talents - that includes your kind as well. But it was necessary for me to know your plans for after you graduate. I can tell that your response was truthful."

Does that mean there's magic with which one can discern the truth? My reply was the truth since I do want to return home and live a peaceful life - and I also wish for Kamii to be happy. Luckily he didn't directly ask where I came from.

"How did you know that I'm a demon?" He has no obligation to tell me, but just in case he will answer, I try it anyway. Even if it's already too late, I still want to know whether it's his personal experience or skill, or an acquired ability that others could learn as well.

"I simply have a nose for such things." Replying while pointing at said hawk nose, Thorvadis leaves it at a vague answer. Then his expression becomes serious, though his attitude remains of one who's aware of his superiority. "Now, as for the reasons I have not killed you already - they are simple."

That was straightforward. I don't like how confident he is without knowing what I'm really capable of. At the same time, he might actually know how strong I am but still feel confident that he can win. Since I can't tell which it is, I'll have to stay quiet and keep listening.

"Firstly, your magic affinities. Demons always have the dark affinity, and some have one or two nature elements." He looks into my eyes with an indiscernible expression - one that doesn't feel good to be on the receiving end of. "Having all affinities is unheard of for anybody but the gods."

I'm as amazing as the gods of this world, then? That doesn't change the fact that I feel like a rat frozen under a snake's gaze, even though he's just a human.

"It is my duty as a mage to learn more about you."

Lab rat frozen under a scientist's gaze.

"I feel honored..." I remark snidely - the only way for me to retaliate under the circumstances. I don't want to take everything he says lying down, even though I know it's futile.

"Secondly, your love for that cursed child is real. An existence that humans shun at best, and will persecute and kill at worst. For a demon to show compassion even humans are rarely able to; I cannot consider your motivations evil." He ignores my remark and continues his explanation.

I'd also like to think of myself as a good person, even if I did kill dozens of humans before. Ultimately, it just comes down to which perspective one looks at things from. The man-eating demons that spread corruption are evil in the eyes of humans, while the demons will view humans as evil because they keep sending large armies to kill them.

Did I just have a very profound realization about how the world works?

"Yes, she's very important to me, and I will do everything in my power to keep her safe." I deliver this statement with unwavering determination. It's an indirect threat that if he ever did something that could hurt her, I would unleash everything I have to pay him back for it.

"I see." Thorvald smiles as if he just heard a child declaring that they're going to become an astronaut in the future. "Explain one thing please: Why are you in this kingdom? The Dominion is too far away for you to have just come here on your own."

"I fell through a transportation network circle and ended up in the wilderness of the Slaettermark." It's partially the truth, which is always better than a straight lie. "I was all alone, and only through the kindness of the humans who found me was I saved from starvation and certain death."

"I see." Once again, the principal smiles, but this time it's filled with gentle warmth. I don't feel as bad about being seen through by him anymore since he really doesn't seem to harbor any ill will towards me. "In either case, I will approve of your enrollment at the academy. However, know that you will be kept under close surveillance. And while you will receive a stipend, it will not be freely available to you without reviewing the spending purpose first."

I certainly didn't expect that. There were two ways I thought this would go; he would deny my enrolment and send me away, or he would knock me out and lock me in a cell so that I can be used as a lab rat. He's letting me lead a normal life at this academy - even if they're going to keep watch over every step I take - and even giving me something like an allowance.

"Will that be alright? If the other students learn about me, won't they try to attack me?" I'm implying that when such a time comes, I won't hold back in defending myself, which will doubtlessly result in casualties.

"Do not worry, Miss Marcott. This academy practices tolerance you will - sad as it may be - not find anywhere else in this kingdom." Thorvald stands up and walks to the large window behind his desk, to look into the sky. "I like to think that demons and humans are not so different from each other - aside from their physical characteristics, of course. They are each born from parents who love them, have people who are important to them, and value life in their own ways."

He turns around to look at me with a youthful gaze that surprises me to the point that I have to suppress the urge to say it out loud - that he's a hopeless idealist. It's a wonder he could retain that idealism at his age.

"And you are not the only demon in this academy. They each have their circumstances, but none of them have a home to return to in the Dominion."

"So I can enroll after all?" I feel like I shouldn't be thinking about joining the academy under these circumstances, but rather about how I can get out of here as quickly as possible. But I'm intrigued by the prospect of meeting other demons at this academy, too. Of course, I also want to learn about magic.

"Indeed, you can. Remember, that your behavior will be judged, and any transgressions, whether they be against humans or your fellow demons, will be punished." Thorvald rounds the desk and walks over to stand behind the couch across from me, putting his hands on the backrest while looking into my eyes. "Do you have any questions?"

"Not a question, but a request. I would like for you to keep my being a demon a secret from the students." I can't ask him not to tell the professors and the staff, but I would like to enroll at the school as a normal human being, as my appearance suggests; I don't want them to keep wondering what I really look like when they know from the start that I'm a demon.

"That will be up to you. If nobody sees through you on their own, your secret will be safe." Stroking his beard with a chuckle, the principal glances at Kamii, as if suggesting that because of her, most will assume that something's off about me, too. "Be aware that we show no tolerance for discrimination among students. Everyone who pursues knowledge and mastery in the arcane arts is equal in this academy."

That also means nobody will be making fun of the little dark elf for her cursed arm. I hope that will indeed be the case because I know from my previous life that even a prestigious school isn't safe from bullying. I can proudly declare that I stood up against bullying in my class; it's one of those things I can never forgive. After all, a friend of mine tried to commit suicide in our third year of middle school due to bullying, and I was just barely in time to save her.

Ahhh, I'm beginning to reminisce about my previous life again...

"You will find that I am the first to condemn discrimination, Grand Master Eklundstrom." Replying with my chest puffed out in confidence, I make my stance clear. Anything to move away from the conversation about me being a demon, so that he won't ask any other questions.

"Is that so? That is good to hear." Thorvald is genuinely happy at my answer. He really is a good person, albeit maybe a little naive. Then again, I think it's most likely all just an act. "I have to admit that I find your existence fascinating, Miss Marcott."

His eyes are moving all over me, and I suppress a shudder. Sexual harassment right after I praised him in my mind! I know he only means it from a mage's point of view of, but there's no way I won't feel bothered by being stared at like that.

"A demon with an affinity for light magic is just as unheard of as having all magic affinities. I hope to learn much from you." His smile appears as nothing but sinister, even though it was most likely not meant that way. But why do I feel like he means learning from my body directly - after putting me in formaldehyde? "For now, a tour around our facilities to help you become familiar with the academy. After all, you will be staying for a while."

He takes up the bell from his table and rings it once. Again, there's a knock on the door almost immediately after, and a man in a black robe enters without waiting for a response. He has long, straight black hair and pale white skin, with piercing crimson eyes and eyebrows that seem to be curled up in an eternal frown. He appears to have a prideful disposition since his posture is very straight and he doesn't lower his head to look at Kamii and me from above.

Everything about him screams vampire.

"Basarab, would you please show the ladies around the academy." The principal speaks to the newcomer in the same tone as he did with Astrid earlier. Now I can finally get away from Thorvald. "Be advised; they are more than meets the eye."

He's smiling at these words. I guess that's the code to tell him that I'm a demon and that he should keep a close eye on me so that I don't cause any trouble or run away.

"Understood." The man named Basarab replies without changing his expression. His powerful baritone voice reverberates through my body, and it gives me a sensation unlike anything I've felt before. "I am Basarab Laiota, professor for dark magic. Please follow me."

I think I just felt something in my nether regions upon

hearing him string together an entire sentence with that voice of his. For that alone, I could become straight!

Kamii nudges me, and I'm shaken out of my trance. I must have been spacing out because both Thorvald and Basarab are looking at me, each with an eyebrow raised in slight confusion. The little dark elf looks up at me with a frown of disapproval.

"Sorry..." I mostly say it to her, though I make it sound like I'm addressing Basarab, and stand up from the couch.

"Have a good day, Miss Marcott, Miss Kamii. I hope you will like it here." With these words, the principal dismisses us and walks back to his desk. We leave the room and close the door behind us. The last sight I see of the interior is the old man smiling while keeping his blue gaze fixed on me through his glasses. There's a sense of foreboding in it, but that's to be expected after what just happened between us.

It would seem that Kamii dislikes Basarab. She's walking behind me and staring at his back with suspicious eyes. It doesn't help that she think I might be attracted to him. In reality, I don't like him either; there's just something about his voice that doesn't feel right. Also, I get the impression that he could turn around and bite me in the neck to suck my blood at any moment. Though I don't know whether I even have blood or not.

"The fourth floor is mostly used for storage, and some of the rooms are reserved for special classes." The vampire-like professor begins to explain while we walk through the corridor of the academy. A shiver runs down my spine each time he speaks. "The third, second, and first floors consist of lecture halls and rooms isolated for alchemic studies. You will find the staff faculty room at the end of the right wing. There are water pools in the basement, which are used for water magic classes."

The entire academy building is shaped like the letter T, but with the bottom line about as short as either of the top halves. On the first floor, he guides us down the middle of the building, into a large hall with four long tables that seem to have been carved from a single tree each. Richly decorated chandeliers hang from the impossibly high ceiling, making me wonder whether some space magic is at work or it's just an optical illusion. It looks like it's higher up than the building is tall.

But that would be a pompous usage of such a rare affinity, so I doubt it. Nothing in this nation so far has shown me that magic is used in such a way.

"This is the canteen. Meals are provided at the appropriate hours, but it is open throughout the day for those who forget the time while studying." Basarab gestures to the right side, where students are getting trays filled with food from the open kitchen.

At the back end of the canteen is a raised podium with a shorter table, at which the professors are most likely seated during meals. It must be a pretty oppressive feeling to be watched by them while eating, but it's most likely to keep discipline.

Wait, the principal said I wouldn't be allowed to leave the citadel, so I'll have to eat dinner here. Then what do I do about Senka and Daica? I didn't bring them with me, and the latter will be waiting in the guild hall for us around sundown. She wants to establish a new store so she won't be joining the academy, but I do want Senka by my side.

"This is the library." The smooth voice of our guide pulls me back to reality. Before I know it, we've left the main building and are proceeding towards a three-story one now. It's behind the canteen, separated by a small square with a cross-shaped path leading straight to it, while the left side opens up to a large grassy field and the right side heads towards a grove.

We walk across the small square, and Basarab pushes open a set of thick double-winged wooden doors to reveal a sight that takes my breath away.

This is the definition of a fantasy library. To the right of the entrance, a young female receptionist wearing glasses is sitting behind a round desk. On the other side is a shelf on which books are stacked messily - I assume it's where students put the books they return after borrowing them.

Beyond the entrance area is an immense hall spanning all three stories, filled with an immeasurable number of bookshelves, connected by circular staircases and straight walkways to allow access to everywhere quickly. I can't even begin to imagine how many books are in here.

On the first floor, right in front of us, is a reading area with several long tables carved from pleasant-looking dark wood. The chairs are cushioned, and I'm sure they're comfortable to sit in. At intervals, there are open spaces with couches and tea tables, for those who prefer the feeling of a small reading room.

The entire library is quiet, even though there are a lot of people of all ages sitting at the tables or on the couches, reading or doing research while taking notes on paper. Some are relaxed, while others are surrounded by stacks of books and looking frustrated.

"Of course, you are expected to be quiet in here." Basarab whispers, and the sound sends another shiver down my spine. I think the effect is amplified even more when he speaks quietly!

We walk through the library to the very back and exit through a single-winged heavy door. This is the edge of a small grove - most likely part of the one on the right - but no path leads into it here. Instead, we follow Basarab towards the left and walk out onto the edge of the grass field. I realize that this is located to the left and behind the main academy building. It resembles a football field and is free of trees; however, it's used for magic practice rather than for sports.

A class seems to be taking place, as students of varying ages are gathered on the field, each wielding a staff. It looks like they are practicing wind magic because I see some people waving their staves to juggle sheets of paper in the air.

Then I notice a girl with short silver hair and huge feathered wings of pure white among the regular humans. I stare at her from a distance and just can't pull my gaze away, fascinated by the beauty of her form. Those wings... I want them too.

We walk past the class, and I notice that there are more girls than boys, and most of them are younger than my real age. Some of them are Kamii's apparent age, although as a dark elf, she's already considered an adult. Judging by the magic they're practicing, this must be a basic class.

Many stop what they're doing and look at us, with the majority of them staring at Kamii's arm. She's used to it and doesn't let it bother her, but I don't like that several of them are whispering to each other while pointing in her direction discreetly. Even though Thorvald said that discrimination isn't tolerated in this academy, there's no way to stop it from occurring anyway.

In either case, if they have a problem with her awesome cursed form, they can come and take it up with me.

"This is the practice field for wind magic. The training arena over there is reserved for the earth and fire elements." Basarab's voice pulls me out of my thoughts. He's pointing at a pit of dirt to our right, where unnatural rock formations - most likely the result of earth magic - rise from the lowered ground. Luna is most likely being tested there right now. "And water magic is only performed at the outdoor and underground pools."

Our guide notices that we're disrupting class, so we quickly walk away and leave the ogling students behind. I can feel all their eyes bore into my back, as we walk on the dirt path next to the library building, towards a collection of four two-story buildings across the field.

Those must be the dormitories. In front of them, at the edge of the field, are rows of clotheslines, on which sheets are hanging out to dry. While it has grown cold and winter is announcing itself, the weather today is quite mild, so many windows are open. That's when I finally notice something: All windows in the academy are made of glass.

It's not the first time I've seen glass in the human territories, but never has it been in this abundance. Most houses in the towns we've passed through so far still only used wooden shutters. It never registered before, because the better inns and all the adventurer guild halls had glass windows.

Some students are sticking their heads out of their windows to take a breath of fresh air. I spot a handsome boy with a distant look, staring at the sky deep in thought. He must be around Rolan's age but looks much less mature - most likely because the leader has been adventuring for years now, while that boy must have lived sheltered in the academy.

"The buildings are separated by gender and age groups. Those before twenty summers stay in these two." Basarab leads me to the one on the right side, silently assuming that I'm younger than twenty. I'm not trying to pass as someone older than I am, but I hope he won't treat me like a child. Then again, he knows I'm a demon so his attitude will be adjusted accordingly anyway. "The female dormitory where you shall live from today onward is on this side. I will introduce you to the dorm mother."

A dorm mother? I've only ever read about their existence in manga since it was a job on the decline where I came from. I wonder what kind of person she'll be; I hope it's not somebody scary.

"Mistress Ninlil, I have brought new students." Basarab calls out towards the clotheslines where the perfectly white sheets are swaying on the breeze.

"Oh my! Yes, I'll be right there~" A somewhat high-pitched voice replies from somewhere between the hanging laundry. My jaw almost drops at the tone; if that voice had spoken Japanese, I would be expecting a certain scientific teleporter to appear before me next.

But the person that outrageous voice belongs to has an even more outrageous appearance. She's a little girl around the height and apparent age of Senka's, sporting a brown bob cut tied with a white kerchief and wearing a white work apron over her maid-like blue dress. But her most distinguishing features are her ears. They are much bigger than those of a human's, covered in fur of a lighter brown than her hair, and pointed upwards like those of a cat.

Those are anatomically realistic cat ears.

Thank you, whichever god processed my reincarnation, for letting me come into a world where I can witness real cat ears! They're even twitching and moving according to the sounds of her surroundings. Coupled with her childlike appearance and her feisty voice, I feel the urge to embrace her and-

No, I have to control myself; I can't be disrespectful towards the dorm mother, no matter what she looks like. She must be a demon, even though I hadn't seen any of her kind when I traveled around with Maou-mama.

"Thank you for bringing them here, Basarab." The tone she employs while talking to our guide makes me think

that she might actually be older than he is. She's almost treating him like a child. "Don't start thinking about people's ages when you only just met them."

Wait, I... what, did she just read my mind or does my face really show my thoughts so obviously?

"I'm Ninlil, the dorm mother. Nice to meet you."

"My name is Chloe Marcott, and this is Kamii." I straighten my back in reflex and introduce myself with a bow.

"A demon and a cursed child, huh?" She states with a warm smile that melts my heart. Her voice may sound like a certain narrator of a strange amalgamation of old Western fairy tales and a modern Japanese slice of life setting, but her friendly attitude and the fact that there's no judgment in her amber eyes gives me peace of mind.

Wait, did Basarab give her a signal or how did she know I was a demon? Did my transformation come undone somewhere or why is everyone seeing through me so easily today? I didn't accidentally leave an arm in tentacle form, did I?

"Even though you're hiding it well, you can't hide it from me." Once again, she reads my mind, even though I was careful not to show it on my face. She says it with an almost mischievous expression, and I suppress the urge to pet her hair. "Umu, you'll be allowed to do that when we get to know each other a little better, Miss Marcott."

I flinch at how well she just saw through my intentions again.

"This concludes the tour, and I will hand you over to the dorm mother now. If you have no more questions, I shall take my leave, then." Basarab makes his presence known again by speaking in his goosebumps-inducing voice. Do all members of the staff have such distinct voices or was I just lucky to have met these two back to back?

"Not right now. Thank you for showing me around, Master Laiota." I remember to address him by his last name and reply with a bow.

"During breaks and in the mornings and evenings you can find me in the faculty room if you need me." With these words, he gives Kamii and me a nod, before turning around to return to the main building. Throughout the tour, he maintained a neutral and professional attitude, and even until the very end there was not a hint of a smile on his features. Still, I don't think he's a bad person.

"Follow me; I'll show you to your rooms." Ninlil beckons me like a cat when I return my attention to her.

"Excuse me, Mistress Ninlil, but Kamii and I would like to stay together in one room." I point at the little dark elf holding onto my sleeve. She's looking at the little dorm mother with an expression of curiosity, but it's not enough to make the latter comment on it.

"There are twin rooms, so that can be arranged." She replies with a smile, assuming that it'll be hard to separate the two of us. She's right about that; I was ready to give up my recommendation to stay with her.

But having a twin room is perfect. This way Senka can have a bed to herself since Kamii will always sleep in the same bed as I do. It's how we've been living ever since I freed her from that cage, and even having Daica around didn't change it.

Ninlil leads us to the entrance of the dorm building, which has a rose emblem made from copper to the right of the front door. I assume it symbolizes that this is a building for females only, though I haven't seen the emblem on the male dorm.

The interior is filled with the muffled voices of girls chatting away in their rooms. We climb the stairs to the second floor and walk through its long corridor. All along the way, my eyes are fixated on the swaying cat tail that peeks out through a hole hidden between folds of her long skirt.

When we reach the very end of the corridor, I find a window showing the inner side of the citadel wall, which is just a stretch of grass away. This must be the edge of the academy grounds, although no fence or any other kind of marker shows it.

Unlocking the door and opening it, the dorm mother gestures for us to go in first. To the right is a door that leads into the bathroom, while on the left, let into the wall, is a wardrobe just like those one can find in a hotel room. When we go further inside, we find that it's unexpectedly spacious. There are two fluffy-looking beds across from the window that shows the same sight like the one in the corridor, as well as a glass door leading out onto a small balcony.

The dorm mother takes out a handful of yellow crystals from the pocket in her apron and puts one of them in each of the desk lamps. She looks up at the small lantern hanging from the ceiling in the middle of the room. It's too high up even for me to reach, so there's no way that she can do it even when standing on a chair.

Is she going to fly up there with wind magic or something?

But the little cat girl crouches down and jumps up nimbly. At the apex of her ascension, she quickly inserts two crystals into their mountings, before dropping back down and landing softly on her feet. Agile and dexterous just like a cat.

"In case you don't know the incantation to turn on lamp crystals, it's *Limino*. To turn them off, it's *Bice*." At the keywords, the crystals switch on and then off again. "They recharge using natural light, so don't leave them on during the day. And they won't last you the entire night, so don't use them that way, either."

"Understood." As expected of a magic academy, the lamps are magical, too.

"Students your age are required to wear uniforms, so I'll bring you yours later. Those with special requirements..." Ninlil looks at Kamii's crab arm while saying that. "... will need to get their measurements taken so a customized uniform can be provided."

"When will you do that?" I ask while glancing out the window.

"That can be done tomorrow. Your enrolment isn't finalized yet so you will have some free time."

"What about my luggage? I didn't come here expecting that I have to stay."

"Hm... since you're a demon, I'm sure the principal doesn't want to let you out of the citadel before he knows he can trust you. I'll talk to him and see if he can make an exception by letting someone accompany you." The dorm mother appears like a radiant saint in my eyes. Can anybody really be this understanding and helpful? "Any further questions?"

"Is there a curfew?" While it seems that I can't leave the citadel without permission and a watchdog to accompany me, I want to know whether I can walk around inside without having to worry about the time - especially since there's no proper timekeeping method as far as I know.

"Normally you're expected to sleep during the night and attend classes during the day. We do have a few students who can only be awake at night, so those are exceptions." Ninlil begins to explain, and I already feel my mood drop. Basically, there's a curfew for those who have no special circumstances. "As long as you're indoors, such as in the library or the lecture halls, it should be fine. Some do train in the specialized rooms all night long to improve themselves or to prepare for examinations.

Needless to say, you're not allowed to be out on the fields and use noisy spells after nightfall and before dawn."

"So I can be in the academy building, but not roam around during the night?"

"Correct." The little cat girl walks up to one of the two desks in the room and opens a drawer, from which she takes out a book. "These are the rules and regulations of the Royal Academy. Most of them are common sense, but it's best if you read through them at least once."

"I will make sure to study them." I don't really want to, but I think it would make her happy if I do it. "I have some friends waiting for me in the main building, and I need to meet them soon."

"Then let me talk to Thorvald for permission to let you out for today at least. Wait there for the good news." Ninlil gives me a reassuring grin and reveals her sharp canines.

"Thank you so much, Mistress Ninlil!" I bow deeply before her and suppress the urge to pick her up and hug her to my chest - knowing full well that she can most likely feel my intentions somehow.

"Thank me later, when I get the permit." Patting my still lowered head while standing on tiptoes, the little dorm mother gives me a reply that implies she will later allow me to do what I've wanted to do with her since I first laid eyes on her. "Now go, meet your friends."

I bow once again and excuse myself, before Kamii and I leave the dormitory and go back towards the main entrance of the academy. I assume that Luna is either still in the middle of her test, or has already completed it and gone to meet the others.

On our way back, we go over the grassy field where magic training is conducted, but the class from earlier isn't there anymore. During the time I was shown my room, their lessons must have concluded, and they moved indoors. We do the same, going through the canteen to head towards the stairwell leading up to the waiting room we left the others in.

I exchange a look with Kamii, but since I don't know who might be listening, I just silently pet the little dark elf's hair.

She understands our precarious situation very well. Despite her innocent appearance and her usually expressionless face, her mind isn't childlike at all. If I can get out to meet Daica at the guild hall, I'll talk to both dark elf sisters, as well as Senka, about the circumstances. Hopefully, they can help me come to a decision.

Chapter 27

Last Evening Of Freedom

When we pass by the front entrance on our way up to the waiting room, I spot Luna and the others already talking to each other. That saves us the time and effort to climb the stairs all the way to the fourth floor again. It seems the assessment test was a success, as the half-elf looks happy in her own reserved way.

"Hey, the missy's back. How did it go?" Gram is the first to notice me and waves me over. "... something wrong?"

My face must be showing that my mind is a little bit of a jumbled mess at the moment. So far, I've thought that my disguise was perfect because even Arcelia, a saint of light magic, didn't find out when she touched my hand. And I also always thought that I had my facial expressions under control, but was repeatedly read by Ninlil as well.

Neither of that was true, so I'm a little shocked.

"Oh, it's just that they want to keep me in the citadel, and I won't be allowed to leave without an escort for the foreseeable future." I reply truthfully, but obviously, leave out the fact that it's not only because of my affinities but the fact that I'm a demon.

"What did the principal want to talk to you about?" Luna was there when Thorvald told me what I just explained, and I wasn't this shaken at the time, so she's probing further.

"Well, he realized that I'm not from this kingdom and asked a few uncomfortable questions." I expected that, so I came up with this vague explanation. Even though it's been about two months since I first met this group - and thus, about as long since I lost my parents in the fake backstory for the persona of Chloe Marcott - I can still make use of it.

"Oh, I see..." The half-elf lowers her head apologetically.

"No, don't worry about it. I just didn't think it would open the old wound like that." Averting my gaze to appear like I want to put this topic behind me, I act a little melancholic.

"S-so, you're both enrolled now? I'm proud of you!" Rolan raises his voice in an attempt to change the topic. It's quite the clumsy method, but I welcome it.

"Thank you." I raise my head and look up at him with a forced smile, and he scratches his cheek in embarrassment. "And not just us, but Kamii, too."

The little dark elf wordlessly raises her crab pincer in a gesture I assume is meant to be a fist pump; all the while she's maintaining an expressionless face, so the others can't really tell what it means and only stare at the giant cursed arm. She has settled into the role of the stoic and silent type when not worrying about being separated from me. That's a real-life kuudere right there.

"Oh yeah, we heard." Gram pats me on the back and laughs. "You're really something, you know that? Going as far as declining the invitation to the academy."

"You are really fortunate to have found such a caring older sister, Miss Kamii." The bard comments, even though he should be aware that she's older than me. But when looking at her behavior, it's easy to forget that fact. She replies with a nod and takes my hand, entwining her fingers with mine in a demonstrative gesture, as if to show off our relationship.

"We most likely will not be able to go on any requests with you for a while." Luna sounds dejected. Rolan takes her face into both his hands and looks into her eyes.

"Don't worry, just think about improving your magic. This is the opportunity of a lifetime, Runa." And they kiss, for the first time openly in front of the rest of the party. I guess their emotions got the better of them, even though they've been trying to keep it a secret. Not like everyone didn't already know.

"I asked to leave the citadel today so that I can get my luggage from the guild." I talk to Gram and the bard, leaving the two flirty lovebirds to themselves. "I hope it won't be long before I get my answer."

"Oh, we would have gotten it for you." The big man says while stroking his mustache. "You wouldn't have to bother about going back and forth again."

"I also want to tell Daica about this." Apparently, he didn't consider that fact, because he's taken by surprise and scratches the back of his head.

"To be honest, I completely forgot about her. We haven't seen her all day long." He says in an apologetic tone.

"Well, she does not have much of a presence." The bard interjects with a mischievous smile. But it's the truth; Daica is about as silent as Kamii around the others, but she dresses in dark colors and usually wears a sullen expression that makes it hard for others to talk to her. It's not her fault that her facial features make her look like the gloomy type, but she could work on her hairstyle and sense of fashion.

Though it seems to be a thing specific to dark elves, as they do prefer darkness and things that I could only describe as occultism - even though that should be just dark magic in this world.

"Are you Miss Marcott?" A male's voice calls out to me from behind. When I turn around, I notice the middle-aged balding man wearing mostly red approaching us. He must be a fire mage, even though his gentle round face devoid of all facial hair runs counter to what I imagined someone wielding such a fierce element should look like.

"Yes, that's me." I assume he's here to either tell me that I can't leave or act as the watchdog for Thorvald. Though I suppose it's the latter, or Ninlil would have come to inform me that it was no good herself.

"My name is Aldebrand Vangir. I'll be your guardian for this evening." He says with a warm smile. Why do all professors feel like actual nice people?

"Thank you so much. I really appreciate it, Master Vangir." I nod my head gratefully.

"Don't thank me; thank Mistress Ninlil for her persuasive power. The principal owes her a lot." Aldebrand waves off my expression of thanks. So the dorm mother and the principal have some prior history together. She did use his first name when referring to him and didn't employ the title other staff members call him by.

With this, we set off to leave the citadel. Luna doesn't have any restrictions for going out - according to Aldebrand, many students live in the city and commute every morning and evening - so she doesn't require an escort. Some of the commuters are nobles, who have their own carriages, and prefer to live in their mansions, while others can't afford the dormitory fees. In other words,

Luna and I are quite lucky that we get full scholarships and can live in the dorms for free.

The sun is dipping under the horizon when we finally reach our destination. It might be a little early to meet Daica since she said after sundown, but there's the possibility that - just like with Luna earlier - she's already waiting in the guild hall.

When we open the door and step inside, the smell of food greets us. But more importantly, it's filled with people. We missed it last evening since we went to sleep really early, but the number of adventurers in the capital is many times more than the one in Hovsgaerden. The Lost Tombs are one of the main reasons, but the fact that nearby townships and villages don't have their own guild branches means they all gather here.

I spot the big dark elf sitting at the outermost edge of one of the long tables, and notice several men surrounding her on all sides; several even sat down right next to her, completely boxing her in. Daica's reputation in Hovsgaerden preceded her so not many would associate with her back then. But here, nobody knows what she used to do, so they judge her by her sultry body - despite her choice of dark and unsexy clothes. The dark purple robe she wore when I first met her was just sleepwear; outdoors she prefers a turtleneck wool dress one size too big for her, which covers everything.

If not for the coat I bought for her in Aekrestad, she wouldn't have anything that does her figure justice. To dark elves, being unnecessarily big and curvaceous is equivalent to ugliness. But recently she has begun to warm up to the idea that her cursed form is something to be proud of. I'm doing my best to make her feel that way so that she no longer has a reason to despise its existence.

Though her prude choice of clothing has its own charm

in my eyes.

The men are swooning over her, taking turns complimenting her good looks. She's being overwhelmed by all the attention, and it looks like her brain will overload soon. My sadistic side is enjoying that helpless appearance, but I need to put an end to it soon. While she's wearing gloves just in case someone takes her hand, the mood is one where a more daring suitor might caress her cheek.

"Wait here for a moment, then you can come to join me again." I whisper in Kamii's ear with a mischievous grin. She looks at me questioningly, but nods nonetheless; if it's just within her line of sight, she's willing to leave my side.

I walk towards Daica, who notices my approach and smiles, hoping that I'll save her from this situation. The other adventurers are entranced by her expression, but one of them realizes where she's looking and turns around to me.

"Oh, hello. Are you her friend?" He says, but I ignore him.

"Sorry, did you wait long?" Looking into the big dark elf's eyes, I speak with a charming smile. She shakes her head and is about to rise from her seat, but I put a hand on her shoulder to make her stay in place. Then I sweep a loose strand of hair out of her face and press my lips onto hers.

When I separate from Daica again and glance around, I find that the flirty men are staring at us with their mouths hanging open. At the entrance I see my party staring at me dumbfounded as well. Judging by this more or less still medieval society, same-sex relationships are not something accepted or even practiced. Demons and dark elves are far more open-minded about such things, which is why my relationship with these two sisters could happen in the first place.

This is the first time I've displayed our relationship in public. So far, we've been keeping it to our rooms, but this is a statement; those in this guild hall are the most likely customers to visit her future store, so I'm making it clear that she's mine. It's both to protect her and those who might try to touch her skin directly since her curse makes her body deadly to those who aren't demons or cursed as well.

"W-what brought this on, C-Chloe?" The big dark elf stutters, and blinks in surprise.

"I just felt like it." Caressing her cheek, I give her a warm smile. Then I turn my attention to the adventurers, who return to their senses when my gaze pierces their eyes. They either awkwardly excuse themselves or act disinterested, walking away to return to their own groups.

"So that's your relationship, huh?" Gram comments when he and the others join us.

"That was pretty bold of you." Rolan says while scratching his cheek in embarrassment. You, of all people?

The bard and Luna still look confused, remaining silent as they glance between Daica and me. Kamii is already aware and gives her little sister a silent thumbs up for managing not only not to faint but keep calm enough to string together a question afterward. Her weak will is the only reason we haven't gone all the way yet.

Aldebrand doesn't say a word and watches. However, the fatherly smile he sported ever since we first met has disappeared as he continues to eye us from the sidelines. Even though the principal said that there would be no discrimination, that only extends to race. Sexual orientation is still rigid among humans, huh?

"Don't sweat the small stuff." Dismissing the men's concerns with a shrug, I sit down next to the big dark elf.

Now that the flirtatious nuisances have left, a lot of space opened up at the table. "We have things
to do here."

"T-that is wonderful." Daica congratulates Luna and me for our enrolment. She doesn't direct it at her older sister, most likely because she still doesn't know what to make of it. She's most likely feeling a little jealous because she won't be able to see me as often now, while Kamii will spend every day with me like she has since the day I first met her.

"How did your search go?" I change the topic and ask the big dark elf about things on her side. She left our group in the morning to start looking for a location where she may be able to open a new shop.

"I-I found something." Unexpectedly, she replies with an endearing shy expression of triumph.

"Wow, you must have been really lucky. How did you find a place in the capital?" I had expected that there would be no free store areas here, but she somehow found a place after only half a day.

"Y-yes, I was fortunate." Even though she's smiling sheepishly, there's an undertone of pride in her voice. "I-it's right next to the southern wall, s-so it's dark all day long."

"Is that not the slum district?" The bard asks with a raised eyebrow.

"Y-yes. It's d-derelict, and they say it's h-haunted, so it's v-very cheap. J-just perfect for me." Even though what she just said isn't a reason to be joyful, Daica gives us a radiant smile - or at least for her standards it can be considered radiant.

I remind myself that dark elves prefer darkness and curses; things that in my previous life are associated with chuunibyou. Her last store was also in a place that never saw the sunlight, filled with things normal people would never buy. But Luna went there for a purpose, so I assume there were legitimate items among them.

"Will your money be enough to refurbish it?" I don't comment on the stupidity of buying a rundown place in the slum district which is also said to be haunted. She got the trifecta of adverse conditions and decided that it was even better that way.

"Ah..." At my question, Daica averts her eyes and laughs nervously. Clearly, even with all her savings, it's not enough, and she didn't want to be reminded of it. "I-I will take it slowly."

"You can tell us if you need any help." Rolan offers his goodwill with a smile, and the big dark elf looks at him in surprise. "We'll do our best in Chloe's absence."

"While I'd love to continue this until late into the night, I think it would be best if we got ready to return." I look out the window and glance at Aldebrand, who's doing the same. The sky has already turned completely dark by now, and according to the professor, it means that the citadel will be closing its gate soon. "We'll go up to our room and get the luggage."

"Please do so, I'll wait for you down here." He replies, remaining seated with his ale. Gram invited him to several drinks, which has loosened his attitude quite a bit. I didn't expect that it would go so far that he lets me out of his sight despite doubtlessly knowing how important it is to keep watch over me.

Luna wordlessly gets up and motions to return to her room, and Rolan naturally follows to help her. Gram and the bard remain to entertain Aldebrand, which means I'll be able to talk to Senka for a bit.

"I-I'll come and help." Daica jumps up from her seat and follows me quickly. I was just about to ask her to do so, but she understands my intentions well enough.

Thus, we leave the guild hall and go up the stairs to our rooms, separating from Luna and Rolan in the corridor. The moment I close the door behind me, I run over to Senka, who's lying on my bed, and pick her up.

"Woah, what is it?!" She must have been deep in thought or even sleeping with her eyes open because she sounds surprised.

"Did you miss me?" I cuddle her and plop down on the bed.

"It looks more like you missed me." The doll girl counters my question with a sassy comment, as always.

"Yeah, I did." My expression turns serious as I separate from her and place her next to me. In reality, there's no luggage to pack since we didn't unpack it after arriving here yesterday, so I'll take the time I bought for us to discuss the situation with everybody present. "The principal found out that I'm a demon, and by now all the professors at the academy should know about it as well."

Daica's eyes widen in surprise, but Senka remains unperturbed. It even looks like she expected as much, most likely because she thinks that I'm the type to mess up where it counts. Is there any precedent she might be basing this on?

"I'm still allowed to enroll at the academy, but I won't be able to leave it without someone breathing down my neck for the time being." I continue, not wasting any time on asking why the doll girl is giving me a look that seems to say 'I thought as much'.

"So you'd like to know whether you should go back there or try to make a run for it right now, huh?" She's quick on the uptake and gets to the heart of the matter immediately.

"Yeah, that's what I'd like to discuss with you." I address the two dark elves as well, not just Senka. If I were alone, it wouldn't be a difficult decision; I could act like I'm going along with the academy and find a way to escape whenever I need to. But Kamii will be in the academy with me, and Daica will have a store in the city. When the time comes for me to leave because of Maou-mama's deadline, it might prove challenging to do so.

"Isn't it fine? You still have plenty of time left." Trivializing my real worries, Senka shrugs. "I'm sure you'll find a lot of useful spells that can aid you in traveling back home."

The dark elf sisters know that I'm the child of the demon queen and that I have this long-term quest to return to the capital of the Dominion within three years to be able to claim the throne. This journey is meant to widen my horizon and let me learn more about the world, and even after just a few months, I can say with confidence that I've gained a lot.

"You think it's that easy?" I'm skeptical about that. While I do think that I'm quite powerful due to the conveniences of my body, the only battle between casters I've seen is when Luna defeated that slave trader mage with the double fire affinity. But in that case, she had a front-liner that allowed her to cast her spells unhindered.

"That's for yourself to decide." The doll girl simply says and then goes quiet. Nothing else to add, huh?

"I-I think it would be better to r-run." As expected, Daica suggests the safe route. Right now, we could still make our escape by getting out of the guild through the back door and leave the city before Aldebrand catches wind of it.

"What do you think, Kamii?" I ask the one who's going to be the one most impacted by this. After all, she will have to share the prison of the academy dormitories with me - even though I don't think that either of us would consider that to be something bad.

"I will go where you go." She replies with a smile so

faint that one could easily miss it. Because I'm always looking at her so closely, I spot it and feel my heart grow warm.

"Ultimately, it's up to me, huh?" I pet her hair, which elicits a noise like a content cat from her, and look between Senka and Daica.

I can hear someone in the hallway outside and assume it's Luna, who finished packing and is going back down. We don't have much time, so I need to make my decision quickly.

"Let's go for broke." I say and stand up from the bed. When things go south, I'll always have the trump card of my real appearance. While I don't know how effective it'll be against mages since I assume they have better control over their minds than petty thugs, it should be enough as a one-time shocker that will allow me to gain the upper hand. "I'll take this challenge."

"It would be pretty lame if you didn't." Senka comments with a grin, and I pick her up again.

"Don't talk like you're not coming with me." I cuddle her and rub my face against hers, but she stays limp like a real doll. At this point, she's already given up on struggling, even when she's reminded of the difference in our chest sizes each time I squeeze her against mine. "Or do you want to stay with Daica?"

"Nope, I'm fine staying with you." Replying drily, she doesn't react in panic as I had hoped she would. Even though her time with the big dark elf was traumatic, just mentioning it isn't enough for her to become flustered.

"A-are you sure?" Daica sounds as unsure as she hopes that I am so that she might somehow find a way to change my mind.

"If you feel that strongly about opposing my decision, you should say it straight." I place Senka back on the bed again and turn to the sullen dark elf. She's surprised at my reply and lowers her gaze. Cupping her face, I make her look into my eyes. "I care about your opinion. If you're really against it, I'll listen to you."

"N-no..." Touching my hand with hers - she removed her gloves at one point - Daica feels my warmth directly. "I-it's your decision after all."

She averts her gaze, and I let go of her face again. It seems that she's still opposed to it, but doesn't want to stop me after all. Maybe my face is showing how much I'm actually looking forward to learning magic and being treated as somebody extraordinary due to my affinities.

"I'll be ready for the day you decide to leave." Suddenly, she fixes her gaze on my eyes and speaks without a stutter. Just like that time when she made her decision about following me, she's showing a rare moment of strong will.

"You keep getting swept along by me, don't you?" I place my forehead against hers and touch our noses, and she gives me a defiant look despite our closeness. Usually, her eyes would begin to swim, and she would flush red, but this is an important issue that makes her forget any sense of embarrassment.

"I'm yours after all, aren't I?" Giving me a resigned but warm smile, Daica shows me that she's more than just a cutely awkward girl - although referring to her as a woman would be more appropriate when talking about both her appearance and age.

"So it's decided then." I separate from the big dark elf and go over to the chair to pick up our still packed luggage. The backpack contains Kamii's part too since her cursed arm makes it impossible to carry one herself. With Senka in my arms, I complete the image I had when I was traveling to the capital. "All ready to go."

Back downstairs, Luna is already waiting. Aldebrand

may not show it on his face, but he has grown impatient. At this point the citadel is most likely already closed, so the procedure to be granted entry will be a hassle. I don't really care since it's going to be his job to get me back inside.

"Sorry, we made a mess yesterday, and it took a while." I lie and pat my backpack with one hand. The members of our party stare at Senka as if remembering that I used to carry something like that around. I didn't have her with me all day long so they may have forgotten about it already.

"You intend to bring that thing with you?" As expected, Luna is the one that does comment on it. She has been most vocal about her dislike for the doll girl's design and has fallen victim to revenge jump scares for that.

"Of course. I bought her for a lot of money." Replying with a pout, I squeeze Senka, signaling her not to do anything in front of the professor. He might grow suspicious because he knows what I am, and think that she's not a doll but a demon as well. Luckily, she remains silent, understanding the situation. She's always been quick on the uptake; much quicker than I am.

"Is that a life-sized doll?" Aldebrand asks, curiously examining the doll girl in my arm. "It looks really well made."

"Yes, I found her in a run-down store and just had to rescue her from gathering dust." Grinning mischievously with a sideward glance at Daica, I reply. The latter understands full well that I'm talking about her and averts her gaze with a self-deprecating smile.

We leave the guild hall and walk out onto the brightly lit square. The entire city is illuminated by an abundance of lamp crystals - the same as the ones Ninlil placed in our room earlier. This must be a benefit from having the Royal Academy in this city; this technology isn't used anywhere else we've passed through so far, and here it seems to be an everyday commodity.

Incidentally, the demon castle in Arkaim must have also been using those, though I never noticed it until now and thought they were electric - despite all evidence I saw at the time pointing to a world where electricity used for household appliances doesn't exist yet.

Even though we tried to persuade them not to, the men are coming with us. They carry our luggage for us, acting like this is a long farewell all along the way. We're still in the same city, and even if I might have trouble getting out of the citadel, Luna will be able to leave whenever she wants to.

"I can get a permit from the principal to come and visit you from time to time." I say when Rolan repeatedly makes it sound like I won't be able to get out for years. Well, I doubt I'll get one as easily as I make it sound. With me being a demon and the fact that I have the potential to reach the level of the gods, the cunning old man won't just let me move as I please.

When we reach the gatehouse at the bottom of the bridge leading across the lake and up into the citadel, it's already closed. The guards stop us and ask for our reason to approach this late in the evening. Aldebrand produces an obsidian plaque with an intricately carved seal on it. After a quick examination and a few questions, we're granted entry.

"All the best to you three. Next time we travel together, it'll be to take down the demon queen." Rolan says with a confident smile. Again with this...

"Don't you cause any trouble, missy. Keep an eye on her, Kamii." Gram, after speaking his farewells to Luna, turns to me and the little dark elf. He makes it sounds like I'm a troublemaker and Kamii is more mature than me. She silently nods and looks up at me with an intent expression that suggests she will do as he asked of her.

"I wish you good luck in your studies." The bard winks at me, but it's one of the rare times when I don't feel annoyed by it.

"I'll be waiting for you." Daica embraces me and whispers into my ear. Her huge breasts press against mine, and I regret not having waited a little longer with the enrollment to get to the point where I can spend a sensual night with her. Now I don't have as much time to further her training so that she doesn't faint moments into it.

The farewells are a little dragged out, as if we're leaving for another country. The citadel is still within the same city, and it's not like we're going to prison.

Well, it's not like Luna is going to prison, but I might as well be.

But at least it's a prison with the benefits of a school, much like in those overblown stories where a transfer student enters such an environment and flips the established order upside down. A so-called school prison. One with a beautiful angel schoolmate and a catgirl dorm mother.

That doesn't sound too bad, now does it?

Chapter 28

Preparation For School

Many windows in the dorm buildings are lit from the inside even at such an hour. It's the same glow as the ones coming from the lamp crystals in the city, meaning that they're as widespread as light bulbs are in my world.

Ninlil is nowhere to be seen, so we enter the female dormitories. Luna apparently shares a room on the first floor with two other girls around her age. She hasn't learned their names yet, but I'm sure we'll meet again tomorrow, and she'll tell me then. Wishing each other a good night, we separate at the stairs, as Kamii and I return to our room on the second floor.

I'm glad that we don't have to share with anybody else since that way I can talk to Senka without a problem. Not to speak of my love life with the little dark elf, which I couldn't have with someone else in the room during the night.

When we enter the room, I find that Ninlil must have come by. My uniform, three complete sets neatly stacked, sit on my bed waiting for me. There's only one cloak, but that's to be expected of outerwear. Kamii's aren't here yet, but the little dorm mother did say that she will have to get hers custom made. We'll have to see about that tomorrow.

Since there's nothing else to do tonight, I'll check out how I look in the school uniform. Luckily, the wardrobe has a large mirror built into the inside of one of its doors, and there's also one in the bathroom - which has a brass tub large enough to fit two people.

Looking at myself in the mirror after putting the outfit on, the first thing I notice is that the plaid skirt is just too long. It reaches all the way down to the ankles and isn't easy to move around in. This makes me feel like a delinquent, even though overall it's still better than those girls who roll up their skirts so much that their panties are on display whenever they move around.

The top consists of a white shirt with a long-sleeved knit sweater over it - much like winter high school uniforms in Japan. Of course, the clothes style and materials are different, as the shirt doesn't have a high collar and the front is tied with strings. The sweater is also quite rough, rather than the soft wool I'm used to. Overall, it's not very fashionable.

White baggy bloomers for underwear are provided in the set as well, apparently being a part of the uniform. As I noted before, they remind me of old lady pants. Japanese anime would like the audience to believe that girls in medieval fantasy settings all wear cute panties, which will be flashed for extra fan-service at least once per episode. Now that I find myself in one such world, I can say with confidence that reality is different.

I know this is a uniform, but I don't really want to wear something like this every day. As an experiment, I'll modify one of the outfits and see whether they'll call me out for it or not. I shorten the skirt to reach only above the knees by cutting the fabric and sewing it up - although I'm pretty bad at it. Still, it's not that hard to do it in a straight line, as opposed to what I tried back then when I first met Rolan and the others, so the result is acceptable.

As for thigh-highs, I have neither the skill nor the materials to make them because the included socks are pretty short. That means it's time to pull out an old trick; I'll use the body paint technique. Since I can change my body's shape at will, I can make it look genuine by adding a small skin indentation to simulate a rubber string around the thigh area.

After all, a skirt has to have the absolute territory.

If someone were to brush against my legs on accident, they would most likely realize that it's just body paint. That's why I come up with a new trick. Just like that time when I recreated a vularen olfactory system inside my human nose cavity, I localize hair growth on my legs, to the area covered by the fake thigh-highs. But I keep the hair so short that it feels like fabric to the touch.

When I stroke my legs, it feels just like the real deal. Such a soft material! Being sent to Yagrath, the Dark Continent, on accident was one of the best things to happen to me because I got an awesome template with that of the vularen.

As for underwear, I go with the ones provided. Proper panties would complete the look of every skirt-wearing girl, but if a breeze flips my skirt, it may flip a few people's lids. After all, that kind of underwear is unheard of in this world and might cause people to grow suspicious of my knowledge - or think that I'm a loose girl.

I've been letting my hair grow out over the past couple of months, but for my academy debut, I'll go back to the style I had in my previous life. I shorten my hair and watch it happen in the mirror. So this is how my transformation looks from the outside?

Ultimately, I'm still blonde, and my eyes are still blue,

so not much changed. But I do look more like a boy this way, and I'm not sure whether that's a good thing. If anybody sees me like this, I'll have to stick with it for a while; no going back once I go through with it. I still have time until tomorrow to decide, though.

With the short skirt and black thigh-highs, I look like a cool older sister-type high school girl. When I close the wardrobe door and present myself to Kamii, she looks at me with big round eyes.

"What happened... to your hair?" Her voice is shaking a little, and she points at my head.

"No good after all? You prefer it long?" I let it grow out again, and she gasps in surprise. Even though she has seen me transform my hand, she wasn't aware that my entire body is capable of that feat until witnessing it just now.

"A school uniform. How quaint. Why does it not surprise me that a high school girl from Japan is doing this even when reincarnating into a fantasy world?" Senka comments with a sarcastic undertone. "Next, you'll be looking for rice and soy sauce. Will we also see a nation that is Japan in everything but name in this world then?"

"Leave me alone. I feel most comfortable this way." Twirling around, causing my skirt to flip up, I strike a cute pose that drives a frown onto the doll girl's features. "Although I actually feel most comfortable without any clothes on... no wait, that came out wrong."

The doll girl is giving me a mocking Glasgow grin, one eyebrow raised in the cheekiest expression I've seen her make to date.

"This body doesn't require clothes, and I can erase the bits that would normally make a human feel shame when they're exposed." Explaining it may just be digging a deeper grave, but I feel the need to do it anyway. I've lost my humanity on the first day of my new life in this world, so I don't care about human conventions anymore.

"You've properly embraced the way of the pervert, so you don't care about conventions anymore." As if having read my mind, Senka twists my wording almost perfectly. Is it showing on my face again or can some people really read minds?

"I guess that's what it would be like from a human standpoint." I shrug, and she clicks her tongue audibly. It seems she was trying to rile me up, but it didn't work.

I can't wait for my academy days to begin.

Our schedules were delivered by an owl the next morning, shortly after I was awoken by bells. Senka's eyes twitched at the sight of the mail bird, and she was looking around as if seeking an escape route. I think I know the reason for her fear, so I took the letter the owl was carrying in its beak wordlessly and acted like it was all just my imagination.

I was actually expecting that there would be a spell which can make letters fly on their own since that is one of the more convenient things I can imagine coming out of a world fueled by magic; of course, technology in my previous world is far ahead of that, with the invention of mobile instant messages. In either case, I still have much to learn about magic - and many false preconceptions to discard.

"There's quite a bit." I lie down on the bed and look at the schedule. Months in this world have twenty-eight days and are separated into two fortnights of fourteen days each. Classes run for six days, with one day off, before everything is repeated. Basically, there are classes on Saturdays, and only Sundays are off.

Though in this nation, the days of a fortnight are named after the seven other planets in this solar system - which don't include the moon. Thus, Saturday and Sunday would be Himinndag and Sjodag, and with a preceding Fara if it's the second set of seven days in the fortnight. I haven't seen a calendar in this world, so this schedule is the closest thing to it so far.

Kamii's schedule looks much less complicated than mine when I take a peek at it. She doesn't have class on either Himinndag or Sjodag, but on four days of a typical five-day school week, it's just combinations of dark magic classes. The fifth day is the same as mine, with history and ritual lessons.

Mine is still only a preliminary one though, with many of my subjects being beginner classes of the nature element affinities, one element a day. Each day is separated into two morning and two afternoon classes, with noon being reserved for lunch.

Here I see that there's a concept of timekeeping after all - something I haven't needed even once in my two months in this kingdom. The morning and afternoon classes each span two time periods with hard to pronounce names, with a lunch break between the middle two.

In the letter accompanying the schedules, I'm told that today is Fara Sjodag and that regular class begins tomorrow for me. The first subject is Basics of Wind Magic, set on the field between the dorms and the library building. While I don't know what time the first period is precisely, a bell is rung at a set interval, so that should tell me all I need to know. Still, I want to learn about this timekeeping system, which doesn't separate the day into numbers but names.

Since today is a day off, I should go and do some self-study in the library. There are no spiritual element affinity classes scheduled for me, so I might as well learn it for myself. If casting magic of any element is as easy as light magic has been for me, it might be much faster to just read it up rather than attending classes.

Of course, I won't skip school to study alone. It would be a waste of the connections I could form here, for a future in which I might try to create peace between humans and demons. If I do manage to learn stuff on my own, I'll keep it a secret from the principal though. I'm sure the more powerful I grow, the closer he'll keep an eye on me, and the less likely it'll be that he lets me go - without a fight, that is.

"I'll go to the library to do some research. What are you going to do, Kamii?" The thing to expect is that she's coming with me, so I'm considering the possibility that she might want to stay in the room with Senka for a change.

"I'm coming too." But the little dark elf does the expected thing and replies with upturned eyes.

"What about you?" I turn my attention to the doll girl, who would be all alone in this room once we leave.

"I'm fine, I have sufficient knowledge about this world." Senka refuses with a distant look out the window. If she knows so much, I should just ask her about the timekeeping thing then.

"Then explain how one can tell what time it is exactly." I hold out the sheets with the schedules and point at the instances of names like Klifralys and Laekkandilys.

"You were awoken by the bells earlier, weren't you?" Beginning with a question, Senka basically gives me the answer already. "That's when Feiminn Verdenslys begins. Here in Kongenssoevn, that should be when the first rays of the sun become visible over the mountains."

According to the doll girl's following explanation, the time around sunrise is called Feiminn Verdenslys, referring to the name of Verdenslys, personification and goddess of the sun. It literally means shy Verdenslys, describing how the sun appears to be peeking over the horizon or mountains shyly.

That's followed by Klifralys, climbing light, when the sun has completely separated from the ground. Then comes Geislun, the time of radiance, when the sun moves towards its zenith. Belysnath - again, a mention of the Lady of Brilliance - means Belys' grace, and refers to the time period between high noon and mid-afternoon.

Finally, there are Laekkandilys and Sistelys - descending light and last light. They correspond to the times when the sun is noticeably falling, and when it touches the horizon and disappears but still illuminates the sky for a while longer. Night time is collectively called Verdenssoevn, world's sleep.

Overall, the timekeeping method of this nation is quite poetic and feels like much more thought went into it than just separating it into hours, minutes and seconds.

"That's pretty vague. Doesn't that mean that every day is different, and sometimes you get much more free time because the days become longer or shorter throughout the year?" I throw out this thought. The days have indeed been getting shorter and the nights longer, as winter approaches in big steps.

"Yeah, it seems to be a very vague timekeeping method, but they adjust things for those days that are nearly eighteen or only seven hours long by adding another period before sunrise and after sundown." The doll girl explains. Considering the length of the days, that should already be in effect now. Did I miss a bell in my sleep? "There's also proper timekeeping in the same vein as what you're used to. It's considered a rare ability in this world, especially since they don't have a concept of clocks. I mean, is it that hard to make a sundial or something like that?"

That reminds me of the bard, who seemed to know the

time even underground. Maybe he has that rare ability, even though I don't really see any practical application for it other than in that particular instance when he could tell us when to have meals and when to sleep.

"So the bell will ring whenever a period moves onto the next?"

"Convenient, right? Almost like in school!" Her sarcasm isn't lost on me, but I ignore it. "But I'm pretty sure that's only here in the academy. Or have you heard bells elsewhere so far?"

Now that she mentions it, I haven't. Even though this world has churches, they don't seem to ring the bell periodically, as far as I remember. The Cathedral of Light has a pretty impressive belfry, but I didn't hear anything when we stayed there for a couple of hours.

"Then I guess I don't have to worry about getting the times wrong." I'm quite relieved to know that I won't mess up and be late for school, despite living in it. But it means that my current sleeping rhythm, in which I go to sleep soon after the sun sets and wake up at the first light of the day, will be messed up. If I don't get enough sleep for one reason or another, it can get difficult with only one bell; I'm not a morning person, after all. "Do you have an alarm clock setting?"

"I see what you did there. Very clever." Her smile is as fake as they come before she rolls her big blue eyes in annoyance. "But yes, I can wake you up if you want me to. I don't sleep anyways. At least not very often."

The dark bags under her eyes are a testament to that, although I wonder how they even formed in the first place if she doesn't have any bodily functions. It'll be one of the mysteries about her that I will or will not find out someday.

"Can you wake me up at six in the morning every day then? I do want to act like a model student after all." Or at the very least, I want to make a good first impression tomorrow, when classes begin.

"Alright." Unexpectedly, Senka is quite accommodating despite her sassy attitude.

With that out of the way, I can go to the library now, and start with magic instead of having to read up about timekeeping. But before that, I remember a small thing I need to do in our dorm room. It looks really dreary in here, and I have a little something to change that.

Opening my shirt and pulling out a skull cleaned of all its skin and meat from my cleavage, I lift it up in one hand and look into its hollow eye sockets. Kamii stares at me while blinking in surprise. She knows that I can store things inside my body, but I guess it's always a wondrous sight to behold when I take something out from it.

It's a Graeber skull. I nabbed a corpse along the way without the others noticing just to see how they taste - I mean, to have the template in case I might need it in the future. While I don't think I will ever have a reason to transform into one of those ugly semi-humanoid creatures, one never knows what the future holds.

The skull features huge incisors with a lot of free space in the jaws before the relatively small molars begin. As if to make space for those teeth, the eye sockets have shrunk, though I know it's because of their life in absolute darkness. The cavity for the brain seems quite small, though to be sure I'd have to crack open the skull.

I place it on the small shelf above my desk, as a piece of decoration in Kamii's and my new love nest, where we'll spend the coming months, if not years. I'd like to make this place as cozy as the room in my previous life felt - or to use an example of this world, Ingrid's office. Hopefully, the little dark elf feels the same way.

A knock on the door pulls my attention away from the skull. I guess it's alright for others to see it; I can always make up the excuse that I picked it up when we went through the mountain, or that it was already here.

"Yes, come in." The door opens, and Luna enters with a curious expression. Her sight wanders through the room and falls on Senka lying on my bed first. A grimace flashes over her face, but then she averts her eyes and looks around.

"This is a pretty nice room." She comments while sitting down in the chair furthest away from the cursed doll. "How does your schedule look like?"

"It's still a temporary one, but it's pretty packed already. I won't be having much free time." I reply and show it to Luna. She scans it quickly and a hard to understand expression appears on her face.

"You will be mostly attending beginner classes, huh?" Returning it to me, she asks with an eyebrow raised.

"Yeah. Like I said, it's only temporary." I reply with a shrug but realize what her expression means. It's a suppressed smug face.

"The professors testing me said that I must be a genius for being able to meld elements so well, even though my incantations are very inefficient - I did teach myself, after all. That's why I'm primarily attending classes on Advanced Incantations and Master-Level Melding." This may be the most Luna has talked to me in a single sitting, let alone in a single breath while also showing a smile - only that in this case it's an annoyingly triumphant one.

She's cocky now, but I'm sure I'll overtake her in no time. When that happens, I want to see what kind of face she makes.

"I am really looking forward to tomorrow." She finally changes the topic on her own while stretching her arms above her head.

"Yeah, so am I." I'm still peeved by her smug attitude,

but there's no point in issuing any challenges. I'll just make a huge impact with my impressive mastery over magic and skip to the most advanced classes as quickly as I can. Then I'll be able to pay her back for that smug expression.

"So we will only see each other during lunch break and after school, then. Good luck in your studies." She does show me a genuine smile at these words and my irritation is fully blown away. Once again, I have to admit that she's quite beautiful - she's a half-elf after all. As expected, the handsome hero-type lands the beautiful mage in every party, huh?

Luna soon leaves my room again to attend to her own matters. She never mentioned the Graeber skull on the shelf, though I'm sure she must have noticed it. Maybe she didn't consider it to be something important to talk about.

Looking around the room one more time, I signal to Kamii to get up from her bed and follow me to the library as she said she wanted to. But just as we move to the door, another knock stops me in my tracks.

"Yes?"

"This is an inspection!" The voice belongs to dorm mother Ninlil, and I'm shocked at her announcement. She opens the door and enters with a mischievous grin that shows off her pointy canines. Her outfit is the same as the one I saw her in yesterday, so I assume it's her work uniform.

"Hm, what is it, Mistress Ninlil?" I relax when I realize that it was a prank, but Ninlil furrows her brows when she looks me up and down.

"What have you done to your uniform?" She frowns while lifting up my skirt and looking underneath. At least that part is within regulations, so she doesn't comment on it.

"I-I thought the design was too old-fashioned." I quickly push down my lifted skirt and step away from the cat girl, whose piercing amber eyes stare into mine unerringly.

"Old-fashioned, huh?" She remarks in a sharp tone. I feel like an invisible pressure is emanating from this little girl before me and making me shrink, as she grows in size. No matter how I think about it, she must be quite old to be talking about Thorvald like he's a child. Saying words like 'old-fashioned' might not be the best thing to do around her. "You're a rude one, aren't you? Stop trying to find out how old I am."

"Huh?" I blink at Ninlil dumbfounded. Was it really showing on my face that obviously? "Are you using some kind of magic to read my mind?"

"Oh, stop it. There's no such magic in this world." The cat girl dismisses my attempt at finding an explanation other than how readable my face is. "If you've lived as long as I have, you begin to understand what others are thinking."

"Wait, did you just-"

"No, I didn't."

"But-"

"In either case, I have come for my reward." Cutting me off and changing the topic with a straight face, her amber eyes shooting me a glare that I better not pursue the matter any further. Then she unties the kerchief and shows off her bob cut and cat ears in all their glory, while her expression softens and she looks up at me expectantly.

"What reward?" I don't remember promising her a- oh. But my words are already out, and it's too late.

"A self-proclaimed fashion designer, a rude girl who constantly tries to guess a lady's age, and now an ingrate, too?" Both her eyes and pupils narrow as her brows furrow again.

"I'm sorry, I remember now!" I quickly pick Ninlil up with one hand and use the other to pet her hair.

That was a mistake. The cat girl's ears and tail stand up straight, as her face takes on a distinctly primal expression. Then, without giving me any time to react, two sets of sharp claws run down my face from the forehead to the chin at the same time.

"My eyes!!!" I scream in pain and drop the cat girl in shock, who lands on all fours and hisses menacingly. Covering my face with both hands, I quickly chant healing magic. "Sano! Sano! Sano!"

Repeatedly casting the spell on my face, I feel the pain subside as warmth washes over the wounds. In reality, I could easily just use my convenient body and heal the scratches by closing them up on the spot. But I'm in a human body template - even though I'm using my pre-death appearance as a base - so I do bleed and feel pain when I want to. Only that the blood will return to my body after running down my skin, and the pain can be shut off instantly.

The main reason for not doing so is that although Ninlil knows I'm a demon, I don't want her to know what species I belong to. After all, the Crawling Chaos species seems to consist of only Maou-mama and her offspring. For all I know right now, that's just her and me since I haven't met any siblings yet. If the dorm mother or any of the other staff members make the connection, I could be in deep trouble.

I hear hissing again and open my healed eyelids, to find Kamii with her giant crab pincer raised, glaring at the cat girl, who's still on all fours and showing off her sharp canines in a threatening grimace.

"Stop it, you two!" I step between them just as they charge forward, stopping Kamii's cursed arm with one hand and quickly grabbing Ninlil's collar with the other.

The former looks at me in surprise, while the latter slackens her body like a cat being picked up by the scruff of the neck. "What came over you?"

"Don't ever pick me up so suddenly again." With a wholly unapologetic expression, Ninlil replies while looking up at me with defiant eyes.

"Sorry." I set her down, and she crosses her arms.

"That's what happens when you surprise me." Not a single word of apology over nearly blinding me. What would she have done if I didn't know any light magic to heal myself with? My beauty would have been ruined by scratch-mark scars!

"Umm..." I'm reluctant to ask whether I can try again or not, but Ninlil's ears twitch, and she looks up at me.

"I came here to take Miss Kamii's measurements." Changing the topic once again, she eyes the little dark elf behind me. "But this doesn't look like the best time for that."

Kamii is still tense and doesn't trust the dorm mother after she just attacked me. Even though it was somewhat my fault for suddenly picking her up - I'm sure a cat would have reacted in a similar fashion - the fact that she wounded me remains. I think it'll be a while before the dark elf can begin to trust her.

"I'll take the measurements and send them to you." I offer, and Ninlil raises an eyebrow.

"You know how to do that?" She looks at me with skeptical eyes, but then her gaze falls on my outfit. I did work on my skirt overnight, so she must think that I have some knowledge about clothes tailoring. I don't really know how to take somebody's measurements, but I'm sure the encyclopedia lying on my bed can help me with that.

"Yes, I'll bring them to you later." Responding with a nervous smile, hoping to mask my thoughts, I begin to guide her towards the door. "Thank you for coming over and sorry for the trouble."

"Let's try it again later then." Tying the kerchief over her hair while walking out, Ninlil turns around with a warm smile. Still not a word of apology, but at least she's not acting like I deserved it anymore. With this, she leaves and walks down the corridor with her tail swaying from one side to the other.

"What was that?" Senka sits up from the bed after the cat girl is out of earshot, and I closed the door behind myself.

"She's the dorm mother." I walk over to the bed and pick up the doll girl, whose eyebrow is twitching even as she remains expressionless. Don't tell me this is another one of those dangerous things that only she understands?

"In either case, before you ask, I don't know how tailors take people's measurements in this world." Preempting the question I was about to ask, she dashes my hopes.

"Nooo, don't say that!" I drop her on the bed and jump onto her.

"Stop it!" She comes to life and fights my grip as I hug her legs.

"Help me, Senkaemon!"

"Who are you calling a big-headed robot ca- no, stop that!"

In the end, instead of studying some new magic spells in the library, I had to sneakily learn about tailoring. I was lucky that there was even a book about measurements in the first place, but it took a while to find it.

Ultimately, it was a pretty fruitless day, although there was one saving grace; I got to pet Ninlil in the evening, when I delivered Kamii's measurements. It was a nice feeling, but it wasn't long before she lost interest and shooed me out of her room. Just like a real cat, a very short fuse and an even shorter attention span.

Chapter 29

Blazing Transfer Student

Somebody is shaking me out of my sleep, and my eyes snap open in surprise. That was a mistake because the visage of a horror movie monster is right before me. Piercing blue eyes that are larger than life, dark bags under them that are signs of a deeply seated psychotic nature, two stitched scars starting from the corners of the curled lips and running across pale white cheeks...

I would have screamed I didn't know that it belongs to Senka, my secret second roommate.

"Rise and shine, Miss Marcott. Rise and shine." She says with a stutter and in a weird accent. "The right girl in the wrong place can make all the difference."

I have no idea what she means, and I'm not in the mood to ask. Waking up unnaturally causes me to become a lethargic morning grouch, as I was almost every morning in my previous life. This bed is really comfy, the room is pretty chilly, and the outside is still dark. Coupled with the fact that I'm weak in the mornings, my first words are as expected.

"Just five more hours." I mutter and pull the soft and fluffy blanket over my head. Kamii is under here as well, and her cursed arm is resting on me. Over time, she has gotten more and more used to sharing a bed with me, so she feels more comfortable to move around in her sleep without hurting me with the spikes on the crab pincer.

"Kamii-chan, it's time to get up. School is starting." I lift the blanket and whisper into her long and pointy ear. It twitches cutely at the sensation of my breath, and I brush a strand of loose hair out of her face.

With a sigh, the little dark elf opens her eyes and looks up at me sleepily. I press a kiss on her forehead, and she smiles contently. Lifting her arm off me, I sit up and look around to find Senka standing by our bedside with her arms crossed.

"If you snooze me for five hours, my batteries will run out." She comments with a sarcastic smile. Then it fades, making room for a serious expression. "Though the part about my batteries running out is true. I need another soul soon, or I'll stop moving."

I'm reminded of the fact that the first time I met her, she only started to move after I gave her a bit of blood from a still living person inside my body, which she used as a catalyst for voodoo or blood magic to take his soul as nourishment.

"How soon?" This is my first day of school, so I don't want to cause any trouble by making somebody disappear on the academy grounds.

"Well, I can keep going for a while longer with what I have now, but it'll mostly be limited to being a glorified alarm clock." It's a vague answer, but I trust that she'll tell me when it becomes a pressing matter. "And that's why I'll go into sleep mode now. Don't do anything strange to me, you understand?"

"Strange like what?" I pick Senka up and cuddle her,

but she doesn't struggle and stays limp. "Aren't you at all interested in some fun?"

"Not at all." With this terse response, she stops moving and hangs her head, although her eyes remain open and stare into nothingness.

It wouldn't be fun with an unmoving doll anyway, but I squeeze her one more time anyway and place her on the bed that Kamii leaves unused. The latter always sleeps with me, so technically, Senka has it all to herself, although she doesn't really use it either.

I go into the bathroom with the little dark elf and begin our morning routine. It's become much simpler for me since I gained this body, as it doesn't require grooming or even washing. If I didn't have some fun time in the bathtub to look forward to with Kamii, I wouldn't really need to take any baths. Within seconds, I can simply renew my body from scratch and take all the dirt inside my body, where I can compress it into a little ball to be flushed down the toilet.

The conveniences of being a shapeshifter.

When we're finished and get dressed, there's a knock on the door. It's Ninlil, who delivers Kamii's school uniform. I completely forgot about it and let the little dark elf wear her white dress, but the cat girl came at the right time.

"I don't approve of that uniform, but there are no regulations against it." Ninlil points at my modified outfit with a frown while walking out of the room. "Don't you go and make that skirt any shorter than that, you hear? Or there will be a punishment."

Even though it's coming from a girl about the same apparent age as Senka - with cat ears no less - her tone and confident expression convince me that she can make good on her threat. When I turn around to Kamii, I find that she's glaring in the direction where the dorm mother disappeared to. Because the latter scratched up my face yesterday, she's considering her an enemy now. Petting her night-colored hair, I sigh.

It's just one thing after another; the dreaded moment of truth is here. Kamii and I have separate classes, so will she be able to go on her own? In other words, can she leave my side? I'm sure it'll take some convincing.

It took a lot more than 'some convincing'. While the little dark elf is not a child - despite appearances - she can be as stubborn and insecure as one. So far, the only time she has left my side was when I went into the Cathedral of Light to meet Arcelia. And Gram was there to distract her with sweets and snacks.

This time, she's going to be all alone with strangers and not have anything to distract herself with until lunch break. Maybe I should have given Senka to her so that she at least doesn't feel too lonely, even if the doll girl said she won't be moving around much until I can get her some sustenance.

Ultimately, I taught her the concept of pinky swearing, telling her that we would meet again during lunch break and that I would swallow a thousand needles if I broke our promise. If something did happen and I couldn't meet her right away, I could take the punishment, too. Such are the advantages of this Crawling Chaos body. Still, I'd prefer not to let her down.

After we had breakfast in the large canteen together - during which her cursed arm was the center of attention once again - I escorted her to her lecture room on the first floor of the main building, before returning to the field. It appears that Basics of Wind Magic comes with practical training.

The sun has risen high enough above the mountain to display its full radiance, and showers the grassy field in its warm rays. It's pretty cold outside because winter is fast approaching; nonetheless, the weather is beautiful, and I'm reminded of morning club practice. Standing on the dirt road at the edge of the field, it almost feels like I'm at my school's sports grounds.

I have an urge to run a few laps as a warm-up exercise, even though this body doesn't need any - no actual muscles means no way to pull one from strenuous activities.

Slowly, more and more students trickle out from the main building, where they had breakfast. I see a few coming from the dorms as well, so they either were really quick in eating and returning to their rooms to pick up some things or skipped breakfast.

I'm thrilled to spot the angel girl among the students of this class. She's only basic level in magic then? When I walk over to the invisible marker everybody seems to gather around, all eyes are on me. More specifically, many are looking at my short skirt with either shocked or slightly indecent expressions. The former are the girls, the latter are the boys.

A blonde girl around my actual age comes forward with two others in tow. I do a double take when I see her and have to suppress the urge to point and shout out loud.

She has drill hair! I'll call her Drills from now on!

Her expression is also one of haughty self-confidence, making it obvious that she must be a noble. No matter how I look at her, she's the stereotypical spoiled rich girl that bullies others with her status. The two goons following her have quite the forgettable faces as they must be either her servants or commoners sucking up to her; one of them is carrying a staff for their leader, whose hands are free to rest on her hips. They are grinning gleefully as if expecting a good show.

They're obviously approaching me to make a statement

and set down the pecking order for the newcomer. Perfect for me; I'll show them that I'm not someone they can mess with.

"Who are you?" Drills asks while trying to look down on me with her dark blue eyes. There's a hint of surprise in her gaze when she stands before me and realizes that I'm a bit taller than her.

Now that she's this close, I can see that she has rosy white skin and would be considered a beauty if not for that overbearing expression of superiority on her face. Her uniform appears to be of higher quality materials than mine. I'm sure she used her money to get a custom-made one to stand out from the crowd even more than her hairstyle already does.

"What's wrong with your clothes? Not enough money to afford a proper skirt?" She's actually playing the money card, in a place that's clearly based on merit rather than wealth. Then again, maybe some people can get in here through money alone; she looks like the oldest of the students in this beginner class after all.

"I thought it was common courtesy to tell others your name first before asking for theirs?" I bring a finger to my chin and ask innocently. At my words, the girl's eye twitches and the proud smile freezes on her lips. "My name is Chloe Marcott. What's your name?"

"Your name sounds so unrefined, just like a peasant's. I am Svanhild. My father is Tofi Akerman, fifteenth head of the prestigious Akerman clan." Not only does she insult my name, she even flashes her father's title.

"Nice to meet you, Svanhild. So, what are you doing in this class?" I look around demonstratively, still acting as if I don't notice how she's trying to mess with me. "You seem older than everybody else here."

That's gotta sting~

"Wha-" Judging by her reaction, my comment did hit a

sore spot. She's glancing at her goons as if asking for help and grasping for a comeback. I'm around the same age as her, but she doesn't seem to consider that fact.

Finally, her cheeks puff up in anger, and she takes half a step forward. Will she get physical, now that she lost the verbal exchange? Bring it, I'll knock you on your ass!

"Umm, please stop fighting..." A soft and mellow voice from behind Drills pulls my attention over. It belongs to the angel girl, who's the only one in the class full of onlookers trying and mediate between us.

Seeing her from up close, she appears to be around the same age as Luna. She has light blue eyes - with the right one mostly hidden behind her silver bangs - and looks up at the both of us with a nervous gaze that just seems to be asking for people to tease her. Her skin is almost translucent white, and she has an ephemeral air about her as if she could fade into nothingness at any moment. She's clutching a short staff, and her legs are shaking.

Then I notice that her chest looks like it's about to burst out of her shirt; it's almost as big as Daica's.

"Stay out of this!" Drills swings her arm to hit the angel girl, but I catch it quickly. A gasp runs through the class, and even the two goons look scared.

Was what I just did such an incredible feat?

"Huh?" The bully is surprised by my speed, but when she looks behind herself to see who came to interrupt her, her eyes widen in shock. Pulling her arm away, she glares at me. "I will remember this!"

Oh girl, don't you know that you just raised the stock bully flag? This condemns your future plans of getting back at me to always fail and backfire on you. But I'm actually looking forward to seeing what she may plan. Watching her walk away with her nose raised in indignation, I can't help myself and chuckle.

Still, what was that reaction when she noticed the

angel girl? Considering she's the only winged person I've seen in the academy, she must be a special existence, so maybe it's because of that.

"Are you alright?" I turn to the girl in question, who looks up at me with upturned eyes, blinking in surprise.

"Ah, yes. Th-thank you." She suddenly expresses gratitude, even though I didn't do anything. Her cheeks grow red as she nods her head respectfully. "My name is Hestia. I-it is a pleasure to meet you."

"I'm Chloe Marcott. You can call me Chloe." I extend my hand for Hestia to shake, but she stares at it as if not understanding the gesture. Maybe such customs don't exist in her culture - same for family names, just like Kamii and Daica. "I'm sorry if it is considered rude to ask, but... what are you?"

"Huh?" She looks up at me in surprise.

I can't imagine that she's a type of demon. It would be the height of irony for an angel to be counted among demonkind in this world. There were some pure and beautiful demons which looked like fairies in the capital, and one of the maids had butterfly wings, so the possibility does exist.

"I-I am a Fata." She looks amazed that I don't know, and replies with a stutter that reminds me of Daica. It doesn't tell me much, but I'll just take it that angels are called Fata in this nation.

"Your wings are so pretty." The feathers look so fluffy and seem to glow under the rays of the rising sun falling onto them. I feel like touching them. Even folded, they're still enormous; I guess their size means that they're functional and allow her to fly. On the other hand, her needlessly huge breasts don't serve any function and will only weigh her down. Well, I do feel like touching those, too.

"Fueh?" She's surprised by my sudden compliment,

and her face flushes red. Then she wraps herself in the wings, and only the upper half of her face peeks out from between them. That makes for an incredibly cute picture.

"Everybody, please line up. The class is starting." A soothing female voice calls out to the students gathered on the field, and I turn around. It's a young woman with curled and fluffy long platinum blonde hair, wearing a cloak of pale blue and carrying a long staff with a large translucent crystal in its tip. She must be the professor. "We have a new student today. Due to special circumstances, she is an irregular enrolment."

I look around and find that all eyes are on me, as expected. That's my chance for a lasting first impression, but I'll just keep it simple; I don't want to embarrass myself by making some stupid mistake, like biting my tongue while saying too much.

"Come forward and introduce yourself." Looking around with her sky blue eyes, the professor finds me among the students and beckons me over. Her friendly smile and drowsy eyes give me the impression that she could fade away with the wind, of which she must be a master practitioner.

There seems to be a common theme among those who wield wind magic since Hestia gives off the same kind of vibe.

"My name is Chloe Marcott. It's an honor to be able to enroll at this academy, and I'm looking forward to learning magic with everyone here." There, I didn't trip over my words and only gave my name. I look over the gathered students, counting fifteen overall. Except for Hestia, all seem entirely human.

"I am Liv Bergfalk. If you have any questions, feel free to ask me." The professor comes over and introduces herself in a quieter voice for a more personal conversation. Glancing over my clothes, she takes note of their state but doesn't comment on them. As Ninlil said, the uniform code isn't so strict that the staff will chastise me for it. This way, I could leave a great impact on the male students on my first day - even though I have no interest in them.

The students form a line before Liv, and she officially begins the lecture. I find myself standing between Drills on one side and Hestia on the other. Between a hollow and a soft place, huh? Everybody has a staff except for me, and the other students glance at me while whispering to each other.

"You don't even have the money for a catalyst? How pitiful." Drills remarks with a sneer while lifting her nose to look down on me.

"If only money could buy talent." I shake my head with a sympathetic expression and shrug exaggeratedly.

"Wha-?! How dare-!" Once again, she's about to explode, but the professor notices the commotion and steps in.

"Did you not get a practice staff?" Liv asks me in a soft voice, which is enough to stop Drills from continuing. I thought Thorvald would make it known to all the professors that I don't need a catalyst for casting magic, but maybe he's letting me decide whether I should reveal it or not.

"It's alright, I don't need one." With these words, I cast Ignis and summon a flame above the tip of my finger. A murmur runs through the class and Drills stares at it with widened eyes, her mouth hanging open in speechlessness.

"So it is as Grand Master Eklundstrom said." Even though she doesn't look nearly as surprised as the students, Liv still has a curious expression on her face as she mutters to herself. The principal did tell everybody after all, but she didn't believe it until seeing it with her own eyes.

Blowing out the flame, I let my gaze sweep across the class to find Hestia looking up at me with an amazed expression. When she notices that I'm returning her stare, she quickly averts her eyes. She's not the only one who is awed by my feat.

"Then you will be able to participate in class normally." With a warm smile, Liv lifts her catalyst and sways it around in a circle, then throws up a handful of shredded paper, before chanting in an unexpectedly firm voice. "Ventus!"

Unlike in anime and manga, the wind is invisible, so the paper is there for the sake of visualization. At her chant, the confetti-like pieces are scattered by a burst of wind.

"Ventus creates a gust that can be adjusted for an area about this large." The professor uses her staff to describe a large circle in the air before her, then lowers it and asks the class. "Can anybody think of any applications for this?"

A strong gust when all the girls wear skirts here? Don't teach boys this age such a dangerous spell! I spot two of them coming to the realization that there's a perverted application for it, as they whisper to each other with indecent smiles. Wait, now they're looking at me because I have the shortest skirt in this class!

"It can be used to blow dust from hard to reach areas." A girl with shoulder-length brown hair answers the professor's question. She has a homely face and doesn't stand out much, so I didn't even notice that she was here before she spoke up just now.

"Hmpf, that's such a commoner's view." Drills snorts dismissively and lifts her redwood staff with runes intricately carved into its entire length. There's a large diamond inlaid into its tip, which features a blossoming rose design. "It's best used for deflecting arrows."

"Both are correct." Liv replies warmly, genuinely happy that her students got the right ideas. I didn't expect that the rich girl, who most likely came in here on her family's money rather than her talents, would be able to answer questions in class. At most, I thought she would just buy a degree and use money to get ahead in life afterward anyway. "Do you have any thoughts, Miss Marcott?"

"Umm..." I'm taken by surprise because I've been lost in thought about other things. I didn't expect that the professor would ask me a question in my very first class, so I haven't even thought of an answer. Searching my brains for something to use, I come up with an impromptu idea. "To blow away smoke or fog?"

"Oh, that is indeed a way to use it. You should never cast this spell around an open fire, but if you find yourself inside a smoke cloud or a dense fog, it can prove useful." It seems to hit the mark as one of the possible applications. "Now, please scatter on the field and practice it."

Everybody does as told, and I'm about to follow suit when Liv comes over and stops me.

"I heard that this is your first time casting wind magic. It is a very difficult element because it lacks the visual qualities of all the others. If you need any help, ask me anytime." Her tone is so soothing, and the friendly attitude really warms my heart. She should know that I'm a demon but still treats me like anybody else in the class.

"Thank you." With a nod, I return her smile. If all the professors in this academy are this accepting, I think this might be the place for me to start with potential future negotiations for peace between the humans and demons - when I'm in a position to do so.

When I walk out onto the field, I see that the students are targeting the ankle-high grass with their staves, pointing the catalysts down so that they can see visual confirmation for whether their spells succeeded or not.

"Ventus!" Drills suddenly shouts as I pass her, pointing her staff in my direction. You're looking for a fight, aren't you!

But the result is just a disappointing breeze that only causes my cloak to sway a little and doesn't even get to the skirt underneath it. I can't even laugh about it, that's how pitiful her display is.

Not like that'll keep me from sneering at her anyway. Her face grows red in anger and the two goons practicing nearby watch in fear, expecting their leader's imminent outburst. Walking past her without saying a word, I find myself a spot near Hestia.

"Ventus!" Pointing at the ground like all the other students, I try to visualize a burst of air like I've seen being performed in fiction many times. The result is an explosion of wind that blows across the entire field and flips all the girls' cloaks and skirts. Their underwear is completely exposed for a good few seconds, revealing that they all wear the standard baggy bloomers - except for Drills, who sports unexpectedly mature side-tie lingerie made from black silk.

Hestia is blown off her feet because her wings give her a larger surface area, and she must be very light to be able to fly. And while her underwear is revealed, my eyes focus on her beautiful white thighs instead.

Even the professor is holding her cloak so that she doesn't share the same fate as all the other girls. She stares at me in utter surprise, most likely trying to think of something to say.

"Professor Bergfalk, can you explain to me why the same spell yields such different results between Svanhild and me?" While looking for an explanation, I throw a jab at Drills. She glares at me with an aghast expression, then grinds her teeth in frustration because there's no way for her to find a comeback when I've shown the difference in our abilities.

"Oh, you have not learned about the flow of this world?" That's an entirely new thing that I haven't heard from anybody else so far; neither Luna nor Senka mentioned it to me.

The principal should have told all members of the staff that I've only been learning magic for a couple of months, though maybe he didn't believe me back then because he realized I'm a demon. I might as well step it up in front of the class myself then.

"No, I have only practiced a little light magic, and Ignis is the only spell I know that isn't of the light attribute." Tilting my head with an innocent expression, I respond to her question. The entire class stares at me in disbelief, and I feel like asking how long they've been studying now. But I think that would be too much and shatter their pride. "What is this flow of the world?"

"It is an energy field created by all living things. It surrounds us and penetrates us; it binds the world together." Liv says in a mysterious tone while twirling around herself like a leaf on the wind. The explanation is vague enough that it could be some kind of common saying nobody knows the meaning of. "I heard that your current schedule is only temporary, but I am sure you will learn about it in more detail in the melding classes before you move onto advanced lessons."

Upon hearing that I'm only attending this class temporarily, Hestia looks disappointed, while Drills sighs in relief. I'm happy to see that the angel girl seems to look up to me, though something feels off about her behavior.

"For now, try to practice the spell without putting too much force into it." That's a vague advice if I've ever heard one, but I assume that she means I shouldn't shout the incantation as loudly as I did earlier and use a softer voice. If that's all it takes to adjust the strength of a spell, I really have to question the sense of balance that the creator of this system had.

I decide that it's best if I aim the spell in a direction without people, so I walk to the edge of the group and face the pit reserved for fire and earth magic. It's practically walled off due to the rock formations jutting out of the ground, so it should be fine even if I reach all the way over there.

Time passes without me noticing, as I'm unable to adjust my output and keep shooting powerful blasts of air across the field until the bell announces that the first period is over. I look at my schedule and see that the following class is called Basic Wind Melding. That's what Liv was referring to when she told me about where I could learn about the so-called flow of the world.

The Basics of Wind Magic class was both entertaining and somewhat relaxing, as it was held outdoors. We could fire off spells as we liked and take little breaks whenever we wanted to. Liv seems to be very impressed by my incredible magic output, as she kept coming back to me while making her rounds. Many students had trouble even casting Ventus correctly, while others were able to master it quickly and started trying various applications for it.

From witnessing some of the more proficient students, which includes Hestia, I found out that wind magic, the most malleable of the nature elements, can be wielded to such a delicate degree that it can even be used to achieve something close to telepathy. After all, air is invisible so one can affect things from afar without being seen.

I question the decision to give so much power to boys at the height of their puberty. The two I saw plotting to abuse the spell since the professor taught it to us have been trying to lift my skirt without being noticed throughout the whole class. And I've been doing my best to foil their plans by casting my wind blasts at the exact same time to counteract their effect.

There's little in the way of a break between periods, so everybody quickly makes their way into the main building. Since it's another basic wind class, everybody remains together so I can follow the others to the lecture hall. Considering this lesson is being held indoors, I'm sure that it won't include casting any magic.

The professor is an elderly man named Sigsteinn Lundgren, who wears round glasses, has gray hair and sports a pot belly barely hidden by his gray cloak. Unlike Liv, he doesn't have the obvious wind mage appearance, though he must be proficient at its theory.

Magic melding is visualization practice. I assumed that the flow of the world refers to something like mana, but in reality, it just meant having a good grasp of the effects on reality that magic has. Thus, Hestia's masterful application of the Ventus spell was due to the fact that she has a great sense for everything around her.

And this class is teaching how to obtain that grasp and a sense for lower level spells. I'm paying an unusual amount of attention for a lesson taking place indoors - which I've always associated with the teacher delivering a boring monologue for a long time before asking a few questions.

Not like this one is any different, and especially so after the practical nature of the last class. There should be no reason for me to be so interested in it, but if it helps me improve my control over my magic output, I'll give it all I got.

Everybody was provided with textbooks at the start, which have to be returned after class. The academy runs a system where students don't have to buy any books, but also won't have any books to study with outside of the lessons unless they go to the library. This is a measure to both make it easier on those who enter the academy through a scholarship that doesn't cover all the expenses and to ensure that students don't slack off on taking notes.

As for things to take notes with - I had to borrow some writing utensils from Hestia. There were some supplies in the drawers of the desk in our dorm room, but I completely forgot about them this morning. The common utensils are fountain pens and ink bottles, employed on unbleached paper. With proper calligraphy, the writing will look like historical texts to be unearthed by future generations.

"W-what are these runes, M-Miss Marcott?" Hestia whispers to me in a stutter. I look down and realize that I've been subconsciously writing in Japanese. Drills, who sits behind us, immediately picks up on that and quickly leans over to see what Hestia means.

"You're not even able to write properly? Are those not simple doodles?" With a laugh I can only describe as that of a cliché rich lady, she points at my notes and announces to the whole class. She lost to me in practical magic, so she tries to get back at me on the intellectual level. "As expected of an uneducated peasant."

The other students in the class turn around to look at the commotion, while the professor adjusts his glasses in surprise.

"This is a short form I developed to make notes quicker." Not playing her game, I reply innocently. Might as well turn this into an opportunity to gain a few more stardom points with the other classmates. "These 'doodles' are more efficient when fast writing is required."

Although I can already read the runic language of this nation fluently, it wouldn't come as easily to me to write them out as it does with Japanese. I never had any need to do it so far, though I'll have to secretly practice in my dorm room so that I can participate in written tests.

All the students quickly surround me and look at my notes with great interest. The professor clears his throat and frowns, but is unable to control the class this way. This is another opportunity for me to garner some points, this time with the staff.

"Please, everyone. You're disrupting class." I employ an empathic tone and get a surprised look from the professor before he quietly nods his head in gratefulness when everybody returns to their seats. He continues with his lesson, and I suppress the urge to pump my fist in triumph at how easy things are in this academy.

Chapter 30

Angels And Demons

When lunch break begins, everybody immediately surrounds me again. Drills glares in my direction with impotent anger, before leaving the room quickly, followed by her goons. She knows that I can blow her away with just Ventus, so she can't try to overpower me through magic. Attacking me physically will inevitably cause her trouble with the staff, so that's out, too. Her attempt at a more passive-aggressive approach failed as well, so she must be racking her brain for another way.

"I'm sorry, but I have to meet somebody in the canteen." When I see that this will take a while, I quickly excuse myself and escape the encirclement. Naturally, they follow me and keep asking questions, such as where I'm from and what my special circumstances for my enrolment are.

This is a situation in which my Japanese upbringing helps a lot. All I give are nondescript answers that leave it up to the listeners to piece things together on their own, and they somehow accept them and run away with their own ideas. At least I told them that I used to be a foreign lesser noble who turned into an orphan and became an adventurer of the guild. It helps me earn sympathy and some more awesomeness points with the students.

When we reach the canteen, someone runs directly into me full force and almost knocks me off my feet. Night-colored hair and the scent of an ancient forest are enough to tell me who it is. Kamii clings to me with all her strength, as if we haven't met in a long time. I pet her hair, and she looks at me with upturned eyes.

"Mahkotoh! Don't ever leave me alone again." She snuggles into my chest and speaks in a muffled voice. It was her first time being separated from me for several hours without having anybody she knows with her. I have to commend her for getting through it without running out of class to try and find me.

The group of students that was surrounding me has distanced itself, most likely because they're scared of Kamii's cursed arm. I notice that Hestia has been silently coming along as well, and her expression is outright frightened when she stares at the blood red crab pincer. It goes beyond the uncomfortable glances the others are giving it.

Maybe Fatas are especially afraid of cursed things? If that's the case, we can't be friends. It's a real shame, but the little dark elf is the most important thing to me in this world. And I'm a demon myself, so I guess things would get difficult on that end too.

But unexpectedly, she approaches us with shaking legs and comes closer than anybody else dares to. Her hands are clutching her staff as if it's a lifeline which she can pull on to escape this situation. I just hope she won't cast a spell when startled.

"Would you like to have lunch with us?" I suggest, and she twitches at the sound of my voice. Her eyes have been focused on Kamii's arm so much that she seems to have forgotten everything else.

"Y-yes, I would be d-delighted to!" Hestia's face lights up, but she still glances down at the crab pincer repeatedly. It seems she's wary of it as if expecting that it could attack her on its own without the little dark elf's input.

All the other students are watching the angel girl's actions with shocked expressions. They were surrounding me so eagerly earlier, but once they found out that I associate with a cursed being, their attitudes shifted completely. Though the principal said that discrimination was not allowed here, shallow people won't keep to that rule.

In that regard, I have to give Hestia credit for gathering her courage to come forward anyway - and apologize in my mind for thinking that she was no better than they are.

The three of us make our way into the canteen, followed by the wind magic class and other students from all over the academy on their way to lunch, who all gather into a group of curious onlookers. I find that Drills is sitting at the end of one of the long tables, a whole clique of followers surrounding her on all side. She looks over to us and notices that my following is bigger. Her eyes widen, then grow narrow in disgruntlement. But when she glances at Hestia and then Kamii's arm, she returns her gaze to the food before her in dignified indifference. I expected that she would throw an insulting comment my way, but she refrains from doing so for some reason.

But everybody else staring at us is already enough for me. I notice that many look at Hestia with starstruck eyes, while others make way for her reverently. With the angel girl, the little dark elf has become secondary in importance, and I'm surprised by that fact. There must be something special about her - aside from the fact that she's the only winged person I can see around here - as I thought when I saw that Drills was shocked to find that she almost hit her.

I decide not to ask about it, though. As someone who has spent time around a hundred maids who each have unique physical appearances, I think it's alright for me to treat Hestia as just another individual, just like I do with Kamii and Daica.

Of course, I do want to learn more about her, but maybe it'll nip our budding friendship if I ask her now. I'm sure Senka knows, so I'll just ask her when we get back later in the afternoon.

"Umm... W-what is your r-relationship with Lady Marcott?" Hestia suddenly asks after we sit down at the table and begin eating. I blink at her, not understanding what she means, but then notice that she's looking past me.

Kamii doesn't realize that she's the one being addressed, as she digs into the food - as always, the same copious amount as I have piled on my plate. This time, it's meatloaf with mashed potatoes and cooked vegetables.

"Oh yeah, I forgot to introduce you." I put an arm around the little dark elf's shoulder, upon which she turns to look up at me with her big amethyst eyes, not forgetting to continue chewing her food. "This is Kamii. We're sharing a room."

"Ah. I-I'm Hestia. N-nice to meet you." Nodding her head and smiling, the angel girl introduces herself with a stutter. I'm reminded of Daica, who acts nervous like this as well, though she does sometimes get a burst of self-confidence and can speak normally for a bit. "So, y-you two are friends?"

"No." Kamii immediately replies with a full mouth, and I'm shocked speechless. She quickly swallows the food and continues while putting her left arm around me and leaning her head on my chest. "We're lovers."

I hear the clattering of cutlery as somebody drops it on their plate, and our section of the canteen grows silent.

Everybody was listening carefully, and they heard my companion's bold declaration.

"I-is that true?" Hestia's eyes jump between the two of us as her face goes blank in surprise. I didn't intend to keep it a secret, but neither did I want to parade it around. I'm sure the whole academy will know about this within the day, and everybody will stare at us when we pass by them in the hallways.

Though I think everybody is waiting for me to deny or confirm it, thinking that Kamii is just a child who doesn't know better. During our journey, I noticed that elves, especially the dark variant, aren't widely distributed enough for their aging process to be common knowledge. Otherwise, the guards wouldn't have thought that Daica was Kamii's mother.

Is this really the moment for me to make a definitive statement, in front of so many onlookers?

"Yes, it's true." I shrug and say, squeezing the little dark elf close to me. The whole canteen breaks out in murmurs, and when I continue, nobody is listening anymore - except for Hestia. "I'll have you know, she's older than me."

"I-I see." She looks doubtful, but doesn't pursue the topic any further and concentrates on her meal silently. The others around us do the same when I glance around.

Maybe this just destroyed all my chances at making friends in the academy. I've already noticed with those in the guild hall and the professor that acted as my guide outside the citadel that humans don't seem to be very accepting of same-sex relationships.

But I don't really care about their opinions since neither Kamii nor I are humans. In both our cultures, it's much more common for two of the same gender to be with each other because having a long lifespan and no biological pressure to reproduce for the sake of survival seems to allow for more opportunities to try new things in life.

Well, at least that seems to be the case in longer-lived species in this world.

The rest of the meal is spent in awkward silence, though I catch Kamii shooting glances at Hestia from time to time. The latter does the same towards me, quickly averting her gaze when she notices that she has been found out. For all I know, Fatas are also a long-lived people so she may be peeking over out of curiosity. It may be my delusion, but it could mean not all is lost. My afternoon classes are also on wind magic so I may get another shot at talking to her some more.

Incidentally, that class is taking place on the fields again, and it's something of great interest to me: Wind Combat Training. I'm looking forward to it not only because it promises action, but also to see whether I can put to practice the things I learned in melding. If I can't, then someone will inevitably get hurt by my uncontrollable output.

After lunch, I have a slightly easier time to convince Kamii that we have to split up again. She understands that we're not far from each other and that we'll have a lot of time together after classes are finally over. At that time, I'd also love to hear about her experiences in the dark magic lessons, especially since I'm interested to know how many of the students there are cursed or maybe even demons.

The little dark elf repeatedly turns around with a frown as she has to go to the dungeon of the academy building for Defense Against Dark Magic all alone because I'm going out to the field with Hestia again. I think her main peeve is the fact that the angel girl can stay with me, while she has to leave.

Back out on the practice field, I find that not all the students from the previous two classes are present and there are several new ones. Drills and one of her followers are though, while they lost one of the two whose names I don't even know. The two mischievous boys aren't here either.

The professor is a woman in her early twenties with short vermillion hair that is kept short and spiky in the back, while left longer in the front and on the sides. Her bangs cover her forehead and eyebrows and reach down to her sharp eyes, which glare with piercing golden pupils across the class like a predator. The staff held firmly in her hand is made from a beautiful red wood, and the top part is carved in the shape of a winged dragon. She's both a wind and fire mage, evidenced by the two rubies for eyes and the white crystal between the dragon's jaws.

"So you're Chloe Marcott." She walks closer and addresses me in an almost unfriendly tone while glancing at Hestia. I notice that all her teeth appear to be sharpened, but with lips unfamiliar to smiles, one doesn't see much of them. She has a slightly androgynous face, so her stoic look makes her come across as a cool beauty that would have girls falling for her - somewhat like me in my previous life.

"I'm Dregana Tarragon. If you need any help, feel free to ask."

The way she delivers that pleasantry makes it sound like it's just that to her, as the tone isn't pleasant at all.

And her teaching methods are as unrelenting as her golden stare. She apparently heard from Liv that we learned Ventus, so she's using wind magic to levitate balls, which the students have to deflect in turn. It's like I'm watching telekinetic dodgeball, with the one throwing the balls being unapologetically violent about it. Several of the boys take shots to the face or where it hurts even more, but she only points out their flaws and failures in a matter of fact tone.

During Dregana's training with the other students, she keeps turning her head to us and glaring at Hestia, to the point where the latter takes her distance from me and keeps her head down eventually. I thought the Fata was a special existence, but maybe she's as much an outcast as Kamii is? The difference between how the students and this teacher treat her is quite striking though.

I'm surprised to see that when it's Drills' turn, she seems to have improved her control over Ventus. Even at the very end of the first class, she hadn't learned how to use it properly, but I guess the melding lesson opened up her mind to a different approach. She manages to deflect the balls several times, though some graze her shoulders and legs. Ultimately, she takes one to the center of her chest and goes down gasping for air, but quickly picks herself back up and joins the others that have been hit wordlessly.

Unexpectedly, she isn't complaining and taking the harsh lesson with dignity, just like all the other students. I have to give her credit for that and reconsider my impression of her being a spoiled rich brat that only cares for her own wellbeing and status.

Finally, it's my turn, and I step forward under the watchful eyes of everybody, and the golden glare of the professor.

"Ventus Fortior!" Swinging her staff around with one hand, as if to guide one of the floating balls, Dregana chants in a commanding tone. That's an addition to the spell we learned this morning, and apparently, it makes it much more powerful. She has been using it a few times on those who have been able to defend against her better than others but is going for it against me from the very beginning. It's clear that she doesn't like me, and I can imagine the reason.

"Ventus!" I shout just in time for the ball to get deflected. There was no leeway for me to try and control the flow, and it still only went off course enough to not hit me. I think she's seriously trying to hurt me.

"Good." Even though it's a word of praise, Dregana's expression suggests otherwise. "Again. Ventus Fortior!"

"Ventus!" Without giving me a moment's rest, she shoots another ball at me with an even more powerful burst of air, and I counter it with my own. At first, I thought I could maybe use this class to try melding, but this feels like an attempted public execution.

I don't get any mercy, as she keeps shooting at an ever-faster rate, and I have barely any time to chant in response. Is this even meant to teach me something or is she just trying to hit me? Her serious expression doesn't give me any indicators as to her mood, but she may be growing frustrated that I've been able to avoid getting even grazed, let alone hit.

"Grandor Ventus Procursus!" Suddenly, Dregana uses an entirely new spell, and there's an audible explosion as three balls fly towards me at the same time.

"Ventus Fortior!" I try out the spell that she has been using so far, and physically dodge at the same time. Even though they're flying at breakneck speed, they shouldn't do much harm to my malleable body. But I can't show to the students that I'm a demon - although I'm absolutely certain that the professor knows and is doing this precisely because of that fact.

Air bursts out from where I concentrate on, and one of the balls heading for me explodes from the air pressure acting on it from two sides. Another is deflected off course, but the third grazes my shoulder. I feel the impact travel through my bones, and there's a nasty popping sound which suggests my shoulder was dislocated.

I could easily heal the damage by transforming only the affected body part back into its real form once, before reforming the human shoulder. Since it's covered by clothes, nobody would see it. The problem is that the sound was quite telling, and everybody should have heard it, so I can't just act like I'm completely fine.

Luckily - or not - I'm quite experienced with dislocated shoulders, because it happened to me several times in my previous life. Four times during training, when I collided with somebody, three times were when I ran into telephone poles after being distracted by an onlooker during marathons, and a few more times when falling out of bed or down the stairs at home.

Yes, I'm a clumsy girl.

"Go to the infirmary right-" Dregana calls out to me, not sounding the least bit apologetic about going overboard against a first-time student, but I crouch down and grab my shoulder with my good hand. Then I place my fist on the ground and give it a good push.

"Argh!" I scream out from the pain as the bone pops back into the joint with an audible sound. This isn't something I would have done in my previous life because unlike now, I wouldn't have been able to shut off the intense pain; the scream was only an act, but I had to make it believable. There are obviously other factors that make this kind of treatment undesirable, such as destabilizing the shoulder bones and making it more prone to dislocation in the future so I wouldn't advise people to try this at home.

Dregana's eyes are widened in surprise, and I see many of the students staring at me with unbelieving expressions. One of the girls has even fainted from witnessing what I just did and is being fanned with fresh air. Hestia's face is drained of all blood as her legs are shaking in dread at the attempt to imagine how much it must have hurt.

"Are you alright?" The professor comes over, finally a hint of concern in her voice. Still no sign of an apology, though.

"Yeah. It hurts, but I'll be fine." I lift my arm shakily and grasp with my hand, then put up a strong front - which is all just an act. I don't know whether what I just did has earned me some more badass points or only served to alienate me. Thus, I need something to tip the balance in favor of the former.

Placing my palm on my shoulder, I chant Sano. A white glow surrounds my hand, and I can feel the warmth seep through my body. Everybody's eyes widen in curiosity, while Hestia looks like she recognizes what I just did. As expected of an angel girl, she must know light magic too.

A murderous expression flashes over Dregana's face and I very nearly flinch at the sight. It's over in an instant, but it was there without a doubt. Is she enraged at witnessing a demon perform light magic?

"Well done. Go rest with the others." She simply comments when I get back up. That's all I get from the one responsible for hurting me just now. "Next."

I walk over to the others who finished the training and line up with them. For once, Drills doesn't shoot a snide remark my way. She acts uninterested, but it's clear that she hasn't come up with anything witty to say after my display of magical and physical prowess. I managed to replicate the professor's spell on the fly, even under such difficult circumstances.

Speaking of which, she used a new spell just for me. Before, she had been using Ventus Fortior against the steadfast students - and me from the start - but that last one seems to have been of a much higher level. Grandor Ventus Procursus, was it? I'll have to remember that one and try it out myself some other time.

Though I'm sure that I'll have forgotten about it by the next period.

The bell announces that the period is over. In the end, Wind Combat Training was just the class being rotated through the dodgeball session several times, with slight variations added in each time, such as curveballs or being attacked from different angles simultaneously.

Throughout, Dregana kept glancing in Hestia's direction, as if to make sure that she stays apart from the rest of the class. If she weren't the teacher, I would go over and directly talk to her about the fact that what she's doing is discrimination.

But when it was Hestia's turn, I was surprised to find that the professor went easy on her. Not only did she not use Ventus Fortior, but she made sure not to aim at her directly. Is it preferential treatment or just another way to keep her down by not letting her improve under actual pressure?

When the students pick up their bags and begin to leave, I walk over to the angel girl to go to the next classroom with her. Now that the class is over, we shouldn't be glared at anymore; what we do in our free time is our business after all.

But the professor asks for me to go follow her, as she has something to talk to me about. I must have made an impatient expression at her curt invitation since her golden glare turns even sharper for a second. Suppressing the instinct to flinch again, I silently go with her.

"I've been informed that you're a demon, Miss Marcott." Dregana turns around and begins the conversation after we round the corner behind the library building.

I have a bad feeling about this.

"I'm a lecturer of this academy, so I abide by its rules. Honestly, I don't care that you're a demon." Her expression gives me a reason to believe that she does care, and the way she puts it makes it clear that there's a catch. "But stay away from Lady Hestia."

I blink, surprised by her bluntness.

"Fatas are absolutely pure existences. Demons spread corruption that is harmful to them." She gives me an explanation for her sudden demand, although at this point my mind has already gone blank. "So I ask that you take your distance from her."

My head is spinning.

"I'll ask Grand Master Thorvald to make sure that you don't meet her in class in your future schedule."

Ahhh, this sucks...

I absentmindedly agree to her one-sided demand, knowing that she won't be convinced by it anyway. After all, I'm a wild card with an affinity for every element, as well as a seemingly uncontrollable magic output. To this academy and nation - and potentially to the entire human world - I'm a special existence, maybe even more special than a single Fata like Hestia.

"You may go now." Dregana states in a firm tone, glaring at me with her golden eyes like an eagle watching its prey. She's signaling me that she will keep observing me, to make sure that I stay away from Hestia.

Damn, that puts a huge damper on my mood. It makes sense though, doesn't it? A demon and an angel becoming friendly with each other just doesn't make any sense, not even in a fantasy world. She's a blindingly pure existence, and I appreciate her for exactly that reason.

At the same time, I feel an urge to corrupt her rise from deep within me. To ravage her purity, destroy her innocence and drag her down to hell-

I disperse the thought as I walk away from the

professor. This is most likely an instinct of my tentacle monster body - however stereotypical that may seem. But I have enough willpower to control it; I'm not a mindless creature that gives in to its base desires.

As I walk around the corner of the building, I find a single white feather lying on the ground. Stepping over it and pulling it into my body through an appendage growing from my leg without letting Dregana notice it, I move it up to the inside of my hand before bringing it back out.

No matter how I look at this, it's Hestia's. So she was eavesdropping on us and ran away when she heard that I'm a demon.

Then I notice that the tip of the feather is beginning to blacken as if it was dipped in ink. More such spots appear all over it and spread quickly until I'm holding a jet black feather in my hand. This is like litmus paper, but for corruption, and it's a very fast-reacting one, too. Does this happen to a Fata's wings when they come too close to demons? But I remember standing very close to her before. Maybe it has to be physical contact?

I remember that she looked at my hand, extended for a handshake, without understanding what it means. If her people teach not to make unnecessary physical contact, then the custom to shake hands would never even develop. It's quite interesting to considering such things, and I'd love to learn more about her, but all of this keeps reminding me of the fact that I'm not even allowed to get close to her anymore.

This really sucks...

Chapter 31

Here Without You

At the door to the canteen, I'm greeted with a tackle from Kamii again. I return the hug and kiss her hair, which causes students around us to turn their heads. If someone in this academy were to tell me that I can't see this girl anymore, I'd snap.

I spent the last period, Application of Wind Magic, deep in thought and didn't hear a single thing. Hestia wasn't there, so she either had a different class or skipped out after hearing my conversation with Dregana. Makes sense that she'll keep her distance from me after learning what I am. She's a pure Fata, and I'm an existence that destroys that purity.

But I still catch myself looking around the canteen to try and spot her distinct winged figure, which is notably absent. That was to be expected because she should know that I would be here at this time to meet Kamii and have dinner with her.

I can't help but think about this aura of corruption that demons allegedly exude. The demon queen's is supposed to reach all the way across the globe and affect nature in this very kingdom, according to the bard's explanation back during our journey. In my case, neither Arcelia noticed it while touching me directly, nor did Hestia feel anything even though we sat close to each other during the Basic Wind Melding class and lunch.

How does this corruption aura even work?

I'm lost in thought during the meal as well, to the point that I've already forgotten its taste when we leave the canteen and make our way back to the dorms. Everybody glances at us when we pass, most likely because the rumors surrounding our relationship has been spread far and wide by now, but I only register it in passing.

"Nya? What's wrong, Miss Marcott?" When we open the door to the dorms, we're greeted by Ninlil. Did she really just make the stereotypical sound of a cat? "Had a rough first day?"

"Mistress Ninlil, let me cry into your chest." I request half-jokingly, which elicits a raised eyebrow from the cat girl.

"You met Hestia and were told by Dregana to stay away from her, and that's got you down, huh?" She sighs and shakes her head. Did she read my mind just now? "I just saw you out on the field, dummy."

If she didn't read my mind before, she clearly did just now - or she interpreted the perplexed expression I catch myself having on my face perfectly. No matter how I think about it, she's way too perceptive. Her ears twitch, and she steps up close to me while ignoring Kamii, who hides behind my back and stares at the little cat girl with a cautious gaze.

"The situation around Hestia is quite difficult, so it's best if you don't get involved with her. Not just because you're a demon." Ninlil explains with an understanding expression. "I'm saying this for your own good."

Why does the way she puts it not sit well with me?

Today is the first time I've talked to Hestia, but my mind is already occupied with her like that. Was it love at first sight?

"I can understand why you're so interested in her. She appears very vulnerable, and people will feel compelled to care about her." The cat girl continues, catching on to my thoughts once again.

"Isn't she?" I find myself asking, and Ninlil's ears twitch again.

"... she is." Lowering her gaze, she replies. "But it doesn't make her defenseless. In either case, don't cause any troubles for and with her. Fatas are revered by many as the messengers of the gods, so if you hurt her, you'll make an enemy of all those people."

That's why everybody was so shocked when they saw Drills nearly hit her, and she must have been secretly thankful that I stopped her hand. And it also explains why so many students looked at her with starstruck eyes in the canteen. She might usually avoid going there, but followed me when I was the first who treated her like a normal person

"Thank you, Mistress Ninlil." I nod with a bitter smile and motion to walk past her, but she stops me.

"Don't you go and do anything stupid, you hear?"

"I won't, don't worry." I excuse myself, and we walk up the stairs, feeling the dorm mother's eyes on my back until I'm out of sight.

Finally, we make it back to our room. After entering, I shut the door behind me and am greeted by Senka sitting on her bed, leaning against the backrest like a puppet with its strings cut. Her larger-than-life blue eyes suddenly turn around towards me, but she doesn't move anything else.

"What happened? You look terrible." She comments without moving her lips. Thank you for being so frank with me.

I fall onto the bed and bury my face in my pillow. Kamii sits down next to Senka and looks at me with a slight frown. I expected her to join me on the bed like always and nestle into my side, but she's sensing that something is going on.

"Can you tell me more about Fatas?" I get up and grab Senka, before plopping down on my back and lifting her above me.

"Those fake angels?" Senka says with her arms and legs slack. She's in low power mode, so just moving her eyes earlier was enough emoting from her at this time.

"Huh?" I'm confused. What does she mean by fake angels?

"Hestia?" Kamii suddenly joins the conversation. "What happened?"

I didn't think that she would be interested in talking about someone she seems to have perceived as a potential rival. At the same time, she already knows that I'm not the type to be tied to a single person, as evidenced by the fact that I'm going after her little sister with her knowledge. She doesn't seem to mind that one as much as she does with Hestia though.

"She found out that I'm a demon." I sigh and avert my gaze.

"You manage to avoid detection for a whole volume, and suddenly everybody sees through you instantly?" Senka's blue eyes stare at me relentlessly, and her voice sounds snarky. Wait, did she just-

"What did she say?" The little dark elf wants to know, and I'm surprised by her unexpectedly mature gaze. Her face remains mostly expressionless, but her eyes are focused on mine.

"Is that really you, Kamii?" I sit up and mutter more to myself than asking her.

"Yes, it's me." Tilting her head, she wonders about my

question.

"... she was eavesdropping while a teacher confronted me about it." Choosing not to pursue the issue of her somewhat out of character interest in the matter any further, I return to the topic at hand, replying to both Senka and Kamii's questions. "I found her feather on the ground in a place from which she could have easily overheard us."

Producing the feather from inside my palm, I show that it has turned completely black. There are no signs of any changes to it other than the color, but the idea that all of Hestia's pure white feathers could turn into this gives me both dread and excitement. It would be a shame that she loses the bright beauty, but the thought that it would be like leaving my mark on her is very enticing.

"Yeah, Fata feathers are like litmus paper, but for-"

"I already made that mental comparison earlier."

"Sounds like you already know everything there is to know then."

"Sorry, please continue."

"Small sources of corruption cause them to display gray spots." That reminds me of a certain alliance of girls with small gray angel wings. "But in extreme cases like yours, the feathers will turn black really quickly."

I don't appreciate her referring to me as an extreme case; I'm a very normal demon - is something I can't say when my real appearance can drive even demons insane.

"What happens to those with completely black wings?" Rolling the feather between my fingers, I stop to consider that this would be quite beautiful in its own right.

"That's unknown since the Fatas have a secret remedy to counteract the effect of the corruption. None of them ever got to the point where all their feathers turned black, so nobody knows what really happens if they do. But I'm sure you can understand the psychological fear of gray and black spots appearing on one's body." Senka explains while remaining an unmoving doll. "Some lose control over their emotions the moment they see some gray, while others become sick and quickly waste away when it spreads a little further than just the tips of their wings. I can't even begin to imagine what happens to their minds when all the feathers turn fully black."

"That does sound pretty awful." I turn to look at Kamii's cursed arm. What if a Fata grew something like that? Would their society freak out over it?

"What do you want?" The little dark elf suddenly asks, and I'm perplexed. It doesn't sound hostile, so I look up into her eyes. She has a serious expression completely different from her usual more innocent self.

"... I wanted to be friends with her." I respond truthfully when I realize what she's referring to. Initially, I was only attracted to her beautiful wings. When I finally got the chance to talk to her, I thought she had a personality similar to Daica's, but lacking in the latter's ability to be unexpectedly self-sufficient. Then I realized that she's actually great at magic, and her behavior stems from the fact that she lacks confidence when interacting with people. At least that's the impression I got after spending half a day with her.

"Then do so." Kamii stands up and puts her hand on my cheek. Her amethyst eyes with the seemingly swirling galaxies in them are peering down on me with a gentle and encouraging gaze. "Have rules ever stopped you before?"

My eyes widen, and I stare up at her in surprise. She's referring to my repeated disregard of rules and regulations when I was in Hovsgaerden - as well as my boldness in kissing Daica for all to see, just to drive some flirtatious adventurers away. Though that one was because I didn't consider that dark elves are quite open to same-sex relationships while human society isn't.

"You're right." Maou-mama sent me out into the wide world to let me gather experiences, but I doubt she did it with the intention for me to also forget about the fact that I'm royalty. And royalty, especially that of demons, take what they want when they want it.

When I think about it

, I realize a small inconsistency.

"You said Fatas have some kind of remedy against corruption, right?" I turn to Senka, whose eyes spin around to me in their sockets. Stop that!

"Like I said, it's a secret, so I don't know what it is."

"Whatever it is, can't she just use it when corruption begins to affect her? It's not like my proximity to her today caused any problems." We never made any physical contact, or she would most likely have noticed at that time. But that also means that as long as I don't touch her, she should be fine.

"You forget the psychological part of it." Senka replies and I can practically see the shrug, even though she isn't moving. That's true; she immediately decided to keep her distance right after hearing that I'm a demon, without confirming it for herself first. Otherwise, she would have waited around the corner and confronted me about it. That just means she really fears becoming corrupted, even if she can revert its effect.

Well, I'll try and talk to her, if we ever meet again. She might try to avoid me entirely from now on. But if I do - when I do - I'll tell her that I want to be friends with her, and try my best to avoid corrupting her. The rest will depend on her answer.

"Mahkotoh?" Kamii tilts her head and seems to return to her usual childlike attitude. Split personality or just an elaborate act to make me feel protective of her? Whatever the case, she's my beloved girl, so I don't mind whichever it is.

"Come here." I pat my lap, and she climbs onto it while facing me. Huh?

"I was lonely today." A smile appears on her lips, and I feel a warm sensation spread throughout my abdomen at its sight. No, she must have been acting just to get invited into this position. "You paid me so little attention."

We were always quite active in the bedroom in Hovsgaerden, but haven't done anything since we left to go on the journey that brought us here - for obvious reasons. I've been too busy to notice my own desires, let alone Kamii's. But for her to be so proactive about it is a first.

"That's my cue to leave." Senka comments, but doesn't move in the slightest. "Or so I'd like to say, but I really need to save energy. Can you please not?"

"Close your eyes or something." I reply with a sarcastic grin. Then I give the little dark elf on my lap my full attention.

The sound of birds chirping wakes me up. I wasn't awoken by the Senka alarm clock, so I immediately sit up and look towards the window. Luckily, the sun isn't up yet, and the sky is still a dark blue, though I have no idea whether or not it's actually the time for us to get up. Classes start shortly before sunrise, and we still have some things to do before then.

Most specifically taking a bath.

I'm naked in bed, and so is Kamii beside me. There's a thick smell of unmistakable origin in our room, and I notice that the doll girl isn't where I left her yesterday. Did she use her remaining energy to escape after all? I hope she didn't go out to get some energy on her own because this academy is full of perceptive people.

"Mahkotoh?" The little dark elf stirs and wakes up when she feels me moving. She turns to look up at me with disheveled hair and gives me a gentle smile while her cheeks grow red at the memory of last night. Her 'morning after' appearance is still a sight I can't get enough of.

When I think back to last night, I remember that we didn't pay attention to our voices too much. But the walls are quite thick and well-isolated, so I hope the sounds of our uninhibited lovemaking didn't travel far enough for the rooms around ours to hear.

"Come on, we have to get ready for class." I caress Kamii's cheek and brush back her messy night-colored hair.

But before we can leave, I want to clean up the bedsheets. For some reason, I don't want the dorm mother to find out, even though I don't know if what we did is against any of the rules. Not like I'd care, but I just don't want to get scolded.

"I don't mind you doing these things, but please keep it down at night." Ninlil confronted us when we leave our room.

Ahhh, it was so embarrassing!

I apologized profusely and was let off the hook after a stern warning with her incredibly fitting voice. But that meant the academy is quite lenient in that regard. The dorms are separated by genders, but about half the students are adults, so it must be something accepted solely for the fact that it can't be regulated too strictly.

Still, we're in a girls-only dorm building, and I think the majority of those living here are around my age or younger. I'm sure some students listening in on us were too young to learn about such things.

And just as expected, breakfast was quite awkward because not only is Kamii's declaration that we're lovers commonly known throughout the academy after the first day, but a new rumor started to make its rounds now. A lot of the girls were staring at us unabashedly, whispering to each other with light blushes on their cheeks.

But unexpectedly, it didn't take much for the previously so clingy little dark elf to separate from me for class. Maybe she charged up on energy from me last night and is much better equipped to challenge being alone now because of that.

Today's classes are the same as yesterday's, but with the water element rather than wind. I wonder why the basic classes are perfectly separated into one per day, but I suppose it's so that those who have control over multiple elements like Luna or me can attend all of them each week.

In either case, not a single student from the classes yesterday are present, so I assume none of them have both the wind and water affinities. That means neither Hestia nor Drills are here. I would have wanted to talk to the former if she had been, but I'm also happy that the latter isn't. She would somehow find a way to mock me for the circulating rumors that even the girls in this class are whispering to each other about - if she isn't the pure-hearted type that will blush at the mention of anything beyond hand-holding.

"Do you all remember the spell we learned last week?" The professor, a man in his late twenties with short, light brown hair and blue eyes, asks the class. His name is Kari Raskop, and he's the scholarly type, wearing an ultramarine cloak over his slim body.

"Yes, Pilos Aquos. It's a spell to summon a ball of water that can be molded for various uses." An overeager boy answers without waiting for his turn.

"Good, you paid attention, Ivor. Now, Miss Marcott. I heard that you have strong control over the flow, so could I ask you to perform the spell for all to see?" Kari praises the boy who replied before turning around and addressing me. He must have heard wrong in regards to my control over the flow because I completely lack any.

But I can imagine that the somewhat airheaded Liv told the other professors about my stupidly strong magic output in a misleading way, which could have led to this misunderstanding.

"Pilos Aquos!" I raise a hand and chant but realize too late that I did it with a lot of force. A pool-sized sphere of water forms above the class and refracts the sunlight falling through it. Everyone stares up at it with open mouths.

Then all of the water begins to get affected by gravity at once and starts falling towards us.

"Aquos Congregos!" The professor raises his staff with a single sapphire let into its tip and speaks a quick incantation. The falling sphere stops in midair and forms an arm, which moves towards the large pool next to which we're training. Within a few seconds, all the water I summoned disappears into the overflow drainage, which most likely directly connects to the lake.

Everybody stares at me in bafflement, and even the girls seem to forget about everything else; this display of magical prowess is, for the most part, more interesting than gossip about relationships and heated voices in the night.

Thus, as with the first period yesterday, I spend the rest of the class trying to control my magic in a place where I won't hurt anybody - or in this case, drench them with water. Though I think if a sphere of water enough to fill an entire school swimming pool falls on a person, they'll get flattened first.

I see from the other students that the spell usually only summons an orb that can fill a mop bucket to the brim. It's much easier to learn by controlling a small amount at first, so just splashing the place with huge water spheres isn't very productive. And due to the weather, the students make sure not to get wet, so I don't get to witness some see-through white shirts either.

Well, at least I'm learning new spells that could be useful in some situations so I won't complain too much.

The second period is Basic Water Melding, but it's with Sigstein, the same professor as the one I had for wind melding yesterday. I assume he either just knows a lot about magic theory or holds affinities for both wind and water.

In either case, it's practically a repetition of yesterday's class with him, only that the topic is water. Wind and water in magic share a lot of properties, but the former is far more versatile and malleable than the latter. Thus, it's much harder to control as well, which is what I take from this lesson.

Other than that, it's already becoming a little boring for me since I know that afternoon classes are going to be combat training, which I'm looking forward to like an overeager elementary school kid. One of the girls told me that it's going to be held at the indoor pool and that we should be going in only our underwear. Most likely that's because of a lack of swimwear technology in this world. A lecture in which an old man is talking about mental images and inner control just can't compare to something like that.

Still, I do try to pay attention and jot down notes on how to control and shape magic with the mind. It may take me a while before I can adequately practice it since I'll need to get my output down to normal levels first.

Otherwise, I'll be only creating bursts of air and pools of water all over the place which I won't be able to control accurately.

Tomorrow I have classes on earth magic and the day after is fire. The former is a more permanent element, and the latter is very volatile. I hope I won't accidentally grow a mountain in the earth magic arena or burn the entire academy down with a fiery explosion.

Lunch break couldn't come sooner. I think that each period takes around two hours without any breaks, although the classes taking place outdoors - mainly the practical ones - are much more relaxed, and students can rest whenever they like. Listening to an old man talking for two hours with barely any involvement is just too much for someone like me, who has enjoyed a modern education and its much more humane system.

When the bell rings, I dash out almost immediately, to meet up with Kamii in front of the canteen. She doesn't tackle me like she did yesterday but still hugs me tightly. I respond by petting her hair.

A lot more people are staring at us now than they did during breakfast, and definitely not only because we're both eating a huge meal. Some boys are whispering to each other as well, so it means that the information has spread to them by now, too.

"Umm, a-are you Miss Marcott?" Suddenly a voice asks me, and I turn my head around to see a girl around the age of Kamii looking at me with an uneasy, almost scared expression. She flinches when our eyes meet.

Oi, I'm not some kind of sexual predator who's going to push any girl she sees to the ground!

"Yes?" I'm a little more careful about my demeanor, to not give her a reason to fear any sudden actions on my part.

"I-I was asked to tell you that somebody is waiting behind the library building for you, b-before the beginning of the next period." She stutters a little, clearly feeling uncomfortable having to speak to me.

Don't tell me it's a confession? Considering a girl this age is bringing me this message, the other person must be a girl, too. After all, at this age, they don't usually associate with boys. I glance at Kamii, but she just returns my gaze wordlessly. I don't doubt that she understands what this situation entails, but she keeps quiet about it.

"I'll come right away." I reply and quickly finish up my lunch. It would be rude not to answer the request as soon as possible, but I also don't want to waste any food.

In either case, is my school life going to turn rose-colored again after all?

Kamii follows my example and finishes her meal just as quickly, before getting up from the bench at almost the exact same time as I do. Obviously, she tags along to this confession, but I don't consider for one moment that she should stay hidden. Whoever it is will have to live with the fact that she won't have me to herself.

My imagination is already running away with this. For all I know, it's Drills and her goons, trying to shake me down with the help of some strong upperclassman. No part of me is considering the possibility that it's a boy calling me out though.

But both my wild fantasies and cynical musings are swept away when I round the large library building and see the person waiting for me a few steps away - in the same place as where Professor Dregana confronted me yesterday.

The person is standing with her back turned towards me, from which a pair of pure white angel wings sprouts. She has short silver hair and an almost ephemeral air about her presence, which comes through even she isn't facing me.

It's Hestia.

Chapter 32

Purity And Corruption

"Hestia." I call out to the angel girl, and she turns around to look at me with swollen red eyes and dark bags under them. She must have been crying and maybe didn't get any sleep last night. It's especially noticeable because of her otherwise pristine white skin and silver hair, so my eyes are immediately drawn to it. Her vulnerable appearance stirs something inside me, but I suppress the sensation and express my concern. "Are you alright? What happened?"

I might be seen as acting dumb since I know very well what must have caused this. But she shouldn't be aware that I found her feather unless she left it there on purpose. In either case, it's better to ask about her wellbeing than begin by apologizing for not telling her that I'm a demon or something like that.

"Miss Marcott..." Hestia's eyes move past me and fall on Kamii, who's following closely behind me. The latter wears her usual expressionless face, not showing what she's thinking about this situation. Then she returns her gaze to meet mine and continues in a sad tone. "... you were the first person whom I thought I could become friends with."

That's certainly not what I expected, but then again, I don't know what I actually expected.

"I was surprised when I first met you." It feels like the onset of a long monologue, but I listen to her intently and without averting my eyes. After all, it looks like she gathered her courage to do this. "You did not know what I was, and you treated me on equal grounds, unlike any of the other humans."

The last part isn't quite right, and she knows it herself. She shakes her head, and a sad smile appears on her lips.

"No, you were not human in the first place." Her voice carries a hint of despair, as her gaze wavers. "Was it all an act to get closer to me?"

I see what this is about, but I don't answer. Is this really what she thought of first thing when she learned I was a demon? Is this how it goes between Fatas and demons?

"Please, tell me." But then I notice that there's more to her words. She wants to believe that I didn't try to deceive her and approached her for who she was, rather than what she was. That I was treating her the way I did out of genuine interest in her person, rather than her race or position.

Maybe it's normal for Fatas to rush things in their heads. We've only known each other since yesterday, so where is she coming from talking to me like we were friends for many years and I betrayed her trust in some way or another?

"No, I didn't think anything when I extended my hand to you." I respond truthfully. "In fact, don't you remember? You were the one who talked to me first."

"Huh?" Perplexed by my response, Hestia blinks at me. Technically, she called out to Drills and me without making a distinction, and I was the one who first initiated a conversation with her specifically. But it still means that she was the one who provided the opportunity for me to talk to her. "Oh, you are right."

"In either case, are you okay being so close to me? Aren't demons like poison to you?" I've been keeping a respectful distance of half a dozen steps, in case she has a group of student admirers secretly protecting her from the shadows, who will blast me with magic when I get too close.

Hestia lowers her gaze at my words and appears torn on how to respond to that.

"You are so kind." She suddenly looks up and shows me a smile. Is my simple concern being perceived as kindness? "I was sent to this school to die."

I'm unable to reply to this sudden revelation and only stare at her.

"That is because I am unwanted in the Fata Triarchy." Still smiling, though it's one of resignation and sadness, she explains her situation. "We Fatas do not kill our own, and it is a great blemish if one's actions are the cause of death for another of our kind. But sending somebody into exile without a means of purification does not count."

So even pure-looking angels still have the mires of politics and darkness of intrigues. Is that why Senka referred to Fatas as fake angels? They sure don't sound like heavenly messengers living in a land of purity and eternal peace.

"If I die in exile, it will be treated as having happened of natural causes, and nobody will be inconvenienced by it." Her empty eyes and weak smile are a shocking sight. I suppress the urge to close the distance and hug her, out of fear that corruption will overtake her body as quickly as it did with her feather yesterday. But her lifeless gaze reminds me of Kamii's when I first met her.

Even though I'm a monster that doesn't bat an eye when ending lives, though only against those that threaten me or those important to me, I'm not a heartless person. I feel deep empathy for her fate, just like I did for the little dark elf behind me when I found her in that cage back in Hovsgaerden.

"I don't know about the circumstances where you came from, but you can't go back there anymore, can you?" I'm not great at making speeches or lecturing people, so I can only say what I think. "So you should live your life as you like."

Hestia stares at me in bafflement, but it doesn't seem to have gotten through to her just yet, as she hangs her head again. A resigned smile plays over her trembling lips, making it clear that her will is on the verge of collapsing.

"You are really strong, are you not, Miss Marcott." Tears form in the corners of the angel girl's ethereal light blue eyes, but she wipes them away hastily. To me, it looks like a conditioned reflex, and I get confirmation by her following words. "I was born the illegitimate child of a very important man in the triarchy. He treated me nicely when I held political worth, but cast me out when his enemies could use me to threaten his position."

Using one's own children for political maneuvering is something the bad guys in stories I've read would do. To think that the Fatas, revered by humans as messengers of the gods, had such worldly and petty issues. What would the people think if they heard about this?

"He made it clear that my life is meaningless now." Hestia is still suppressing her emotions and putting up a strong front. She didn't look like the most cheerful person in class, but my judgment couldn't be so bad to not notice that her fun in casting wind magic and her interest in studying were faked, could it? "I am sure he - and many others - would be happy if I died quietly in this corner of the world."

"Don't talk about dying!" I burst out and chastise her. She flinches at my harsh tone, but I quickly bridge the few steps separating us and grab her shoulders. She's a little smaller than me, but it feels like she has shrunk under her self-destructive thoughts even more. Her body is trembling in my grasp.

"M-Miss Marcott?" Hestia stutters in a surprised tone.

"Live!" I stare into her eyes and speak firmly. "Make the most of your life and live it to the fullest. Don't give those bastards the satisfaction!"

Her wings quiver and the feathers rustle as if an immaterial breeze is blowing through them. She is staring at me, her lips flapping open and closed in lack of words. Then her legs give out, and I quickly guide her to her knees before letting go of her, in fear that my corruption is affecting her. I don't see any gray spots on her wings yet, but that may just be a matter of time.

"But I... I am just a worthless being that is not allowed to have any happiness..." Talking herself down, the angel girl looks up at me with one last attempt at maintaining her crumbling facade of self-control.

"Tell me who said that to you!" I fall to my knees as well and cup her face, ignoring the warning bells in my mind signaling that this should be bad for her. "I'll beat them up for you!"

"Haha... you would do that... for me?" A broken laugh emerges from Hestia's mouth, but she can no longer control her emotions. The dam in her heart breaks and the tears come flooding out. "You... you are so kind to me... are you really... a demon?"

I embrace her, and she lets her voice out freely as she cries into my chest. My initial impression that she must have been feeling the same as I did, when I came into an unfamiliar environment all on my own, was plain wrong.

Unlike me, she has no place to return to, and she has neither a great power nor an unshakable spirit that allows her to live alone in this world. She also had nobody to open her heart to, while I quickly made friends, including with some of the humans I met - though it was quite easy to hide from them what I am.

Knowing that her own father sent her to a faraway land to die in a place where she wouldn't cause anybody trouble, while at the same time being placed on a pedestal in that very exile must have been an enormous burden on her. Alienated by everybody around her in this foreign land, she finally thought she found someone who could become her friend - only to learn that this person is a demon with a harmful effect on her.

However, right now she's holding onto me with all her feeble strength, to make sure that I'm not leaving her again, without a single shred of care for what I am. And it's really too late now; I've come into contact with her and touched her skin directly. But it seems that she doesn't care anymore. The warmth she was looking for all along is enveloping her now, and she might even think that it wouldn't matter if she died from it.

I've done it now, haven't I? Dregana didn't seem the type to let things slide, so when she finds out, there's going to be hell to pay. Though I wonder what Hestia's fans and the professors protecting her would say if they knew she was doing this out of her free will?

"Class has started." Kamii suddenly remarks next to my ear, and I flinch. The angel girl hastily separates from me with a flushed face, most likely being reminded by the little dark elf's voice that she has been watching us all this time.

Wait, don't tell me the warning bells I thought I heard in my head just now was the bell for the next period?

"Please, do not mind me." Wiping her tears, Hestia

smiles at me. Unlike earlier, it's no longer one that attempts to hide deep sadness and despair, but a genuine expression.

"Let's meet at dinner. It's a promise, alright?" I take her hand and lock my pinky with hers. From the corner of my eyes, I can see Kamii's eyebrow twitch at my action.

"Huh, what does this mean?" This isn't a custom of this world, so Hestia doesn't understand.

"It means that it's a promise that can never be broken." I hope the little dark elf doesn't think that pinky swearing has an inflationary value, which drops with each one in effect at the same time. As long as I don't make contradictory promises this way, everything should be fine.

"You are incredible..." The angel girl mutters with a giggle and looks down on our connected fingers.

Thus, we split up and go to our separate classes. I'm really looking forward to having a long conversation with Hestia later, but I don't let my anticipation mess with my concentration during the first afternoon period. It's Water Combat Training at the underground pool, and all the students appear in their underwear.

The heated indoor pool halls in the basement of the academy building seem to be connected to the lake, and boys and girls are separated for this class, which is only to be expected of this somewhat medieval society. I'm sure even the staff knows about my relationship with Kamii by now, so they should be careful with letting me participate in an underwear-only class.

But my mind is comparing all the girls I see with my memory of the little dark elf's body in the glow of the lamp crystals last night. Did she pick such a timing on purpose? She couldn't have known that this is how this class is held, right?

I don't find joy in watching half-naked girls anymore - who are by no means ugly - when I can still vividly remember the perfection of a dark elf's delicate shape. I hope this doesn't turn into a mental condition for me, or Daica would be very sad to learn that I can't get excited by her mature body. Kamii is more devious than I thought - although I may be wrongly accusing her here.

The professor is a woman in her mid-twenties, named Eydis Vinterstrom. She wears her brown hair in a ponytail and a streamlined light blue leotard that reminds me of a swimsuit, even though the material isn't quite the same. Her lean body is just like a professional swimmer's.

I have to say, many of the professors are quite young. While Liv may be the type to look younger than she actually is, Dregana and Kari appear to be in their twenties, as does Eydis. While that may have something to do with the fact that they're teaching beginner classes, it does make me wonder about their mastery in magic.

I assume the only reason we're here is the time of the year; I'm sure this class would have been held at the outdoor pool if it was summer right now. This is combat training after all, so people are bound to get wet - and sick if it's not at least as warm as in here.

"You have been learning to manipulate *Pilos Aquos*, is that correct?" Eydis asks the class this rhetorical question. Rhetorical, because she summons a water ball in the middle of her sentence while brandishing her staff. Of course, the professors share with each other what they taught, to build the classes around the knowledge the students have.

So one can speak the spell's name with the intention to cast it while otherwise talking normally. That could be useful for some sneaky incantations, and I'll make sure to remember it for when I need to act like I'm talking my way out of a situation.

The students reply to Eydis' spell with their own, creating hovering water spheres of varying sizes above their staves. When the professor sees that I'm not following suit, she glances at me with a stern expression but doesn't say a word. Clearly, she must have heard about my stupidly big output so she won't comment on how I can't really participate in class.

I hold out my hand towards the pool and cast Pilos Aquos with a whisper. A large sphere of water, enough to fill a large wine barrel, forms in midair. The students stare at it in wonder, and Eydis is looking surprised. It's much less than what I did in the morning class but still too much for me to maintain the shape of.

But that's what I wanted. The excessive water falls into the pool, and a smaller ball remains floating in place. I didn't have an opportunity to practice this move, so this is the best I can do at such short notice. Still, it's better than flooding this underground hall.

"Impressive." The professor simply comments and brings around her staff. Then she addresses the whole class. "I am sure that the wind mages have told you that it's a more versatile element than water and that it can achieve everything water can."

She sounds zealous for some reason. Maybe there's an ongoing feud between advocates of wind and water magic because the elements are quite similar in how they're wielded. I think that it's a moot point because they ultimately fulfill different purposes in life - although the academics might only look at it from a theoretical standpoint.

"But water is something material, and it possesses real weight." With these words, she swings her staff, and a small orb separates from her water ball. It shoots across the pool, where a row of wooden targets has been set up. The water splashes against one of the boards and pushes it down, but it immediately rights itself again. They're most likely mounted on a spring mechanism.

It seems that the focus of this class is achieving intricate control over the sphere of water one creates from a simple spell. There are no incantations involved in the shooting part, so that means Pilos Aquos is quite versatile on its own. The objective is to use the least amount of water to push the board down.

My output is stupidly large, so controlling the spells is even harder than usual. Not only can I not make the water fly in the right direction since it gets affected by gravity - unlike light magic, which I could use to hit with pinpoint accuracy - but when I do hit, it's not nearly enough power to topple the targets.

I find a little solace in the fact that none of the other students display much mastery over the spell either. While some do manage to hit the boards with enough force to push them down about halfway, they use up their entire water sphere in the process. Magic doesn't seem to require any resources, so it's not like it's a waste of mana or something. But I can understand the reasoning behind using a single spell to the fullest because recasting it requires an incantation and a little time for the water to form.

This is quite exciting, and I find myself enjoying this class a lot. Unlike during the wind class with Dregana yesterday, everybody is participating at the same time, so there's no waiting around for one's turn.

Slowly, I begin to appreciate the fact that everybody is in underwear, too. Water is splashing everywhere, and everybody soon becomes thoroughly drenched. A few have opted for colored undergarments so that when they do get wet, they don't become see-through. Others didn't think that far ahead or just didn't care because we're all girls here. It provides me with great insight into their individual growth or lifestyles when I see what they look like downstairs.

However, I'm comparing them to Kamii's perfection, so I can't bring myself to get excited by these practically naked girls swinging their hips while waving their staves to cast magic. One advantage is that it allows me to concentrate on practicing my magic better, so I won't complain too much.

At the end of the class, I still haven't been able to knock the targets down without employing the entire water ball. Strangely enough, I'm a little happy to realize that I'm not some kind of genius that does everything perfectly on the first try. It would be pretty boring if that were the case, and I'd be able to just learn the incantations for the most powerful spells to become a godlike existence. This way, I know that I have to practice, as well as choose my fights - if I ever get to that point.

It's highly likely that the academy doesn't want to let me leave when the time comes for me to return to fulfill Maou-mama's mission, and I'll have to fight my way out. By that time I'll make sure to have learned teleportation magic and make a run for it through the transportation circle I came through when I first arrived here - unless I find a closer spot.

"What's down there?" I ask when we leave the dressing room and walk down the hallway. There's a set of stairs that goes up to the first floor with periodic lamp crystals in wall mounts, but another set leads deeper underground. It lacks illumination, and there's a massive chain blocking the path.

"It's off-limits to students." One of the girls responds in a secretive tone. She's an unassuming girl with short brown hair and freckles sprinkled across her nose and cheeks, and I think her name was Helga Stenberg. "The professors tell us that it's a storage area, but rumors say that it directly connects to the Lost Tombs."

I'm a real sucker for such things. Glancing over, I imagine myself exploring that place sometime during the night and discovering the secrets buried in its depths.

"It really is only a storage area." I feel a hard knock on my head and turn around to find Eydis looming over us with her staff, which she used to hit me just now. It didn't hurt and wasn't meant as some kind of corporal punishment. She's slightly taller than me, and I'm the tallest in the class, so she does make for an imposing figure though.

"Of course you would say that." Helga comments with a mischievous grin and quickly runs away when the professor lifts her staff threateningly.

A strange feeling of warmth spreads inside me. This is only the second day I've been at the academy, but I've met so many interesting people. There are laid back lecturers like Liv, as well as those that command respect with an authoritative attitude like Dregana. Some have a balanced friendship-like relationship with their students, as Kari and Eydis do, and others are the type that prefers to convey as much knowledge as they can in the little time they get with their students, such as in the case of Sigsteinn. It brings me back to my time in high school.

I shake my head of the thoughts of my previous life welling up inside me. Once I let myself go down that road, I'll start missing the people I left behind there. After all, unlike the usual main characters in these reincarnation stories, I wasn't a shut-in who had no social contacts and whose parents were dead. I had a loving family and friends at-

No, I'm in a relationship with two loving dark elves, I have a close friend in a sassy living doll whom I can crack all kinds of jokes with, and a friendship with an angel girl is coming along. There's no reason for me to think about the past life I can't return to when I have all that now.

I'm interested in that so-called storage area though.

When I come to the canteen, Kamii is waiting for me outside already. She seems to arrive before me all the time, most likely hurrying here after class right away. I agreed to meet Hestia out here, so we wait until she shows up a few minutes later. She must have had wind magic classes on the field outside, which is much farther away than the classroom where I just had Application of Water Magic.

Speaking of that class, I couldn't participate at all, because the spells that were required had to be cast at a tiny scale. I didn't even try casting Pilos Aquos once, because I knew that the whole room would have been flooded. The contents were mostly about how it could be used for work in narrow spaces which require the fact that water is incompressible. I'll get to that eventually.

The canteen is bustling with activity already, and the benches are filled with students eating their meals and chatting. Many notice the three of us and go quiet though, and in our wake, many begin to whisper in hushed voices. As always, Hestia draws a lot of attention due to her large wings, but wherever Kamii passes, students are cautiously staring at her cursed arm.

I'm just an extra in the middle of these two, although the rumors about my magic output and my relationship with the little dark elf have already made their rounds through the entire student body by now. We're a trio of curiosities in their eyes, huh?

The sideways table at the back of the hall reserved for professors is full as well. Even the principal is among them. I'm sure all of them must have heard from Ninlil what went down in my room last night, and they can now see me associate with Hestia closely. Aldebrand, the professor who acted as my guardian when I left the citadel to get my luggage, is giving me a gaze of clear disapproval, and some others do the same. He must be one of those who revere Fatas for their purity and who would hate to see a demon corrupt them - just like he doesn't approve of same-sex relationships.

For now, none of them are taking any action like Dregana did yesterday - who's missing from the table. But as we walk down the aisle my eyes are on Thorvald; his reaction is the most important one here. After all, he was the one who approved my enrolment, knowing full well that I'll meet the Fata sooner or later. And I'll see how far his rule of no discrimination goes, and whether or not it's as progressive as I hope it is.

His gaze sweeps across us, stopping on Hestia and noticing how happy she seems to be while talking to me as she forgets about the silent stares from all the other students around her. Closing his eyes for a moment, as if to gather his thoughts, he opens them again and meets my gaze. A smile emerges on his face which extends all the way to his eyes, as they look directly into mine, and time seems to slow down. Then he blinks and turns his attention back to his meal, and the moment is over.

I think he doesn't really care about my sexual orientation, and he's approving of me being friends with the angel girl, as long as it's what she wants too. She wouldn't be smiling in such an easygoing manner if she feared to become corrupted, so it's clear that she has made her choice.

The three of us sit down together after some students make way for us - though I do notice that they hadn't finished yet and just did so out of respect for Hestia, or fear from Kamii.

As I glance over to the professors' table, I spot Thorvald saying something to Basarab sitting next to him, who gives a short reply. Then the principal turns around to address Aldebrand on his other side. The latter's eyes widen at the words spoken to him before he puts down his cutlery and wipes his lips with a handkerchief while trying his best to maintain a composed facade. Placing the cloth down on the table with more force than necessary, he stands up from his seat and walks out of the canteen briskly. Three other professors do the same and follow him out; those must belong to the conservative faction among the staff.

But apparently, everybody else quietly decided that they would approve of me associating with Hestia, but most likely only as long as nothing happens to her.

"So you live in the dorms?" The angel girl asks me, and my attention is pulled back to my companions.

"Yes, Kamii and I share a room." I reply, and a blush spreads on her cheeks. I'm reminded of the fact that she heard the little dark elf's declaration of our relationship first hand. And she must have heard the rumor about the voices coming from our room at night, so an image might have filled her mind just now. "Oh, what's this?"

I almost extended a finger to poke her in the side, but keep myself from doing so. Even if it's over the clothes, I still want to avoid touching her again until I can see what kind of effect my earlier contact with her had.

"N-nothing." She averts her gaze and pokes her food. I realize that she's only eating vegetables, and only boiled rather than grilled ones. It perfectly fits in with her image of a pure being, who only eats lightly seasoned things and never anything that has breathed at one point. I couldn't live without meat though, and I appreciate that she doesn't try to talk me out of it like certain people I've met in my previous life.

"Want to come over and hang out in our room?" Without thinking too much, I invite Hestia. The moment my words leave my lips, their implication dawns on me.

But it's already too late.

A wave of whispers spreads from around us, as the angel girl spins her head around to stare at me with round eyes. Her face is flushed red, and she flaps her lips in surprise. No taking back now; I stand to my decisions, however bad they may seem, so I keep a poker face as if it was all intentional. Wait, isn't that even worse? It will look like I just confidently invited her over for some *casual fun* of the lewd kind.

"Umm, i-if you do not mind." Hestia replies with a trembling voice, as she beats her large wings subconsciously. The students sitting on the chairs behind her duck, as they brush over their heads. She's so easy to read.

"Please come in." With these words, I gesture for Hestia to enter our room. I did use wind magic to dry the sheets in the morning and kept the windows open for the smell to disperse, but apparently, the entire room has been fully cleaned in our absence. It looks new - aside from the Graeber skull on the shelf - and I'm impressed by how quickly and thoroughly Ninlil works.

I spot Senka sitting on a chair facing the door like a puppet with its strings cut. Her eyes are silently staring at us, or more specifically, at the angel girl. The fact that her hair seems to have been combed and her clothes look cleaner than before - although they weren't exactly dirty either - makes me think that the dorm mother gave her a makeover, too.

"W-who is that?" Hestia points at the doll girl and doesn't want to step into the room, as if fearing that she may come to life at any moment and jump at her with a knife.

"That's just a doll." I walk over to Senka and pick her up to cuddle her. "Isn't she cute?"

The angel girl's expression says otherwise, but she'll understand the charms of creepy-cute eventually when she associates with me more. Then her eyes fall on the skull, the only piece of decoration in this room. Rather than the expected disgust or fear, she shows interest in it, to the point where she forgets about Senka.

"What is that?" She asks me and walks up to the skull with a curious expression.

"Will you keep it a secret?" I speak in a hushed tone, and Hestia is hooked. Nodding with excitedly glittering eyes, she looks up at me. "On our way here, we went through the capital of the dwarven kingdom Rathgolim. I accidentally startled the Graebern, and we had to fight our way out. This is the head of one of them."

"Ohh, tell me more! What happened there?" She sounds like a sheltered princess hearing about the outside world from an adventurer for the very first time. Maybe that's even the truth, considering she's in exile all alone.

Seeing how interested she is, I start from the very beginning, when we decided to go through the kingdom under the mountain as a shortcut, so that we could deliver Ingrid's message in time. Now that I'm recounting the story, I realize what an adventure that was. Before coming to this world, I would have never dreamed that I could one day experience something like that myself.

"Miss Marcott?" Hestia calls my name, and I'm pulled back into reality. After finishing my story, I must have lost myself in a strange sense of nostalgia, even though what I just talked about happened only a few days ago.

"Oh, sorry. I was a little out of it. In either case, call me Chloe." While that's a bastardization of my Japanese surname, it's the given name I go by and react to. Only Senka and Kamii have been calling me Makoto, though the latter's pronunciation is a little bit off. I won't correct her since it sounds cute.

"C-Chloe." With trembling wings, the angel girl tries saying it. She didn't hesitate as much as I thought she would. A lot of girls in middle and high school remained overly respectful with me even after I told them to call me by my given name.

Then again, this isn't Japan, and people here don't have as much apprehension to become familiar with one another. She stuttered because that's just the way she is.

"So, what do you normally do for fun?" I sit on the bed across from her and place Senka on my lap. Kamii lies down behind me and remains as silent as she usually is when I'm talking to others. I remember her encouraging me to initiate things with Hestia against Dregana's warning last night. She must be looking forward to seeing how it goes now.

"I like to do coal sketches." That was a wholly unexpected response, delivered in a rare moment of pride. She must be sure of her skills to be able to declare it with such a bright expression.

"Oh, that's incredible. Can you show me something you've drawn?" I'm quite interested to see what subjects an angel will feel compelled to put on paper, and I wonder what it would look like to see her fingers darkened by coal.

"I have them in my room..." This time she doesn't answer with as much enthusiasm as she did before. Maybe she's losing her confidence after being asked to show her work.

"Could we go over and take a look?" Probing cautiously, I try not to be too pushy.

"My room... is in the tower keep." With an avoidant glance, she explains why it's hard to just head over there. She means the tallest tower of the castle, which juts up into the sky like a spear.

So she's living all the way up there, huh? She must be

flying up and down on those wings of hers every day. I'm imagining the liberating feeling of soaring under one's own power, and the urge to get Hestia's genetic material is welling up inside me. With it, I could get those wings too.

A kiss would be enough, wouldn't it?

"Umm... how do I say this..." Her words pull me back, and I find her fidgeting. It seems to be a subject that's hard to broach.

"Yes? Don't worry about things, just say it." Encouraging her just once, I stay quiet and watch her gather her courage, to speak her mind.

"The rumor of you and Miss Kamii..." She finally begins, and my left eyebrow shoots up. "What were you doing?"

Is she asking about the details, or does she actually not know about the activities that create the sounds everybody in the vicinity of this room seems to have heard? If it's the former, I'd question her innocence. If it's the latter, I'd be overwhelmed by her innocence.

"Hm, so you want to know, huh?" The distance between the beds is pretty small, so I lean over to Hestia and look into her light blue eyes with a suggestive and seductive smile. "Do you want me to teach you?"

The pure-hearted Kamii last night, this pure-bodied angel tonight? What a feast!

"I-I..." It seems that understanding dawns on her. But she's unable to avert her eyes from my searing gaze.

"I've been surrounded by raging lesbians!" Senka suddenly shouts and pushes herself between us. Hestia stares at her, the doll I promised her was harmless, and blinks. That very doll girl spins her head around to face her, and I see a wide Glasgow smile reflected in her round eyes.

"Ah..." She faints from the shock.

"Hey, what're you doing?" I spin Senka around, but she

slackens again like a puppet with its strings cut. This is giving me a feeling of déjà vu; something like this happened in a similar constellation before. "Wait, didn't you do the same thing with Daica?"

"You're rushing things too much. These days it seems like your lower body is beginning to control your mind. What happened to the thoughtful Makoto?" Senka explains the reason for the clam jam without moving her lips. "I get the adage 'the more beautiful and pure a thing is, the more satisfying it is to corrupt it', but this isn't somebody you should corrupt so easily."

I turn to look at Hestia's unconscious form and glance over her pure white wings. It's true; I forgot that I wanted to keep an eye on things to see how my physical contact at noon today affected her body. But her asking about what I did with Kamii last night made my desires flare up.

"Thank you, Senka." A part of me is unsatisfied, especially since the mood was going in the right direction, but another one is relieved. I think the latter is the rational part. If I judged her reaction correctly, this could have been a step toward a deeper relationship. But if I were wrong, it would have left an irreparable mark on our still young friendship. "But if she wants it herself... you know."

"That's where things were indeed heading towards, but remember that she's a Fata and you're a demon."

"I think we're past that point, now. I touched her directly earlier today." I sigh. So far, her wings don't show any signs of corruption, but it may just be a matter of time.

"Then hope that it was brief enough that it won't result in what happened to her feather." At Senka's words, I involuntarily glance at the drawer in which I stored her shed feather, which turned jet black in a matter of seconds. I thought of using it as a piece of interior decoration, but am happy that I didn't. Hestia would have been shown proof of my effect on her the moment she entered this room.

"Wh-what...?" Hestia suddenly sits up after regaining consciousness and stares at Senka in my arms. "I could have sworn..."

"You must be tired; you dozed off just now, in the middle of our conversation. Maybe it would be best if we called it a day." I act like nothing happened, to keep Senka's secret. She may even believe that it was just a hallucination, resulting from lack of sleep. I already noticed at noon that she most likely didn't sleep last night.

"Oh..." Her expression reveals that she wanted to be in my company for a while longer, continue our conversation that led to me almost making a move on her, and then climb the stairs to adulthood with me. The last part is just my imagination though. "M-may I stay the night here?"

Or not?

"Hmm, would you normally ask that, knowing there are only two beds in this room?" It's a rhetorical question, implying that I'm thinking Hestia may be asking to share a bed with me. Her flustered expression shows that she picked up on what I meant. "You can sleep on that bed if you don't mind keeping the doll company."

"Eh?" She glances at Senka's scarred face and blinks. I shouldn't tease her too much, or she might remember what she fainted over.

"Kamii and I sleep together in this one." I state in a matter of fact tone while pointing at the bed I'm sitting on. My relationship with her is already a well-known fact throughout the academy, so there's no point in keeping it a secret.

"So it was true?" Hestia looks between the little dark elf and me. "Two... girls?"

"Yes, I have no interest in boys." I cross my arms and

declare in a definitive tone.

"Then Kamii is really older than you?" Yesterday, after Kamii started the rumor mill with her quite public announcement of our relationship, I did tell her that.

"Yeah, several summers older." I don't know her exact age, and I don't really feel the need to ask, either. She's from a long-lived people, and I'm most likely the same. There's no point in knowing for sure, considering we could be together for centuries from here on out.

"T-tell me more about your relationship." Even though it's a pretty personal question, Hestia's expression of innocent anticipation is persuading me to answer it. Maybe she'll awaken to the allures of this side, and I could have a chance with her.

The night is still young, a lot can happen.

Chapter 33

A Fruitful Day

"Onii-chan, it's time to wake up. You'll be late for school." A girl's voice with the incredibly sweet and even more incredibly stereotypical 'little sister pitch' wakes me up in the morning. My eyes snap open, and I'm instantly wide awake because I've never heard someone with that voice before. I find Senka leaning over me with a deadpan expression. "Ah, you're finally awake, onii-chan."

As if to demonstrate to me that it was her, she adds another line that would normally be unnecessary. It's delivered in a pitch that would fit a happy go lucky girl her apparent age, but it's completely out of place for her.

"So it was you! Can't you just wake me normally? And what's with the onii-chan?" I rebut, but seeing that I'm awake, she collapses back onto the chair I banished her to and ceases all her movements. Thanks to that, I don't even feel my usual morning sluggishness, but it's not good for my figurative heart to be startled awake like this every time.

I look over to the other bed and find Hestia sleeping there. She's curled up like a cat, and her wings cover her in place of a blanket. That's right, she stayed over for the night, so that Senka had to sit out in the cold.

And nothing happened between us after all. I told her about how I met Kamii and how our relationship progressed to the current point. Of course, I also revealed my work in progress with Daica and the fact that she's the former's little sister, assuring her that both are perfectly fine with it.

I'm sure it reminded Hestia of her father, who had a wife but still sought an illicit relationship, which ultimately resulted in her birth. But the thought that somebody could have too much love in their hearts to remain devoted to just a single person intrigued her. She even said that it may be a sign of greatness.

Sighing, I turn to look at Kamii, who's still asleep. I don't know about things like greatness, only that I fell for both dark elves and was unable to choose. People from my previous life would call what I'm doing cowardice or dishonesty, and that I'm just making excuses when I say that exclusively staying with one would deprive the other of the happiness I believe both can find with me. But I don't care what people think. I love both of them, they both love me, and all's right with the world.

I kiss Kamii on the forehead and shake her shoulder lightly, then get up from the bed and walk over to Hestia to do the same - but without the kiss since we're not there yet.

But I stop dead in my tracks. She lost a single feather in her sleep, and it's lying on the ground between the two beds. I pick it up and stare at it. Its tip has turned gray, and just a moment later, blackness spreads all across it.

"Mmm... Chloe?" Hestia wakes up and rubs her eyes.

"Good morning, Hestia." I quickly pull the feather inside my body through the palm and let it dissolve instantly. No need to cause unnecessary concern right when she wakes up; after all, it was only the tip.

I can't see any other feathers on her wings that have turned gray or even black. Maybe it only happens that quickly with ones she has shed. At least that's what the last two instances have been like. I guess her body has at least some defenses against it or the effect of me touching her directly yesterday noon would have been as noticeably imminent as those feathers.

"The first period will start soon, so we should get ready to go and have breakfast." The matter of corruption will be left for another time.

"Then I need to return to my room first." Hestia sluggishly drags herself out of bed and covers her mouth for a yawn, while her wings seem to still cling onto the sheets as if reluctant to let go of their warmth. She seems to be just as bad in the mornings as I usually am.

"Let's meet in the canteen then." I motion to walk over to the door to open it for her, but she wobbles over to the balcony and unlocks the glass door. "Huh?"

"Yes, see you there." With these words spoken in a lethargic tone, she falls over the handrail. I stare at the spot she disappeared from and remember that this is only the second floor. Even if she fell, she shouldn't have hurt herself.

I know she has wings, but Senka referred to Fatas as fake angels, so I thought that maybe they're just decorations and don't allow her to fly. That aside, she doesn't seem to be in any state to take to the air even if she could. But as if to prove me wrong, she comes up and glides past the balcony.

I run out and look up to find that she's beating her wings gracefully, as she soars towards the castle. Her room is located in the tallest tower, but for someone with the same freedoms as a bird that must be the best place to live.

When I turn around, I find that Kamii is rubbing her eyes after witnessing Hestia's flight. She's not as bad in the mornings as the latter and I are, but that just made her question her eyesight. I guess she didn't consider that those wings were really made to fly on.

Now I want the Fata's genetic material even more than I already do. It looks so liberating to freely travel wherever one pleases on one's own power. Well, I aim to get it eventually, one way or another. After all, that would allow me to travel back to the capital much faster than I could on foot, even when I'm in the vularen form. There's always teleportation magic, but I'll need to learn about it first.

For today, I have earth magic classes though.

"Good morning, Miss Marcott. The principal would like you to visit him in his office before breakfast." When we come down the stairs to the first floor, Ninlil greets me with this announcement while carrying a broom too big for her size.

"D-did he say what this was about?" I have a bad feeling about this.

"Hurry now, or you'll miss breakfast." Ignoring my question, she ushers me out by sweeping the dust around my feet. "Don't dawdle and go there right away."

There goes my cheerful mood for the day. I'm sure this is about my friendship with Hestia, which he did seem to approve of when I saw him in the canteen yesterday. Maybe he thinks I've taken it too far by inviting her to my room right after and making her stay the night. Though I'm surprised to see how fast news travel - unless he saw her taking off from my balcony directly through his office window.

But there are no two ways around it, so I'll have to get it over with as quickly as possible. I ask Kamii to go ahead and meet the angel girl in the canteen so that she doesn't have to wait too long in case things do take a while longer.

When I climb the stairs of the academy's central tower, I feel my heart beating faster. I'm in my full human template, so I do have all the functions of one. In my previous life, being called to the principal's office was something reserved for delinquents and problem children. Maybe it's a conditioned reflex in students?

"Come in." Thorvald's voice beckons me inside before my hand comes down to knock on the door. Nothing surprises me anymore in this academy; he must have a magical surveillance system in place or something.

"Did you want to talk to me about Hestia?" I enter and get to the issue right away.

"Oh, no. This is about your new schedule. It took a while, but it has been finished." The old man shows not a hint of surprise when I take such a confrontational stance. He's holding up a sheet of paper between his long and thin fingers. "You can choose to remain in the basic courses for the remainder of the waxing fortnight, or switch over to this one right away."

"So, this isn't about my..." Before I make a mistake and probe the matter too deeply, I shut myself up and walk over to take the new schedule.

"But do keep in mind that you should not come into too much physical contact with Lady Hestia." Just as I pull on the sheet of paper, he holds it tightly and adds this warning, before letting go. "You have to understand that I am taking a great risk in letting you do as you please."

"Then why do it in the first place?" It's hard for me to remain respectful when I'm told something like this.

"Because I see that you are good for Lady Hestia's heart. And it is indeed a testament to the failure of us humans that she could not feel at home at this academy until you, a demon, showed her the kindness she was longing for all this time." Thorvald's sharp blue eyes grow softer at these words.

"If you knew she needed friendship, not veneration, why couldn't you do something about it?" This may be an unfair accusation since I don't know all the factors involved in this matter. However, things could be much easier, if people didn't have to overcomplicate relationships. "Even though you knew this place was meant to be her exile - her grave!"

"As I said, it is the failure of us humans." He glances up at me, and the youthful glint I saw in him on our first meeting appears all but gone, replaced by weary old age. But his gaze grows sharp again, as he silently reprimands me for my disrespectful tone before a person of his standing. "Just like we regard demons as evil, we cannot see Fatas as anything but divine. Even if her circumstances are just as human as yours."

I realize what he's getting at. It stems from lack of knowledge of this world and possessing knowledge from my past life, that I found Kamii's cursed arm cool, while my first thought upon seeing Hestia was that she was simply beautiful. People born into this world would have reacted differently in both cases since they know what to expect in either of them.

He's not saying that everybody is that way; he himself is an example for one of those who can see beyond the stereotypes associated with races and cultures. But the vast majority of people don't have a worldview as broad as his, so they can't do the same.

"Whatever." I shrug to shake the oppressive feeling that Thorvald's imperious expression is laying on me. He deserves respect for many things he's done, including not ordering my death after finding out that I'm a demon and not discriminating against Kamii, so I shouldn't give him such a hard time. "Just know that I won't ever betray her."

This is a statement that shouldn't be delivered when one is flustered, but I intend to keep my word. Of course, it only stays in power as long as Hestia doesn't betray me. If she found out that I'm the demon queen's child and decided to use me as a bargaining chip so that she can return home in glory, I would not hesitate to end things right there.

Surely, she won't do that; she's much too pure for that.

"Thank you." With a nod, he expresses his gratitude, and I instantly feel bad for the tone I employed so far. "As for your new schedule, please make your decision now, so that I can inform the professors before class begins. And you better hurry, the first period is beginning soon, and you still have not had breakfast yet."

I take a look at the paper in my hand. When I see the subjects, my decision is made instantly.

"So you decided to continue taking beginner classes until the next fortnight?" Hestia asks me after breakfast when we make our way out of the canteen.

"Otherwise I wouldn't be able to have another magic class with you." After all, my new schedule doesn't have any basic classes aside from the seemingly universal History and Ritual Day every Hringurdag - the Fridays of each week. And I'd prefer being able to practice magic with Hestia rather than just sit next to her in a lesson where I have to pay attention and take notes.

"O-oh, I see." The angel girl blushes but looks happy to be incorporated into my decisionmaking like this. Her confession yesterday and Thorvald's silent apology today have already shown me that she was feeling alienated and lonely here, so I'm glad that I can alleviate it.

"So, see you at lunch break." I say to both Kamii and Hestia, and we go our separate ways. I'm quite looking forward to learning earth magic since it's something different from wind and water. It's also the only permanent magic that leaves behind solid matter. Surely, one can master it to the point of creating architecture with it, right?

When I make my way towards the training arena, I notice that other students are also converging on it. There are a few more than in the wind and water classes, and almost all of them are male. Furthermore, most of them are older than me, too.

Don't tell me affinities discriminate between genders and make it more likely for men to get the earth element, which is traditionally associated with physicality and steadfastness? It sure is the image I'm getting right now.

The training arena is a large pit dug into the ground, its walls surrounded by both rounded and jagged rocks jutting out from the dirt. These formations are the results of previous classes being held here and seem to be left on purpose. Some surfaces show heat marks, which must be what the last fire magic class left behind. It's an entirely different environment compared to the open field and the underground pool and has a raw feeling to it.

"Gather around." The teacher is a man in his early thirties with a bass voice to match his muscular frame, just like Halfdan, the earth mage adventurer in Hovsgaerden. However, unlike the latter, he's taller and has the stereotypical appearance of a PE teacher rather than a fur trapper. It even extends to his choice of clothes, which look like a medieval version of a sports jersey. He has short brown hair and kind dark brown eyes, but I'm sure they can grow serious when necessary. "As you may have heard by now, this academy has a new celebrity."

He gestures at me, and everybody turns to stare. This is the first time so many boys have had their eyes on me, but at this point, I don't care whether or not they're interested anymore.

"I'm Chloe Marcott, and I possess all magic affinities." With this short introduction, I get the surprise out of the way. The rumors about my relationship with Kamii and my apparent closeness with Hestia have drowned out the thing I should really be famous for. I can tell because my having all affinities seems to be news to the students here.

"My name is Bjorndal Svarteka, you can call me Bjorn." His approach seems to be one where he tries to become friends with his students. The fact of the matter is that most of them are men who also appear to have well-toned bodies, so this is like a fitness group. And unlike the traditional mages, they don't carry staves either.

Many students are wearing steel gauntlets with citrines let into the backs of them, and I finally understand what catalyst Halfdan must have been using. The adventurer didn't seem to have any when he placed his hands on the ground to cast his magic, but they must have been hidden under his sleeves all along.

"For now, try to keep up with everybody." Bjorn says and signals for the students to get ready. They take off the cloaks that protect them from the cold and place them in a pile on a stone bench, before forming two rows in front of him. Do earth mages need to perform hand or even body movements to cast spells? Then the professor begins to jog ahead, and the students follow him.

It's track and field!

My heart jumps into my throat at the familiarity of this sight, even though nobody is wearing proper sports clothes. Their pace is also slower than what I'm used to since they lack the proper running technique of the modern days. Nonetheless, this is the kind of warm-up exercise I can get behind.

That's when Bjorn switches things up and begins shadow-boxing while running. The students mimic his movements, and soon the arena is filled with the crunching sounds of dirt under soles, clothes rustling, and the rhythmic breathing of more than two dozen people.

I get a lot of wondrous stares when they notice that I'm not only keeping up but also showing no signs of tiredness. While my body is quite convenient and doesn't tire, this kind of exercise wouldn't have been enough to make me sweat even in my old body. I ran full marathons at competitive times even for adults, so this much is nothing for me!

After ten laps around the inner circle of the rocky arena, which already has many of the students breathing hard, Bjorn makes everybody line up in staggered ranks with a lot of space between everybody. It seems this is still part of the warm up, as he faces us to demonstrate moves for us to copy.

He draws one foot back and plants it firmly on the ground, and everybody follows his example. Then he performs a straight punch with his left fist, which looks incredibly powerful. I can tell that he has mastered his body far more than any of the students have. Even though many sport muscular frames, they don't have even half of his force in their punches, which only look like imitations of his movements.

"Put your minds into it. Feel your body, see the point you target and know how to get there." Taking a heavy step forward with his left foot, he delivers a straight with his right fist. "Pilum Gradum!"

With this chant, the ground around his feet cracks, and a circle of dirt in front of him rises up a little. He opens his hand into a palm facing down, and as if physically pulling up the ground, he lifts his arm. The dirt breaks to make way for a stone pillar, shooting up to about two meters in height. I was wrong, and this is already the magic portion of the class.

The students each go at their own pace, and the results are different for everybody. Some manage to pull out a pillar similar in size to Bjorn's, but they crumble right away as they're made of dirt rather than stone. Others rise up really slowly and don't reach nearly as much height as intended. Some barely make the earth move.

"Pilum Gradum." I'm standing at the very edge of the group and try to face away from the others when I perform the step and punch. The ground in front of me wells up slightly, but it's nothing too big, so I continue. Putting my intent into the invisible stone underneath the dirt covering the ground, I pull it up.

Like a breaching whale, a giant pillar shoots up in front of me and quickly grows to the height of a two-story building. However, it crumbles into fine sand almost instantly and returns to the earth. It seems I put too much force into it, but at the same time, I lacked control over the solidity of my spell.

As always, my output is ridiculous, but my control is mediocre at best. I've tried by whispering the incantations, with mixed results. I'll need to study melding and require a lot more time to practice before I can get better at this, but I didn't expect otherwise.

"That was great." Bjorn comes over to praise me, but I know that his next words will be a lecture. "But focus your mind on the shape, before trying to perform the motion."

What he's saying could apply to a physical exercise as much as it seems to apply to earth magic. Just copying a motion isn't enough, if the intention behind performing it isn't right. Running with your arms at the same angle as the fastest sprinter in the world is nice and all, but if it doesn't help to balance your body as it does for them, copying it will instead hinder you. It's a good lesson.

In either case, I feel unexpectedly pumped for earth

magic, even though I always considered it to be the least interesting of the nature elements and only useful for utility. After all, its destructiveness couldn't measure up to that of fire or water - or at least it's what I've been thinking so far. Now that I've raised a pillar that could shatter an entire building from below, I know otherwise.

In fact, I'm learning that wind and water magic can be employed for utility as well, while earth magic can easily match the others in its damage potential. I have a feeling that this has helped my understanding of magic in this world greatly.

But of course, I kept overshooting my spells in the quantity department, while messing up the quality department. If I hadn't already expected this, I would have been frustrated. Learning all kinds of magic couldn't be as easy as how I learned a few low-level spells, or everybody with an affinity would be able to do the same.

Though it doesn't explain why I was able to wield light magic so quickly, and Ignis doesn't cause a massive explosion of fire for me either.

The melding class that followed was practically the same as the previous two, except for a small difference in the end product. Unlike wind and water magic, earth is permanent; at least that seems to be the underlying philosophy of earth mages. Whatever structures and shapes they create through their spells should be done so with the intention to last as long as the mountains they use for inspiration.

If I think about it that way, maybe I'll do better in it, too. I'll see the fruits of this new way of approaching this particular element in the combat class after lunch.

"You are covered in dust." Hestia motions to pat it off my cloak, but I gesture for her to stop and quickly do it myself. "Oh."

Even though we don't care about each other's heritage, she seems to have forgotten way too quickly that I do spread corruption. Maybe there's no harm in touching just the clothes and keeping contact brief, but Thorvald warned me about it again just this morning, so it's fresh in my mind.

"Sorry, but... you know." I feel the need to apologize, but the angel girl doesn't look discouraged at all, and a beautiful smile spreads across her face.

"You are looking out for my wellbeing, are you not?" But her words carry a hint of loneliness, as she glances at our surroundings.

There are many students in the canteen, and many can be seen clinging onto one another, patting each other's backs, or just making physical contact with people involuntarily. For two friends to maintain such a distance does feel a little sad.

I'm the physical type as well, and I have to consciously hold myself back from just putting an arm over her shoulders as I would have done with my friends and club mates in my previous life.

As if to spite her, Kamii clings onto me while looking forward with a deadpan expression. Both Hestia and I stare at her, but she doesn't return our gazes and stoically walks alongside me as we head for the open kitchen to pick up our food. Maybe she feels neglected, now that I've been paying my new friend so much attention.

Over lunch, we talk about our magic classes and how we've been progressing. Hestia tells me that she only came to this academy about half a year ago and that she hadn't learned any magic before then. Apparently, her father had her carefully groomed to become a political tool, and that didn't include being able to defend herself with magic.

It explains why we met in the beginner class, though her proficiency and ease in utilizing wind magic is astounding. She must be a natural talent, who was finally given the opportunity to find out about it.

Also, she obviously has an affinity for light magic, so she's highly valued in this nation for that. All Fatas have it, but none of them live outside their isolationist country. They live in a theocratic feudal system with humans in a subordinate position, so the latter conduct all the foreign relations and trade for the ruling class.

The more I hear about Fatas, the less I see them as pure angels. They're just winged people who use their beautiful appearances and humans' misconception of their divinity to get ahead in life; Senka's comment about them being fake angels was very appropriate. Some of them possess the same kinds of ugly hearts that humans do.

"We'll have class together again on Fara Silfurdag." I look at my schedule after lunch is finished.

"Do you not have history and ritual day?" With her head tilted, the winged girl tries to peek at the piece of paper in my hand. "Oh, you do."

"You mean on Hringurdag? Will we be in the same class?" I have my doubts since everybody has the same schedule for that day, which means the students will be split across different classrooms.

"I hope so." Hestia gives me a shy smile, and my heart skips a beat.

"Me too." Kamii says without looking in our direction. Even though she remains expressionless, I can tell that she's sulking a bit because I haven't been paying her as much attention as I have Hestia since yesterday.

"I want to see how you do in classes." I put an arm around the little dark elf's shoulder and pull her closer. Now I see Hestia watching us with a sad smile. I feel bad for her, but I won't touch her until I figure out whether corruption accumulates in her infinitely or slowly disappears with time. The former would mean that from now on I shouldn't ever touch her again, and the latter that it's fine as long as it's in moderation.

I'd like confirmation as quickly as possible, but it's something that takes time specifically, so I can only wait.

I thought that the Earth Combat Training professor would be Bjorn again, but it's an old man with magnificent white sideburns and a bald head. He's a bit taller than me, but his form still appears stocky, sporting a muscular body that even his baggy clothes can't hide. His entire midsection is incredibly broad, but I don't doubt for a moment that it's made of muscles rather than fat.

His name is Magni Svarteka, and I immediately understand that this is Bjorn's father. I even spot the resemblance right after the latter's image floats to the surface of my mind.

"My son taught you *Pilum Gradum*." Just as he says the name of the spell, he takes a powerful step forward and delivers a punch that looks even more impressive than Bjorn's. The students in front of him take a step back in fear, but the stone pillar doesn't erupt where everybody expected it. Instead, it shoots out from behind him at a perfect forty-five-degree angle. "Now you'll learn to wield it not as an extension of your body, but as an ally."

I thought that earth mages were disadvantaged in that they have to use the ground under their feet while the others seem to be able to summon elements out of thin air. But it's actually an advantage because in all the other elements, the spells seem to appear near the catalyst, while in earth magic the very ground the enemy stands on can be manipulated and used as a weapon.

"But first, let me demonstrate the Svarteka family's

traditional earth magic form!" Magni announces in an excited voice and takes off his robe and shirt to reveal a muscular body befitting of a thirty-year-old rather than someone I assumed to be over sixty.

"Oh no, not again." One of the few girls in class complains in a hushed voice, but the professor hears it.

"Silence! I expect you to be able to do at least one-hundredth of this by the end of winter!" He points at the girl, who quickly stands at attention and nods.

"He's only doing this to show off to the new student." A boy mutters while glancing at me. I assumed as much, considering everybody here already seems to know whatever the old man's talking about.

Magni takes the starting stance for Pilum Gradum that Bjorn taught us in the morning. With a strong forward step, he chants the spell and pulls a pillar up from the ground. However, he doesn't stop there and takes a step towards the formation to deliver a punch to it while calling out a new incantation I haven't heard before.

"Volantem Lapim!" The fist connects with the pillar, and the upper half of it breaks off. It flies in the direction of his punch and turns into a spike in midair. But Magni doesn't stop and spins around, delivering a backhanded swing at an invisible enemy, while chanting yet another spell. "Ortum Terram!"

The ground rises up where his swing is the strongest so that whoever stood there would have taken it in the rib area. Even though he's walking a form, it feels like he's putting his all into it; every punch gives me the impression that it could break bones, the effect of every spell flows perfectly into the physical attacks, and I can practically see the shadowy figures surrounding him, which he's fighting off all on his own.

"Guttam Terram!" Another spell, which causes the ground in a small area to sink down, is followed by a knee thrust that would shatter an opponent's nose if one had stood there.

At one point, I can't keep up with each incantation, even while the speed remains a slow rhythm that seems to show off the mage's steadfastness and signal to attackers that their defeat is an inevitability. Every bodily movement is accompanied by an earth spell that just brims with power.

By the end of it, Magni's naked upper body is steaming in the cold air, as he exhales a long breath and returns to a ready stance. Then he turns around to the students, of whom most have become captivated by the display even though some complained about having already seen it many times at the start.

"Let the lesson begin." With his intense voice, the professor finally declares the official start of class.

Now I understand why the vast majority of earth mages are men that extensively train their bodies. Pretty much everybody got knocked around by emerging pillars they accidentally created outside of their fields of view. One broke an arm upon getting hit by his own spell from behind, while another suffered a concussion when he launched himself through the air and impacted the ground hard.

I was one of them too, though luckily the hardness of my pillars are flimsy at best. When I intended to pull up one from behind me, it came from the front and hit me in the stomach. While it did knock the air out of my lungs, it was nothing more than sand. If it had been a solid block of stone, my insides would have been turned into mush.

In times like these, I can appreciate that I wasn't reborn as a human, or my life in this new world would have ended right there.

The students who broke something were carried off to

the infirmary, where they will get healed by a nurse who can use light magic. To have one of the only twelve people in this nation - thirteen with me - who have an affinity for light working as a nurse; this academy really is something else.

The Application of Earth Magic class that came afterward required intricate control that I still don't possess. Earth magic's utility is far more evident than that of the other elements, in that it can be used to create permanent structures, both above and underground. Halfdan made a stairwell and closed off a tunnel in seconds, and the professor built a crude two-story house over the course of a few minutes, which he returned to the earth right after.

Of course, the students weren't required to do the same, but they were shown their goal, just like Magni showed it to us in regards to combat abilities. It motivated people to strive for something, rather than being told to blindly practice a spell they just learned. Ultimately, I didn't create anything permanent, as my output was still too strong - though I'm feeling that it's slowly getting better.

I'm confident that things will improve soon from here on out.

Chapter 34

A Crimson Magic Dream

The dreaded fire magic class has arrived. It's the one thing I've been scared of when I first noticed that my magic output was ridiculously over the top, but the issue with Hestia has successfully distracted me from those thoughts.

I know I can cast Ignis without causing an explosion, but I have no idea why. The flame that was meant to range from the size of a candle's light to that of a torch's fire follows my will perfectly, and I can adjust its size according to what I want it to be.

"Miss Marcott, I have heard that your control over the flow is still lacking. Please be cautious of where you release your magic." The professor is Astrid, the first member of the staff that I met at this academy, and she pulls me aside to warn me before the lesson starts.

Thanks, I'm feeling extra pressure now.

We're in the training arena which was somewhat reshaped in the earth magic classes yesterday but still remains a closed off area where no fire can spread. Astrid is teaching us a spell called Mico Ignis, an addition to the

Ignis spell that everybody here apparently already knows. The defining characteristic is that it's a remote flame that can't be maintained, and it used to be the go-to spell for lighting candles on the high-hanging chandeliers in the canteen. Lamp crystals became widespread in the academy and made that obsolete, but it can still be useful for igniting something from a distance.

That's like the worst spell to teach somebody with poor control. Just like with the stray stone pillars yesterday, I might accidentally create a flame right under somebody's cloak - most likely my own.

"Mico Ignis!" Astrid is using a walking stick-sized short staff. Upon chanting the two words, a small flame appears a dozen steps away from where she's pointing. It flickers out almost instantly, just the way she had said it would.

And then it's already our turn. The class is smaller than any of the previous ones, though I don't know whether that has anything to do with the rarity of the fire affinity or is pure coincidence, so there's plenty of space in the arena to spread out in.

"Ignis." I ascertain myself of the fact that my control over fire is still as I remember it. Who knows, maybe all the melding lessons has also messed with this element. But the flame that appears over my hand is as small as I intended it to be.

"Woah." The nearby students make, and I notice that many have taken a larger distance from me than they have from each other. Thank you for your trust in me!

"Without a catalyst..." A girl with dark reddish-brown hair mutters, unaware of the fact that I can hear her. It's not something I can pride myself in since it's always been like this for me; it most likely comes with being a Crawling Chaos.

"Mico Ignis." I try adding the extra word to the

incantation and extend my hand towards the arena wall. A small explosion of fire occurs right on target, albeit slightly larger than I had intended for it to be.

"Incredible!" Another girl with crimson eyes and short brown hair covered by a pointy witch hat exclaims. She wears a black cape rather than a cloak and wields a gnarled staff with a large red orb set into its top section. Her eyes switch between the smoke rising from the explosion site and me, an excited glint in them. That appearance is somewhat familiar, but I can't remember where I've seen it before.

In either case, I'm surprised to find that my control over fire, the most volatile of all elements, is much better than that of the others. The first time I cast Ignis back in Hovsgaerden, it was as intended too, unlike all the other spells I've learned at the academy so far.

I feel something stir inside me.

"Mico Ignis Fortior." I aim at the same spot again, but try adding the word that modified the Ventus spell to be stronger as a test. This time, the explosion is more than twice as large as the first one. The same girl that expressed her amazement before is clutching her staff and staring at it with glittering eyes.

"Miss Mar-" Astrid calls out to me, but my lips are already chanting again before my mind is ready.

"Grandor Mico Ignis Fortior!" This time I'm combining the spell Dregana used against me in Wind Combat Training, Grandor Ventus Procursus, with the Mico Ignis Fortior from just now. I noticed a pattern in incantations, wherein the modifiers have a different ending than the actual effect of the spell. In this case, it's Grandor and Fortior.

A gigantic whirling ball of fire appears where I aimed the spell. However, unlike the smaller versions of the spell before, it stays in place and continues to burn even though there's nothing to feed it.

Is it just me or is that fireball growing? Uh oh.

I cancel the spell in my mind, but it's already too late. Instead of fizzling out, it collapses on itself before disappearing in a massive explosion that shakes the ground. A shockwave whips my hair and cloak around, as I stare at the crater in the wake of my overeager experiment.

The entire class is speechless, but Astrid walks over to me with the silently seething anger that only a female teacher can both hide and openly display as skillfully as she's doing. I prepare myself for yelling or even corporal punishment - that's still a thing in this world - but her first words baffle me.

"Are you unhurt?" She asks with a level voice. I was the closest to the explosion, but it was still far enough away that only some of the heat reached me.

"I'm alright." I'm too dumbfounded and realize too late that it was an opportunity to get myself out of the scolding. Which follows now that she knows I'm fine and don't need to go to the infirmary.

"What were you thinking? The objective of this class is not to learn how to burn down the entire academy, but achieve the fine control over one's magic to light a candle across the room." She lectures me in a stern voice. "Anybody can make something bigger and brighter; it takes far more time and skill to go in the opposite direction."

I feel like I've heard that last one somewhere before, but keep my mouth shut and simply nod. This was my fault, so I should just accept my punishment - although it's lighter than I imagined it would be considering what I've witnessed in other classes so far. But at the same time, Astrid is relentless, as her preaching continues for quite a while.

When I'm finally released, and she turns around to look at the class, everybody quickly acts as if they've been practicing on their own while she didn't pay them any attention. The only person who keeps staring at me is the witch girl. She now appears ecstatic and comes over to talk with me, ducking past some of the other students to not look too obvious. When she stands in front of me, I notice that she's slightly smaller than even Kamii.

"That was amazing!" Her first words are not a self-introduction but a profession of admiration. "Mico Ignis!"

She then suddenly chants the spell and swings her staff towards the crater that I made in an overly dramatic gesture. However, only a small flicker of a flame appears in midair and instantly vanishes without much of an impact. It would have been barely enough to light even oil, so it sure as hell can't be called an explosion.

"I love fire magic, but I just don't seem to be very talented at making it work at a distance." With a derisive comment about her own proficiency, she turns to look at me. Her eyes are hopeful as if expecting that I can teach her to overcome that weakness. "Please tell me how you could scaled up such a weak spell with unrelated modifiers like that."

"I don't really know how I did that either, umm..." Not trying to sound rude when asking for her name, I act like I'm trying to address her. Unlike Drills, she came to me with a friendly demeanor after all.

"Oh, I'm Lenoly Emberwake." She catches on quickly and gives me her name.

"... Emberwake?" I repeat the name because it sounds like a made up title she gave herself. Especially after telling me that she loves fire magic, introducing herself as Emberwake is adding oil to the flames of my doubt. This girl must have chuunibyou.

"Yes, we bakari don't have family names and are given

titles when we cast our first spell in life." She doesn't seem to think anything about my skepticism and explains.

Wait, bakari? Maou-mama told me about the Bakari clan, one of the Four Great Clans of the Dominion. They're made up of humanoids that have goat-like features, such as horns, square pupils, short tails and patches of fur on the center of their chests - and other regions of their bodies. I can't see the latter because of her clothes, but that witch hat might be hiding the horns. Her pupils are human though.

"Are you a demon?" I ask and raise my eyebrow - maybe making too much of a skeptical face because Lenoly is taken aback by the straightforward question combined with my expression. Then she loses her carefree demeanor and looks away troubled.

"Ah... yes I am..." Her answer is delivered with as much enthusiasm as should be expected coming from somebody who was asked an uncomfortable question.

"That's awesome! I've been wanting to meet one of the demons attending the academy for a while now." Luckily, I was able to contain my excitement enough to avoid revealing that I'm one as well by saying 'a fellow demon' just now.

"H-huh?" Lenoly looks even more surprised than she was before. She most likely didn't think that I'd be happy, and instead felt that I'd start avoiding her after learning she's a demon.

"I can't really teach you how to do what I just did since it just happened, but we can practice together from now on." Giving her a gentle smile, I explain my situation.

"You don't mind me being a demon?" She's staring at me curiously, most likely thinking that I'm strange for feeling this way. Maybe she has been facing some discrimination because of her race, though in her case it's not as evident as it is with Kamii and Hestia.

"No problem at all. The love of my life is a cursed dark elf." I don't feel embarrassed announcing this to the entire world; everybody in the academy should know about our relationship anyway. And just as expected, she blinks her eyes in realization.

"Ohh, you mean Kamii?" But I didn't expect her to know the name.

"Yeah, that's the one." I confirm it.

"You're quite bold, aren't you? Announcing that so openly and all." With a somewhat gloating grin, she comments on how readily I revealed my sexual orientation in a place that doesn't look too kindly on it.

"Not as bold as you, announcing that you're a demon." I return the favor. Expressing love towards a fellow girl is already frowned upon, but that girl is a pariah too, so people will avoid me for being strange. However, being a demon in human territory usually only invites fear or hostility, so she's one step above me.

"Huh, when did I do that?" She tilts her head and raises an eyebrow.

Damn, I feel like punching myself. Now I know why she told me that she's a bakari without a care in the world; humans don't know demon clan names and lump them all together as enemies. She might be treated as a foreigner or some ethnic minority from a backwater place where traditions like giving names based on magic casting exist. But in the Dominion, the Bakari clan is one of the most respected, and their kind are the most numerous of all demon species.

"Umm, never mind." It doesn't seem like she did it intentionally, to test whether I'm a demon or not. Luckily, she seems to be a little of an airhead, or she would have instantly picked up on how I associated bakari with demons. Or maybe she already did but doesn't want to blurt it out in front of everybody. "Let's practice together."

"Yes, let's do that!" All other thoughts seem to be cleared away at my words, as she nods enthusiastically.

Phew, dodged a bullet there.

I practiced moderation with my spell output afterward and tried to explain to Lenoly how I visualized creating a flame a distance away from me rather than right above my palm. It's hard to put it in words, as I'm not doing it consciously. Astrid showed how this new spell worked, I knew how its basic version worked, and the rest just happened.

But Lenoly is a hard worker, and by the end of the class, she was able to conjure a somewhat larger burst of flame at a shorter distance away than she tried to cast it at before. Maybe she just aimed too high at first because she aimed for maximum effect and range at the same time.

In the second period, we sat next to each other and theorized about using the spell in creative ways, rather than listen to Astrid - who also happens to be the melding professor. Until she noticed our behavior and put a stop to it with a small Mico Ignis right above the notes on our table. I think it singed my brows a bit, and Lenoly fell off her chair in surprise.

Of course, the entire class laughed about it, but I took it in stride. It was our fault for not paying attention and talking about unrelated things in the middle of lessons.

Also, I got to see under Lenoly's skirt where I noticed that she has a brush-like tail sticking out from a hole in her bloomers. She already admitted that she was a demon, but this confirms it. She quickly covered herself in embarrassment, and a fuzzy feeling of familiarity spreads in my chest.

This is the school life I've been wanting.

"Kamii!" Lenoly runs ahead of me and jumps at the

little dark elf with a hug. The latter used to do that to me just a few days ago, but now the tables have turned.

"Stop. I can't breathe." Kamii says unenthusiastically and makes a half-hearted effort to push the bakari away. They're both about the same height, so they look like classmates in middle school.

As someone who has a relationship with one of them, I should have left out the 'middle' part there...

"Don't be so cold, you always leave me during meals to sit with Miss Marcott. Now that we know each other, we can have meals together." From Lenoly's words, I glean that she and Kamii have become friends. I had feared that the latter would avoid associating with other people and that her school life would be a lonely one in which I'm her only bond to remind her of this important time in life.

Well, it doesn't seem like school has that much of an impact on the lives of the people in this nation as it does in Japan. After all, this is a magic academy, and life is quite different in this world.

Kamii is way beyond the age of a school kid anyway.

Soon, Hestia joins us, and we enter the canteen together. She glances at Lenoly repeatedly, wondering why our trio has suddenly increased by a member. Or maybe she fears that I'm being taken away by this newcomer and won't have as much time for her anymore.

"Vitalis, over here!" Waving across the heads of the students already sitting at the tables, the little bakari calls over another person. It's a girl with long curly brown hair, purple eyes, and an unnaturally white complexion. Her expression is straightforward, and her clothes are so orderly that she's only missing a pair of glasses to complete the appearance of an honor student who could make president of the student council.

My first thought is that she's a demon in disguise too.

And when she comes closer, I find that every inch of her skin, including her hands, is covered in fine white powder. Is she purposefully using makeup to hide her usual skin tone? It instead makes her stand out - at least it does to me - but if she's normally blue, this would be better than nothing.

"This is Miss Marcott. I finally got to meet her directly after hearing about her so much from Kamii." Lenoly says to Vitalis, who looks up at me with a curious expression. I see that Kamii has been talking about me to her friends, huh?

When I turn to the little dark elf, she averts her eyes at the exact same time. Her face doesn't betray any emotions as she maintains a neutral facade, but she's either embarrassed that I found out, or fears that I'll ask what she has been saying in particular.

"It's nice to meet you. My name is Vitalis Alacinea." She nods stiffly, though I assume it's not because she's nervous. Her voice is completely unlike what I expected; it sounds mellow, and she drags her words as if she's sleepy.

"I assume you already know me, but I'm Chloe Marcott. You can call me Chloe. Both of you." I include Lenoly as well, who isn't shy to take me up on that offer immediately.

"Let's go get lunch, Chloe." She says and takes my hand to pull me along. But she instantly lets go again as if an electric shock just ran through her.

"What is it?" I look down at my hand; if it was static, I should have felt it too.

"N-no, nothing." Forcing a smile, Lenoly gestures for me to follow her, but she doesn't try to take my hand again. I take a closer look at it to see if I botched my transformation somewhere and created a sharp or pointy thing on it, but that's not the case. Maybe she realized that holding hands was too much for friendship. Are bakari that prude?

It would be funny if a demon feared my touch, while Hestia seems to actively seek it. But in the end, I'm sitting on the side of the table opposite from Lenoly and Vitalis, so I can't try to find out what happened back there.

To my dread, I find that the professor for Fire Combat Training is Dregana. She's the one person I didn't want to meet ever again - not like I could have avoided her on Fara Silfurdag when I have Wind Combat Training with her. She told me to stay away from the Fata on my very first day, but I went and ignored it for all to see.

The second she spots me, her eyes hone in on mine, as she gives me a deathly glare with her piercing golden irises. In her last class, she tried to seriously hurt me, and it was only wind magic then. Now it's the much more dangerous element of fire, and I believe the damage from that is something a Crawling Chaos can't just regenerate. In fact, it seems to be the only element that my kind might be weak against.

"Today, you learned the addition of Mico to fire magic." I'm sure she's itching to burn me to cinders in a 'magic accident', but she maintains a professional tone in front of the students. However, even they can tell that she's in a bad mood, as many are looking nervous under her gaze.

"Today is going to be a blast..." Lenoly whispers next to me with an uneasy expression, and I can't help but snort at her pun.

"It appears that Miss Marcott would like to volunteer to demonstrate the use of Mico." Obviously, Dregana would hear it and make use of that to get at me. "Set fire to the hay without making a sound."

She's asking me to cast the spell in a way that it doesn't

explode, thinking that my control over the flow is as bad as it is with all the other elements. Astrid must have not informed her that - ironically - I'm quite good at controlling the most volatile of all nature elements.

"Mico Ignis." I mutter and point at one of the prepared bales of hay. A small flame flashes under it and disappears almost immediately, but it was enough to jump over to the dry hay. The fire quickly spreads and soon the whole thing is burning.

"Well done." Despite her obvious dislike of me, she has her voice and facial expression under control. "You can adjust *Mico Ignis* to achieve either a small silent flame or an explosion that comes with a bang."

Again, I'm seeing an incantation being integrated into a sentence. The professor points her staff at another hay bale, which explodes from within, blowing it to pieces instead of setting it on fire. It seems she placed the spell inside her target, and I suppress a shudder at the thought that she could do the same to me anytime she wanted to.

"You will learn to master both, and you will be tested by the end of the lesson." Dregana paces in front of us like a drill inspector and announces with a cold and firm voice. "There are enough targets for all of you to practice on. Get started."

Her eyes stop on me, and I can practically feel the seething anger in them. I'm sure that she'll chew me out at the end of class, if not before.

"Let's practice together." Lenoly turns to me and motions to come closer but stops dead in her tracks like a deer under the headlights of an oncoming car. The car in question is Dregana, and the headlights are her golden eyes that are just as glaring.

"Don't worry, you'll do fine." I mutter to her, and she responds with a nervous nod, before turning away and getting to work on her target.

"Mico Ignis!" I call out since I intend to cause an explosion this time. However, the spell goes off-target and detonates the ground next to the bale. It doesn't even catch on fire, and I almost flinch when I see a pair of golden eyes turning towards me from the corner of my eyes. Fortunately for me, she doesn't say a word and continues to let her gaze sway across the class.

Glancing over, I find that Lenoly is having trouble getting the small flame close enough to light the hay, so I'm sure she'll have even more difficulty creating the explosion. The testing distance is a dozen steps, which is almost twice the range at which she can conjure fire reliably.

And it seems she's not the only one having trouble. In that regard, I'm the most proficient fire mage in this class, as I was able to do it with the silent flame on the first try. Could it be that I'm actually a genius in this element?

I cast Mico Ignis, but more quietly, to adjust my control over it. But it doesn't appear where I want it to and flickers out uselessly. Once again, Dregana's eyes fall on me, and this time they show clear disapproval.

I'm sorry for getting ahead of myself. The first try was just a fluke, and now I may fail the test at the end of class.

"I'm beat." I hang my shoulders and walk alongside Lenoly, as we head towards the academy building. In the end, I was somehow able to reproduce my first lucky hit and used a big explosion to cover for my lack of pinpoint control. The first earned a nod from Dregana, which looked very reluctant, and the second garnered me a glare. But luckily, she didn't say anything and moved on to the next person.

The little bakari is hanging her head and seems to be breathing out her soul. She wasn't even close in any of her dozen attempts, and the professor decided to stop her so that others could get their turn. It must have been quite the shock for her after her successes in the first period.

"Come on, cheer up. I'll practice with you on Sjodag." We have the day that is equivalent to a Sunday off so I could dedicate some time to training magic with her. I need to get better myself so that I won't get glared at by Dregana again. Next time I'm sure she'll make me repeat it several times to test my consistency.

It was a surprise to find that she let me go after class. I seriously expected that she would call me over to scold me because I ignored her warning about Hestia. Maybe the principal forbade professors from confronting me about the matter.

In comparison to the tiring couple of hours, which felt even longer than the melding classes in which a professor talks us to death without a break, the Application of Fire Magic class with Aldebrand was quite relaxing. He didn't make his dislike of me as obvious as Dregana is doing, but he also didn't engage with me like he did with the other students. In fact, he pretty much ignored me for the entire duration of the lesson.

Well, I'm not here to be familiar or even friendly with the professors - though I wouldn't say no if it were with Liv or Eydis. As long as they teach magic properly, and I can interact with the students, I'll happily take any glares or silent treatment from most of the staff. It would hurt if Ninlil were that way with me though; I really do like her.

With a rather tiring afternoon, another day of school is over, and I can look forward to dinner with Kamii and Hestia. Now Lenoly and Vitalis are joining us too, and it really begins to feel like high school again.

Chapter 35

Demon Mages Society

Early History of Magic, History of Demons and Magic, Theory of Rituals, and then Ritual Practice; that's the program for today. For the former three, I'll be in class with Kamii and Hestia. Lenoly and Vitalis are in a different group, though everybody has the same lessons.

With both girls flanking me, I can barely concentrate on the content of the classes. It doesn't help that the professors seem to be elderly people who speak slowly and without much motivation in their voices. At least I take away from the first period that magic was created by the gods, and made available to the populace through the founding of the Royal Academy.

I'm not that interested in history lessons though, so I don't retain much more than that; it was the same in high school for me. Legends and fairy tales, on the other hand, those tickle my interest. When the bard accompanied the tale of Gulbrand, Lord of the Forge, with mysterious music and used a clear voice filled with imagination to deliver the story, I was utterly captivated. Even though that was most likely a historical account as well.

I force myself to pay attention during History of Demons and Magic because it directly affects me. It seems that the Royal Academy came into existence shortly after the demons were first encountered. As if the founder understood the threat they would pose to humanity a century later, she did her best to spread magical knowledge among the people.

Around the same time, a similar academy sprung up in the Empire of Terminus, back then only a small kingdom with a different name. It aided them in the conquest of the surrounding nations and propelled them towards the formation of the empire.

Magic was first used as weapons before more peaceful times saw their application in everyday life. There were some prolonged periods of stability and even peace with the demons, so the figurative swords were turned into figurative plowshares. Fascinatingly, some spells in existence today were copied from tribal magic innate to demons.

It's ironic to think that humans were able to get so far with their magic because they learned from their mortal enemies, whom they can't reconcile with on the most fundamental basis; that of survival.

The fact that there were periods of peace intrigue me though. I think this will be the first time that I'm going to read history books in the library out of my own volition.

Theory of Rituals and Ritual Practice are different from what the labels suggested in my mind. I thought they would be about drawing magic circles on the ground, wearing dark cloaks, and sacrificing animals to commit some sinister deeds. Instead, the classes teach the proper steps one has to take in alchemy and the creation of magic goods such as wands and staves, of which the processes are considered rituals in their own rights.

Well, the former does also seem to teach ritual magic -

spells that require many to perform together - but just not today. The latter then puts the theory learned before into practice, as we're given raw materials and told to put together potions under close supervision.

Even then, a boy managed to botch his concoction and created a flammable liquid that sticks like napalm. But instead of being scolded for practically melting down his table, he was praised for the discovery, and the brew was taken in for analysis - most likely for military application.

Is this how chemistry in ancient times worked? People just had accidents, and they found out substances that could be used for warfare?

The intended result is what Hestia achieves on her first try; a transparent bluish liquid that reinvigorates and clears the throat from hoarseness. A mage's voice is his most important tool after all, next to a catalyst that is.

"I assume you're good at cooking too." I comment when I eye the brown stuff I created somehow. It smells terrible and doesn't look like something a person could ingest without incurring the wrath of their own bowels. The angel girl is just perfect all around, huh?

"Y-yes, I do like to cook for myself from time to time." She actually replies in the affirmative.

"I'd love to eat a dish you made someday." I pour my poison into the sink located at the side of each long table and turn to look at the result of Kamii's mixture. Hers looks far less dangerous than mine, but she isn't confident in its effects either.

"Don't drink this." She says after taking a whiff from it and pulling a grimace. It's a darker blue than Hestia's, but it also appears to be continually bubbling without any apparent heat supply. I have no idea how either of us could create such failures from natural ingredients like herbs and minerals.

The class ends uneventfully for us, though others had

their mixtures blow up in their faces as smoke and foul-smelling fumes. None were as bad as the napalm boy's, but maybe he got off better than the others who essentially only failed. We clean the earthen beakers and dishes we used, before packing our stuff and leaving the class for dinner.

"Hey, I'm Akyna Requin. I was told to deliver a message to ye." A man - or boy, I can't really tell his age from his appearance - with pale grayish skin and combed-back ultramarine hair chats me up at the dinner table. I never noticed him before, but now that he stands before me, I can tell that he's clearly a demon.

His body is incredibly top-heavy, with his head flowing into his broad shoulders almost seamlessly through a thick neck. Unnaturally small and nearly perfectly circular eyes dot his face, but his dark blue irises leave barely any room for the sclera to be visible. He lacks eyebrows - and indeed, any kind of facial hair - but has a pronounced brow ridge, which makes it look like he's always frowning. Adding the fact that several rows of sharp triangular teeth line his constantly open large mouth, he has the appearance of a shark walking on two feet.

"Though ye can't be..." He scratches his head with a webbed hand and looks at me skeptically.

"Can't be what?" I ask, feigning innocence and faking a smile. Hestia next to me is feeling uneasy and tries to appear inconspicuous. Kamii doesn't seem to care about this person standing at our table and is continuing with her meal, letting nothing come between her and the plate full of delicious food.

"Hey, leave her alone." Lenoly stands up from her seat across the table and points her staff at Sharkface.

"Oy, careful with that." He has an accent that makes

him sound unrefined, and it's clear that he isn't from this nation. "Don't kill the messenger, aye?"

I correct myself; he sounds like a pirate.

"Go on, do your job then." I don't know what to think of this individual, so I'll wait and see.

"Professor Laiota wants to speak to ye after dinner." Despite seeming brutish, he has the presence of mind not to point in the direction of the table where the professors are eating. Basarab is there and eyeing me as if he heard what his messenger just said.

"Did I do something?" I doubt he knows, but I still ask.

"No, it's more about what ye are, if ye catch me drift." With the ugliest and least skillful wink I've ever seen, he implies that he knows I'm a demon. I wonder why the professor chose someone like him to deliver a message that clearly requires secrecy. "And, umm..."

Now he's at a loss for words while glancing at Hestia and Kamii, even though his expression makes it obvious what he wants to say. He's telling me to come by myself since it must be something secretive and have to do with demons.

"Wait, what?" Lenoly stares at me in surprise and her jaw drops. She seems to have finally understood what Sharkface is implying and then realized what that makes me.

"I understand. Where should I meet the professor?" I'm secretly looking forward to hearing his voice again; everyone needs some ear stimulation from time to time.

"Come to the staffroom. Well, the prof's still eating so ye can take yer time." He points behind himself after all and shrugs. "Looking forward to seeing ye there later."

"What is this?" A familiar voice says behind me, and I turn around to find Drills standing there with her whole clique of around a dozen people. She's in the presence of the professors, so I doubt she wants to start a fight using them. But it seems she prefers to have the security of numbers on her side since my group has grown as well. "All kinds of sideshow artists gathered in one place, I see."

"You do know you're talking about Lady Hestia as well, right?" Even though I wanted to say that, Vitalis is unexpectedly the one who delivers this snappy retort. She didn't seem the type to be this quick-witted, but I stand corrected.

"No, I was not talking about her." Slightly flustered, but keeping her imperious facade, the bully girl avoids addressing the person in question directly.

"What are you doing here? I thought a servant would deliver your meal to your seat, so why does the noble Lady Svanhild Akerman need to walk on her own two feet?" I act genuinely surprised, and her cheeks redden.

"I... I was going to talk to... yes, to Professor Bergfalk. This big oaf was just blocking my way." Flicking her hair back, Drills points at Sharkface, who looks at her with a perplexed face. Liv isn't sitting in her seat at the table of the professors, so that was a bad lie. Clearly, she came here trying to rile me up but didn't think things through far enough in case I didn't go along with it.

"Huh, me?" He looks behind himself, but nobody is there. Maybe he's actually a little dimwitted. "Come on, there's enough space to walk past me."

If he tried to smile, it was a resounding failure. With rows of sharp teeth on full display, Sharkface appears to be threatening Drills and her group of goons. It's quite obvious that he's a demon, and he's taller than any of them even though his back is slightly hunched forward, which only makes his expression scarier.

"What is going on here?" Eydis comes down the aisle and asks. "Are you scaring the students again, Akyna?"

"Wha-? No, I'd never." Sharkface spins around and makes an exaggeratedly offended expression. Was he actually threatening them then and isn't even trying to hide it now?

"Of course you would not." With a sarcastic reply, the water magic professor knocks her staff on the ground loudly, and several members of Drills' clique flinch. "Anyway, it is mealtime right now, so get to your seats."

"I'm already finished, so I'll be going that way." With obvious glee, Sharkface points at the door. The path there happens to lead through Drills and the others. Their eyes are wide open in fear, and some seek help from Eydis with their gazes.

"As expected of a fast eater like you." But she ignores their silent pleas and walks away. Is she actually turning a blind eye to this because it's a deserved comeuppance for Drills?

Then I remember that Eydis dislikes wind mages, so that may be the actual reason. No discrimination at this academy, huh?

"Would ye be so kind to move? Yer in the way." With a wide grin that shows off his rows of sharp teeth, Sharkface turns Drills' earlier words against her.

She and her goons immediately step aside and open a corridor for the physically imposing demon, who walks past them slowly, as if savoring the feeling of superiority.

I feel like we could be friends.

Lenoly, Vitalis and I leave the canteen shortly after Basarab does, and follow him from a distance. I asked Kamii and Hestia to return to our room first. The former didn't want to leave my side if the latter didn't accompany her back, so I feel sorry for forcing her into that role.

"So you know what this is about?" I ask the bakari girl,

who keeps stealing glances at me along the way. My question surprises her, and she flinches.

"Y-yeah, Professor Laiota is the overseer of the Demon Mages Society." She explains, and I'm instantly hooked. It sounds like some kind of secret society, which is exclusive to demons.

Oh, that's why she was so astonished by Basarab inviting me to it. Those who know about it will instantly understand that I must be a demon as well.

"So, are you shocked to learn that I'm a demon?" I grin at Lenoly, and she stares at my face with scrutinizing eyes.

"You hid it really well. What tribe or clan are you from?" She asks me, but I wave her off and laugh. "Huh? Come on, tell me."

"Another day." Knocking on the staffroom door, I end the topic by turning the attention to the matter at hand. Astrid's voice calls me in, and I open the door slowly.

I've been called to the principal's office and now the staff room, all within the first week. It almost seems like I'm a problem student. Although I'm guilty as charged because I did cause a few problems to the professors by associating with Hestia.

Speak of the devil; I spot Dregana's golden predator eyes peer across the room and bore into mine. She's sitting at her desk, and it seems like she was doing paperwork, but stopped just to give me a death stare. I'm getting used to it by now and ignore her.

"Yes, Miss Marcott?" Astrid asks my reason for being here, but Basarab comes over.

"She is here to see me." He explains, and she nods in affirmation, before leaving us. I feel a tingle in my spine when I hear his voice, but it seems everybody here has grown used to it; Lenoly, for example, isn't reacting at all. "Thank you for coming so swiftly. I called you to inform you about the Demon Mages Society."

According to Basarab, the society convenes in the evening of every Hringurdag, which is tonight. While the demons in the academy aren't required to join it, most do because they look for kindred spirits to converse with.

"The meeting will take place shortly, so please head there. I will join you right after." He gestures at the door, signaling for us to get moving.

There refers to a room in the basement reserved for this occasion. The image of cloaked figures performing some dark summoning ritual in a dungeon cell pops into my mind again. But aside from the pools used for water magic, regular classrooms can be found down there as well.

"Can you tell me a bit about this Demon Mages Society? What do you do there?" I ask my companions along the way downstairs.

"Ah, yes." Unexpectedly, Vitalis is the one who answers. Normally, Lenoly would jump on this opportunity, but her mind seems to be occupied by trying to figure out what kind of demon I am. "We talk about everyday experiences in human society. Many of us hide their identities, while others have been found out already."

I assume she means those like Sharkface, who have a hard time trying to hide their inhuman appearances. Lenoly, on the other hand, is doing a pretty good job at it - even better than me lately. That witch hat must be hiding her horns, or she doesn't have any as a female bakari.

"Some face subtle discrimination, including from members of the staff." Vitalis continues in a hushed voice after looking around with an exaggeratedly watchful gaze. "I'm sure Grand Master Eklundstrom told you that such behavior would not be tolerated. But it's still ever-present."

As I learn more about the activities in this secret society, we reach the designated underground room.

Lenoly and Vitalis look around on either side to make sure nobody was following us, before knocking on the door.

A pale boy with an eternally evil gaze in his eyes opens it. He looks across our faces and stops on me for a while longer, his sharp red pupils seemingly glowing from within. Combined with his combed-back blond hair and refined features, they give him the stereotypical look of a vampire.

"A new member?" He makes way and gestures for us to enter. Even his voice sounds practiced, and every tone is delivered exactly the way he wants it to be. If it weren't for his evil eyes, he would be considered handsome - though I guess some people like that, too.

The interior is like any other lecture hall, only that most desks have been stacked against the walls to make space for people to stand together and mingle. There are about two dozen people, all around my age and looking mostly human. I suppose adult demons either don't attend the academy or don't feel the need to participate in something like group therapy. Or just like with dark elves, I'm projecting human physical ages on other races with different biologies.

"Welcome to the Demon Mages Society." Sharkface comes up to us and states proudly. "I'm looking forward to learning what kind of demon ye are."

While he's saying it with a genuinely interested and innocent expression, it sounds like a line coming from a pervert. He realizes it and turns away in embarrassment.

"Finally, I can relax." Vitalis sighs next to me, and there's the sound of bubbles bursting on the water surface coming from her. The powder on her face looks like it's being steeped in water before some places start caving in.

"Ugh, you should learn of another way to do this." Lenoly comments while taking off her witch hat. It reveals two curved horns growing from her forehead, poking out from between the root of her bangs.

Vitalis' transformation speeds up, and she pulls off her hair, which was actually a wig. By the end of it, her skin has become translucent, and I can see right through her blue body. There are bubbles and distortions as if looking through a water bottle. She's a slime.

Was she keeping all that makeup on her body through surface tension or even consciously holding it up, preventing it from mixing with her matter?

Then she begins to strip.

"Waah! Idiot, stop!" Lenoly jumps in and covers her with her cape.

"Oh no." Vitalis really seems to be an airhead. She quickly pulls down her shirt again, which she had already taken off halfway. "I forgot this isn't our dorm room."

"I'd say you lack a brain, but that wouldn't even be a joke." The little bakari sighs and cups her forehead with her palm. She's right, I don't see any internal organs in the slime girl, though just now she revealed a purple sphere in her chest region, which must be her core.

"Welcome, Miss Marcott." Basarab voice comes from behind me, and I suppress a shudder. I spin around and find that he has entered the room after us without me noticing. "Let me introduce you to the members."

He goes through the students and begins from the closest ones, skipping those I already know. The evil-eyed boy is a vampire as I had suspected, and his name is Elestair Sheason. I seem to recall that Maou-mama once mentioned the Sheason name, but I can't remember in what context.

The others don't have any clan names that ring any bells, which means that they must be either members of minor clans or individual demons. I learned during my weeks in the capital that sometimes new types of demons crop up in the Dominion, seemingly without the involvement of parents. Usually, they're completely alone, and many die without ever leaving behind offspring. Some members of the Maid Corps are of that kind too.

Obviously, I can barely remember any of the names moments after, and only those that made a strong first impression remain in my memories.

"This society exists so that demons within the academy can socialize. Here, you can speak about the problems you face in daily life, and report discrimination against you." Basarab explains what Lenoly told me before. "You can exchange information with your fellow demons, such as how to deal with instinctive urges of your kind, how to best hide your identity, and many other topics."

As I expected, this is basically a support group for demons.

"Everyone, let us begin." The professor announces the official commencement of the society meeting, and everybody comes together in a circle.

Each student gets a turn to talk about their issues and experiences, presenting things they may see as problems or new discoveries that may help others. Many of those I can't tell apart from humans because they either still wear their disguises or are practically indiscernible from them don't participate. Since their identities are a secret, they face no discrimination.

Sharkface reports that it becomes harder for him to keep his instincts under control. He feels like pulling people underwater and rip them up whenever he has water magic classes at the pool. As I thought, he's a shark demon.

The other students seem to be afraid of him, and only a few gather their courage to give him advice. Basarab finally suggests that maybe going hunting in the lake periodically could help relieve that tension and stress he must be feeling. It sounds like a pretty good idea, and I'm surprised to find that this is really helping people.

Elestair speaks like someone suffering from chuunibyou, but considering he's a vampire, I can forgive it and successfully suppress the urge to cringe at his words. He speaks of the darkness in his heart telling him to prey on the weak humans in the city. Their lights at night entice him to swoop down and take their blood, to create an empire of thralls at his beck and call.

Several girls immediately take the opportunity to present their opinions on the matter. Despite that evil look, he really is popular with the females; I wonder what humans think about him though. The answers all involve what I perceive to be a suggestion for him to create a harem in the academy and take girls' blood in turn so that he won't kill them.

Not only is that a valid proposition from the girls, who I thought were only interested in gaining his favor, but Elestair is also thanking everybody and seriously considering their suggestions. Despite his appearance, he's actually a nice guy, huh?

Vitalis complains about difficulties with her makeup, as some people have already pointed out how strange she sometimes looks. Lenoly says that it's quite dangerous on the field during winter when strong winds blow and could take her hat off to reveal her horns. They are two of the few more or less successfully disguised ones that do present their everyday problems to the group.

I don't have anything to add since I have neither been found out by the students nor troubles keeping my real appearance hidden. Most of my urges are being taken care of by a certain little dark elf, and those that aren't get suppressed by having common sense. That is, I have enough presence of mind to hold myself back from trying to corrupt Hestia simply because I'm curious to see what would happen.

But at the rate I've been going, it's only a matter of time before I get exposed in one way or another - possibly even by members of the staff who dislike my relationship with the Fata.

"There's something I need some help with." I decide to speak up after all.

"Is it about Hestia?" Vitalis immediately asks with an inquisitive gaze. Even though she's half-transparent, I find that she's pretty expressive, now that the thick layer of makeup is gone. I've always been fascinated by slime girls - unlike simple slime monsters - though this is the first time I see one in such high definition. In reality, that is.

"Yes, it is. It would seem that there are professors who dislike my relationship with her." Glancing at Basarab while saying this, I reply.

"I think it's best to talk with Grand Master Eklundstrom about that." But it's Lenoly who speaks up first. I expected the professor of dark magic to be the one, but he remains quiet and waits to see whether other students have any ideas or not. Maybe he's trying to stay neutral or not reveal his stance for the time being.

"Did something happen?" Elestair asks with a concerned look. No matter how I think about it, he just didn't seem the type to make such a face, but I need to reevaluate my judgment of people.

"Professor Vangir ignored her existence for the entirety of the Application of Fire Magic class on Annathdag." Before I can say a word, the little bakari already replies in my stead. She was in the same class when Aldebrand treated me like air. I consider it to be much worse than what Dregana does because she still lets me participate. And she seems to glare at everybody equally.

"I see. That is indeed troublesome." Basarab steps in and raises his voice. "Please understand that Professor

Vangir is a deeply religious person. Despite seeing one first hand, he still treats Fatas as divine and untouchable beings that live in a world different from ours."

While it's an acceptable explanation for the discriminatory behavior, it doesn't excuse it. I can fully understand that he's just a human, like the teachers in high school, of whom many played favorites and disregarded problem students based on personal preferences. It's disgraceful, but such is life.

Not that I expect demons to be different in that regard since they have personalities just as diverse as humans do.

"Can you please talk to the grand master about it? I'm here to study, but being left out of class is a clear obstruction of that." I'm not in a position to complain, considering I ignored Dregana's warning and associated with Hestia - even if she was the one who approached me. In either case, I was told to leave her alone and I couldn't. How could anybody do that after she poured her heart out like she did to me?

"Yes, I will talk to him about this matter, as such behavior sets a bad example for professors and students alike." Basarab agrees with a nod, and we move on from me.

When I'm free again, I notice one of the students, a black-haired boy with blue eyes, staring at me from the sidelines. He looks quite young and wears loose robes that completely hide his physique, but he has the most human appearance out of everybody here, aside from me.

He realizes that I spotted him and turns his head away, not in a hurried manner like someone who was caught, but naturally, like something else got his attention. Maybe he's interested in me? But I don't care about boys so he won't have a chance.

"That is Flann Umratawil." Vitalis says, and I blink in surprise. Oh, she saw that I was looking at the boy and gave me his name. But that name sounds sufficiently inhuman - though I might be doing some nation or culture injustice by thinking that way. "He never participates, but never misses a day. Professor Laiota doesn't address him though, so he has kind of just become an observer."

"So, what kind of demon are ye?" Akyna comes up to me and asks. The therapy round has ended, and it's free time to socialize now, so his first course of action was to inquire about my private matters.

"I would prefer to keep that a secret." Averting my gaze while feigning an offended expression, I dismiss his question. I know quite a few clans from the lessons with Maou-mama, but each one has distinct non-human features such as horns, claws, and surplus body parts. Demons usually don't have shapeshifting abilities, and even if they do, they aren't as perfect as ours, so revealing that I can transform would expose me as a Crawling Chaos.

"Come on, yer among fellows here." But he remains persistent and gives me a grin filled with sharp teeth.

"Take a hint." Lenoly comes between the two of us and glares up at the much taller shark boy. I can see her legs shaking a little and suppress a giggle.

"Alright alright. Geez, just trying to be friendly." Shrugging, Akyna sighs and returns to his group. Even though he's pushy, he's not a bad guy. His appearance would have suggested that he belongs to the bully type, but that's not the case.

Well, the same is true for Elestair, who looks like the kind prone to narcissism and holding a superiority complex. But he seems to be entirely down to earth and well-liked among the other demons, and not just for his good looks.

In the end, I stayed with Lenoly and Vitalis most of the time, and they gave me some background information on those I inquire about. One girl among them leaves the biggest impression on me. She has reddish skin, violet eyes, and a pair of twisted horns growing horizontally from right above her eyebrows. Even though she's supposedly only fifteen years old, she already stands a full head taller than me. Her name is Tamariki, and just like me, she apparently never revealed what kind of demon she is.

Each and every one of these students in the Demon Society has circumstances that led them to come to this kingdom. Some are the descendants of those exiled generations ago, others are the children of new species of demons that decided to live far away from the wars between the Empire of Terminus and the Dominion.

I'm the only one with a wish - a reason - to go back and the only one who has a place to return to. I shouldn't let that stop me from trying to make friends with them though.

When the society meeting is over, we're told to go in pairs one after another and make sure to leave the main building through different ways, to not attract attention.

I'm happy to know there's a place where I can meet like-minded people in this academy.

Chapter 36

The Cradle Of Chaos

"Can anybody quickly summarize the history of the previous demon king Aldeath Rangatira?" Snorri Hyrst, the elderly history professor, asks the class. The top of his head is bald, but fuzzy white hair forms a wreath open in the front which seems to rest on his temples. While he's on the skinny side and doesn't have a thick mustache, he still has the typical professor appearance. The first time I saw him, I had to look twice to make sure I wasn't seeing things.

"You're asking the impossible, professor!" One boy exclaims in a half-joking tone. The other students begin to laugh, and I look around in surprise.

"Aldeath reigned as the demon king for nearly five centuries." Vitalis leans around Kamii's back, who's sitting on my right side, to whisper to me in a rare moment of clarity. Usually, she's in the clouds and spends more time fixing her makeup - not because of vanity but to hide the fact that she's a slime - than paying attention in class.

It's only my second weekly History and Ritual Day at

the academy, but she seems to have paid close attention to me not only during the first time but also when we talk during meals. Otherwise, I don't see how she would know that I seem to lack a lot of common knowledge about the world, and the history of demons in particular. Maou-mama just never saw fit to teach me anything outside of combat as a Crawling Chaos and how to be a ruler, so it's not my fault.

"Indeed, Miss Vitalis." But the professor overhears her and points his chalk in her direction. She flinches, and the makeup on her face crumbles a little. Hastily taking out her powder box, she fixes it with skilled movements. "According to the empire's records, Aldeath first rose to prominence five-hundred and thirteen summers ago."

And even though he asked the students to do the quick summary, he instead begins to do so himself, relating the story of Aldeath's steep rise in power and eventual overthrowing of the hated king that reigned before him.

Even though it's the history of the Dominion, the enemy of mankind, it's being told neutrally and factually; I'm surprised to see that the humans aren't unnecessarily demonizing them. I expected that they would use as much propaganda as possible to influence the impressible youth, but maybe this is all due to the principal's influence.

After all, several demons are attending this class, including Lenoly, Vitalis and me. Tamariki is sitting a few rows behind us, and she's listening with sparkling eyes.

Her red skin and horns are on full display, making her the only demon in this class who doesn't hide it. Well, she would have a hard time due to her incredible height for a girl her alleged age. And as expected, the seats around her are empty, but it doesn't look like she cares at all.

Snorri continues to relate how Aldeath proved to be not only an invincible warrior and infallible military commander, but also a capable administrator and wise ruler. His physical prowess and charismatic leadership over outstanding individuals from all walks of life won him the throne, but his eye for talent and good decision-making allowed him to remain on it for nearly five hundred years.

Even though he's the one who reigned before Maou-mama, I never heard her mention him. Judging by the fact that this human history professor seems to speak of him in praise, she must have had to fill incredible shoes.

However, I wonder how somebody like him could die. It sounds like he's from an incredibly long-lived race of demons, so old age wouldn't make much sense. If he was as invincible as Snorri makes him out to be, he couldn't have been killed in combat either.

Unless, of course, Maou-mama was the one who killed him and took the throne, which would mean that she's even more powerful than he was. In turn, that implies that I can grow to such heights as well.

This is just my wishful thinking. It's a common thing in these stories where somebody gets reincarnated into a fantasy setting: They always end up as a human hero who will become the most powerful warrior in that world. Or in a new trend, start as a member of a supposedly weak race that possesses the potential to become godlike through evolution - no matter how little sense that makes.

Maybe the latter is true for me, although I can't see the end of my road yet.

While I was deep in thoughts, Snorri seems to be nearing the end of Aldeath's history. He's talking about things that occurred only thirty-one years ago when the previous demon king began to raise an army to invade the human lands.

"He went on to crush Emperor Lucianus III's offensive in an overwhelming display of strategy and cunning.

Three of history's most powerful Champions were lost in that war, and the Empire of Terminus was dealt a crippling blow." While the professor makes it sound exciting, from a human's perspective, the content is anything but.

"The emperor abdicated afterward, and his eldest son and last remaining Champion of his era, Prince Lucianus the Younger, took the throne at the age of twenty summers, becoming Emperor Lucianus IV." A boy finishes Snorri's narration to speed things up.

"Ah, yes." Blinking in confusion, the professor can only concur while letting his gaze sweep across the class in an attempt to spot who spoke up just now. "But that is where today's lesson begins."

"Class is already almost over, Professor Hyrst." A girl giggles.

"Huh?" Snorri looks out the window, but there's no real indicator that such is the case. "Oh, then I will tell you as much as I can in the remaining time."

"Hurry up! This is the most interesting part." Tamariki suddenly calls out from the back, and everybody spins their heads around to her in surprise. Not only does she not care about people's opinions about her race, but she participates without a worry in the world.

"Yes." Clearing his throat, the professor continues with renewed vigor, now that he knows at least somebody is paying close attention and even considers the things he speaks about so passionately as something exciting. "Two summers passed, and Aldeath was amassing his troops to initiate the first demon invasion on the Alliance lands in nearly seven centuries."

These are events that people of today have lived to see. While to the young students here it may be considered history, Snorri himself must have heard war reports and rumors as a contemporary who witnessed this great demon king's final years.

Shortly before Aldeath was ready for full mobilization, a report of a grotesque creature made up of black matter that sprouts countless tentacles terrorizing the countryside came in. It was a roiling unidentifiable mass that covered an area as large as the demon capital Arkaim. Nobody knew where it had come from, only that it indiscriminately devoured whatever it touched, save for the earth it moved across, growing rapidly and leaving only a barren wasteland in its wake.

The moment I hear that description, my attention grows sharp. While I love hearing lore - although it's history in this case - this is something else. That strange creature made of black tentacles sounds suspiciously like a Crawling Chaos.

It had appeared in the most fertile south-eastern region of Atirior, also called the granary of the Dominion. If left unchecked, the food stores of the entire nation would be at risk, and the creature would grow even larger.

Furthermore, it exuded a miasma that caused all kinds of rapid mutations in both plant and animal life ten leagues around it. The demons weren't spared either, but they were further stricken with a strange sickness, and those that saw it directly were often overcome with madness.

"Thus, it was given the name Crawling Chaos." Snorri explains, and I very nearly jump up with a scream. Only Hestia, who's sitting to my left, stretching her wings at that exact moment, and the sensation of her feathers brushing across my neck, stop me from doing so.

Empire scholars regard this monster's emergence as the reason for Aldeath's ultimate downfall. He oversaw a massive evacuation campaign while leading an army against this monstrosity. Hundreds of powerful demon mages bombarded it with magic, while his troops kept it occupied, sacrificing thousands in the process.

Finally, Court Magician Mithra proposed a grand ritual through his space magic affinity. The purpose was to launch the entire creature into the heavens and have the sun itself destroy every last trace of it.

Once again, I sew my mouth shut from the inside since my urge to shout out something at the mention of another familiar name is becoming overwhelming. Kamii stares at me questioningly, and I shake my head quickly. Obviously, that response was so awkward that she raises an eyebrow in curiosity.

"Are you alright, Chloe?" Vitalis looks concerned, but I nod my head frantically while releasing my lips.

"Yeah, it's just such an interesting topic." It's a half-lie, but the professor overhears me.

"I am happy you feel that way, Miss Marcott!" He points at me just like he did with Vitalis earlier. "Here comes the best part!"

Mithra's grand ritual was a success but at the cost of thousands of demon warriors more, who had to lure the creature to the place where the magic circle had been set up. Finally, the Crawling Chaos disappeared into the sky, never to be seen on Dominion ground again.

"Spies and demon collaborators who relayed this news to the Alliance created a panic in the military brass, and a covert search across the entire human realm was initiated, in case it came back down within their borders." Speaking in a mysterious tone in an attempt to scare the students, Snorri bends forward and shifts his eyes left and right.

During the year that followed, living pieces of the Crawling Chaos appeared all over the world, as if they had rained down from the heavens. They were easily destroyed with few to no sacrifices, and the biggest ever discovered was one that had grown to fill the inside of a barn after consuming all the livestock in it. Their appearances ceased soon after, and no sightings have been reported since. Even today, there are lookout towers employed solely for that very purpose all across the human nations.

At the time, when Aldeath's remaining troops scoured the battlefield for survivors, they found a naked woman lying unconscious on the path of destruction the Crawling Chaos left behind. She was the only survivor ever found.

When she awoke a few days later, her memories had been damaged, and she didn't even know her own name. She was a stunning beauty, and the lustfulness of the demon king was not a secret, so nobody was surprised when he took her in as a concubine. However, since he possessed an enormous body and a bigger sexual appetite, those who would be called to attend to him at night dreaded his company.

At this part, I see the boys straighten their ears in anticipation, while some of the girls whisper with distraught expressions.

Many thought that this woman would be broken and tossed aside, but she surprised everyone by giving him all the satisfaction he needed on her own. In less than a fortnight, he raised her status from concubine to queen; she was the first person he ever considered worthy to take the throne next to his.

However, the Dominion's forces had been significantly weakened by this creature. Seeing that weakness, Emperor Lucianus IV launched a campaign two years after the incident. Personally leading an army of half a million fresh conscripts, he sought to capitalize on that opening. Aldeath had been unable to adequately replenish his army in those two years and was quickly pushed back all the way to Arkaim.

The demon king, seeking to take the emperor's head and end the human invasion, sallied forth with his most elite troops. However, severely outnumbered and surrounded, he met his end at the hands of Emperor Lucianus IV himself.

Historians are divided over what exactly happened at the end of that confrontation. Some argue that Aldeath wasn't killed in combat, but tied down the emperor and activated a grand ritual spell, sacrificing himself to eradicate the enemy army.

Others support a more far-fetched theory that his queen, seeing her husband fall in battle, came down on the empire's army in a blazing vengeance. She single-handedly annihilated a large portion of the troops, and the citizens of Arkaim rose up in arms to chase down the remaining stragglers to avenge their king.

The truth of the matter is that not a single human returned that day. Following the death of Aldeath, who never had children, a power vacuum developed among the Thirteen Great Clans of the Dominion. A bloody battle for the throne seemed inevitable.

I thought there were only Four Great Clans, but maybe the following bloody battle eradicated a large portion of them.

However, against all expectations, at the gathering of the clans, the queen announced that she would reign in her late husband's stead. She was met with ridicule from the powerful individuals that sought to take the throne for themselves and received no support from those that only wanted stability.

That day, her enemies among the Great Clans disappeared behind the closed doors of the meeting hall. Rumors have it that she killed them all in a single motion of her hand. Whatever happened, the remaining four clan leaders pledged eternal loyalty to her. She proclaimed her hegemony over the Dominion the very same day, and none would ever stand in her way.

When she ascended the throne, her corruption spread from Ceogath all the way across the Empire of Terminus and even reached the Kingdom of Lares halfway around the globe. Even Aldeath's corruption had not been this powerful and only ever extended to the shores of the empire. Her existence proved to be a slow but steady poison on the entire world.

At the same time, the demons revel in her madness, as she has been steadily solidifying her influence, raising a formidable army to eventually overrun the world of man, as her late husband had intended to.

"She is Queen Pelomyx, also called the Cradle of Chaos." Snorri finishes the history lesson, moments before the bell announces that class is over.

That happens to be the name of Maou-mama, though I never knew she had a title like that. It sounds like they're referring to her having given birth to me when they called her Cradle of Chaos, but they may have realized that rather than a survivor, she's a progeny of the Crawling Chaos that was launched into space and that the small ones appearing all over the world were her offspring.

"Huh, are you crying?" A girl behind me asks, and I bring a hand up to check my face. Then I realize that she couldn't have seen it from her position, and I turn around to see who she was addressing.

"No, I'm not." Even though tears are rolling down her cheeks, Tamariki answers with a stoic expression. While she doesn't look sad, the story seems to have touched a nerve in her. Maybe she heard Aldeath's exploits from her parents and the emotions overwhelmed her.

Considering she's openly showing the fact that she's a demon, nobody should be surprised to see that she would be emotionally invested in the history of her people in one way or another. Maybe someone from her family died fighting against my grandma - which is what I'll call the progenitor Crawling Chaos that gave birth to my mother from now on.

The students begin to pack up, and I look at Tamariki, who appears to be suppressing the urge to express her admiration for the people in the story. She's just like me, though in my case I had to stop myself from shouting in surprise whenever I recognized something - such as when Maou-mama appeared in it.

"Hey, let's have lunch together." I walk over to her and ask, immediately feeling several sets of eyes on me. They must belong to the human students who are surprised to see me trying to make friends with a demon.

Why is that so surprising? I'm also more than friends with Kamii, and while Hestia is on the other end of the spectrum compared to demons, she's not very human either. They don't know about Lenoly and Vitalis, but so far I've only made friends with non-humans here.

"Who are you again?" Standing up from her seat, Tamariki looks down at me with her eyebrows furrowed. She seems annoyed, but I don't let that discourage me. If this were high school, she would be the delinquent-looking student, but I've made my fair share of friends with some of their type after getting to know them better.

"Chloe Marcott. My friends call me Chloe." I respond without a care in the world and give her the option to bridge the gap she's most likely created involuntarily.

"Oh, that one." But she doesn't take it and tilts her head with a bored expression. Did I misjudge her, and she's actually not the accidentally awkward type? "What do you want from me?"

"Let's be friends." I get straight to the point.

"Why?"

"Huh?"

"Why do you want to be friends with me?" She isn't asking in the tone of somebody who actually wants to make friends but can't because of what she is; it really sounds like she's inquiring about my motives, and whether or not they're in her interests.

"Because you're an interesting person." I respond truthfully. This feels wrong, but if she wants to go down this way, I'll accompany her.

"Is that it?" Her eyes narrow in disdain.

"Let us go..." Hestia pulls on my sleeve, intimidated by Tamariki's attitude.

"Come on, don't be like that." Extending my hand towards the demon girl towering a head over me, I maintain a friendly smile. I sure hope she's not the type that would prefer to talk through fists, but her appearance does suggest that we might be headed down that route.

"Did you forget about Chloe?" Vitalis suddenly joins us and speaks in her usual carefree tone.

"Wait, don't-" Lenoly steps in to stop the slime girl from saying anything that could expose any of us for a demon. But when I look around, I find that everybody has already left the room in a hurry so that they don't get dragged into what could be a fight. Even Snorri left since he's most likely not the type that can fight. How irresponsible of a professor.

"I'm a demon just like you." I come out with it directly.

"I doubt that." Tamariki fires that reply pretty quickly, turns away and leaves through the door.

"Hey, wait!" I don't want to give up here, but I know that it'll be hard to get through to her.

"Don't bother." Even though she doesn't sound very interested in what's going on, Vitalis holds me back. "She hasn't made a single friend at the academy, and except for History and Rituals Day, she's never seen in any other classes."

"That's because Tamariki is a special case." Lenoly squeezes past the slime girl and into our circle to join the conversation. She made sure to avoid touching Hestia because she doesn't want to corrupt her. "She takes special lessons, and nobody among the students even knows what affinities she has."

"The academy keeps it a secret, huh?" I mutter under my breath, but everybody hears it.

"Unlike you, huh?" Vitalis pokes my cheek, and a little powder crumbles from her fingertip. "Oops."

"Yeah, unlike me..." What's so special about Tamariki that they're keeping even her affinities a secret? Both she and I are demons, and I have all magic affinities, but the academy didn't do anything to keep that hidden

.

"Maybe she's of political interest." Hestia suddenly says, and I spin my head around to her. She hasn't told any of the students about her status as an exile from the Fata Triarchy. Her gaze when she looks at me assures me that this isn't the time she will reveal it to others either.

But that could explain why she actively avoids having friends, especially if they're demons.

"And she got you that interested?" Senka asks when I bring up the topic after Hestia leaves for her own room in the evening.

"Well, she seems like an interesting person." I respond while playing with Kamii's hair. This time, I doubt she'll say the same thing as she did when my mind was occupied by the angel girl. Unlike back then, I'm not that deeply troubled by this case.

"I'm sure this is going to be revealed in a later volume." Shrugging, the doll girl uses a wording I can't just ignore, but at the same time don't feel like discussing.

She sometimes says things that make me doubt reality, and it's not healthy for my mind.

"Stop that."

"Stop what?"

"Alright, never mind." I don't want to think about it.

"In either case, you don't need a resolution to everything. Some can live alone in this world, while others need people to survive. Hestia is of the latter type, but you just met one of the former." Once again, Senka shrugs, and it looks like the topic is done now.

"Then there's the thing about my origin." The doll girl called me a Cosmic Horror the first time we met, and it sounded like she meant I literally came from space, which seemed ridiculous to me. Now that I heard my grandma was a gigantic all-consuming mass of tentacles that just appeared out of nowhere, I begin to believe it myself.

"You heard the story of the Crawling Chaos, huh?" Senka's expression grows unexpectedly serious at these words. "Yes, you're from space."

She pauses, and I anxiously anticipate what comes next. This may very well explain everything about my existence in this world, and maybe even my reincarnation, which may not be one in the first place.

But time passes, and she doesn't continue speaking, instead only watching for my reaction.

"Umm, go on?" I gesture at her, slightly confused.

"What do you mean? That was it." She tilts her head and blinks her eyes.

"Huh? That can't have been it. You can't just leave me hanging at 'yes, you're an alien', damn it! Tell me where I came from. What is my purpose?"

"Right... 'Why are we here? Are we the product of some cosmic coincidence? Or is there really a god?' Everybody asks that question." For the third time in a short while, Senka shrugs. Then she points at Kamii, who has fallen asleep in my arms, even though I didn't control the volume of my voice just now. "Didn't you find it already?"

Wow. I didn't expect that kind of answer, and it hits me pretty hard. I look down at the little dark elf; her sleeping face calms my heart, and all my questions and misgivings are wiped away. I've always been someone who lived in the here and now, so why did I even begin to wonder about things such as what I'm doing here.

"Success." The doll girl says and pumps her fist.

"Huh?" I turn my head and stare at her.

"Nothing." She smiles to herself.

Chapter 37

Night At The Academy

I've been at the academy for two weeks now. Starting tomorrow, I'm going to have a different class schedule specially tailored to my needs as the only person in the world - that anybody knows of - who possesses all magic affinities.

I don't really feel up to the task of learning advanced techniques when my control over the flow is still this bad. Maybe I should have asked the principal to postpone the switch to the new schedule, but now it's too late.

To be more specific, it's already late at night, and most people are asleep. I can still see some lights shining in the dorms, and there are some classrooms in the main building being used by advanced students for personal research. The same is true for the library, where the main lights have been turned off, but individual reading lamp crystals are visible through the tall windows.

Kamii is sleeping already, but I have different plans for tonight. Wiggling free from her embrace without waking her up, I get out of bed and pick up Senka.

"You sure about this?" She whispers to me while

staying in my arms acting like a doll.

"Of course. What fun is there in school life, if you can't explore the school building at night?" I respond while sneaking over to the balcony. Silently unlocking the glass door, I slip out without a sound and close it behind me.

"Why do you need me with you though?" The doll girl asks this legitimate question.

"If I'm caught, I'll pin this all on you." Joking, I squeeze her to my bare chest. I'm not wearing any clothes, instead sporting a dark purple skin coloration that looks like a bodysuit to blend in with the night - including my face. My hair is covered in a bandanna made from my own matter. Of course, all the important bits have been removed as well, so that they don't get in the way. On the outside, I look like a ninja.

"And why do you need to sneak about? Can't you just get permission for studying at night?" She ignores my answer and moves on to the next question.

"I could, but that wouldn't be fun." And I doubt they would grant it to me. After all, I'm a demon with the potential to learn all the magic in the world and combine them into the most powerful spells in existence. They either want to be in control of what I'm capable of or slowly learn whether or not they can trust that I won't abuse power when I can gain it freely.

And the former is easier than the latter.

"Now shush." I peek down from the balcony and activate my night vision. Ninlil is a catgirl, so she most likely has a great nose, even better hearing, and night vision just like I do. She's the first obstacle between me and the main building; once I get away from the dorms, it's much less likely for me to be discovered.

Making sure nobody is looking out of their windows, I quickly lower myself from the balcony by extending my arm like a rope. I'm always impressed by the physical strength and resilience of my real body. I can support my entire body weight and that of Senka - which is admittedly quite light - on an appendage as thin as my thumb.

I went barefoot even though it's freezing outside so that I can use the vularen's paw pads to soften my step. Not that I'm actually affected by the cold. Touching down on the grass silently, I look in both directions once again while quickly pulling the tentacle back into my body.

The improved hearing of the vularen also helps me pick up on any potentially approaching footsteps, whenever I get close to a corner. Swiftly running along the wall and staying low to avoid the windows on the first floor, I make my way towards the opposite dorm building.

Staying in the shadows, I leave the dorm area and run along the tree line that separates the southern edge of the main building from the citadel wall. There's a path, but I stay off of it because it's easy to be spotted from one of the many windows.

I feel like I'm in a spy game - the type of games I was worst at. But this is an opportunity to improve through real-life experience. There are tons of scenarios playing in my mind, and I'm coming up with all kinds of answers to them.

But I reach the window of the bathroom that I left a crack open without any incident. A part of me is even a little disappointed that everything went so smoothly.

Pulling myself up to the window and peeking inside to make sure nobody is there, I push it open and enter with Senka in my arm. My heart beats faster now that I've come so far; unlike when I was outside, I can't make the excuse that I was going for some fresh air now.

"So, what are you going to do?" Senka mutters into my chest, and I look down. She's buried between my breasts, furrowing her brows in annoyance.

"The basement of the academy interests me." I reply in a whisper. I've passed by the cordoned-off staircase leading deeper than the underground pools for water magic several times now, and it has always been beckoning me to explore it. The so-called storage area rumored to be connected to the Lost Tombs; if that isn't a school mystery, I don't know what is.

But I also want to peek in on advanced students conducting secret magic training sessions at night.

Or maybe other kinds of secret sessions.

Putting my ear against the bathroom door, I check for footsteps of potentially patrolling professors; the hallways echo when only one person walks them. When I hear none, I open it silently and step outside on the vularen paw pads.

This is so thrilling. Hugging Senka, who must be hearing my quickened heartbeat, I sneak through the dark school. I did this with a friend in middle school as a test of courage, using the exact same entry route as the one I came in through this time. The old ways work all the same in a new world.

Suddenly, I hear the clacking of heels echoing through the hallway. With my enhanced hearing, I can tell that they're coming from the front, so I immediately backtrack towards the last corner. However, just at that time, somebody opens a door, and I nearly run into it. In the last moment, I create a third leg that stops me dead in my tracks.

"Thank you, professor." A female student says at the door, but I can't see her from this side. Then she hears the footsteps as well and quickly pulls the door inward behind herself again. "Somebody is coming!"

It's the last thing I hear before the door closes again and leaves me alone out in the open. Did I just stumble upon an illicit teacher-student relationship? But rather than worry about that, I need to get away from here and hide.

The safest bet would be to return to the bathroom, but that would just mean I'm going back to the start. If I did that each time someone patrols my way, I wouldn't get anywhere tonight.

I look around and then up. The architecture in this academy features gothic arches that split the hallway into square segments. With the highest point being only visible from almost directly below, I can use that as a hiding spot.

Extending a set of tentacles from my back, I grab onto the protrusions at the bottom of the arches with them and lift myself up like a giant spider. No matter how often I use the appendages of my real body, I'm left in awe at how strong they are.

Nestling my tentacles into the grooves in the architecture, I prop myself up against the ceiling and look down. It may be a little late to regret having brought Senka because I'm quite limited with her in my arms. If it was me alone, I could change my surface color to match the background and blend in even better.

The footsteps approach my location without slowing down, and the light of a lamp crystal illuminates the hallway. Finally, the person carrying it comes into view, and I squeeze the doll girl tighter. It's Astrid, the one professor that seems the most uptight about school rules. The only ones to discover me that could be worse than her are Thorvald or Dregana.

I switch off my night vision just to get an idea of what it looks like for a normal human and find that I'm surrounded by complete darkness. The circle of light from Astrid's lamp doesn't reach all the way to where I'm hiding, so I'm sure she wouldn't be able to see me if she looked up right now.

As if that jinxed it, she suddenly stops right below me.

I undo my heart transformation because I fear it could start pounding so loudly that she'll hear it. But when I do, Senka twitches and her joints creak. Hearing my heart come to a stop like that must have surprised her.

Astrid looks around, then tilts her head to concentrate on her ears, hoping to catch that noise again. I turn my muscles into bones to suppress any chance of creating any sounds through trembling. If she finds me now, there's no way to hide what I am anymore.

But she walks towards the door beyond which the female student is hiding with a professor, and opens it without knocking. A surprised squeal comes from inside the room before a male voice starts making excuses.

Even though I do want to hear the drama, it's more important to make my escape right away. Lowering myself halfway down from the ceiling, I extend my tentacles and climb through the hallway by using the small protrusions in the architecture as footholds.

Silently distancing myself from the site of imminent carnage, I round the corner and drop to the ground. My legs give out for a moment, and I slide down against the wall. If it weren't for the fact that my real form has no heart that could beat out of my chest, it would have happened long ago.

My breathing also stopped completely for the past few minutes, and I didn't even notice it. Only now that I'm taking a breath do I feel how my human lungs are burning. Quickly undoing their transformation, I create a fresh set from scratch. I'm fortunate to have this convenient body.

"Enough of a thrill?" Senka whispers with an unmistakable undertone of irony.

"Yeah, but let's keep going." I reply with a determined grin. This is exactly what I wanted, and there's no way I'm going to stop after coming only this far. The night is still young, and there are a lot of things waiting to be explored.

Maybe I actually want to get caught?

On my way towards the underground pool, I passed by several classrooms where lights were shining through the crack at the bottom of the door. While it would have been easy to stick a tendril through the keyhole and create a tiny eye on top of it, I held back my curiosity and didn't stop to peek inside them.

My goal is clear, and it should be enough for my first exploration tour through the academy. It wouldn't be funny if I were discovered because I dawdled along the way, and then lost my freedom to live without constant surveillance from then on. Even if the depths underneath the academy building really only serves as a storage area, I'd rather know than let it consume me when I don't have a chance to find out anymore.

Speaking of surveillance, this is a magic academy so there may be some way I'm being watched without me knowing. Though if that were the case, they should have apprehended me by now.

Finally, I reach the place where Helga told me about the rumor regarding the underground connection to the Lost Tombs. It was here that my curiosity was tickled, and this is the starting point of the real exploration tour.

"So this is the place?" Senka asks while stirring in my arms. There shouldn't be any professors down here at this time of the night, so she's a little bolder now. "Should I scout ahead?"

"Are you alright? Did you stock up on energy without me knowing?" I'm surprised to hear such an offer from her, even though I haven't been able to provide her with a soul to recharge her battery with.

"All I can say is that I'm fine for now. In either case, scouting is all I'm really good for in this world anyway." Shrugging, the doll girl says something pretty sad.

"Oh no. You're cute and good for hugging, too." I cuddle her and rub my cheek against hers. She just lets it happen with a less than amused expression. "In either case, this is my exploration tour, so I'll do it myself. There's no point if someone stealthy like you will just tell me of all the patrols and traps."

"This isn't a game; better safe than sorry. But it's your choice." Senka shrugs again. This must be her way of looking out for me.

"It's so cute how you care about me." Squeezing her, I blow into her ear.

"Stop that!" She shudders at the sensation and raises her voice, to the point that it echoes up the stairwell. Slapping both hands before her mouth, she ceases all movements.

We both remain completely silent and listen for any potential footsteps. I've done away with recreating a heart because there's just no point in having it right now, but it would have started racing again if I hadn't.

Breathing a sigh of relief, I turn Senka around and look into her eyes. There's only silent reproach, and I stick out a tongue; I know it was my fault, so I can't say anything. I'm sure if this were an anime, she would have popped a vein. But she holds herself back from commenting.

"Let's go." I whisper and hug her to my chest again.

The path is blocked by a heavy chain, and I make sure not to touch it when stepping over it. I can't help but think that an alarm will go off at even a little bit of contact. If this place is actually important, I could see a siren going off the moment I step on the floor beyond it though.

But no such thing happens, and I begin to descend the stairs. My night vision allows me to see everything quite clearly even without any light. So far, there hasn't been anything extraordinary, and we keep spiraling deeper into the earth.

We have traveled downward for a while now, but it just keeps going.

Thus, we continue to go deeper, passing one more floor where we find the same. However, the path leading even deeper has turned into a narrow circular staircase. This may be a sign that I'll find something interesting down there.

Turns out it's as boring as I expected it to be.

One floor down, we come to an unlocked door, beyond which is only a hallway with more doors on both sides. The raw stone walls tell me that this is a storage area, just like ones I found in the demon castle. There shouldn't be anything especially interesting down here, but just in case I check a few of the rooms.

My sense of distance has become muddled, and when I look back, all I can see is the bend of the circular staircase. While I don't tire, my mind isn't entirely immune to psychological effects. That's why I brought Senka; if I ever feel lonely or scared down here, I'll just start talking with her.

"Umm, let's play shiritori." I suggest playing word chain because it's something where both people speak. It's not ideal, but I suck at initiating a conversation while under stress.

"You're scared. That's why you brought me." Muttering in a flat tone, the doll girl sees through me effortlessly.

"N-not at all. I just wanted to... yes, share the fun." But this is a sorry excuse for an excuse. Even I know it, so I hug her tightly and confess my real thoughts right away. "Yes, I'm lonely and scared."

"Not only was that a sorry excuse for an excuse, but also are you a sorry excuse for a Cosmic Horror." While she doesn't employ a harsh tone, her words still hurt. She even said the exact same thing that I thought regarding my lousy attempt at saving my dignity.

"What does that even-" I start, but we reach an abrupt end to the stairs. A large wooden door studded with steel is on the right, and I'm sure that it's locked without even trying. "Well..."

"You want me to pick it?" Dropping the previous conversation, Senka offers to help.

"No, I can do this." I place her down on her own two feet and extend a hand towards the large lock. Sticking a finger into it and filling the interior with my mass, I try to turn it, but nothing happens. Using various shapes, I repeat the process under the watchful eyes of the doll girl. "Don't rush me."

"I didn't say a word." She keeps staring at my fruitless work, her gaze as merciless as it is emotionless.

"Alright, I give up." After trying out all kinds of shapes that I could think of, I pull back my finger and turn to Senka.

"You can do this." She looks down at me with unrelenting eyes. "Go on, show me how you can do this."

"Please forgive me. Even though I'm just a simple high school girl, I got ahead of myself." Shooting off these self-deprecating words, I prostrate myself before the doll girl, who has her arms crossed in a victorious pose.

"If you go that far." Speaking in a tone of sarcastic graciousness, she steps forward and places her palm on the lock. I can't see what she's doing, but there's the sound of a complex mechanism moving behind the door, as it goes through various metallic noises before finally ending with a satisfying and echoing click.

"What did you do?" Staring at the door swinging outward slightly, I mutter in bewilderment.

"Unlock the door." Her answer is as deadpan as I expected it to be. I won't pursue this any further, but it feels like she just used some kind of cheat ability.

Shrugging, I pull the thick door open further. That's when I notice that the doorframe is layered, and each one has holes for the locking mechanism. It's basically a bank vault door hidden under a wooden one.

Maybe a silent alarm went off in a security office somewhere, but I can't turn back and run away now. If I'm going to be caught anyway, I'd like to find out what for first. And this level of security means that there has to be something very important down here.

"This is so exciting." Picking up the doll girl and stepping over the threshold with determination, I continue this exploration quest with an uncertain destination.

The other side of the vault door is a vast hall where wooden tables, chairs, and crates are stacked up high. There are all kinds of pieces of old furniture that would be considered antiquities in modern times, but must be broken or not fitting the interior decoration of the academy anymore. Thick curtains and other sheets of cloth cover some piles half-heartedly as if whoever put them there didn't care about appearances.

If it weren't for that over the top measure to keep people out from here, I'd have no trouble believing this was just some oversized storage vault. Whoever created this place failed at the attempt to make things look inconspicuous at the door itself. No matter what they try on the inside now, I won't be fooled. There has to be some kind of incredible secret here.

Turning the interior of nostrils into that of a vularen's, I sniff the air and look around. There's no hint of mold, so this room must be regularly cleaned and maintained. However, there's a hint of a familiar smell coming from deeper inside.

"Undead." I mutter. Maybe the rumor that this place was connected to the Lost Tombs is true. At least I assume that a place with that kind of name will have a lot of undead in it. Or maybe there's a corpse hidden down here. Whichever it is, I'll uncover the body in this academy's basement.

Following the faint smell, I find a path through the piles of furniture and crates. When I knock on them, I can hear that the majority are empty. Upon closer inspection, most of the chairs and wardrobes have some defects, such as broken legs or rusted hinges. Rather than a storage room, this is like a dump then.

But along the way, I pass a small open space in the center of which a glass cabinet with some expensive looking jewelry and golden goblets stands. If I were here as a thief, this is the thing I'd be looking for. However, that's most likely a diversion, and the real thing being hidden in here is wherever that corpse smell is coming from.

Finally, I come upon a large wardrobe half-buried under the biggest heap of items in this place. The stench of decay is coming from here. Rather than a body in the basement, this is the classical case of a skeleton in the closet, huh?

"It's locked." Trying the door, I find that it won't budge.

"It would appear so." She states without a care in the world.

"Help me, Senkaemon." Rubbing my face against hers, I ask in a feigned helpless tone.

"Stop making that reference!" Struggling free, she hops down and puts her hands on the door.

"What a tsundere." I poke her cheek, and she snaps her teeth at my finger, biting it off effortlessly.

I stare at the stump near the first joint of my index finger silently. Then she swallows audibly, and I blink. What...?

"Just insurance." She simply says.

"Against what?!" I regrow the finger and point at her.

But she ignores me and concentrates on unlocking the wardrobe door. Don't tell me she'll use her strange voodoo-like abilities to suck out my soul when I mess around with her too much?

With a click, the lock is undone. This time it was much quicker and had far less of an impact compared to the one for this room. Opening the wooden door wide, I find that there's a hollow space hidden inside what only looks like a pile of crates and furniture from the outside. It's an elaborate dummy.

There's a walled-off staircase in the center of this space, from which the unmistakable stench of decay is wafting up. The architecture is completely different from that of the academy, and the floor is made from another kind of stone too.

It's the same as the large mausoleum that serves as the entrance to the Lost Tombs in the city square, next to the guild hall. So the rumors were true, though I have to wonder where they even came from. Who else could have gotten this far and gathered all this evidence without a convenient Swiss Army Senka?

"You're thinking something rude, aren't you?" The doll girl glares at me, and I quickly shake my head.

"So, what do you make of this?" Quickly diverting her attention, I point at the staircase. While the smell of undead is rising from there, those it belongs to are nowhere in sight. The wooden door behind us is unlikely to keep them out, so there must be another barrier deeper inside that blocks their advance.

"This is definitely the place this security was meant for." Looking around, Senka replies earnestly. "The jewelry is only the beginning of it, I'm sure there are some even more expensive items down here, but I'm sure nothing compares to this."

"It's that, isn't it? An entrance to the Lost Tombs." I take another whiff and frown. Switching off the vularen olfactory systems, I try again. It's almost unnoticeable for a normal human's nose, and I can see why they could hide this here. If it's always at this level, then nobody will ever notice it from the outside.

"I'll go back to the vault entrance." With a thoughtful expression towards the wardrobe door, my companion expresses her wish to leave.

"No, don't make me go in there alone!" I'm only half-serious. The main reason I took Senka along was that I'm confident that the deeper I get into the secrets of the academy, the more easily scared I would become. But if it's the Lost Tombs and the enemies are undead, I should be fine.

"I'm going to be on the lookout. If somebody comes, I'll signal you." She ignores my comment and walks away.

"After this is over, let's get married." Her dependable side really made my heart skip a beat just now, but I'm mostly joking.

"Yeah yeah." She just waves me off instead of sending a snarky rebuttal my way; even though I tripped a death flag on purpose, she doesn't comment on it.

Watching her disappear beyond the wardrobe door, I turn back to face the stairs leading into the ominous darkness below. Putting my thoughts into remembering the spell that banishes undead beings, I start my descent.

The staircase is straight, unlike the circular one that led down here from the underground pools, but even my night vision can't seem to penetrate the pitch black path ahead. I'm too scared to use a light spell and awaken an army of creatures of the dark like I did in Rathgolim. If those came pouring out, I'm sure I won't get away with just a slap on the wrist when I'm found to be the one responsible.

I soon reach the end of the stairs. Actually, rather than

ending, the path turns into a dirt slope that leads deeper still. Judging by the looks of it, the ground gave away at one point, and the stairs broke off. Instead of stone walls, it's bare dirt supported by wooden beams.

It resembles a mineshaft more than a tunnel now, but I don't have to walk long before I come upon the continuation of the stairs. There's a faint blue light illuminating the steps ahead of me, and even without night vision, I can see it. The stairs soon give way to a short level path. An arch awaits me at the end of it, but as there's no door, I can see inside the room beyond.

Rather than a room, it's a circular hall with arches just like the one I just came in through all around. The smell of undead is coming from one of those passageways, which is blocked off by thick steel gratings. That must lead into the Lost Tombs.

The blue light comes from the elevated platform in the center of the circular hall, which looks awfully familiar. It's a transportation network entry point, but this one seems to be glowing even without being activated - unless something is teleporting in right now.

"Someone's coming down the stairs." I suddenly hear Senka's voice, and my entire body jumps. The surprise almost made me lose my human form.

"Huh, what?" Looking around, I try to spot the doll girl, but I'm alone in here.

"Never heard of telepathy? Anyway, no time to lose, get out of there." Even though this was an opportunity to be sarcastic, she's more worried about me being found out.

"There's a transportation circle down here." I say out loud while taking in the layout of the room one more time before I make my getaway. If I don't get caught tonight, I'll have an opportunity to come again. This place won't disappear anytime soon so I can take things slowly.

"Thought so. Now hurry." That's all Senka says in

response.

I quickly run out of the room without looking back again and transform into a vularen to travel up the stairs as fast as possible. At the top, I turn into human form again and jump out of the wardrobe door, quickly closing it behind me. The lock clicks shut and try opening, but it's locked.

If I had closed it from the other side, SenkaI wouldn't have been able to get out without Senka's help. I'm really glad I brought her, not just for company and unlocking doors, but for having somebody to rely on. When I reunite with her at the entrance, I'll shower her with my love.

Taking the shortest route through the piles of furniture and wooden crates, I make my way towards the vault door. My nose picks up the smell of several humans coming from that direction, but they're still far enough. But how will we get out of here? The stairs leading down here are narrow, and there's not a single hiding place like an alcove or branching path.

Maybe it's time to take my transformation abilities to the next level. The moment I reach Senka, I snatch her up and leap out the storage room.

"Lock it, quick." I whisper to her frantically, while looking up the stairs, where a few sets of footsteps are drawing closer. The faint yellow glow of a lamp crystal grows stronger, signaling that they will be here in just a few seconds.

The vault door closes and I spread out my mass to cover it as the echoing metallic sounds of its locking mechanism plays out. Then, when the final click is done, I quickly return to my human shape and look towards the light. The fact that their steps haven't sped up means my sound-suppression worked just now.

"Woah, what are you planning?" The doll girl's surprised voice speaks in my mind when I swoop her up into my arms. Not answering her, I let her sink inside me completely.

This is the moment of truth: Does my body really defy the laws of physics?

Pressing myself against the wall opposite from the door, I flatten my shape to the point where I'm barely thicker than a sheet of paper. Taking on the color and texture of the wall, I literally turn into a wallpaper, just like those that ninja in fiction use to blend in with their backgrounds.

Even then, I can somehow see without eyes and hear without ears in this form.

The people finally come into sight, and I'm glad that this form has no muscles that could flinch. It's a group of professors consisting of Astrid, Basarab, Aldebrand, and Dregana, led by Thorvald himself. An alarm must have been tripped somewhere after all, or there would be no reason for them to be here at this time of the night.

The principal stops a few steps away from the platform at the end of the stairs. He begins to scan the area as if searching for any signs of a break-in, his inquisitive eyes moving across my camouflaged body. The other professors do the same, and I think I would have had a heart-attack if I had a heart right now.

But it seems I successfully fooled him, as Thorval

d finally turns to the door and takes something out from his robes. The vault door begins its unlocking sequence, during which he and the other professors look around one more time without noticing me. When it's done, and the door swings outward slightly, he immediately pulls it open with unexpected strength, before disappearing beyond it.

Astrid, Basarab, and Aldebrand follow him quickly, but Dregana stops on the threshold for a moment. She turns around and lifts her lamp crystal while audibly sniffing with her nose. Her intense golden glare pierces my wallpaper body, and for a moment I'm convinced that she found me. But then, she blows air out of her nostrils as if getting rid of a strange smell, and turns away.

Pulling the vault door nearly closed, Dregana disappears inside the storage area, and her footsteps grow more and more distant. I wait a while until I can't hear anything, before peeling myself off the wall and turning into my human form.

Without losing a second, I run up the stairs on silent vularen paw pads and make my way back to the bathroom where I first came in through the window. I'll slip out of the academy building the same way and make sure to cover my tracks. Getting back to the dorm will be easy when I get that far.

Once again, I can't thank Maou-mama enough for this body, which requires neither a heart nor sweat glands. Both would have given me away back there.

I think I'll make do without either for a while until I can calm myself down again.

Chapter 38

The Lost Tombs

Two moons have passed since the group moved to the capital of Kongenssoevn, and jobs from the guild are unexpectedly pouring in steadily. Not only the Lost Tombs, but guarding merchants to nearby cities, and resolving friction between nobles provide great income. However, while accommodations in the guild hall are relatively cheap despite the excellent service, they can't live on their earnings alone.

Rolan and Runa have met every single time on her day off, and they even had the opportunity to explore the upper levels of the tombs together once - although it was more of a sightseeing trip than a serious attempt at finding treasure.

But this time is different; they have decided to start a fortnight-long expedition into the deeper depths of the dungeon. Since they lack the firepower that Runa and Chloe provided - especially the latter's against the undead - they put up a notice for a group collaboration a few days ago.

Then, yesterday a group in need of people in a

frontline position left a note on the one they posted and arranged a meeting for breakfast today.

"Nice to meet you, my name is Rolan Helt, these are Gram Vestegard and Sigurd Nurmi." The introductions are done in a booth reserved for group meetings.

"I'm Hreidunn Grefrun, these are my nephew Leif and niece Vigdis Harturn." Their leader, a woman in her mid-thirties with red hair in a ponytail and green eyes, introduces the group of three. "We arrived here four days ago and challenged the tombs on our own, but learned that it's difficult without somebody to defend our backs."

"So you are a fire and you a water mage?" Rolan asks Leif and Vigdis respectively. They have red hair and green eyes as well, but have freckles that distinguish them from their aunt - and mark them as siblings. The note said that they were adept at magic, with the latter knowing healing spells.

"Yes, we thought it would be easy to get into the deeper levels using our abilities..." Leif says but averts his gaze with a hint of shame. He gives off the impression of somebody who used to be sure in his skills but was shown that they were lacking.

"The floors close to the surface are easy to maneuver, and all the traps have been cleared out." Gram explains. "But soon after you leave the areas illuminated by torches, you'll start encountering the undead."

The Lost Tombs are a massive underground complex layered by floors, which have been in existence even before Castra Custodis, the name of this city before it was renamed Kongenssoevn after the final resting place of the first Nordur king, Lares Stigsson.

It was the tomb city for a civilization predating the Nordur, long before any present-day nation existed. The most magnificent mausoleum in the world was being built for a legendary ruler here. However, that ruler died overseas, and his body was never recovered, so the construction was abandoned. The civilization soon fell into ruin and the mausoleum slowly sunk into the ground as if disappearing along with its creators. That turned into the foundation of the catacombs.

Throughout the ages, tribal chiefs, nobles and even kings had their bodies laid to rest in its depths, many of them with slaves and mountains of wealth to accompany them in death. One theory has it that the slaves who died during construction were buried where they fell, turned undead eventually, and are even now continuing to expand the underground tombs mindlessly. Some say that one day the entire world will be hollowed out by their work.

While impressive in its own right, the craftsmanship of the tombs can't be compared to that of Rathgolim. The imposing grandeur of the dwarven capital stands in stark contrast to the claustrophobic experience that these catacombs provide. After all, one was built to house the living, while the other was intended for the dead. Though ultimately, both now share the same purpose.

While the Empire of Terminus disregarded the sacred nature of the location and built Castra Custodis on top of it, the stationed governors and soldiers continued the age-old tradition by burying their deceased in the tombs. Only under King Lares Stigsson was that tradition abandoned in favor of burials in the lake, a custom he brought with him from the Slaettermark. Since then, the tombs have been open for exploration.

One theory has it that Graebern are the ones responsible for the mausoleum to sink down initially. Rolan has had enough of those creatures of the dark and prefers to think that they won't appear anywhere in the Lost Tombs, not even the deepest depths nobody has ever explored before.

"We'll split half-half." The leader makes this statement when it comes to how they will distribute the earnings and neither Gram nor Sigurd object.

"Are you sure? We're far less experienced than you are in this, so shouldn't you get more?" Hreidunn believes that their inexperience warrants them less of a cut. She's disproving the saying on the northern plains that southern valley-people are all money-grubbers.

"Yeah, each member is equally important, so I want that to go all the way." Knocking on the shield strapped to the big man's back and putting a hand on the bard's shoulder, Rolan confirms his decision.

"On another note, what do you think of my proposal to try a slightly unconventional route?" Sigurd brings up when the opposite side has nothing more to say after the leader's declaration. He's referring to the idea of using a vertical shaft they discovered on their last run.

"Are you sure that place is a passage?" Gram isn't convinced, but mostly because he dislikes cramped spaces where he could get stuck.

"I know I can trust in your sense of direction and intuition, but climbing down a shaft which may never end isn't the best idea." The same goes for Rolan, who usually goes with the bard's suggestions.

"My intuition whispers to me that there are no dangers on that path." He says with a confident smile. It is in times like these that his demeanor will instill a sense of security in his friends; he has led them through many dangerous situations by trusting that intuition alone.

"Climbing isn't exactly our expertise." Leif speaks up almost sheepishly and gestures at his sister and himself. While their bodies aren't exactly untrained, they're mages first and foremost; strenuous physical activities aren't their forte.

"We can build a simple pulley." Glancing at the big

man, Sigurd implies that the former's strength will be required for that. "It will also be useful on our return trip."

"Yeah yeah, I get it." Rolling his eyes, Gram crosses his muscular arms before his broad chest. Vigdis has been stealing fascinated glances at him since they first met, and having the focus of the conversation shifted in that direction gives her an opportunity to stare unabashedly.

"There have been few injuries or fewer deaths over the past two summers, so we will not encounter many undead." Sigurd proceeds to lay out the information he has gathered. "There will be skeletons in the lower levels, but those should not pose any problem for our group composition."

"I take that you've also learned everything about the traps in those lower levels already?" Rolan asks, but the bard responding with a smile is all the confirmation he needs. "Alright, then we'll proceed there after lunch. Until then, please prepare supplies to last a fortnight."

The topmost level of the tombs is considered a tourist attraction, and many merchants and peddlers are selling goods that daring delvers will need on their descent into the dark. There's no clear starting point since several entrances lead deeper down, but the deepest point someone was willing to set up a tavern in has become the unofficial base camp for exploration parties.

This is where the newly formed group starts their journey, packing plenty of provisions and camping supplies. Aside from his shield, Gram is also carrying a hook and several sets of pulley mechanisms, with three long ropes to last for thirty paces each.

Soon after they leave the area illuminated by torches, he hands the tools over to the three redheads and readies his shield since this is a place where traps may still function. The most frequent type are pitfalls, but darts shooting from hidden mechanisms are nearly as commonplace.

Sigurd is taking the role of the navigator and cartographer, recording their path on a map and putting chalk symbols on the walls. He also marks traps that have become functional again to warn those that come after them.

Whoever built the traps and rearms them is still a mystery, even after centuries of exploration. Some say that the tomb is a living creature in itself, possessing a will to keep the invading humans out of its belly - or kill them to create more servants for a day when its undead contents spill forth to overrun the world of the living.

It's at times like these that the existence of magical maps is most appreciated. Before its invention by a cartography enthusiast at the Royal Academy, people had to draw them by hand and had to use stacks of paper to account for depth. In these catacombs, where the only path may sometimes continue downwards in a spiral, creating a map using the old method would be a tedious task on some occasions, while almost impossible on others.

Sigurd eventually informs everybody that they have reached the hole. Last time they passed here without even noticing its existence, and only when Rolan dropped an old coin he was playing with straight into its depths did they find it. It's located in a small alcove along the path, which seems to have been hidden on purpose.

There's a stone crossbeam above the half-circular hole, which suggests that this is either a well or was used to transport construction materials deeper down. Gram immediately gets to work on installing the pulley since he's the only one tall enough to reach it.

"Sorry to make you always do the heavy lifting, big man." Rolan is standing by with his hand on the hilt of his sword. This is an area where undead may appear, so it's best to remain on guard.

"It's alright. I got enough strength to go for days." Grinning under his mustache, Gram replies, and Hreidunn glances at him with her eyebrows raised. He threads the rope into the last pulley, and with this, three mechanisms have been installed. The redundancy is for a case in which someone is on the way down while another needs to come up quickly. "So, who goes first?"

"I will." The leader turns around and picks up a torch, which Leif uses fire magic on to light it for him. "Depending on the number of undead, I'll signal you. If there are just a couple, I'll be able to handle myself until you come down."

If it were any of the others - aside from Gram, who has to remain here until the end to operate the pulley - they wouldn't be able to defend themselves against multiple enemies like someone skilled in swordsmanship is.

"See you down there." Rolan hooks one foot into the saddle stirrup attached to the rope and holds on with one hand. The big man begins to lower him into the darkness of the shaft.

Soon, the leader's figure in the torchlight becomes harder to see, until only the flame remains. The rope is nearing its end when his voice echoes up from below.

"There's an exit here!" He says in an excited tone. Judging by the remaining length of rope, he was lowered around fifty-five paces, and Sigurd quickly marks it down on the map. "I can't see very far, but the tunnel seems to go on quite a bit in both directions."

"Then I'll be coming down next." Hreidunn calls down the shaft and Gram secures the first rope, before getting to work on lowering the next person. She's a seasoned hunter and tracker so she can tell if others have passed through before and when, or if undead have dragged their feet along the ground.

After she reaches the bottom and confirms that there are no recent human tracks, as well as no signs of the undead, everybody begins to descend one after the other. Finally, after the luggage has been lowered on its own, Gram climbs down a rope he has fastened on the crossbeam without a pulley.

"Phew, I'm getting old." The big man jokes upon reaching the exit where Rolan extends a hand to pull him into the tunnel.

"If you're feeling old, what about me?" Hreidunn feigns a peeved expression, and everybody laughs.

"You look a lot younger than I do, Miss Greftrun." Gram says while picking up his equipment.

"Hreidunn is fine." She replies with a smile before suddenly readying her bow. "I hear something."

"It sounds like a single Risen." Sigurd confirms that the ranger's hearing wasn't just her imagination. The Risen are undead in any state of decomposition, but before they have become fully skeletal. It usually indicates that the person died within the past few months. "Wait, I hear four feet."

Usually, only humans turn into undead because they bury their deceased so that decomposition and animals don't break down the body within a few days. However, there are cases like in the Lost Tombs, where the air is dry, and flies are very rare. When an explorer's animal companion dies, there's a high likelihood for them to rise again.

"It's down that path." Pointing to their right, Hreidunn signals where the sound is coming from. "Is it only that one, or are there many more in that direction?"

"Which way should we go?" Rolan asks Sigurd, who thinks for a moment.

"While I would prefer to avoid a brush with any danger,

my intuition tells me that we will find more riches that way." He naturally points in the direction of the risen animal.

"What do you think?" Turning to the whole group, the leader asks for their opinion. Personally, he would prefer the more risky path because he trusts the bard's intuition; if he says there are more riches, then it will be substantially more than in the other direction. And any path without risk means that it's more likely somebody already found it before they did.

"I'll trust in our guide's judgment." Leif responds and looks at his little sister for her thoughts.

"Nothing ventured, nothing gained, right?" Vigdis shrugs in resignation and seems to have preempted her aunt's comment; the latter stares at her niece with a perplexed expression, looking like she wanted to say the same line.

"Into danger then." Hreidunn sighs.

Soon, the group rounded a corner and came upon the undead they heard earlier, and found that the source of it was a large dog with a metal dart stuck in its head. It was scuffling around half a dozen corpses, all in a similar state as the canine. The humans hadn't risen yet, but it was only a matter of time.

Rolan quickly beheaded the dog that noticed their approach too late, and the party got to work decapitating the corpses as well. Leaving behind the grisly site, they ventured deeper down the tunnel.

Under Sigurd's and Hreidunn's guidance, they avoided all kinds of traps, while Gram used his large shield to block those that had to be triggered before the path opened. Leif almost fell into a pit with spikes at one point, but Rolan was able to grab him just in time, while on another occasion the lute on the bard's back blocked a dart flying straight at Vigdis' face by pure chance.

Finally, they made camp in an empty room that looked like treasure may or may not have been there before, to spend their first night in the darkness of the Lost Tombs. With Hreidunn taking the first shift, they settled down for an uneasy sleep, surrounded by millennia of history and dust.

"The air is becoming more and more stagnant." Gram comments and holds his torch forward. It doesn't penetrate the darkness beyond a few steps because of the dust particles dancing in the light.

"There may be hidden rooms with servants, walled in with their dead kings around here." Sigurd says and pays close attention to the details on the ground and the walls. "We do not want them to get out, so take care in your step and where you touch."

"I wouldn't mind some action, but I'd rather not face a horde of undead while the air is so hard to breathe." Hreidunn has covered her face with a cloth, so her voice is slightly muffled. The copious amount of dust comes from the bodies of which only bones are left now, meaning that skeletons could be lying in wait around any corner now. While they encountered some more risen after the undead dog and the wiped out group on their first day, they only met brittle skeletons in the last two days.

This is their fifth night in the darkness, and while torches are still abundant, the deeper they get, the more dangerous it is to use fire as a source of light - especially in closed rooms where they make camp. They purchased a few lamp crystals with their savings to illuminate those camping grounds, but they are close to losing their stored magic by now.

Provisions will still last them for about eight more days, but their minds will give out from the constant darkness before then. Maybe they underestimated that factor since they haven't spent more than four days in here at a time before.

While Rolan, Gram, Sigurd, and Hreidunn are holding on well, Leif and Vigdis have been tiring more quickly, and their faces show not only physical but also mental fatigue. At this rate, they will suffer mentally before finding any treasure.

"This is a switch for opening a door." Pointing at a stone plate let into the wall, Sigurd explains when they come upon a wall section carved full of runes. "Judging by these inscriptions, there's something of importance beyond it. The door is still closed, so nobody has been here since it was first sealed."

"In other words, we might find some treasures in there?" Rolan asks with a skeptical expression while looking around to spot where that door may be. He's certainly not a greedy person, but this is the sole reason they came this far. And they can't continue like this without at least a little success; the two siblings will break down if things go on like this, in a seemingly aimless fashion. "What do you think, big man?"

Rolan asks Gram for his opinion. He has a fear of undead, but the ones they encountered so far have only been a few deceased explorers, so there was no reason to be afraid. If they opened this door and an army of skeletons streamed out, it would be an entirely different matter.

"Well, that's what we came for, right?" The big man gives the leader a resigned grin. Skeletons are fragile, even when they're numerous; especially ancient ones are so brittle that he could tackle his way through them with his shield and shatter them easily.

"What about you?" Rolan turns to the others, who look ready for anything to break the monotony of the past few days.

"Let's do this." Hreidunn says and nocks an arrow. Leif and Vigdis nod, standing back to back, as the location of the door is still unknown.

"Then be ready." The leader holds his sword with one hand and presses the plate with his other, once Sigurd signals that his crossbow is prepared. The ground below their feet begin to shake and everybody looks around in anticipation. However, no wall opens up to reveal riches or an army of undead.

"Below!" The ranger yells in surprise and motions to pull the two mages away, but it's already too late. The entire floor opens and turns into a giant slide, and everybody staggers from the sudden movement. Rolan stabs his sword between two bricks in the ground and grabs onto Sigurd. However, Gram's heavy shield brings him off-balance, and he stumbles and crashes into the two, causing the leader to let go of his sword. The three of them

roll down the tilted floor, after the other three already on their way down.

Unexpectedly, they don't drop into a pit filled with spikes, snakes or skeletons, but reach solid ground more or less safely.

"Anybody hurt?" Rolan quickly gets up and looks around at his companions. Hreidunn has stayed on her feet and already picked up one of the dropped torches to illuminate their surroundings. Leif is buried under his sister and groans but doesn't seem injured, while Gram is helping Sigurd up already.

The leader then gazes up at where they came from to find that they have fallen quite a distance. The slope is too steep for him to climb, and his sword is nowhere in view.

"Here, take this. I know it's not as good as your sword,

but it's better than nothing." Hreidunn comes up to him and hands over her sidearm. It's a baselard and has only three fourth the length of Rolan's arming sword. But just as she said, it's better than being unarmed in case of a battle.

Suddenly, eerie green flames light up in bowls attached to the walls, and an unnatural wind blows past them towards the double-winged door at the end of the hallway. They open up with a mighty creak stemming from hinges that have rusted after centuries of neglect, but only darkness waits beyond. A whisper around them extends a ghostly invitation.

"There's no other way, so we'll have to take it." Rolan mutters and looks at his companions once again. None of them seem to have been hurt, so they're good to continue.

"The runes on the walls date to a time before the empire came to Blereath. Considering the way this place opens, nobody has been here before." Sigurd uses the illumination provided by the green flames to analyze their surroundings.

"And everybody knows the legends describing the riches kings and nobles of yore were buried with." Leif adds with excitement in his voice. The pain from having his sister fall on top of him has already subsided so he can dream of piles of gold and jewelry.

"Let's just hope that king will be so generous as to give it to us without making a scene." Gram picks up his shield and walks forward, closely followed by the leader.

"Ignis!" Leif chants and raises his staff. A flame the size of a torch's fire appears above the ruby that acts as a fire magic catalyst, and he readies himself to cast fire magic the moment trouble presents itself.

"Stay in the discussed formation." Hreidunn mutters and takes up the very rear alongside Sigurd.

When they pass through the doorway, braziers between

two rows of stone pillars light up with the same eerie green flames as the hallway outside. The ceiling remains cloaked in darkness, and so do the walls on both sides.

At the end of the hall is an elevated platform, on which a throne forged from solid steel stands. Upon it sits a gigantic black plate armor with a crowned close helmet of a king. It's leaning against the backrest with its thick gauntlets on the armrests. Despite looking almost lifelike, whoever wore it must be long dead. In front of it, a massive double-bladed battle axe is mounted like a tombstone.

Around the platform are large piles of gold, jewelry and various luxurious objects, glittering under the green light. Behind it is a mountain of the same, its peak disappearing into the depth and darkness of the throne room.

"I believe that should be enough to buy the missy a meal or two?" Gram remarks sarcastically, but it's clear that he can't wholly suppress the excitement at the sight. Even if all six of them discarded their luggage to carry only riches, they wouldn't be able to put a dent in that mountain.

"We did it!" Leif shouts out and jumps into the air.

"It would seem that the king whose tomb we have violated has very loyal subjects." Sigurd comments and Hreidunn reacts immediately by loosing an arrow between the pillars. A dull impact followed by the shattering of bones is a telltale sign of what was the target.

"Of course it's not going to be that easy, huh?" Rolan comments with a sigh and draws the baselard he received from the ranger.

From behind the pillars and out of many hidden alcoves pour clattering figures. Pieces of armor still hang onto their skeletal bodies, and they're wielding rusted swords and shields. Those are the remains of fallen warriors rather than simple slaves, so they're much more skilled and powerful than normal skeletons.

Once again, an unnatural wind blows through the room, and this time, not only do whispers accompany it but also ethereal green mist in which one may recognize tormented human visages.

"I have a bad feeling about this." Gram's eyes follow the aether as it streams towards the black armor on the throne. Its pieces are lifted into the air and assemble into a gigantic knight that towers more than a head over the big man.

The armored figure takes a heavy step forward, and a gauntleted hand lifts the axe from its mount. The moment the armored fingers embrace the weapon's handle a red glow lights up inside the close helmet's eye slit.

Without waiting for anything else to happen, Hreidunn shoots an arrow at the lich king. It bounces off the thick armor without even scratching the surface. And judging by the bands of runes embossed on it, it must be enchanted too.

"That is a lich king." Sigurd states in a somber tone. "They are practically impervious to weapons."

"We just woke up something terrible..." Vigdis mutters in horror and backs away slowly. The lich king's weapon looks like it could cleave right through her entire length with force to spare.

"What do we do, leader?" The big man asks while bracing his shield. Among everybody here, that looks to be the only thing that can withstand a blow from the enemy's weapon.

Rolan glances behind himself. They could try to escape into the hallway outside, which is narrower than the throne room; the huge axe would become a hindrance there. The armored skeleton warriors are slower than the kind wearing only rags or nothing at all, so they haven't been surrounded yet.

However, the lich king, as if understanding what the group of explorers is thinking, gestures at the open wings of the door, which promptly shut, moved by a ghostly hand.

"I think the decision has been made for us." Rolan says and readies his unfamiliar weapon. Runa and Chloe would have helped greatly in this situation, as they both have magic that could take out this opponent in a single hit. His old sword was enchanted with wind magic that increased its sharpness, but even that one wouldn't have done anything against plate armor. Though even if he could cut through it, the interior is most likely empty.

"A lich has a phylactery, an object to which its soul is bonded." Sigurd informs them hastily. "They are immortal as long as the phylactery remains intact."

"What if it's the entire armor?" Gram suggests this terrifying possibility questioningly.

"Then we have to destroy it." The bard replies but looks to be at a loss in regards to how such a feat could be achieved.

While the skeleton warriors slowly approach from all sides, they use their shields to box them in. They're creating a favorable situation for their master, rather than attack on their own. With echoing footsteps that shake the earth, the lich king approaches.

Leif begins to concentrate on his staff to cast magic, and Rolan decides that their best bet is to rely on their fire mage. If his spells prove insufficient, they'll be in a real bind though.

That's when the skeleton warriors decide to attack, to stop the mage from completing his incantation. Undead with an intelligent leader are different from the uncoordinated and mindless risen they encountered before. They're far more organized and dangerous even to well-equipped groups of humans.

The leader turns to the closest enemy approaching from one side and kicks the first one's shield, causing the arm holding it to shatter under the impact. Despite moving in a coordinated manner, they're so old that the bones are close to crumbling to dust on their own.

On the other side, Gram is swinging the edge of his shield, scattering several skeleton warriors at once in one motion. Sigurd shoots a crossbow bolt into the helmet of an enemy, which makes the head pop off its spine. Hreidunn aims at exposed bones and breaks the long limbs with her thinner arrows, as they don't have as much stopping power as bolts. Vigdis is shivering in the center of the group, unable to move out of fear.

"Imperatoro Effero Flammis, Incenderentis Mundum!" Raising his voice, Leif finishes his preparation and performs a circular movement with the tip of his staff in the air above him. A ring of fire lights up and spreads outward, to a diameter that could fit the whole group. He smashes the bottom end on the ground, and the ring descends.

The moment it touches the ground, the small flames spread explosively in all directions, except inwards. With Leif as the eye of the storm, a massive blaze rages all around them and burns the skeletons to cinders.

Suddenly, the lich king's axe parts the wall of fire and swings at Gram. The latter angles his shield and ducks just in time for the giant weapon to slide across its surface and glide off without doing any more harm than create a few sparks.

Noticing that the enemy has come this close, Leif undoes the fire magic and begins to concentrate once again, most likely to cast a destructive pinpoint spell.

Rolan takes note of their surroundings and sees that the skeletons have been mostly burned away, with only a few remaining on their feet, although the ragged remains of their guard uniforms are on fire. Hreidunn does the same on the other side while releasing an arrow into the gap between the armor under the lich king's armpit. The chainmail underneath stops the projectile, and it drops to the ground harmlessly.

The steel giant turns around its focus on the ranger now. Gram quickly rushes forward and bashes the chest plate with his shield, while the leader takes a stab at the pit of its knee, which is also protected by chainmail. The sword doesn't even penetrate the mail, but even if it did, there's nothing to sever under it.

But from the lich king's reaction, Rolan judges that whatever he was in life, it wasn't a trained warrior. While it swings the axe around with strength no mortal could ever muster, it lacks both focus and coordination. As if especially vengeful, it only attacks whoever hit it last too.

Dodging underneath the axe blade swinging towards him horizontally, the leader stabs his baselard into the armor's right elbow joint and lodges it in. Rolling away from a backhanded swing by the gauntleted left hand, he takes his distance and lets the big man take the front again.

Picking up a rusted sword from the ground, he rights himself again and smashes it against the shield of one of the few remaining skeleton warriors. The steel giant motions to pull out the sword stuck in his joint, but Leif's next spell is finished, as he raises his voice.

"Mico Ignis!" He points his staff at the head of the lich king, and a flame explodes from inside the close helmet, bursting out of every opening. However, it only serves to make this unholy enemy look even more infernal. Then the fire mage continues. "Ac Effero Implodis!"

The flame is sucked back inside, and the helmet rattles like a boiling teakettle, before flying off and revealing that nobody is occupying the suit of armor. Then, an eerie green mist lifts the severed piece of armor and returns it to its rightful place atop the breastplate.

The lich king pulls out the leader's sword and drops it carelessly, before pushing Gram aside with his left hand, seemingly enraged. Even though the big man's weight with his shield should be substantial, an animated armor has far more strength than even the most powerful human of the same size.

"Hreidunn, go search for something that could be the phylactery around the throne!" Rolan calls out to the ranger, whose arrows have been useless against the armor while heading back towards the group. She immediately does as she's told without wasting time on nodding or replying. She obviously has experience in tense situations, as opposed to the two siblings.

"Mico Ignis!" Leif hastily chants the first part of the same spell again when he sees the approaching steel giant, though this time it explodes near the chest rather than inside the armor. He staggers back in fear and accidentally walks into Vigdis, who's caught off-balance. She falls over, and her staff rolls out of her hand.

Silently, the lich king raises his axe and aims at the water mage on the ground. Rushing over as quickly as he can, the leader knows that there's no way he can stop that monstrosity of a weapon. The rusted sword in his hand looks like it could crumble away any moment now, and his gambeson will only ensure that his body turns to mush rather than get split in half.

However, somehow Gram steps between the falling axe and their healer, and braces his shield to take the full brunt of the attack. With a mighty impact and the sound of bones breaking, the big man's shield dents and his left arm gives out. But he stopped the attack.

"Mico Ignis ac Effero Implodis!" Leif gathers himself

and unleashes his fire spell at nearly point blank range, which explodes from inside the suit of armor's left elbow before the heat is pulled back together. Even though there's no flesh to burn, the imploding force causes the chainmail to rip apart and the arm to come off.

"It won't stay like this for long!" Rolan spots the green mist creeping around the severed forearm and quickly drops the rusted sword to pick up the gauntlet. Then he rolls across the ground just in time to avoid a fatal one-handed swing from the lich king's axe. Getting back to his feet, he runs away with the enemy's arm in his grasp.

"I-I am so sorry!" Vigdis crawls over to the big man on her knees. His right arm looks clearly broken, and he can't lift his left arm either. The water mage's staff is a distance away, so she can't use healing magic right away.

"I'll get it!" Leif runs over and swings his staff against a skeleton warrior along the way, thinking it would be easy to shatter. However, the attack is blocked by the shield and the unexpected resistance causes him to lose his balance.

Rolan rounds one of the pillars just in time to hide behind it from another swing by the lich king. The axe crushes stone under its sheer weight, but becomes stuck in the pillar.

"There's nothing here!" Just then, Hreidunn's desperate voice calls out to the leader from behind the throne, and he turns to look in her direction.

It's impossible to search for a phylactery without knowing what to look out for. Not only could it be buried beneath the mountain of treasure behind the throne, but it could be inside a hidden compartment in the walls, or even forged into the solid steel throne itself.

"Leif!" The ranger screams in horror and Rolan spins his head around to find that a skeleton is standing over the fallen fire mage with a rusted sword raised high.

At the same time, two more skeletons are approaching the downed Gram and Vigdis kneeling beside him, who can't defend themselves. He's too far away to run over in time, and he would still have to pass the steel giant to do so.

The group is coming apart.

Sigurd suddenly appears from behind a pillar and releases a crossbow bolt into the skull of the skeleton warrior about to attack Leif. It knocks the head off its neck and the entire undead falls apart.

"There is a square piece of obsidian embedded in the head of the lich king's axe!" He points at the massive weapon before moving to reload the crossbow.

While the gem's color matches that of the steel around it, its slight sheen gives it away. When it's swung around quickly, one won't have any time to try and look for something out of place - especially when the massive axe head is heading for oneself. The bard had been hiding behind a pillar in an area where all skeletons had been cleared, and observed everything from the outside to finally spot that discrepancy.

Hreidunn slides down from the elevated platform and nocks an arrow. It finds its way into the spine of one of the skeleton warriors heading for Gram and Vigdis. She quickly shoots another on the run and grazes the other undead's helmet. It doesn't even serve to slow down its advance, and she reaches down to pull another arrow out of her quiver, before noticing that she's out.

The big man gets up to his feet and throws his dented shield with all the strength he can muster in his left arm. It crashes into the last skeleton and scatters it into its pieces. He falls back down to his knees and both his arms dangle down uselessly. Apparently, the previous impact broke not only his right arm but also his left collarbone.

"Take this, Hreidunn!" Rolan throws the lich king's

gauntlet towards the ranger, although it's too heavy for him to reach all the way to her. However, it's enough to delay the animated armor's reassembly, so he rounds the pillar while drawing his skinning knife. A giant hand comes down on him in an attempt to grab and crush his skull, but a crossbow bolt hits the back of it and penetrates the armor, causing it to swing off course. The leader takes this opening to ram the small knife into an opening in the armor comprising the knee, lodging it into the joint.

"Here, Vigdis!" Leif has found his sister's staff and throws it across the room towards her. She catches it and immediately begins to chant a healing spell; after witnessing Gram's heroism, she has gathered her courage again.

The lich king silently motions to pull out the knife stuck in its knee, but another bolt hits its left elbow joint. With a creaking sound, the wooden shaft is broken and the animated armor forces the movement through.

"Mico Ignis ac Effero Implodis!" But the little delay gave the fire mage enough time to finish an incantation. It's aimed at the gauntlet with the bolt still stuck in it, causing the delicate hinges to break and come apart under the force of the implosion.

At the same time, Hreidunn has reached the severed forearm thrown her way and brings her entire weight onto it to stop it from returning to the lich king.

As if in desperation, the armor lets itself fall forward and lunges with its spiked pauldron aimed right at Rolan. Its speed has increased because it's not wielding the heavy axe, and it takes the leader by complete surprise.

"Ah, wait!" Vigdis raises her voice in surprise. That is because Gram has jumped up again before she could complete her spell, and is now tackling the giant armor from the side. It veers off-course and crashes into the pillar, causing the stuck axe to come out.

Rolan doesn't let this opportunity go to waste and rushes towards it, but the lich king raises a leg to trip him. The leader stumbles and rolls across the ground, just past the weapon.

A crossbow bolt lands right next to him, and he looks over to find that Sigurd has thrown it rather than shot it. Understanding the message, he crawls over to the axe and wields the bolt like a dagger, slamming its steel head down onto the square obsidian. Under the impact, the volcanic glass cracks and a black plume of smoke rises up from it, shaping a tormented face.

A voiceless scream mixes with the storm of eerie green mist swirling about the animated armor, which attempts to stand back up and stretch its ruined arm out towards the destroyed phylactery. Its entire form rattles and then begins to come apart before the helmet falls off and a stream of aether escapes from the chest armor. Alongside the black smoke face from the piece of obsidian, the mist disperses in an immaterial breeze.

The ghostly green flames in the braziers flicker out and darkness returns to the room, except for the still burning torches the group dropped at the onset of the battle.

With horror, they all watch as the mountain of treasure behind the throne loses its golden shine and turns into a massive pile of bones. It was all an illusion to decorate the lich king's throne room; he may have been a poor lord in life and had no riches to bury with him.

However, among the bleak bones something shines and attracts Rolan's attention. He walks up to it and notices that there's a metallic sheen. Digging it out, he finds a rusted bronze sheath with the naked hilt of a sword sticking out from it, as the leather and wood that covered it has long since rotted. However, the hilt itself is in perfectly pristine condition, and there are ancient runes carved into it, which he's incapable of reading.

"Roshanee." Sigurd reads out loud as he stops by the leader's side. "... Sword of Light."

Rolan draws it from its sheath, which completely crumbles away after having faithfully performed its duty until this very moment, revealing a radiant golden blade that glows from the inside, illuminating the darkness of the throne room with a holy light.

Chapter 39

One Day In Town

Winter is over, and spring has arrived.

I've been at the Royal Academy for five months now and learned many new spells in that time. My control over the flow has improved substantially, to the point where I'm on the higher end of normal output at this point. In exchange, I've increased my accuracy and consistency, which is far more important than size.

The rumors around me have changed into common knowledge by now, and nobody really cares about the fact that I swing that way anymore.

Some human girls have started admiring me the same way my juniors in middle and high school had been doing in my previous life. Obviously, none of them would ever take the step beyond that.

Drills has tried many methods to bring my popularity down. Even though we don't share any classes anymore, she hasn't let up trying to smear mud on my name. After all, before I arrived, she was the diva of the academy.

Her success has been mediocre at best, though it did

work to keep away normal students. My bonds with special cases like Hestia, Lenoly, and Vitalis has strengthened instead, and among the members of the Demon Mages Society, I've become well-respected.

Unexpectedly, Drills herself has improved her skills in magic significantly. At least that's what I heard from Hestia, who was in wind magic class with her until a month ago when the former was given an individual lesson plan. While her affinity is wind alone - confirming my suspicion that she came in here through money rather than talent - the staff seems to have discovered something special in her.

It's the first Sjodag of the fourth moon, named Bryaleditid - the month of the mad god - and the first time I'm allowed to leave the citadel. I've been behaving myself, and the principal decided that I wasn't going to run away after making so many friends here. Of course, my bag was searched on the way out, to make sure I wasn't stealing any books from the library - or bringing luggage to run away after all.

While I've been outdoors a lot, it's an entirely different feeling being outside the confines of the academy grounds. Looking across the sprawling city from the citadel gate, I breathe in the fresh air and gaze beyond the walls, where the snow has thawed completely - except for the blanket still covering the slopes of the Kongensgrad in the distance.

The Maw is baring its sharp teeth far away, and I'm reminded of the adventure in the dark we had back then. I've been in this new world for over half a year now. Time sure flies, when there's something new to discover every day.

"Where are we going?" Hestia asks with a smile, leaning forward from beside me and looking up into my eyes. My friendship with the angel girl has become so close that we feel like we could tell each other anything. Of course, both of us are still holding back the most important information, which is our lineage. She doesn't know that I'm a child of the demon queen, and she hasn't told me more about her father since her initial confession.

"Hm, you're coming with me?" I ask with a deadpan expression, and she looks shocked. Last evening I agreed to go down into the city with her, but that was right before going to sleep. Now she may be thinking that it was just a dream. That idea causes me to grin, and she pouts.

"Please do not tease me, Chloe..." She's so cute that I want to hug her, but I can't. Even though we've grown so close, we've had to avoid any and all physical contact. She had told me that a few of her feathers had become gray and then fallen out a week after I had touched her the first time, so I've refrained from making things worse since then.

"I want to eat some sweets." Kamii gazes ahead and makes a show out of ignoring our flirting. She seems to be learning from Senka when I'm not looking because her attitude has become more and more like the doll girl's.

While she hasn't been as clingy publicly as she used to be, her shows of love in the bedroom have become even more intense lately. It's not like she doesn't enjoy sitting in my lap and being coddled though, it's just that these days, she no longer keeps hold of my arm as if fearing I could leave her.

"We're going to visit Daica's store in the afternoon." I've been in contact with her through Luna, as well as by mail - which I kind of strong-armed Thorvald into having delivered by express messenger each time. He's been trying to make it seem like I'm a special guest, so I'm having him treat me as such, too.

The half-elf told me that Daica's store is doing unexpectedly well despite its location and the strange rumors surrounding it. Unlike the last one, it also doesn't smell anymore, as she must be taking my advice on workplace hygiene and proper sealing of containers to heart. So I'm actually looking forward to visiting it.

"But first we'll meet up with the crew." It seems that the men from our old party have grouped up with another that lacked front-liners, and they've been making a name for themselves in the guild as prolific challengers of the Lost Tombs since.

"I am looking forward to meeting those companions you spoke of." Hestia smiles expectantly, and her wings quiver, acting as the angel's equivalent of a dog's tail.

Out of the corners of my eyes, I notice the reverent gazes from the gate guards; they always put on neutral expressions, but seeing a Fata has them all excited now. If they knew I was a demon they most likely would have attacked me to get me away from her. For some reason, I feel like stirring up trouble by revealing myself in front of them and putting a hand around Hestia's shoulder demonstratively.

"Let's get going. We have to be back before the citadel closes." I hold myself back from doing something stupid and point at the city.

Our first stop is the guild hall, where we can meet Rolan and the others. Luna has told him that I would come today, so they'll be in for sure. She couldn't join us because she has special lessons today. The academy is researching her unconventional spell-casting methods, and she's helping out voluntarily.

After having lunch with the party, we'll visit Daica, either together or just Kamii, Hestia and I. It all depends on how they feel about going all the way to the slum district on their day off.

The path to the adventurer guild is practically a straight

line from the bottom gate of the bridge. Walking down the main road, I catch the angel girl looking around curiously. She told me that she has been confined inside the citadel ever since enrolling in the academy, so this is the first time she has the opportunity to look around the city.

It's sad to hear that a girl who can fly through the air so freely like she can has been living in a somewhat self-imposed cage all this time. What if I hadn't come here? Would she still be all alone, isolated from the people around her and bottling up the feelings that spilled out before me back then?

"Smiling." Kamii comments, and I notice the gentle expression on my face. Dammit, Senka is having a bad influence on her! At least she didn't say 'creepy smile' like the doll girl would have done in the same situation.

We soon reach the city square, and my eyes naturally fixate on the monolithic entrance to the Lost Tombs. The constant stream of adventurers and merchants going in and out of it is unabated, so it's clear that Rolan's party didn't clean it out. Maybe reports about their exploits have been a little exaggerated; they have the bard after all.

Everybody's eyes are on us, or more specifically, on Kamii and Hestia. Like always, I'm like an extra who doesn't really belong in the company of these two fantastical girls. But if they knew what I really was... they would be running away screaming, if they didn't die from fear on the spot.

I guess it's better that they just consider me a normal human.

"What are you be doing here, destitute noble?" A familiar voice speaking in a derisive tone echoes across the square, and I roll my eyes.

"Oh, if it isn't... umm, what was your name again?" I turn around and try to greet Drills in a friendly manner. It always throws her off when I don't go along with her provocations. But I've been calling her by that nickname in my mind for so long that I actually can't recall her name.

"Wha-? How dare you!" The blonde girl with the drill hair is standing a distance behind us, flanked by her usual flunkies. They don't look comfortable at all, glancing at me, Hestia and Kamii with worried expressions. My abilities with magic are well known, the Fata is an existence they don't dare to provoke, and the corrupted dark elf could curse them with a single touch for all they know.

"I'm sorry, I really forgot." That didn't make it better, as Drills begins to stomp over while visibly gnashing her teeth. But when she stands before me, she remembers that I'm just a smidgen taller than her.

"Svanhild Akerman! Remember that name!" She stabs a finger into my chest repeatedly, unconcerned about the fact that I could blow her away with a single one-word spell. Even though she supposedly improved substantially, neither she nor her goons are carrying staves, so they wouldn't even be able to retaliate.

But instead of doing that, I appreciate her courage, however misguided it may be. She's standing up for her pride even against somebody she knows is most likely beyond her, no matter how much she might have improved in recent times. I know that she isn't a one-dimensional idiot like the bully types seen in fiction after all.

"Alright, I got it Svanhild." I repeat her name to better memorize it, but she shows me an exasperated expression. Huh?

"That's Lady Akerman for you!" With a roar, she tries to make herself appear as tall as possible by standing on tiptoes. It's one of the rare situations where she's this close to me, and I can't help but...

"How cute." I mutter without thinking, and she overhears it.

"H-huh?" She recoils in surprise. Then her face flushes red, and I'm the one to be surprised; is she actually harboring feelings for me like a tsundere? Then she balls up her fist, and I see that she's shaking from anger. "You dare make fun of me?! Fylgis, my sword!"

"L-Lady Akerman, y-you said it wasn't necessary to bring it today." The goon named Fylgis - the first time I hear her name even after such a long time - replies in a quivering voice.

"You are useless!" Svanhild flares up at the poor girl.

"Hm, isn't that the missy?" Another familiar voice echoes across the square, and I turn to look in the direction it came from. It belongs to Gram, who towers above everybody else around him. Rolan, the bard, an unfamiliar man, and two unfamiliar women are with him. Those must be the new members, huh? "Are you causing trouble again?"

"Ah, just talking to a friend from the academy." I reply and hear a shocked gasp behind me.

"W-who are you calling a friend!" Unexpectedly, Drills may really be a tsundere. She hasn't actually done anything malicious to me, so I don't hate her; in fact, she enriches my school experience, so I'm quite thankful for that. "I have no time to waste on the likes of you. Hmph!"

And with these words, she turns on her heels and walks away, her two minions hurriedly following behind her. In the end, what did she come here to do?

"I-is that the Fata?" The younger of the unfamiliar women asks with an awestruck expression.

"Let me introduce you. These are Chloe Marcott, Kamii and Lady Hestia." Rolan has heard a lot about Hestia from Luna, so he isn't as surprised to see her as the newcomers are. His expression tells me that he's still captivated by her appearance though. "These are our new members, Hreidunn, Leif, and his sister Vigdis."

If this were a role-playing game, I could tell each of their roles with one glance; none of them are wearing their equipment, but it's quite evident to the trained eye. Hreidunn is a ranger, Leif is a fire mage, and Vigdis specializes in water magic. The latter two are easy to identify because they wear the robes in the respective color schemes, while the former has a nimble step and sharp eyes. Her clothes also remind me of Arni's in Hovsgaerden, and he was the most stereotypical ranger out there.

"It's nice to meet you. I've heard that those three would have been stranded without you." I nod to the new members and glance at the three men with a mischievous grin.

"No, not at all. We wouldn't have been able to make it this far if not for them." Although Hreidunn clearly understands that it was meant as a tease, she answers truthfully and with a warm smile on her lips.

"Let's go inside and speak about this over some ale." Gram scratches his mustache with an expectant look in my direction. He already wants to drink with me, even though it's still morning?

"Just one jug." I do want to share a drink with him again though, and since we don't have time to stay until dinnertime, this is a good enough time as any other today.

"As expected of the missy!" The big man is already swaying under the influence of the alcohol when he puts down his fifth empty jug. I do the same and wipe my mouth with the back of my hand.

"This is nothing. Another!" I wave over the waitress, who's staring at the two of us in bewilderment.

"Umm, Chloe..." Hestia speaks up, and I jolt my head around; I completely forgot about her presence after the drinking contest with Gram started to heat up. "Did you not want to meet Miss Daica?"

Oh damn. I look out the window but find that the sun has barely reached its zenith - at least I think that's where it is since, at this time of the year, it's hard to tell. And here I thought it was already evening, with the alarming way in which the angel girl phrased it.

"It's alright, we got time." Replying with a carefree grin, I take the new jug that's placed in front of me and lift it to the big man's. "To you and your achievements in the Lost Tombs! I'm looking forward to going adventuring with you again!"

Rolan and the others are still only on their first jug. While he and the bard know this side of me, the new members don't. They blink their eyes and are speechless to find that I'm most likely not what they expected of someone attending the prestigious Royal Academy.

The same is true for Hestia, and she seems equally shocked.

"Indeed, we look forward to seeing the magic that you have learned. I feel that with you, we could challenge even the deepest reaches of the darkness." Surprisingly, the bard is the first to join in on my toast, and the others follow suit after him.

Kamii and Hestia are only drinking water, though the former is having sweets that Gram bought her for this occasion. She munches on the pastries silently while watching our daytime drinking with her usual expressionless face. But I think I'm gleaning a hint of disapproval in it. Maybe I'm overdoing it?

"A jug for me too, please!" The angel girl suddenly stands up and calls out to the waitress, who's startled by her request. In fact, the entire guild hall, which is becoming more and more crowded after word got out that the famous Fata of the Royal Academy is visiting it, goes quiet and stares at her.

"Wooh, you're feeling it too!" I put an arm around her shoulder and touch cheeks with her while lifting my jug in another toast. "To Hestia's beauty!"

She flushes red at my words and the physical contact but doesn't shy away. The whole guild breaks out in cheering and joins the party at our table, and the waitress quickly brings a jug filled to the brim for the guest of honor. Staring at the giant container before her, she has an expression that suggests she made a huge mistake.

But gathering her courage, she lifts it with shaky hands, puts her lips to the jug and begins to drink. After only two gulps she quickly sets it down and coughs, as the sensation in her throat must have been an unfamiliar one. It doesn't even have that much alcohol content, but this is most likely her first time.

Nobody cares that her ale wasn't downed in one go as how Gram and I have been doing it, and applause rises all around us.

I made a huge mistake.

In the heat of the moment, I touched Hestia - and it wasn't just a little bit of contact, but a lot and for a long time. We had lunch with the party, and I was all touchy-feely with her throughout, hugging and rubbing cheeks without any restraint. Only towards the end did I regain my senses, but it was already too late.

"D-do not worry, Chloe. I-I am really fine." She gives me a flustered smile when I apologize to her profusely outside the guild hall after we left the still ongoing party behind. Her face is flushed from drinking alcohol - even if it was only one jug - and she's a little unsteady on her feet, but I don't dare to brace her.

"I got drunk and forgot how dangerous it is for you when I touch you..." I can't believe that I let this happen. Last time I drank this much this quickly was in Birkas, which was my first experience with alcohol in the first place. And even then I didn't lose control, although I drank much more.

Then again, neither did I lose control here; it's just that some very important inhibitions temporarily disappeared. This time it could have grave consequences though.

"It is alright. Look, nothing is wrong with me." Twirling around herself demonstratively, Hestia tries to cheer me up. But she stumbles and very nearly falls, and catches herself against a lamp post just in time. She's clearly drunk as well. "I... I was actually happy."

"Huh?" I blink. Her expression suggests that she's bashful, but I can't tell if that's a blush on her cheeks or just the alcohol.

"Even though we have been so close recently, I always wanted the same as what you have with Kamii." Bringing her fingertips together before her chest nervously, she averts her eyes and mutters shyly.

"Like what I have with Kamii?" I turn to the little dark elf, who returns my gaze without saying a word. Then I look at the angel girl with a mischievous grin. "Are you sure?"

"Oh." Hestia looks nonplussed. She knows that Kamii and I are lovers and that we do what lovers do. And it seems her imagination conjured up an image at my words because her face flushes a much deeper red than the ale did before she covers it with both hands and turns away. "W-what are you saying?!"

"No, what are you thinking?" It's quite fun to tease her because she's so innocent.

"Are we going?" Kamii suddenly asks in the most indifferent tone imaginable. With one glance at her face, I can tell that she's not amused by our infantile flirting.

"Yeah, we should get going. Daica is waiting." Scratching my cheek with an embarrassed smile, I break up this back and forth.

Luna marked the location of the big dark elf's store on a magical city map. It's the same kind as the one the party had for the surroundings of Hovsgaerden, and it's activated with the same voice command. I'm really glad that it tracks my current location with a black dot because the closer we get to the southern city wall, the more slum-like it becomes. Streets cease to be named, and it's like they put in less effort since they knew that this place wouldn't be inhabited by picky people.

Speaking of people, they're loitering in the streets and staring at us with shady gazes. Many of them are dressed in dark tones and wear stitched clothes, unlike those walking on the larger streets closer to the city center. This is like another world compared to the bright place we've been in until only moments ago.

Just to be sure, I prepare for when thugs might decide to attack us. I'm sure despite reverence and awe, some would try to kidnap Hestia either to sell her to some nobles or for some ransom from the academy. And Kamii is a curiosity that people would keep as a pet in a cage - the exact way I found her in, too. I would just be a little bonus in that case.

It's a little disheartening when I think about my status compared to these two, but I don't envy them for the kind of attention they're receiving around here.

"Is that it?" We reach the marked area and find ourselves in the depths of a dark alleyway. Even though it's only midday, this nation is high up in the northern hemisphere, so the sun doesn't climb very high around this time of the year. The building is leaning on the southern city wall, but aside from its looming shadow, it doesn't look much different from her old store in Hovsgaerden, where I first met her. In fact, this alleyway might be even filthier than the one back there.

"Nightwane's Nest." Kamii points at the signboard above the windowless building and comments. I can't read the letters or runes, which look entirely different from those of this kingdom's language. Since she could, they must be dark elf ones. While they're written in graceful calligraphy and are beautiful to look at - quite out of place here - only dark elves will be able to read them and remember the store name.

"Guess it is." I shrug and push open the door, bracing myself for an attack on my nostrils, even though Luna said it's completely fine now. And I find that while it smells strange, it's not a penetrating stench of decay. That's the scent of herbal medicines.

"Y-yes, I'm coming." Daica's voice reaches us from the depths of the store. When I opened the door, a small bell announced our entry, and she quickly reacted to it. She has become a proper storekeeper, huh?

I walk towards where the voice came from, and upon rounding a shelf, nearly walk into her. As usual, she's wearing a knit robe in a dark shade of red or purple - the former this time - which attempts to hide most of her bountiful figure but still fails to do so. Her amethyst eyes, filled with the same kind of seemingly swirling galaxies as her older sister's, look up at me in surprise, before joy settles in.

"C-Chloe!" She stutters, but throws her arms around my neck in an unexpectedly assertive move and hugs me tightly. "I missed you!"

"Me too." I whisper into her long and pointy ear and nuzzle my cheek against hers. Her body is cursed to poison and kill everything that isn't a demon or corrupted, but I'm obviously unaffected.

She suddenly leans back and looks up into my eyes with an expectant gaze. I immediately bring my lips to hers, and we share a deep kiss. During the past few months, she must have interacted with many people and learned to keep her wits in situations outside of her comfort zone. While her stutter still remains, her expression suggests that it's not because she's nervous. It might actually just be a verbal tic.

We separate, and she takes a deep breath. Her face is reddened, but she looks up at me with a smile filled with affection. Before, she would avoid eye contact and be deeply embarrassed after a simple kiss, but it seems she's much better with it now.

"Maybe we can go all the way then?" I breathe into her ear, knowing that her mind can't be that strong yet.

"H-huh?" T-that wasn't m-my intention." And just like I thought, she becomes flustered, and her cheeks flush an even darker reddish-purple. Despite her mature appearance, she's much more childlike than Kamii and just as cute.

"Daica." The latter calls out to her little sister in a flat tone before rounding the corner. If she's thinking anything about our embrace, she isn't showing it on her face.

"O-oh." Surprised, Hestia blinks when she sees us, before looking away embarrassedly. Please stay this innocent forever~

"W-wah!" Separating from me, Daica stares at the angel girl's wings, and her mouth flaps open and closed without making a sound. She's awed speechless by the Fata's presence in her store.

"This is Hestia. I told you about her in my letters." I introduce her. "Of course, speaking about you only in the highest words of praise."

She waves off my joke with a smile and performs a

curtsy before the big dark elf. The latter bows in return, not knowing the proper Fata mannerisms to reply with the same.

"And this is Daica, Kamii's younger sister." Gesturing at the woman in question, I state in a matter of fact tone with a particular goal in mind. And as expected, Hestia glances between the two dark elves, before looking up at me with a frown.

"You are not fooling me this time." She puffs up her cheeks and pouts. I've been telling her many unbelievable stories that people with common sense could easily judge as being made up, but she has taken each and every one of them at face value so far. Each time, I couldn't bring it over myself to keep her in the dark and told her the truth, but she still trusts me.

"The one time when I'm not messing around, you decide to use common sense?" I cross my arms and tilt my head at her in disapproval, and she stares at me perplexed.

"Y-you really are the younger sister? But..." Once again, Hestia looks from one dark elf to the other, and I can practically see the question marks floating above her head.

"M-my body became like this b-because of a curse." Daica clears up the situation with a lonely smile. Even though I've been teaching her to feel good about her body shape whenever I'm with her, she still can't get used to revealing it about herself to a new person. "Kamii is the more n-normal one between the two of us."

Cranking her head around, the angel girl stares at the little dark elf beside her, who returns the gaze with a deadpan nod. I feel like she's overdoing it with the kuudere behavior, although it's pretty cute in its own way.

"Daica, did you get anything from home?" Kamii turns her head and asks her younger sister.

"Y-yes, I did get a basket of jivana phala." The latter replies and immediately goes into the back of the store. Hestia and I wait curiously until she returns with a small straw basket covered with a cloth. She pulls it aside and reveals orange banana-shaped fruits.

My mind is going places.

"What are these?" Shaking my head of the thoughts, I pick one of them up and look at it from different angles.

"They're... life fruit?" Kamii tilts her head and answers in an unsure tone.

"I-I think that would be the c-correct translation." Daica takes one of the fruits and lifts it in front of her face, and I suppress any indecent thoughts welling up in my mind at the sight. Kamii picks out a big one for herself and bites into it from the side unceremoniously, and my mind is cleansed.

It seems the fruit doesn't need to be peeled and is good to eat just like that, so I try it myself and bite into it from the longer side. As if being true to its appearance, it tastes like a mix between a banana and a mango and is just as incredibly sweet and juicy as the two combined.

Daica hands Hestia one as well, and my eyes widen into camera lenses when she brings the tip to her lips. Cupping it with her mouth, she hesitantly bites down on it, and juice overflows. She quickly licks it up before it can run down the shaft's length and covers the tip with her mouth again.

Thank you for the meal, in more ways than one.

We're shown around the store and learn that unexpectedly, the majority of customers are servants of noblemen who buy medicine for their lords - mainly ones that increase vitality and virility. I didn't know that Daica was dealing in those kinds of things, but apparently, they're just considered magic goods too in this world.

She ditched the cursed item-looking things she used to have in her old store though, and the jars are all opaque and adequately sealed. While some of the labels do make me wonder about their contents, I banish the thoughts from my mind quickly. It's better if I don't know.

There are a collection of wooden staves without any catalyst crystals leaning on a rack, and wands are lined up on a display shelf. I don't remember seeing those in Hovsgaerden, but the store was quite run-down and dark whenever we visited. Here, she's using many lamps to keep the place inviting.

"You did really well." I pet Daica's hair, and she looks happy. "I assume that you're making a killing."

"I-it's not to that extent, b-but I can save up on the side." She replies with a modest smile. It seems that she has become a proper bread-earning member of society now, while I have returned to being a student mooching off somebody else. I miss the times when I was making money from healing people in the guild hall, even if it was nowhere in the figures of what my stipend at the academy is like - of which I don't see anything yet since I'm not at the level where I can do independent research.

I learned about how much money the tuition costs a few weeks in, and felt dizzy afterward. They're investing that much into me with the expectation that once I have the basics down, I'll be studying magic on my own and contribute to magic society with all kinds of discoveries only a person possessing every affinity can make.

Of course, I won't tell them that I've been plotting how to get back to the Dominion in secret and that whenever I visit the library, it's to find information about the locations of the transportation network and how to make use of it. While I did discover the circle in the basement, I haven't found any information on how to activate it in the publicly accessible areas though.

"We'll be heading back to the citadel then." I look out the window and see that it's beginning to get dark. Well, darker than it already is under the southern wall. The days are still rather short - though they have been growing noticeably longer - so one can't judge time just by the position of the sun. "You two, go ahead and wait outside for me, I still have something to talk to Daica about."

Kamii simply nods and walks away, but Hestia glances at the big dark elf and me repeatedly while following after her. I'm sure both are thinking their part, but they show it in different ways.

"I'm sorry that I can't stay longer than this." When the store bell rings, and the door closes, I turn around to Daica and quickly bridge our distance. Embracing her, I mutter to her with an apologetic expression. "I'll find a way to come alone sometime soon."

"D-don't worry, Chloe." She wears a lonely smile, and it's clear that she's a little disappointed after all. Then she lifts her face to look up at me, and once again, we kiss. This is all we can do for the time being, but her assertiveness in employing her tongue shows me that she's ready for more next time.

"You've grown." When we separate, I look into her eyes and whisper with a smile. She doesn't avert her gaze in embarrassment and shows overt anticipation.

"Done?" Kamii asks when I leave the store, and I grin in response.

Hestia steals glances at us but doesn't say a word; she must be wondering how the little dark elf can be fine with me two-timing her with her very own sister. We actually never explicitly worked it out between the three of us, but both of them seem to be completely fine with it so I won't stir up any unnecessary problems by bringing it up.

We walk back the way we came from and chat away

the time, and soon the angel girl loosens up again. She talks about the taste of the life fruits, which reminded her of a jelly-like sweet snack she had back in the Fata Triarchy. All I can remember is the sight of her eating it, and I quickly disperse the fantasy that my mind conjures up on its own without being asked to.

"Surrounded." Just when I turn around to ask Kamii about her home, she mutters while casting a sideward glance.

I look around and find that there are two masked men in the dark alleyway to our right. On the other side are two more, and five men are approaching from behind, while four are sitting on the ground acting like the destitute inhabitants of these slums in front of us.

"Hestia, fly and get out of here." I mutter to the angel girl, but she doesn't understand the situation and looks around in surprise.

The masked men take this as their signal, as they run towards us. Those in the front jump up and block our way, and I see that one of them has a cane with a translucent crystal embedded in its handle.

"Pilum Gradum!" I stomp my foot, and a pillar of stone shoots up, blocking the entire alleyway to our right.

"Confractum Murum!" A voice from behind the stone barrier chants and the pillar conjured by my magic crumbles away. It's a spell that undoes earth magic specifically; one of the two on that side is an earth mage. They know what kind of magic I might use and put the right people in the right places.

"Mico Ignis!" Pointing at the one in the front, I chant a spell that only serves to cause damage rather than shape the area to my advantage; it's less likely to be rendered useless this way.

"Aerus Inanor." The man in front swings his staff around just when the flame appears under his feet, and it flickers out. Not only do they know my favorite spells, but they can also predict where I usually aim them at.

These guys are from the academy, or at least they were hired by somebody who can get information from within it.

"Hasta de Lumin!" But I haven't shown off any spells in light magic.

I launch the spear of light into the alleyway to our left, and it pierces the shoulder of the man in the back, who falls backward clutching the wound. I chose that direction because the other one has drawn a sword, which means that he isn't a mage, so he should be easier to deal with.

"Kamii!" I point in the direction, and the little dark elf immediately reacts by grabbing Hestia's hand and pulling her along. I stomp on the ground again. "Pilum Gradum!"

Another pillar rises up, but this time halfway between the group surrounding the wind mage and me. Then I fire another light spear behind us without aiming it, just to keep them occupied, and follow the two. The little dark elf lifts her cursed arm and threatens the man with the sword, whose eyes under the mask go wide at the sight, and I smile to myself. She's learning to use her assets.

But he has enough discipline to not just run away, as he swings his sword to slash Kamii. The latter uses her crab pincer to catch the blade. She twists her arm and pulls the sword out of the man's hands, who stops in complete bafflement.

Then he gets the back of the pincer to the chin and stumbles out of the way. It was only one hit, so it's not very heavy. Taking the opening, the two girls run past him and the wounded mage sitting on the ground.

"Pilum Gradum!" I chant right when my foot comes down on the ground, and another pillar shoots up from the ground behind me. It blocks the alleyway we're escaping into, but I know it won't hold them for long.

Just as I pass by the thug who's bending down to pick up his dropped sword, I deliver a knee to his temple that knocks his mask away and sends him crashing face-first into a wall. He stays down after that.

The hurt mage sees it and lifts his wand with a shaky hand, before pointing at me. There's a ruby embedded in its tip, and my eyes widen. If he casts fire in this tiny alleyway, it could spread to the surrounding buildings and burn down the entire slum district!

Whipping my hand around, I bring out the bone blade I first used on Yagrath against the pack of vularen and slash the mage's extended arm. I was aiming to decapitate him, but because I haven't used it in a long time, that's the best I can do. When he lets out a scream and drops the wand, his incantation is interrupted, so I consider it as good enough.

"Ventus Secaror!" I still decapitate him with a wind blade when I pass him by. Unlike the swordsman, this one would fire magic at me from behind if I don't do so. But just in case this is really related to the academy, I make sure those on the other side of the pillar hear me chant a spell; I don't want to reveal that I can transform my body.

When I round the corner, which Kamii and Hestia have before me, I find that they're standing in front of a dead end. Don't tell me the guys on this side were decoys so that we would run this way. The earth mage on the right was there to imply that they could close off the escape route behind them. The front and back had too many people with unknown abilities, so this was the best path to take.

"Confractum Murum." I hear from behind me, and the sound of stone crumbling tells me that they're going to catch up.

"Climb the wall!" I would have told Hestia to fly again, but this alleyway is too narrow for her to spread her wings.

Furthermore, clotheslines are hung up above us haphazardly, so she would get entangled in them even if she could fly. Maybe I'm giving our assailants too much credit, but this might have been part of their plan as well.

I quickly create an angled stone pillar, which Kamii runs up to climb on top of the wall. Then she holds out her cursed arm for Hestia to hold onto

"Ventus Secaror!" A man's voice chants behind me and I stomp on the ground to make the pillar raise up straight. It blocks the wind blade aimed at the little dark elf but causes Hestia to slide back down next to me. Then I hear another spell before I can turn around. "Ventus Fortior!"

A burst of air sweeps through the small alleyway and blows Kamii off the wall. I hear a loud crash on the other side, but it's followed by shuffling sounds as she quickly tries to get back on her feet. Good, she wasn't hurt.

"You bastard..." I glare at the man in the dark robe and the blank gray mask that hides his identity. He intended to kill her with that first spell so I won't forgive him.

"Kill the demon. Don't hurt the Fata." He seems to be the leader, as he orders the warriors to move towards the front. All in all, there are three mages, and the other eight all wield swords, daggers or axes. They're most likely hired thugs to distract from the real threats in the back.

I turn to glance at Hestia, who looks terrified. Just when the day was looking to end well, this happens...

Chapter 40

Collateral

"Guttam Terram!" I take a step forward, and the ground under the enemy frontline sinks down. This time, I deliberately don't hold back on the output, so that they'll be stuck in a deep hole when the spell's effect runs its full course.

"Ortum Terram!" The earth mage who destroyed my wall twice before uses the counterspell that raises the ground again. But the melee fighters have fallen to the ground due to the sudden movements and scramble to get back on their feet, which buys me a little time.

Still, I'm one against three, so this tactic won't work. Judging by their catalysts, they have at least one mage of every element, with the leader - who stopped my fire spell earlier - possessing both the wind and fire affinities, while the water mage also has the wind affinity.

"Hasta de Lumin!" I create a spear of light and shoot it at the earth mage.

"Pilos Aquos!" But the water mage creates a sphere of water which deflects the projectile as if it was just light. That's cheating, using physics in a magic battle!

"Pilum Gradum ac Volantem Lapim." Stomping on the ground before himself and then punching the pillar that the first incantation raised, the earth mage counterattacks with a stone projectile. It's nowhere near as big as the ones Bjorn and Magni can conjure, but it's still a dangerous spell to be hit by.

"Grandor Ventus Procursus!" I shout and create a burst of wind that deflects the flying rock into a wall. However, while I was occupied with this spell, the water mage has time to speak his incantation.

"Inebrios ac Grandor Aerus Inanor." He points his staff at me and my whole body is soaked, but in the next moment the air around me disappears, and I feel extremely cold. The clothes clinging to my body freeze up, and soon I'm covered in ice particles.

"Coruscaris." I mutter through chattering teeth, and heat bursts out from around me. The enemy mages stare at me in surprise, not expecting that I would use fire magic on my own body like this. Before I'm completely dry and my clothes catch on fire, I disperse the spell.

"What are you doing? Get her!" The mage leader commands the warriors again, who have stopped to watch our magic battle in awe.

"Cover your eyes, Hestia." I don't see any other way out of this.

"H-huh?" She sounds surprised. No wonder, to her it might seem like I'm expecting to be cut to pieces, and that I want to spare her the sight.

"Don't look no matter what you hear, you understand?"

"Y-yes..."

I give her a second to comply, and the first warrior reaches me with his sword. It cleaves me from the shoulder to the center of my chest.

"Wha-?" When he doesn't see the blood spurt out of the wound, his eyes widen behind the mask in surprise.

Before he can even think of pulling out, I burst out into my true form and use my tentacle arms to rip his body in two down the middle.

"Ah." The ones following closely behind him stop their charge in shock at the sight of blood and guts splattering against the walls on both sides, before they see me emerge from behind the curtain of flying viscera.

The eyes of one of them roll back in their sockets, and he faints on the spot - or maybe he died - while the two in the center drop their weapons as they stand frozen in place. Two more scream at the top of their lungs, before one bends forward and begins to vomit his guts out, while a darkened area spreads on the other's pants. The one furthest back turns on his heels and runs away, pushing past the stunned mages.

And as always, there's one who attacks, hoping to kill before being killed.

"Nobody gets away." I shout after the one trying to run, and my voice causes him to lose control of his legs. He runs face-first into the wall at the alley bend, and I hear a mighty cracking sound. Whether that was just the mask or his skull, I don't know, but he stops moving.

I bring all my tentacles forward and embrace the one swinging his axe at me. He calls out for his mother as he tries to push himself away from me, but soon all of him disappears into my depths.

Shifting my gaze to the mages, I see that the leader is staring directly at me with widened eyes. The earth mage has fallen to his knees and is holding his head, muttering to himself like a madman. The water mage has dropped his staff, taken off his mask, and is now clawing at his own eyes in hopes of blinding himself so that he doesn't need to see me anymore.

"That hurts, you know? Even though I'm like this, I'm still a girl at heart." I let my horrific voice ring out, and the earth mage slams his head against the ground repeatedly, breaking his mask in the process. That doesn't discourage him from continuing until his forehead cracks, and his body goes limp. At the same time, the water mage has drawn a dagger and is stabbing himself in the chest repeatedly, until he keels over.

I step forward on legs made of tentacles and as if in passing, stab the one still screaming through the throat to shut him up. While walking past the two warriors standing still, I pull them into my body with tentacles spreading from both sides. Then I behead the one on the ground lying unconscious in his own vomit. Lastly, I pull the one who fainted into my body and realize that he really died of a heart attack the moment he saw me.

Finally, I approach the leader.

"It's only you left." Recreating my human face where I lack one in my true appearance, I crack an impossibly broad grin at the mage. "I commend you for your bravery in staying."

"W-what... are you?" He mutters through his mask.

"You don't need to know." Surrounding him with my tentacles, I bring my face close to his so that our eyes are at the same height. "Instead, there's something I need to know from you; who sent you?"

But he doesn't answer and bites his own tongue.

"Sano." I whisper into his ear and revel in the terror that fills his eyes when the wound he inflicted on himself is healed. Pulling off his mask, I find that the man underneath is somebody unfamiliar. Of course, it couldn't have been one of the professors personally coming out here to ambush me. "You're not getting out of this so easily."

"A-!" He opens his mouth, but I plug a tentacle into it to stop him from trying again. The sensation clearly horrifies him, as he shakes his head in an attempt to escape, but I embrace him with all my appendages to hold him in place.

"Tell me, and I'll end this." Bringing my face closer to his as a lover would, I speak softly and remove the gag to let him talk - keeping it close enough so that I can insert it before he can bite down on his tongue.

"Mico Ignis!" He shouts, and flames burst out of every orifice in his head. I'm so shocked that I let go of him and watch as he brings his hands up while screaming in a nerve-grating pitch that sounds like music to my ears. Within moments, all the skin and flesh is burned away, and only a scorched skull remains.

He killed himself so readily so that he wouldn't reveal anything. Well, he knew I wouldn't let him die before he gave me what I wanted, but seeing my true appearance guaranteed his death, so he chose not to be tortured since his life was forfeit anyway.

Returning to my human form, I remember that my clothes were ripped this time. Unlike that time in Hovsgaerden when I pulled them inside my body before transforming, a sword cut into me before I could do it. Well, there are plenty of clothes to choose from among the dead.

I hear a gasp behind me and spin my head around.

Hestia is sitting on the ground and stares at me wide-eyed. How long has she been watching? Is she only surprised to see me naked, or is that a delayed reaction to seeing my true form? Or did she watch all of it and just regained her senses now that I'm back in my human shape?

"C-Chloe..." She mutters.

I climbed over the wall of the dead end to find that Kamii was trying desperately to break it down with her cursed arm. Apparently, her hits didn't increase in strength like they did against the Graebern, so it was a futile attempt. There must be some special rules to that ability, which I had no opportunity to explore further after enrolling in the academy.

She jumped into my arms, close to tears; she must have been anxious when she heard the battle on the other side.

We quickly left behind the scene of carnage and returned to the academy before the citadel could close its gates. Hestia remained completely silent throughout, but it was clear that she was brooding over what she witnessed in that alleyway. The fact that she didn't lose her mind tells me that she's either very strong-willed or only saw me at the very end.

In either case, I wanted to talk to her about it when we got back to the dorm, but when we entered the citadel, she excused herself and flew up to her room in the tower keep. She escaped to think things over on her own. I can't fault her for doing that after she was reminded once again that I'm a demon - and a pretty dangerous one at that.

"And that's the story." I explained to Senka after giving her the blood of one of the two who were still alive inside my body. One of them died, and the doll girl stood up with fluid motions. I hadn't been able to give her any sustenance since enrolling at the academy, but she was somehow able to acquire some herself from time to time.

"You love to get yourself into situations that further the plot, don't you?" She commented with a resigned expression. I thought the same, though I wouldn't have used the word 'plot' for what was really happening to me. But I had to admit, that this was the kind of development I've read in stories before, and I could identify it as a turning point in my relationship with Hestia.

Or so I thought, but the next morning the angel girl

awaits me in front of the dorm like usual. I do notice that she has a shadow under her eyes, but there are no signs of her having cried. Maybe she couldn't sleep because my appearance gave her nightmares? If that were the case, she wouldn't be here though.

"How are you feeling?" I ask, and she tries her best to give me a radiant smile. It falls a little short from what I'm used to, but it's nonetheless charming.

"Thank you for saving me yesterday." She avoids my eyes, clearly remembering what I looked like. "I am sorry for leaving just like that after returning to the citadel."

"No, it's alright. I thought you might not be feeling too well after that." From the corner of my eyes I spy Ninlil watching us, so I don't say anything that could implicate me. For all I know, all the staff of the academy could be involved in it.

Then again, if they had been, they would have just attacked me openly on their home ground, announcing that I'm a demon that tried to attack some humans or something like that. I've suspected it so far, but now I know that no matter how powerful my flow is and how many spells I learn, I won't be able to fight several mages at once unless I use my true appearance.

I won't let this discourage me from leaving the citadel, though. They can only send so many assassins before the realization that I'm not somebody they should mess around with dawns on them.

We head for breakfast, and I pay close attention to the table of professors. As always, not everybody is present, so I can't tell whether it's just their usual absence or because they were involved in the assassination attempt and don't want to give anything away through how they look at me.

There are no indications that any of the students know what happened yesterday, though I doubt the ones who do would show it on their faces.

Shaking my head of the mounting paranoia, I finish the meal with Kamii and Hestia, split up from them, and head off to class. Today I have private lessons in wind and fire magic. It makes sense to nurture my talents like this, but it also serves to isolate me from the other students.

Throughout the day, I see no signs that would indicate anybody in the academy has learned about what happened in that dark alleyway in the slums, and we leave the canteen after dinner together.

Hestia suggested going to the bathhouse in the dorms together. I've heard of it but never paid it a visit before because we have a bathtub that fits two people comfortably. When I think that the angel girl is willing to expose herself before me, I obviously can't say no to that.

When we enter the changing room together, everyone's eyes turn towards us. This must be the first time the Fata has visited this place because she was never close to anybody to the point she would want to come here with them.

I hear the rumor mills turning in an instant. My relationship with Kamii isn't much of a secret, and we haven't stopped doing what lovers do at night. It's just that people grew tired of talking about it. However, now it looks like I've pulled Hestia along to extend my tendrils towards her.

"How shameless..." I hear someone whisper, but neither of my companions seems to notice it.

"Ahhh, so jealous..." Someone else mutters. I stop myself from spinning my head around to spot who said it. Surely, it's a misunderstanding, and she's referring to being able to talk to the Fata as openly as I do. I'm sure of it.

Kamii and I strip down quickly and don't even bother hiding our nudity with a towel; whenever either of us takes a bath alone in our room, we would walk out naked to get a change of clothes unabashedly, even when people could see us through the windows.

Hestia is more reserved and takes off her clothes in an almost reluctant manner, even going so far as to hide around the corner of a shelf. Even though she was the one who suggested this, she must be having second thoughts now. But since the little dark elf and I are ready and waiting for her, there's no way she can back out now.

And really, when she does it slowly and with shy glances at me, it's even more stimulating than if she were to just undress normally like we did.

When she's finally done, I'm given a short glimpse at her bare breasts, before they disappear under her towel. So she's the type to look smaller under her clothes, huh? She's almost on the level of Daica in terms of size, but rather than the latter's mature body, she has one more like my age.

"What did you do for them to grow so big?" I'm genuinely interested and ask while staring at the bountiful mounts under the towel and scratching my chin. She's living on a vegetarian diet, so I wonder how she was able to put on that fat.

"Uhh, please do not tease me..." Hestia turns away from me with a blush and murmurs in a troubled tone.

"Miss Marcott?" A familiar voice calls out to me from behind, and I turn around to find Luna in her birthday suit, covering her front with her towel. Even though she's as tall as Hestia, her body is quite disappointing. "Huh, what is with that look?"

"Good evening." I greet her nonchalantly and lift my gaze to meet her eyes. "Care to join us in the bath?"

"I just came out." She replies while flicking her straight blond hair over her shoulder. Her skin has a rosy gloss to it, so it must be true. I guess she used wind magic to dry her hair quickly then. "How did it go yesterday?"

"Oh, we had a great time with the guys and visited Daica's store. They're all doing well, it seems." Of course, I don't mention what happened on our way back to the citadel.

"Did you see Rolan's new sword?" Luna's expression suggests that she isn't happy about it.

"No, I didn't. What about it?" Now I'm curious. None of the party had any weapons because we were only meeting in the guild hall. And the leader isn't a braggart and lacking self-confidence that he would show off his achievements without being asked.

"He found it in the depths of the Lost Tomb. Sigurd identified it as one of the lost treasures of the deep, the Sword of Light Roshanee." She explains with a frown. "But I do not believe it. That must be a cursed sword."

"Why do you say that? That name sounds like a holy weapon." Of course, a cursed weapon won't be called something like 'Dark Blade of Doom' in reality, as the creator would want to hide the fact that it has a detrimental effect on the wielder. Why else would anybody create such weapons in the first place, other than to cause people trouble?

"Because whenever he wields it, he becomes much stronger and faster for a moment. However, afterward, he is always completely exhausted" Luna's expression suggests that she saw it first-hand. Did he show off the weapon when they met and was then too tired to satisfy her? "He does not listen to me when I tell him to stop using it, and neither Gram nor Sigurd are on my side in this matter."

"You want me to tell him to stop using it when I next meet him, huh?" She nods almost sheepishly when I guess her intentions correctly. "Do you really think he'll listen to me when even his most beloved can't change his mind?"

"H-huh?" Luna's cheeks redden when she understands what I mean, and she averts her gaze. "What are you saying?"

"No, what are *you* saying?" I loom over her with a glare, under which she flinches. It's becoming tiresome to see her act like a pure maiden when her joyful voice in the bedroom was audible two doors over. "Anyway, you better tell him again. And this time, put your foot down on the matter."

Her expression grows serious again, and she considers my words. Really though, he has a sword that grants him special powers now, huh? It's like he's the hero in a typical fantasy story, and that's his unique weapon with which he's destined to slay the demon lord or something.

Not when I have a say in that matter!

"Thank you, Miss Marcott." Luna expresses her gratitude and nods with a smile. "I will give him a piece of my mind when I meet him next time."

"Glad I could help. We'll be going in now, so see you around." Gesturing at Kamii and Hestia, who are waiting behind me, I conclude our conversation.

"Have fun, but do try to practice some modesty." The half-elf's meaningful glance at my two companions makes it clear what she means. Does she think I'm some kind of sex-fiend who goes at it wherever I get the urge to?

The inside of the bath is a steamy hall with a square pool, at the end of which stands an intricate statue of a woman with a pitcher pouring hot water down. I finally realize what has felt off about this academy after such a long time; the architecture in the citadel is unlike any other building in the city. It has a different style and reminds me of conceptual images I saw of ancient Rome.

After all, this looks like one of those thermae I read up about due to my interest in hot springs.

But this is actually paradise! It's the fountain of youth! There's an abundance of naked girls walking around casually, heading in or out of the pool, talking to each other, and enjoying the water. Holding myself back from ogling them, I try to maintain a dignified facade.

I observe proper bath etiquette and move to first wash myself off before entering. The other students are doing the same, so it isn't just my Japanese upbringing, it seems.

Looking over at Hestia, I'm reminded of the fact that she has wings. It has become such an everyday sight for me that their existence faded into the background, but now that she's sitting on a small wooden stool and cleaning her hair, I get a good look at her back.

The wings sit underneath her human shoulder blades, and there's a patch of feathers spreading onto her back where they connect. She has strong back muscles like a gymnast's, and her body is more on the lean side. The most interesting feature is the vestige of a feathered tail. Birds use it for balance while gliding and for making sharp turns, but it seems that angels don't have a need for it since they most likely don't hunt prey in midair.

But this means that rather than an angel, she's a bird person.

Then I notice a few gray spots near the base of her wings. It's in a place she can't see, but I'm sure she would be very alarmed if she found out.

"Woah?!" I lose control over my voice as Kamii suddenly pokes me in the side. I'm really weak there! "What-"

She pokes me again, and my whole body convulses violently at the sensation. I fall off the small stool and stare at the little dark elf, whose frown makes it clear that she doesn't like how I'm staring at Hestia.

"... are you jealous?" I dare to ask, and the little dark elf jumps on top of me, pinning my right arm down with her knee and grabbing my left with her crab pincer. "It was a joke. P-please stop?"

"No." She remains deadpan, but I can tell that she's pissed. Then she begins tickling me relentlessly.

We sit in the bath, and I'm exhausted. Kamii is sitting in my lap now and has calmed down. She only stopped when I was lying on the ground like a twitching corpse. I could always harden my skin to make her poking useless, but my mind was too occupied with the shocks running through my body. And it would have been a betrayal of her sentiment, whatever that may have been at the time.

Hestia is only sitting at the edge of the pool and dipping her legs in the hot water, making sure to keep her wings from getting wet. If they're anything like hair, they'll soak up a lot of water and become really heavy, and they most likely don't dry quickly either. She's wrapped in her towel, but it has already become damp from the steam. It now serves to outline the form of her large breasts, while obscuring enough to retain a sense of thrill.

From here, I can't see her back, but the image of the gray spots are vividly before me. Other people don't seem to have noticed, but it's most likely because they aren't specifically looking for it as I do. This time, the corruption showed its effect much faster. Was it because I touched her much more than last time?

"Is something the matter, Chloe?" My face must have shown that I'm troubled because Hestia asks me with a concerned expression. Even though she must be suffering because of me, she's still such a nice person.

"No, it's nothing." I give her a reassuring smile. "How are you feeling?"

"The water is really nice." She says and lifts a beautiful and smooth leg out of the pool. Then she looks at me, and her cheeks grow slightly reddish, whether from the heat or her emotions, I can't tell. "Just being near you gives me a warm feeling."

"I-I see." Somehow, I feel embarrassed by that; it's practically a confession, although the feeling is quite different from the ones I've received so far. It doesn't stem from one-sided admiration, but from having been around me for quite a while. "Same for me."

Despite having Kamii on my lap, I still say this. The little dark elf is leaning against me and resting the back of her head on my shoulder. From her expression, I can gather that she silently approves of this step in the right direction.

Then what was that sudden burst of jealousy earlier?

We soon get out of the bath and separate for the night. Hestia has stayed in my room on several occasions now, but it seems that she needs some time to herself after all. But after what she said earlier, I would have liked if she talked to me rather than brooding over it alone.

Over the following few days, I had to watch as Hestia's health visibly deteriorated. The rings under her eyes grew darker, and she looked more and more tired whenever I saw her. Her beautiful white wings began to appear tattered, but when I realized the meaning of that, it was already too late.

"You're pulling out your own feathers, aren't you?!" On the sixth morning after the incident in the alleyway, I finally confront her about it when she's waiting for us to come out of the dorms like she always does. I should have done it much sooner, but I was an idiot for not understanding.

"N-no, this is... just the season when we Fatas change our feathers." She averts her lifeless blue eyes, and it's obvious that she's lying.

The problem is that not only does she have no means of reverting the effects of my corruption, but it's also getting worse without me doing anything.

"I think we should tell Grand Master Eklundstrom." I bring up, but she quickly shakes her head.

"Everything is alright, please." She pleads, no longer able to maintain her facade. I think I know why; if the principal orders for us to remain separated from now on, she'll return to being alone in this academy. So she would rather lose her life than my friendship.

"Hestia." I look into her eyes firmly and come to a decision. "I'm going to tell him. Things can't go on like this."

"T-then we cannot be together anymore!" Bridging the distance between us in quick strides, she throws her arms around me in a desperate hug. I have to hold myself back from pushing her away, as that would betray her honest feelings.

"Sorry, but I don't want to see you like this." I don't return her hug and mutter into her ear. It pains me to do this, but her life is more important than my feelings right now.

"C-Chloe..." She lets go of me and stares into my eyes with a shocked expression. When I'm this close, I realize just how haggard she looks. And with our contact just now, it should have gotten even worse for her. "W-why..."

Then she closes her eyes and falls forward, and I quickly catch her. She has lost consciousness, and her breathing is rugged. Her face is red, and when I put a hand on her forehead, I find that she's burning up. Willpower and fear of losing what we had so far must have been the only things keeping her on her feet.

Even though I'm only in contact with her over her clothes, gray spots begin to appear and spread on her wings quickly.

"Get the dorm mother!" I set Hestia down in the grass and step away from her, before telling Kamii to call Ninlil over. "Quick!"

Chapter 41

End of Innocence

"This is a troublesome development, Miss Chloe." Thorvald comments and peers over his glasses to look into my eyes. I can't bear the silent accusation in it, even though it may just be my guilty heart imagining it.

I'm sitting in the principal's office by myself, where I was called to right after Hestia was taken away. Some of the worst possible professors are surrounding me right now, several of whom I remember as those that left the canteen in anger after learning of Thorvald's decision to allow my association with the Fata. Among them is obviously Aldebrand, but Dregana is also here.

While the former has a disparaging look, the latter is glaring at me with even more intensity than usual. It feels like she would have attacked me if not for the Grand Master's presence.

"I told you that this would happen, but you wouldn't listen." With an expression that suggests the victory he feels is more bitter than sweet, Aldebrand shoots off a thinly veiled insinuation that the principal is in part to blame.

"It's clearly because Miss Marcott ignored the warning I issued on the very first day." Dregana suddenly says while never breaking eye contact with me. Her golden gaze skewers me just like her piercing words do.

"Now now, did Lady Hestia not approach Miss Marcott on her own the day after?" Thorvald steps in with his calm voice. It seems that everything is being unraveled from the very beginning in this attempt to find the person responsible for this matter. "It was her own decision, so Miss Marcott is not to blame."

"I wonder." Aldebrand comments and shoots me a glance like one would regard a pest. I have to actively suppress the urge to argue with him that if she hadn't been treated like a trophy pet before my arrival here, none of this would have happened.

"Do you know what may have caused this? Everything went well over such a long time." Liv is with us as well, because she's the professor closest to Hestia in terms of classes.

"We always avoided physical contact." I explain, remembering what I did to her in the guild hall. "Last Sjodag, we went to visit some friends in the city. We had some ale, and I forgot to maintain my distance."

Also, it may have to do with her witnessing my real form, but I can't say that. In either case, it's my fault, and I own up to my mistakes. Hestia can't be blamed for anything, even if she did try to hide it from me until the very end just to remain by my side. It all comes back to the fact that I'm her only friend here.

"I see." The principal simply says, but it seems both Aldebrand and Dregana have something to add. The only reason they don't is that Astrid enters the room, and all eyes are on her.

"Madame Idunn is tending to Lady Hestia, but we do not have the means to purify her." She informs everybody of the Fata's status.

Idunn Bystrom is the school nurse, and I've met her several times when I took wounded students to the infirmary. I always made sure not to get injured beyond what can be repaired with my light magic because I feel like she might be able to tell what kind of demon I am upon closer anatomical inspection. She's also one of the only thirteen mages with a light affinity in this nation.

"The Saint of Luminosity is on her way and should arrive here shortly." Thorvald directs this at me. Is it just me or is his gaze implying that he knows even she won't be able to help Hestia? "Let us pray that she can help."

I think he's saying this to calm the others, who put a lot of faith in her powers. Even now, I don't know what makes her a saint other than her affinity for light magic, but it must count for something because I see hope appearing on some of the professors' faces. Only Dregana continues to stare at me without being swayed by the principal's words.

In either case, Arcelia is going to come, huh? I haven't seen her since the day she wrote Luna and me the recommendations. I did want to pay her a visit next time I get the chance to leave the academy, but things are looking bad on that end.

How will she react when she learns that I'm a demon? I'm sure she'll be shocked and angry, thinking that I deceived her.

"The Saint of Luminosity has arrived." Basarab enters the room without knocking and announces Arcelia's arrival. I've gotten used to his voice by now, although it still gives me a warm feeling.

"Good morning, Grand Master Eklundstrom, Miss Marcott." The woman in white comes in after the professor of dark magic and greets us. Her eyes are closed, but I can feel her gaze on me. She must have been informed about the fact that I'm a demon, but if she has an opinion about that, it's not showing on her face.

"Thank you for coming so quickly, Lady Crux." Thorvald stands up from his seat and greets her. He pays her respect like one would a superior, even though he's the older and arguably wiser of them. Is it because she's in a higher position as a saint, or is he just that religious?

"Of course. The Fata is a symbol of purity that we cannot allow to fall." She says with both a neutral expression and tone of voice. The way she puts it irks me, but I hold myself back from saying anything. Under these circumstances, I should keep my head down.

"Let us go to the infirmary right away. Please return to your classes, everybody." The principal rounds his desk and walks towards the door. Before he leaves, I gather my courage and call out to him.

"Can I... see her?" I say, and he stops dead in his tracks. Aldebrand makes no secret of his indignation, but Dregana's glare increases a level of intensity at my words. Ignoring them both, I continue. "I know it's a selfish request, but still... she's an important friend."

"How dare you ask for that after what you did to her." Dregana finally bursts out and jumps up from the couch. Even though she has been angry so far, she has never shown it on her face as clearly as she's doing it now.

"Please, Miss Tarragon." Gesturing for the hot-headed red-head to calm down, Thorvald steps in. "I can let you see her, but you may not approach her too closely."

Aldebrand and Dregana stare at him with unbelieving eyes, but his expression suggests that he will not discuss this here.

"I understand..." This is the best deal I can get under these circumstances, so I'll take it. After all, I might never be able to see her again from now on; this could be last time I get to look at her face.

The infirmary is a church-like hall filled with rows of beds covered in clean white sheets. They are all empty, except for the one at the very back, next to which an elderly woman in a black and white nun habit sits. That's Madame Idunn, the resident healer, working on maintaining a glowing barrier around Hestia lying on the bed.

"Up to here, and no further." About halfway into the hall, Dregana suddenly extends her arm, and I run into it before coming to a stop. I can barely see the angel girl's face from here, but there's no way I can ask for more.

I feel helpless; I talked big about how she should live her life the way she wants, but in the end, I can't help her realize it. Even with all my affinities, including light magic, I couldn't save her from my own corruption. It's frustrating to be so powerlessle I have the ability to cast spells with incredible force.

The other professors follow Thorvald and Arcelia, but Aldebrand and his clique stop at one point, maintaining a respectful distance to the sickbed. Dregana is still next to me as if to make sure that I won't suddenly run over to Hestia, but I can see that she must be itching to go there as well.

In the end, Arcelia is the only one who goes all the way. She sits down beside Madame Idunn and mutters an incantation, upon which the light surrounding the Fata shines with greater intensity. Her pained expression softens a little, and she slips into slumber.

"This is terrible." I faintly hear the saint's voice as she looks at Hestia's blackened wings. The gray spots from earlier have turned much darker than before, and while they aren't propagating as quickly as they were in my presence, it doesn't look like it will stop this time.

Arcelia discusses something with Madame Idunn, but

it's too quiet for me to hear. Then she takes another long look at the patient before turning to Thorvald and waving him over. He quickly bridges the distance and leans down towards the saint.

"I see." I hear him say when she finishes, and he comes towards us to announce the outcome of Arcelia's first impression. "Lady Crux informs me that unfortunately, she does not know the magic Fatas employ to clear away demonic corruption."

"So even the Saint of Luminosity can't do anything to help her?" Dregana asks with an expression full of despair. Today is the first time she has shown so many emotional expressions on her face.

"Without the right method, there is nothing we can do here. I can only alleviate her pain and stabilize her so that she can be moved back to the Fata Triarchy for treatment." Arcelia joins us after having set up another barrier spell around Hestia. It seems that she doesn't know that the angel girl has been exiled.

"I am afraid that is not an option." Thorvald states with a bitter expression. "Miss Hestia cannot return to the Fata Triarchy."

"What do you mean by that, Grand Master Eklundstrom?" Aldebrand asks with a frown. I look around and find that the other professors are also surprised to hear those words. Only Dregana is casting her gaze down and remaining quiet as if she knew.

"She has been exiled due to political reasons that I am not free to divulge." The principal replies. He basically gave it away with that, but nobody presses further at this revelation.

"I see..." The saint's beautiful face is blemished by a frown of disapproval. She truly thinks that leaving a child to die for any reason is wrong, just as I do.

"Thank you, Lady Crux..." I bite my lower lip in

impotence and bow before her. "If Hestia wakes up, please tell her that I'm sorry."

With these words, I turn around and leave, deciding not to stop for anybody calling out to me, which nobody does.

Instead of going to class, I headed back to my dorm room. This wasn't the time to be studying, and I was sure the news about what happened were already circulating because Hestia collapsed in front of the dorms at the time when everybody was heading out to breakfast.

"That somber face makes you look even more tomboyish than you already are." Senka says after I finish explaining the situation. I know she's trying to lift my spirits, but she's not doing a very good job at it.

"Thanks." Picking her up from the bed and squeezing her to my chest as I plop down on my back, I sigh. She doesn't struggle like she usually does whenever I bury her between my breasts while cuddling her; it seems she's reading the mood now.

"While corruption does turn Fata wings black, everything else is a nocebo they associate with the visual effect." She mumbles into my shirt. "You just need to find a way to make her associate the corruption with something positive."

She makes it sound so easy. I never had much interest in psychology, so I don't understand how a person's mind works. In fact, I don't even know how my own mind works since I got this body. Killing people never felt as easy as it has that day when we were attacked by the hired assassins.

Kamii is sitting on the other bed and watching me. She also skipped class to be with me but hasn't said a word. She seems just as concerned about Hestia as I am, and there's actually a worried expression on her face.

"And you really don't know any way of reversing corruption in Fatas?" I lift the doll girl up and ask just in case, although I already know the answer. Senka looks me in the eyes and shakes her head.

"For some reason, it's a well-kept secret that only their clergy knows." She replies. I expected some kind of joke that breaks my reality, but she refrains from doing so under these circumstances.

"Then what should I do?" Bringing her close to my face so that our noses touch, I find myself asking as if I'm at my wit's end. Before she can answer, I avert my gaze and mutter. "If only I didn't start associating with her back then..."

"That-" Just when she's about to say something, she's snatched away from me. I look up to find that Kamii has grabbed Senka with her crab pincer and is looking down at me with a frown.

"Kamii?" As I try to sit up, she places a hand on my chest and pushes me down again, while carelessly dropping the doll girl behind her.

"Why are you so weak?" The little dark elf gets on top of me and stares into my eyes with a deprecating expression. She's referring to the fact that I lost my cool the moment I'm facing trouble I can't deal with by using my physical abilities and the magic I learned.

I can't even say anything in response, and when she sees that I remain silent, her frown sharpens into a glare. This is the first time she has shown me such a face, and it scares me.

"This doesn't suit you." Her expression softens, but there's a hint of disappointment in it, as she moves away from me. Picking up her school bag with her cursed arm and shouldering her cloak, she walks out of the room and leaves me behind.

The fact that I'm not going after her means that I really

lost my touch, huh?

"Is that what you're reduced to when things go wrong?" I hear Senka's voice from the ground and sit up to look at her. She has remained in the pose she most likely fell in and is looking away from me, out the window. "Kamii's anger is understandable."

"But there's nothing I can do. Hestia's state is my fault, so wouldn't it have been better if-" I start to complain, but Senka gets up like a marionette on strings and snaps her head around.

"No." She interrupts me sharply. Rather than disappointment, there's anger in her big blue eyes. "Were your feelings for Hestia really so feeble that you can so easily wish to have never had them? Do you think she would be happy that way?"

Once again, I can't reply at all. It feels like I've read this kind of a cliché development somewhere before. About how, given a chance, there are those who would rather suffer pain and death than rewind time to prevent it all from ever happening. But I've also watched a movie where the exact opposite occurred in an act of self-sacrifice by the protagonist.

Not like there's any way to turn back time and undo the things that already happened.

"Exactly. That's why you shouldn't think that way." As if Senka read my mind, she suddenly says. "Even less, say it."

"I'm sorry..." I understand now why Kamii was so disappointed with me. Despite her childlike behavior, she's the more mature one between us.

"Good night, Kamii." I say and speak the incantation to switch off the lights in the room.

She returned in the evening after classes, while I remained in bed all day long, brooding over the situation with Hestia. At one point, Senka had disappeared to somewhere as well, leaving me to my thoughts.

Kamii doesn't respond, lying in the other bed and facing away from me. She's still not in the mood to talk to me after I showed such an unsightly side of me. This is the first time since I met her that we aren't sleeping together. But I can't complain because I brought this on myself; it's going to take a while before she can get over it.

I close my eyes and prepare to sleep, but all the thoughts swirling in my head don't allow me to get any rest. What will I do if Hestia never gets better again? Even though I swore not to regret what I've done to her, I will draw a line when she dies because of me. Then I think I might just as well leave this place and start my journey back to Maou-mama's side.

Though I don't know what Kamii and Daica would do in that case. The former has been following me because of her attachment to me, but in recent times she has grown more and more independent. The latter came along because of my coerciveness - although I didn't really force her. Then what would I do if neither wanted to come along this time?

But I shouldn't think this way. It's like I already expect that Hestia is going to die.

Suddenly I hear the balcony door to our room opening, and my eyes snap open immediately. A figure is stepping inside on silent, bare feet, and I activate my night vision. The first thing I see is a pair of disheveled wings which are spread out to fill almost the entire room. The feathers are all shades of gray, with those near the bottom being completely black.

"Hestia?" I mutter in surprise, as I look up at her face. It has regained its color compared to when I saw her in the infirmary earlier today. In fact, her cheeks are flushed, but the rings under her eyes have become darker.

"Chloe..." She breathes with a feverish smile on her lips. Her hair is a mess, and she's only wearing the thin nightgown she was changed into in the infirmary. Through its almost translucent fabric and the moonlight falling into the room from the window behind her, I can see her alluring form. Sweat moistens her skin despite the cold air of this early spring night and runs down her elegant white neck to disappear into the bountiful cleavage.

Without warning, she grabs my arm and pulls me up from the bed with unexpected strength. She had been comatose just this morning, so is this the final flicker of the candle before it goes out?

"Wait, y-" I start, but she silences me with her lips and embraces me tightly. Pulling me out of the room onto the balcony, she takes off effortlessly despite the state of her battered wings.

The ground grows distant as we ascend higher and higher. The wind cuts through my clothes, and I find myself worrying about Hestia's health, before realizing that she's hot from the fever ravaging her body. Although being in close contact with me will have worse repercussions than these variations in temperatures.

We land on the terrace of the library's uppermost story, and the moment my feet touch the ground, I'm pushed to the ground. Hestia gets on top of me and looks down with an unfocused gaze, as her tongue flickers over her lasciviously smiling lips. If I didn't know better, I'd say that her eyes have heart-shaped pupils.

"Finish... what you started..." Her voice has a sultry undertone, and her rugged breath creates white plumes in the cold breeze. She tears off her nightgown, and her almost translucent white skin is shining under the moonlight in all its naked glory. This is a sight that should be framed as a piece of art. "Corrupt me!"

That forceful demand, as well as the almost violent kiss, blow all the reason out of my brains. Her tongue seeks mine and coils around it awkwardly; despite her aggressiveness, she clearly has no experience.

Then I feel something hot touch my chest and find that Hestia has ripped open my shirt. Her bare breasts are squeezing against mine, and through them, I can feel her drumming heartbeat. She slides a hand down my side, which causes a shiver to run down my spine, and motions to pull off my pajama pants.

Finally, I grab her shoulder and push her up. She stares at me in shock, but I sit up, bring an arm to the back of her head and pull her in for a continuation of our kiss. It's my turn now.

The recreated human heart in my body beats in a rhythm that joins hers, as our bodies coil in a heated embrace that seems to radiate steam in the cold night. We separate for just a second to give each other a moment to take a breath. Hestia's eyes are filled with unimaginable lust and at that sight, my own overflows.

My transformation comes partially undone, as my instincts take over. Even then, I still have enough presence of mind to maintain my human face. The angel girl gasps at the sight and shies away slightly before her lips curl up into an almost crazed smile. She runs her hands across the tentacles that form my arms and looks down between her legs, where my entire lower body has turned into the same.

"You are... beautiful." She mutters as her form shudders in mad anticipation. Those words, coupled with that expression, serve to break the last fetters of common sense that held back my desires.

God created angels so that they can be ravished by tentacles!

Unraveling my limbs, I run my tentacles all over her body, while I lock my lips with hers. Our tongues move in a mutual dance of pleasure, as the shivers running across Hestia's skin flow into me and guide the undulations of my many appendages.

My tongue grows longer and coils around hers, running over her gums and exploring the insides of her mouth thoroughly. She gasps for air at the foreign sensation, but her hands don't push me away, instead greedily grasping my head to keep me in place.

When we finally separate again because her breath has run out, I see that a wave of darkness spreads across her feathers, changing every remaining white and gray one into inky black. The corruption of her wings are complete, but the expression on her face shows that she yearns for me to do the same to her body.

More and more parts of my body unravel into individual tentacles, which run across her entire body. If somebody were to see us, they would think that I'm about to eat her; except for her wings, she's disappearing in a mass of wiggling appendages, which massage every inch of her skin.

Well, I am about to eat her. In the sexual sense.

My hair is running across her scalp, my shoulders turned into tentacles licking both her collarbones at the same time. Arms that were holding her in place before have fanned out to massage every sensitive spot across her entire back. My breasts have opened up to welcome her large ones into their undulating embrace, squeezing the mounds softly while sucking on their cusps. In my current sitting position, the legs that would normally remain useless are now embracing hers and stroking them all over.

Finally, the tentacles around my abdomen find the hottest place on her body and immediately begin to slide against it. Hestia lets out a surprised squeal but then starts to move her hips to grind herself against me. She's already drowning in pleasure from being caressed all across her skin, but she still seeks more.

Feeling overflowing wetness, I guide the tip of a large and slimy tentacle to her opening and look up into her eyes, before looking down again. She follows my gaze and sees what's about to enter her, but rather than showing fear, she only brings her own body down in impatience, impaling herself on me.

"What a naughty girl you are!" I press out between my teeth at the overwhelming pleasure coursing through my body through that one appendage. "I need to punish you."

"Yes, punish me!" She giggles hysterically like a child who just succeeded in a prank and stares into my eyes. Her expression shows that she has already lost all semblance of self-control, as she wiggles her hips to make me scrape against her insides.

Then I bring several more tentacles to her openings, both front and back, and thrust them in at the same time. Hestia's back arches at the sensation of several thick tendrils pushing into her depths. I relentlessly wiggle them about inside her, and she gasps.

With Kamii, I only ever used my human form because she doesn't know my true appearance. So tonight, as I'm doing this for the first time, I learn that the sensation is out of this world. Our bodies seem to have melted together, and every wave of pleasure running through Hestia's body is transmitted to me as if our nerves are connected.

Her eyes are moving more and more up in their sockets, while her voice becomes incoherent the more I squirm my tentacles inside her. Gasps and moans of rapture travel on the wind, and I realize that she's nearing climax. Just before it happens, I form up several bundles along the shafts and pull them out in one go. Her entire body convulses in an incredible orgasm, and a forceful spray of her love fluids explode out.

She's the type to get incredibly wet, huh?

"You're not done yet, are you?" I run my tongue across Hestia's cheek and ask with dark amusement. Her eyes are filled with a mix of horror and hope. She most likely both dreads and looks forward to feeling even better.

"I'm falling!" Speaking in a voice that sounds as sloppy as she looks, the angel girl looks into my eyes with an expression that suggests she has already lost her grasp on reality.

"Now is not the time to lose your mind." I breathe into her ear as I get my tentacles back to work. She flinches and lets out a lovely shriek like a person getting pleasantly surprised. "That comes later."

I will have her show me many more ahegao that I'll eternalize in my mental photo album.

Chapter 42

Aftershock

There's no going back from this. I look down at Hestia, who lost consciousness after her last toe-curling climax but has since slipped into slumber and is breathing calmly. Her wings are jet black, without the sign of even a single gray spot left, let alone a white one.

To me, she's more beautiful now than she ever was before, her sleeping form presenting a breathtaking contrast to the bed of tentacles she lies on.

But I'll have to do something about our location; at this rate, she'll catch a cold. I cover her with the ripped hospital gown that can barely act as a blanket now and move to peek over the terrace railing. We're on the third floor of the library building, the door is locked, and I wonder how I can get down with her without damaging its surface. There's no way she can fly in her current state after all.

Looking at her black wings, I remember that I should have gathered plenty of her genetic material through all the bodily fluids we swapped. It's the first time in quite a while that I'm doing this, though. Ever since I met Rolan and the others in Birkas, I haven't used my ability to copy appearances through genetic templates.

Closing my eyes and searching for Hestia's template, I feel my body change down to the very last molecule. I have more than enough biomass to replicate the wings after eating those assassins too. When the process is finished, the bangs cover my right eye just like Hestia's do, and I find that the feathers on my wings are white. So that means the corruption didn't change her genetic makeup.

The sensation of the extra limbs is completely different from controlling the countless tentacles that make up my body. They're like an extra pair of arms, and I feel the second set of shoulder blades underneath the human ones when I extend my hands to touch the pure white feathers.

I look down at myself and note the size of my bust. Without thinking, I begin playing with the two mounds, realizing just how big they are relative to the body. Hestia is a bit smaller than me, but this part alone is several numbers larger than mine. There's another pair of chest muscles underneath the human ones to power the wings, but they're hidden by the breasts. Maybe that's the purpose this size serves.

Now, for a test flight. I was able to run on all fours perfectly after consuming the vularen, as I may have also inherited its genetic instincts, but better safe than sorry. I don't want to crash with Hestia in my arms just because I cut some corners.

Spreading my newly grown wings, I beat them on the spot and feel their air resistance. I jump up into the air and let the instincts of this form take over. With several strong beats, I gain altitude and look down to see Hestia's sprawled out figure growing smaller.

This is the most liberating feeling I've ever had since coming to this world. Even running across the plains like the wind in the vularen form was nothing compared to this. I ascend, higher and higher into the sky, aiming for the clouds.

Throughout, I realize that it must be taking a lot of strength to fly like this. Large birds apparently use rising warm air to glide higher and higher in circles, but there's no such thing above the academy. Luckily, this body doesn't tire so I can make full use of this new template without any of its drawbacks.

I turn my eyes downward and realize that I've already risen to several hundred meters. I can overlook the entire citadel, and even the tallest tower of the castle is far below me. Hestia is just a tiny dot on the terrace of the library building, which looks like a child's building block.

This may be the worst moment to remember that I have a slight fear of heights. When we went up to the Tokyo Tower observatory deck, my friends led me to the glass floor while covering my eyes as a prank, and my knees gave out when I looked down. The abyss in the underground kingdom of the dwarves was less scary because it was too dark to see the bottom - and I made sure not to use night vision.

But I can fly. This could be an opportunity to get over my vertigo. Staring down while gliding in circles at around the same height, I take in the view of the sprawling city and the lake shining in the light of the nearly full moon of the waning fortnight.

Slowly, I get used to being so high up in the air with no ground anywhere near my feet. The wings are my support now, and I feel safe, knowing that they will never fail me as long as I'm in control of my own body.

I look down and visualize the flight path with my newly gained instincts, before folding my wings and letting myself fall. My velocity increases with every passing moment until the library building fills my vision. Opening my wings at the perfect timing, I come to a stop just a meter above Hestia.

My heart is beating out of my throat, but I think with this, I'm free of my fear of heights. If I can perform such a dangerous maneuver just like this, I should be more than fine flying normally from now on.

Now, to do that with someone in my arms. I wrap Hestia and her wings in her ripped nightgown and put my arms around her. She seems to feel my warmth and nestles into my chest - which is actually hers. Her life weighed so heavily on my mind, but her body is incredibly light.

Carrying her in a tight embrace, I beat my wings again and rise into the air, flying towards our dorm room where the balcony door is still open. Landing silently, I peek inside to find that Kamii didn't even notice I was gone and is sleeping soundly in her bed. I wonder what she'll say when she hears what happened just now.

A pair of big blue eyes reflecting the moonlight are fixed on me the moment I enter the room. They belong to Senka, who sits on my bed after having been gone for the whole day. Her gaze moves across Hestia in my arms, as well as my wings and face, and an eyebrow goes up at the sight.

"At least you didn't do it in the room..." She frowns at the sight and smell that wafts in with us. "You went all the way, huh?"

"Yes, and I'm proud to say that I got her to do the legendary ahegao several times." I reply in a whisper with my nose held high. But then I notice her frown deepen as she lifts a hand with a creaking sound to point at the Fata's black wings that can't be hidden under the clothes wrapped around her. Oh, she was talking about the corruption.

"Now we see what happens to a Fata when her wings turn fully black." Making a show out of ignoring my unrelated comment, the doll girl wears a serious expression.

She's clearly not dying, even though she might have sounded like it earlier. The fever ravaging her body has disappeared, and her breathing has completely normalized too. No matter how I look at her, she seems to have stabilized.

I carry her into to my bed and place her next to Senka, before going into the bathroom while turning myself back into my usual appearance.

"Pilos Aquos ac Coruscaris." I fill the bathtub with a water sphere and heat it with the fire spell I used when the mage assassin froze me. Dipping a finger in, I feel the temperature and find that it's slightly too hot. Thus, I add a little more cold water with another spell. Letting in water normally by using the tap would take too long and be too loud at this hour.

Walking back out, I find that Kamii has awakened and is staring at Hestia's sleeping form on my bed with her glowing amethyst galaxy eyes.

"So you did it." She comments without letting any thoughts show on her face. Unlike with Daica, whom I never passed the kissing stage with, I went all the way with the angel girl - anybody can tell from her appearance and smell.

"Yes, I did it." But I remember Kamii's attitude towards my indecisiveness this morning and answer without hesitation. She made it abundantly clear that she dislikes it when I'm weak-willed. Thus, I'm living up to her expectations by not apologizing for taking her silence at my advances on other girls - which had been only towards her little sister so far - as consent. "Do you hate me for it?"

"I wouldn't be here if I hated you for what you are." Her words drive a stake through my conscience, but at the same time liberates my heart. In my mind, I apologize that I'm like this, but on the outside, I give her a warm smile.

"Thank you, Kamii." Whispering more to myself than to her, I watch the little dark elf's long ears twitch. She must have overheard it anyway, but it doesn't show on her face, as she lies back down facing Hestia.

"Go give her a bath." She sniffs the air and says with a frown.

"Ah, right." I move over to shake the angel girl's shoulder and whisper into her ear, and her eyes flicker open. That's when I notice that her light blue irises have turned a bright crimson, which seems to glow in the dark just like Kamii's amethyst ones do.

"Chloe..." The first thing she sees is my face, and a warm, affectionate smile graces her lips as she breathes my name softly. Then she notices the little dark elf on the bed across from her, and her face stiffens. She opens her mouth to say something but is preempted by her opposite.

"Don't apologize." The thing she didn't tell me directly, she does with Hestia. There's neither a smile of approval nor a frown of disapproval on her face. She's becoming harder and harder to read for those who don't spend as much time with her as I do.

"I understand." The Fata mutters and averts her gaze.

"Let's go." To bridge the awkward moment between the two, I step in and lift Hestia from the bed. She's surprised at how easily I carry her and freezes up.

In the bathroom, I first wash Hestia down with the warm water from the tub I filled earlier. She can barely move her body due to the exhaustion from our strenuous activities. Despite that, she has a very serene expression and doesn't seem to be in any pain from the corruption. She looks at her black wings but rather than fearful, she appears content.

"How are you feeling?" I ask when she lowers herself

into the bathtub.

"I have never felt better." Her crimson eyes lock onto mine, and I glean something in them I thought was impossible in reality. That's the gaze of a person so madly in love that they would do anything to remain by their beloved's side.

Those are the eyes of a yandere.

Even though I should be scared, it's an indescribably uplifting sensation to be at the receiving end of such a gaze, and I feel my heart beating faster.

Though I'll have to set down the rules with her. If she's really one, then everybody around me could be in danger. While her short exchange with Kamii should have set the boundaries between the two, I wonder about other people and potential future girls.

"That's good to hear." I return her smile and don't let any of my thoughts show on the outside. "Can you tell if something changed about your body?"

Aside from her wing and eye colors, I can't see any other outward change. Her personality did perform a one-hundred eighty, though it may just be that she has discarded her common sense after seeing my true form.

"I am no longer a virgin." She whispers happily while looking at the trail of red rising from her crotch in the bathtub.

Fair enough... I'm sorry that you lost it in such a violent way.

"And I no longer have any fear of corruption. I welcome it." She returns her gaze to meet mine again, and my heart skips a beat. If we weren't cooling down from our earlier round of lovemaking, I would go for another one right now.

Perverted thoughts aside, I don't think she can be considered a proper Fata anymore. The purity that defines her people is gone - in more ways than just the physical sense - and maybe she even received some sort of unique cursed ability from this, similar to Daica's poisonous body and Kamii's increased strength after consecutive hits with her crab arm.

In either case, for the time being, I'll have to keep an eye on the fallen angel, to see how this is affecting her health. Also, I'm sure the professors won't be happy to learn what happened to her.

Aldebrand and his clique will most definitely accuse me of doing this on purpose, and this time Dregana might not let herself be stopped by Thorvald when she tries to rip me a new one. Tomorrow, I'll have to preempt the professors and go to the principal with Hestia in tow, to explain that everything was out of her own free will.

"What have you done to Lady Hestia, you monster?!" Dregana spits this accusation in my face the moment she lays her eyes on us. Her usual intense but stoically emotionless glare has been replaced with a grimace of anger. It looks like the flaming red hair on the back of her head is standing on end like bristles.

Hestia's absence from the infirmary was noticed in the morning, and a group of professors immediately assumed that I'm somehow responsible. They assembled in front of the dorm building in a half circle as if prepared for a physical confrontation. Even Arcelia and Madame Idunn are among the more obvious suspects like Aldebrand and his clique. I spot Ninlil on the sidelines, who looks worried about both sides in this tense situation.

"It was my will. I will not forgive any disrespect towards Chloe." Hestia steps forward firmly, her wings half spread to shield Kamii and me. Their pure blackness stands in stark contrast to her pearl white skin and silver hair. At their sight, Dregana's expression of anger mixes with despair.

"Why did you do this, Lady Hestia?" Arcelia employs a calm tone, but still wears a concerned expression. It's practically confirmed that she can see through her eyelids. "Does your kind not fear the influence of corruption?"

"I am no longer one of that kind you speak of." She spreads her majestic wings fully and shows off the depths of their blackness. They're just as beautiful as the pure white ones she had before, if not more so in my eyes. I'm the type to prefer sleek black to eye-catching white. "It feels like I have reached perfection."

"How can that accursed form be called perfection?" Dregana raises her voice and points at the evidence of her corruption, then turns her gaze to me with murderous intent. "You're controlling her heart, aren't you?"

"I am not being controlled. If you disrespect Chloe any more, I shall not forgive you." Hestia raises her voice with a deathly glare, and Dregana is shocked at the unfamiliar expression on the former's face. There it is; her madness is surfacing.

I'd rather we don't start a battle here because I'm sure that the professors are in a completely different league from the group of assassins I faced in the alleyway. I think especially Arcelia and Thorvald would spell trouble for me.

If push comes to shove, I'll have to show my real form in front of Kamii as well. I'm sure nobody here knows what I am, so witnessing my transformation will leave them stunned just like it did with every human before.

Howcver, if these professors have greater mental fortitude or even experience fighting my kind, I'll checkmate myself. After all, aside from Maou-mama, I'm the only other member of my kind that I know of. If the humans are aware of that too, then they'll know that I'm the demon queen's child. That will only give them a reason to go all out and eradicate me.

"Cease this foolishness right now" A mighty voice thunders across everybody's heads; it belongs to Thorvald, though it sounds like he used some magic to amplify it. The professors open the encirclement to let him through, as he approaches us with Basarab and Astrid by his side. His face has the sternness of a parent reprimanding a child, and it looks completely different from his usual serious side.

Dregana and the other more hostile professors each take a step back, but their staves are still held at an angle that suggests they will cast a spell to kill me in case something goes wrong.

"Lady Hestia, I see you have recovered from your fever." The principal walks forward and stops a few steps before the fallen angel. He doesn't say anything about the change in her physical appearance, as if it doesn't matter to him.

"Yes, thanks to Chloe." Hestia's expression softens as she turns to look at me with an affectionate smile. "It would seem that I lost my white wings in the process, but she was able to save my life."

Of course, she doesn't say how exactly I managed to do either, though I'd prefer to keep it a secret. While I don't think anybody observed us on top of the library's roof, I can't be sure that there's no magic for remote viewingor not. This cunning old man may have peeped on us using a crystal ball or some other fantasy-like method.

"I wish to extend my thanks to the Saint of Luminosity and Madame Idunn for tending to me." With a graceful curtsy that incorporates her wings into the motion, she eases the tension in the air. Nobody can say anything when the person they were trying to defend is fine with the situation herself.

Both Arcelia and Madame Idunn look unsure about what to say, so they take the gratitude silently. My theory is that the affinity for an element derives from one's personality, and those two must be very compassionate to have that of light. I could never see them get seriously angry, and they certainly aren't putting the blame on me like some others do.

Dregana looks like she wants to kill me, and she takes a step forward as if to go through with it. Just in case, I prepare myself, but Hestia rights herself and returns her glare with a calm gaze of her own.

"What are you trying to do?" She asks and looks down on the professor even though she's smaller than her.

"Let me kill that monster. I'm sure you'll turn back to normal when-" The latter begins, but stops when the Fata takes a step forward herself. I can't see her expression from my angle, but it must be something really shocking. "Lady... Hestia?"

"Go back and tell father that I am dead." Speaking with a chilling voice, the fallen angel orders Dregana in a tone that suggests she is her superior. "You do not need to watch over me from now on."

"That isn't what I-" Her face grows increasingly desperate, and she can't find the right words for a comeback.

"You are no longer welcome by my side." She delivers this with the gravity of an irrevocable statement.

It seems these two have a history that runs deeper than just that of a student and her professor. I glance at Thorvald, and he appears to know something, but his face doesn't reveal his thoughts at this unfolding drama.

"... please, don't do this..." Dregana realizes that Hestia is serious, and pleads in a heartbreakingly shaky tone.

"Go home."

That's all she gets in response, and her eyes widen in anguish; it was the final blow. Collapsing to her knees and dropping her staff, she stares into empty space with unfocused eyes and a blank expression of disbelief.

"I would like to apologize for the troubles I have caused you all." Hestia turns to the other professors and performs another curtsy. "I am completely healthy now."

"It appears that Miss Marcott has found a solution to the corruption - albeit a very counterintuitive one." Thorvald's gaze shifts to me for a moment, before returning to the fallen angel's black wings. "You are the first Fata to whom this has happened. Since we do not understand the full extent of the effects from this... transformation, we would like to keep you in the infirmary a little longer."

"As you wish." She nods, before turning to me and giving me a reassuring smile. "Do not worry, Chloe. I will be back soon."

Oh, I'm not worried that something will happen to you. I'm worried about the professors attacking me in your absence. While Dregana seems to have lost her will to do anything, the subtle glare from Aldebrand, and the less subtle and more murderous ones from those following him tell me that I'm still in danger.

"Now, I believe you all would like to have breakfast." Thorvald raises his voice to let it echo across the gathered people, claps his hands, and spreads his arms in a grand gesture. Only now do I realize that all the windows are occupied by students watching curiously, and many who were about to leave the dorm building are now waiting behind us.

The professors leave only reluctantly, while Hestia steps past Dregana to follow Thorvald, Arcelia and Madame Idunn to the infirmary.

"Raaaaaah!!!" The red-headed professor suddenly screams, as tears begin to roll down her face and she jumps to her feet. Then I watch in surprise as she bursts out in flames, which burn away her beautifully carved staff. From within, a dragon covered in red armor and golden eyes emerges. Streams of fire are shot into the sky from spaces between the armor plates on its back, as it slowly stands up.

It stomps the ground with its front paws, which double as its wings, and roars in my direction. The golden eyes are filled with hatred, as it opens its jaws, and I see an intense heat build inside it. Hestia spreads one wing and steps in front of me as if to shield me.

Flaring its nostrils in surprise, the dragon stares at the fallen angel for a moment. Then it lowers its head and bares its teeth in impotent anger before it turns around and runs away across the open field on all fours. It accelerates until it nearly reaches the wall of the citadel and performs a mighty jump. Crushing the battlements with its powerful claws to leap off them, it spreads its wings and takes to the skies.

I and many others watch with mouth agape, as the giant figure disappears beyond the wall.

"Umm, was that alright?" After I get over my initial shock, I turn to Hestia, who doesn't look the least bit surprised to see Dregana turn into a dragon. "She seemed to really care for you."

"Do you remember when I told you that I was sent here to die?" The fallen angel says this without a hint of melancholy. It seems that she no longer cares about such a thing, now that she has me and the ultimate proof of our relationship in the color of her wings. "My father sent Dregana with me to act as a guard. On our journey, she began to get the wrong idea about our relationship."

When she looks at me, her demeanor changes completely. Gone is the dependable girl who can stand up to the entire academy staff and face them down on her own. Instead, eyes of mad love shine through her calm exterior.

"She is a dragonkin my father bought as a slave and freed, even before I was born. Her loyalties lie with him, not with me." Her dismissive tone makes it sound like she has lost interest in the topic and would rather talk about our relationship.

I know the term dragonkin from games. They're half-dragons who have human bodies but some dragon-like features like scaly forearms and legs, a tail and wings. However, Dregana is different from that; her human appearance can't be seen as anything but that, while she can turn into a full-fledged dragon at will.

The other thing I mull over in my mind is the fact that the Fata Triarchy, a place governed by angels, still has slavery, while this nation of humans abolished it. Why anybody thinks they're a race of pure beings is beyond me.

"But she looked really desperate when she saw you like this." I still can't get over the fact that the usually straight-faced and glaring Dregana showed so much emotion over her. Even when Hestia first collapsed, she looked very anxious and flared up at me.

"Maybe she hoped that I would die from corruption, but lost her calm when she saw that I am healthier than ever now." Hestia sounds like she actually believes what she just said.

That's a really harsh thing to assume. To me, Dregana seemed to care for Hestia a lot; more than somebody who's only duty-bound to remain by her side.

"She is no longer here to bother us now." Concluding the topic, she turns to me and puts her arms around me in a tight embrace. Touching her forehead to mine, she gazes into my eyes with an expression full of love. "I will show them that there is nothing wrong with me so that I can return to your side as soon as possible."

Following Thorvald and the others, she looks back with a sad and longing gaze. I wave at her with an uneasy smile, as I regard the surrounding professors. Aldebrand shoots me one more glare, but follows the principal, and so does his clique. Finally, the area in front of the dorm building clears of people, and the students begin to stream out.

Of course, most of them make sure to keep their distance from me, but Lenoly and Vitalis stop by to ask what happened. They saw Hestia's black wings, so they already have an inkling as to the reason for this visit by the staff.

"Guess the cat is out of the bag." I mutter, referring to the fact that I'm a demon. The students should think their part now, and I'm sure a rumor will start to go around immediately.

"A nasty rumor has it that says you are a demon, Miss Marcott." Luna confronts me during lunch break. It seems she didn't see what happened in front of the dorm building in the morning and only heard it from others. "And that you are responsible for the Fata's corruption."

The Fata in question is still in the infirmary and receiving a checkup. Kamii is the only one sitting by my side, while Lenoly and Vitaly are across the table. They're acquainted with the half-elf but watch in silence to see how things play out.

"What do you think about them?" This question takes her by surprise. Did she expect me to deny them or admit to them straight away?

"I do not care about what you are. You are a member of our group." She makes up her mind and states while looking into my eyes confidently. Now I'm the one who's surprised.

"You truly are Rolan's beloved." I finally smile and earn a blush from her. I may have messed with her for a while after we first met, but in the end, I endorse their relationship. "All of you accepted Kamii into the party, even though she's a cursed child shunned by everybody else. For that, I'm really grateful."

Petting the little dark elf's hair, I bow to Luna, and she looks at me with an astonished expression. I'm quite fine with people hating me or avoiding my presence since that's how people in any world work. I've faced quite a bit of opposition in the track and field club due to my seniors insisting on their superiority based on seniority rather than skill. Other club members were jealous of my talents and free-spirited attitude. I never cared about others' opinions and just did my thing.

However, when they target another person, especially one I care about, I won't sit back and remain silent.

"As for the rumors, they're true." I shrug and confess, but make sure to keep my voice down so that not everybody in the canteen hears it. "I'm a demon."

"I see..." She has a difficult expression on her face. "But you are here. That means you do not eat humans... right?"

She somehow sounds doubtful, and she has all the reason to be; I actually ate quite a few humans - even some while she was lying unconscious right next to me. But she doesn't need to know that, and neither does anybody else at the academy.

"I don't." For now, I'm satisfied with the canteen food and the salt of maidens.

I gesture at the plate in front of me. There's quite a lot of meat, but obviously, none of it is human. "As you can see."

Throughout our time in Hovsgaerden and the journey here, my definition of 'enough' has caused her enough headaches, but she knows that I'm alright with eating normal food.

"I would like you to keep this a secret for now. While

you may be accepting, others are not so much."

"I understand. I appreciate your honesty." Luna shows a reserved smile. "I will not treat you any differently from before. You are Miss Marcott, and nothing has changed about that."

"So, want to sit down and eat with us?" I offer the empty seat next to me. In fact, there's a respectful circle of free space all around me, and only some of the demons are sitting anywhere near me.

"Oh, sorry, I just finished my meal." She has always been a light eater, so it makes sense for her to be done shortly after we just started. We did arrive late after all. "And I still have some research to do in the library before the afternoon class."

Unlike me, she's a model student through and through. Not only do I see her carrying books under her arm wherever she goes, but I heard from some of the members of the Demon Mages Society that she's a top performer in class. I haven't been to the library for a few months now.

Being on its terrace last night doesn't count.

"ChloeMarcott is a demon." Rolan mutters, causing Gram and Sigurd to stare at him in surprise. It may have been a stroke of luck that the message arrived at a time when Hreidunn, Leif, and Vigdis weren't around.

"What did you say?" The big man asks, thinking he misheard the leader. The bard heard him just right and wears a look of disbelief on his face. It goes beyond doubting the message; if even he was unable to tell, then Chloe Marcott must be an extraordinary kind of demon.

"Remember that Runa sent me a message that Lady Hestia had collapsed yesterday? Now she sent me an update, saying that she has completely recovered, but now her wings have turned black like a raven's." The leader explains. He can't even imagine what she looks like now, but it would mean her symbol of purity is gone.

"Black wings...?" Sigurd furrows his brows. "As far as I have heard, there has never been a case like this before. Do Fatas not become sick and die long before that can happen?"

"You would know that better than I do. Apparently, Lady Hestia is really happy that way, too." Rolan hands him the letter from Runa.

"And that part about the missy being a demon?" Gram asks while scratching his chin nervously.

"When Runa asked her, she admitted to it." The leader sounds like he doesn't want to believe it, but she wouldn't joke about something this serious.

"What happened to her afterward?" He's more worried about Chloe's well-being than he is about the fact that she's a demon. It brings a smile on Rolan's lips, as he suppresses the urge to shake his head in resignation.

"The Royal Academy doesn't discriminate against demons, so she's probably doing fine." Shrugging, he explains what he had heard from Runa before.

"The missy is something special, alright. All magic affinities, incredible magical powers, a straightforward attitude and a heart of gold." Gram is speaking of her in high tones. "Her being a demon only means that she's so much greater of a person then, doesn't it?"

"Yeah, that's true." The leader agrees with the big man. He always considered the demon corruption a plague upon humanity, but if the situation surrounding Hestia is true, then it means that Chloe has just found a way to make an exception. And if the option of an exception exists, more can be made until the rule can be overturned eventually.

Furthermore, she has shown compassion towards a cursed being like Kamii that even humans didn't bring forth. After all, while her right arm is inconvenient, she suffered all her life because of human prejudice and malice rather than the effects of the corruption.

"We have to be careful in our judgment." Sigurd says with a serious expression after going through Runa's letter silently. "I was unable to see through her disguise."

Rolan knows that this part of the issue is an important matter for the bard. He has always possessed an extraordinary ability even he doesn't fully understand, which allows him to see through curses and corruption. He told the other members of the group not to touch Daica's skin directly because he somehow felt that it was dangerous to do so.

While they don't have any proof whether or not that's true and always wondered about Chloe touching her without a problem, the fact that the latter is a demon could be the explanation for that.

They'd rather not try it for themselves.

"I think Runa is in the best position to judge what she's up to, so I'll tell her to keep an eye on Chloe." He trusts her and doesn't like to suspect a member of the group, but it's a necessary evil. He hopes from the bottom of his heart that she isn't deceiving everybody.

"Right..." The big man doesn't look too happy about it but doesn't say more. He spent the most time with Chloe out of everybody from the group, so he must have seen sides of her the others haven't, which lead to him believing in her being a good person.

"Let's just hope she doesn't do anything dumb." Rolan sighs and looks out the window.

Chapter 43

The God Internship

"To not arouse suspicion, make sure to leave in pairs and wait between departures." Basarab says as he always does after a Demon Mages Society meeting.

"We know already, Master Laiota." Vitalis replies as she always does whenever he worries too much. Even though my first impression of him was that he was the stoic haughty type, I learned over the past few months that I was wrong. His appearance, unfortunately, makes him look hard to approach, but he's a pretty nice guy.

"Miss Marcott, Miss Kamii, Lady Hestia, could you please stay?" He calls out to me. This is the first Sjodag after Hestia was corrupted, and she has been asked to join the meeting. After Arcelia and Madame Idunn checked up on her health, she was released with much head-scratching; the girl that had been on the verge of death the morning before was healthier than ever.

Kamii has been allowed to come shortly after my first time at the society meeting because the professor of dark magic noticed that she was facing problems similar to those of demons. She never complained to me about such things, and I assume it's because she just doesn't care that people's whispers. She really is strong.

The only person remaining aside from Basarab and us is Flann. Even though she hasn't verbally participated in these meetings even once, even less than the little dark elf has, the professor doesn't question her presence here. It would seem that he puts a great deal of trust in her, and she's allowed to do what she wants.

"How are you doing, Lady Hestia?" He asks the fallen angel after the last pair of students left the room, and the sound of their footsteps grow distant.

"I have never felt this great before." She caresses her black wings and answers. Even though her attitude is polite, her eyes make it abundantly clear that she has become sick of hearing that question again and again over the past week. "Is that all you wished to ask?"

Hestia's attitude towards others has changed drastically. She used to be reserved and friendly to people, albeit keeping a respectable distance the same way they did to her. However, after her corruption was completed, she has lost all interest in anybody but me. She only shows friendliness towards Kamii, Lenoly, and Vitalis because they have been friends since before the corruption too.

"That is not what I meant." Basarab maintains a professional attitude despite sensing that he's being considered a nuisance. "Have you faced any discrimination?"

She didn't really participate in the self-help session, while her overbearing presence caused the demons around her to shy away. Fatas are as much of a symbol of fear to the latter as corruption is to the former because of their races' mutual history with each other.

"I have noticed Master Vangir's contemptuous gaze several times, but nothing I feel concerned about." She replies with an empty smile. Aldebrand and his faction have turned around in their attitude towards her. While they used to wish to protect her from the shadows, now they make no secret out of their scorn for her fallen form. Just like a zealous idol fan club whose target of affection publicly revealed that she's in a relationship.

"I see. That is indeed unfortunate. I will communicate this with the grand master and see what he can do." Sounding apologetic even though it's not his fault, Basarab nods his head with a troubled look. "In either case, the reason I had you remain behind is that I have to tell you something. There will be an important announcement on the field the day after tomorrow."

Now I'm interested. This is the first time something like this has happened, so I wonder whether that has anything to do with us or not.

"Tomorrow, everybody will receive a letter that tells them the exact time and place, but the grand master wanted me to talk to you now." The professor continues. "Miss Kamii and Lady Hestia are to remain in their dorm room."

"Huh?" I make with a blank expression.

"The honor of presenting champion candidates to the gods has fallen onto this academy once again." He sounds a little happy, and a shiver travels down my spine. Usually, he speaks in a level tone, so I've gotten used to the almost aphrodisiac-like effect of his voice. But just now, he put some honest emotion into it, so it was like the first day all over again.

Though I have to wonder about the contents of his statement. When I hear champion of the gods, I think of the chosen hero. Are they going to do some kind of test where they make people try and pull a sword from a rock? I guess Rolan isn't the hero after all, huh?

"If you do not want to be taken away by the Mage of the Beginning's Curiosity Collectors, it would be wise not to show yourselves." Basarab addresses the two girls next to me directly.

I don't know what to think about that one. Kamii and Hestia were just called curiosities, but he said it in a tone that suggests he's really worried about their well-being. It does sound like those so-called Curiosity Collectors are religious nuts; after all, Mage of the Beginning refers to Alkupera, the god who created all life in this world.

"So the church is conducting this selection?" I ask with a frown. Even though I know Arcelia is a good person, she must be an exception.

"No, the Curiosity Collectors are the direct subordinates of Lord Alkupera." In the most natural tone, he's basically saying that the god in question is real.

I glance at Kamii and Hestia. Of course, gods can exist for real; this is a fantasy world where angels, demons and intangible corruption with actual effects are real. However, accepting that they exist opens a huge can of worms in regards to my position in this world. Especially when it sounds like the gods are helping the humans. They are the gods of humans I guess, so it's to be expected. I didn't hear about demons worshipping any either.

"Thank you for telling us. We'll make sure to stay away." I say with a grateful nod. I want to get out of here and ask Senka about this matter as quickly as possible.

"Oh no, the grand master specifically requested for you to be present during the selection process." Even though I expected these words, they still hit me like a truck. He only said that Kamii and Hestia should hide away, but there was no mention of me. I just hoped that I was included by default, being a demon and all.

"I see. I'll be present, then." Putting on my best smile, I try to sound cheerful. On the inside, I breathe the longest sigh of my life.

This is awful.

"And that's what happened." I finish my explanation to Senka, and she thinks for a moment.

"I'm not omniscient." Those are her first words, as she frowns. Hestia is staring at the doll girl, suppressing the urge to ask what she is. I haven't introduced them to each other so far because the incident of her corruption and its aftermath have been occupying our time.

Among other things, Hestia was kicked out of the tower keep and should have been given lodgings in the dorms. She immediately attempted to smile out the inhabitants of our neighboring room, but I told her she could stay in ours because Kamii sleeps in my bed anyway.

"But I can tell you that the gods are real entities." Shrugging, Senka slips down from the bed and walks over to Hestia. "And that they wouldn't take kindly to seeing her like this."

"Hm, what is that supposed to mean?" The fallen angel's smile is murderous.

"You've been warned not to attend, right? While the Mage of the Beginning is a special case, other gods are more purist." The doll girl doesn't falter under the deadly crimson gaze in the slightest and turns around to me. "You can be certain someone like the Lord of the Sky will be angered to learn that one of his precious Fatas has fallen to demonic corruption."

"Taivass..." I mutter that name. He was mentioned in history classes many times and is the leader of the pantheon. As far as my impression of him goes, he's arrogant and thinks so highly of himself that it's almost comical. "You think any of the gods could show up?"

"They have only ever shown themselves before humans under the direst circumstances, so I don't think any of them will be there for a recruitment session to what is essentially just an internship."

"Internship?" That's a word I didn't think I'd hear here.

"Yeah, the direct followers of the more active gods periodically scout for promising individuals across the Alliance nations. It's the reason why those nations join the alliance in the first place."

"What do they do there?"

"Do I look like I've been to one of those?" Senka makes a point in giving me a fake smile at these words.

"Umm, Chloe?" Hestia finally gathers her resolve and points at the doll girl standing in front of her. "What is this?"

"That's rude." Spinning around with feigned indignation, Senka steps up to the fallen angel with her head tilted. "I'm Chloe's most beloved girl."

"Huh?" Hestia and I both make in surprise. Kamii suddenly smirks, and I'm taken aback by how fitting it is for her to make such a face, that I don't know how to react.

"In either case, the gods are real, and they're very powerful - in case you couldn't tell from the title." Her sassiness is at its best again today. Then she suddenly grows serious. "The champions are chosen to help in a war against the demons. They must be aiming to start another campaign."

"Were there champions in the battle half a year ago?" I thought the conversation was going to fizzle out just now, but she got my full attention with that again. The battle in question is one that happened the day before I first woke up in this world. Maou-mama said that an army knocked on her doors, but she dealt with them.

"Nobody survived that one, right? So most likely not. They're practically one-man armies, and if they had died, the news would have spread all across the world." Crossing her arms, Senka paces through the room thoughtfully.

"What is this about, Chloe?" Hestia asks.

"I'll have to explain to you another time..." It's too big of a reveal to make right now; neither Kamii nor Hestia know that I'm the daughter of the current demon queen.

But the gods are helping in a new campaign against Maou-mama, huh? That's certainly bad news. Even though the demon kings in stories are generally the final bosses for the human heroes, I don't think someone who is only a king could stand up against entities titled gods. Or in this case, a queen.

There's too little information to say for sure that they're aiming for another campaign, but if the gods - most likely beings with such immense powers that humans and even demons call them that - are involved it means that my mother is posing such a significant threat.

"On another note, I'd like to confirm something." I change the topic. The matter about this new army will have to be shelved until I know more the day after tomorrow. "What are your affinities again, Hestia?"

"I have the wind and light affinities." She responds, wondering why I ask after all this time. I've seen her cast both types before, but now that she has become corrupted I think that she might have lost the light affinity.

"Have you tried casting light magic since that night?"

"I have not had the... oh." Before finishing her sentence, she realizes the aim of my question. "I see. Let me try it."

She holds out her palm towards me and speaks a very short incantation that seems to defy my hearing. A murky dark glow surrounds her hand, and I almost shy back, but the effect I feel is that of the Sano spell.

"H-huh? What did I..." With a perplexed expression, Hestia stares at her own hand.

"It seems you retained the light element, but it was

visually changed into darkness." I scratch my chin. How does that even work? I've seen her use wind magic afterward, so that's also still there. She retained her affinities even though she's corrupted.

"I do not understand." She sounds confused and looks at her own hand.

"Well, you were corrupted by me, who has all affinities, so maybe there's something special about that." When she looks up at my words, I can tell she's thinking that being corrupted by me is something special anyway. "Maybe you got a curse. Do you feel anything strange about your body?"

"My eyes have been feeling a little strained since then." I didn't expect her to tell me something immediately. Usually, I would pin that on lack of sleep or being stressed, but that's obviously not my first thought now.

"Have you ever felt something similar before?"

"I have never had problems with my eyes before... am I going to go blind from the curse?" She looks fearful. Losing one's vision is always scary, but for a being that can fly through the skies freely, that would be the worst possible ailment. "I would not be able to see you anymore, Chloe."

That's what she's afraid of?

"Let's observe the situation for the time being. If it gets worse, you should see Madame Idunn about it..." I'd prefer not to rely on anybody from the academy side for this because they might find signs for what I am, but I have no idea how curses work. If she really is cursed and something happens to her eyesight, I wouldn't be able to help her at all.

It might be time to seriously search for a way to utilize the transportation circle and leave this place.

Sjodag came and passed. Neither Hestia nor I were allowed out of the academy for obvious reasons. Then came Fara Silfurdag, when classes were canceled for the day, and everybody was gathered on the field between the main building and the dorms.

A huge wooden stage has been erected in the front, while a stand overlooks it from behind. Clearly, the envoys will be sitting up there to watch the selection process. The students were asked to line up in columns separated by elements and ranks.

Since I'm still considered a beginner, I should normally be standing somewhere at the very back; however, nobody else possesses all magic affinities, so I was told to form a column all by myself. In fact, I think I might be the only beginner present; I see very few familiar faces, and I'm surprised to see Svanhild among them.

As far as I know, she only has one elemental affinity, but she somehow still found her way into this gathering of people who could be selected to become champions for the gods. I really don't think her abilities are on that level.

On the platform itself, representative professors of each affinity and discipline are sitting in a row of chairs, waiting for the principal and the envoys of the gods to arrive.

Aldebrand and his faction glare at me with pure hostility as always, but some students have started doing the same since a few days ago. I think my reputation has been getting progressively worse after I corrupted Hestia, even though I was on relatively good terms with everybody before then. They can't look past the prejudice of me being a demon, and they can't forgive me for tainting their symbol of purity - while not caring how that symbol feels.

But I've already made up my mind to leave the

academy before things become too dangerous.

I hear murmurs from the students behind me and look in the direction of the main building entrance. There, Thorvald is leading a procession of a dozen men and women in white leather coats that look strangely modern. They have high collars and sleek designs, unlike the typical robes and cloaks of mages.

The people wearing them are all blonde and blue-eyed, and their pace is like that of a ceremonial regiment. It's quite clear that those are the envoys of a god, though I can't tell which one.

What follows them is a group of around twenty people wearing masks and baggy cloaks that remind me of lab coats. Their color schemes range from pure black to those found in modern art paintings. If they had come in performing acrobatic tricks, I would have thought they were a band of clowns, but they walk in an orderly fashion, albeit not as strictly as that of the previous one.

The third group comprises of three females in beige and one Fata in pure white. At the sight of the latter, I involuntarily stare in surprise; I certainly didn't expect this, and judging by the reaction of the students around me, neither did they. Many perform the religious gesture of reverence at her entry.

But the single person who comes after causes me to almost scream out in shock. It's someone with an androgynous physique and an ambiguous gender, clad in dark blue robes and wielding a gnarled staff with no visible catalyst. The face and hands are completely covered in bandages.

It's Mithra, the court magician of the demon castle.

I physically turn my face into a rigid mask, as I feel my insides churn from fear and stress. What is he doing here? Is he an agent for Maou-mama? Or did he betray her and is helping to overthrow her by fostering the next generation of these champions? Didn't he consider the possibility that I would be at this academy since I was sent to this nation?

Due to his bandages, I can't tell at all where his eyes are looking, let alone what he's thinking. For now, I'm kind of in disguise, but it's flimsy at best when somebody who has seen my previous face every day for three weeks looks at me. After all, I only changed my features slightly to match the ethnicity that I'm posing as.

However, the fact that he isn't calling me out means that he either doesn't recognize me or doesn't want to reveal himself before everybody. If it's the latter, it would mean he's working for Maou-mama, but if it's the former, there could be many reasons for his presence. Many of which are troublesome.

For now, I can only wait and see what happens.

"Thank you for gathering here today." Thorvald raises his arms and addresses both the students and the envoys with a grand gesture, once all the groups have settled on the stands behind him. He slowly turns around himself to look across everybody like a skilled orator. "It is with pride and honor that I can announce the commencement of the Trials of the Chosen."

He proceeds to explain how it will be conducted: The professors will choose the most proficient students under their tutelage and present them before the envoys. They will then judge whether they are worthy to demonstrate their abilities or not. Then, these students will have to show some skills that make them stand out among other mages, be it unique multi-elemental spells or great control over their element.

Of course, I can feel several sets of eyes on me from the stands, even while others are being led up to the wooden platform. Some of the so-called students are at least thrice my age, and they're usually immediately sent away again. I guess people who are too old may not have the same future potential as somebody much younger but at nearly the same level.

Then I see Luna get on stage, and my eyes almost pop out. What is she doing there?

Rolan does harbor the ambition to bring down the demon queen, so I guess it's only natural for her to take the opportunity. And her magic is quite powerful, even if her cast speed is lacking. Or was, considering she had special lessons for the past few months and might have improved there.

"This one will do." Suddenly, one of the men looking like clowns crossed with scientists raises his voice. Although he wears a colorful grinning mask, his tone is level. Luna is the first they have deemed worthy to even show off her magic, though there have only been eleven other candidates so far.

"Thank you, Your Excellence!" The professor who presented Luna lowers her head with an excited but reverent expression. "Allow her to demonstrate her unique nature magic."

At these words, the half-elf has the attention of all the envoys at once. I hear students muttering at these words, but I wonder what it even means. Maybe possessing unique nature magic at her age is something incredible?

Luna raises her staff and begins to chant. While it does take longer than the spells I've learned, it's nowhere near as long as it used to be. Within a few seconds, she finishes her incantation and points the catalyst towards the sky. Above its tip, a ball of plasma forms, and I recognize the spell to be the one she used against the double-fire affinity mage in the slavers' den.

Last time, it took her more than a minute to cast it, but now it's almost at the level where it could be used in single combat. If she improves further, that could be quite dangerous to face.

She lowers the staff slightly, and a laser beam shoots down into the grassy field with pinpoint accuracy. It describes a perfect line, and the earth is scorched from the heat. Quickly dispelling the glowing ball, she glances at her mentor apologetically, before facing the envoys with a nervous look.

"Magnificent!" Another masked man says in an excited voice. His coat is the most flamboyant among his group, and his tone is a perfect match for the deranged mind that finds such an explosion of colors aesthetically pleasing. "What is your name?"

"Runa Sigint." Even from here, I can see that her legs are shaking, but she answers in an unexpectedly firm tone.

"I see, a descendant of..." The one with the pure black outfit says, but trails off. Since Luna is facing away from me, I can't tell what kind of face she's making, but I'm sure she either knows what he's talking about or is itching to hear whom he's referring to.

"Is anybody else interested in her?" The color-explosion man directs this at the other two groups of envoys. He's talking about Luna like she's an object that's being auctioned off, and the way she grips her staff tells me that she's not feeling comfortable about it either. "Then we shall take her under the wings of Lord Alkupera."

So those are the Curiosity Collectors? Are they even considering her spell-casting capabilities when saying they want her? To them, she might just be a curious object because they recognize her heritage.

"Thank you very much, Your Excellency." Luna bows before the group of clowns, but her voice doesn't sound as firm as when she announced her name. Instead, there's a hint of doubt in it.

"What is it, my child?" A fourth member of Alkupera's

envoys asks. It's a female's voice, and her outfit would be considered moderate among them.

"I was wondering... what does it mean for me to be under Lord Alkupera's wing?" The half-elf asks the question I've been wondering about myself. Senka, who usually knows everything, didn't have an answer to that question. Judging by the fact that I don't see anybody silently mocking her for her ignorance, it's safe to assume that it's not common knowledge even for the staff of this academy.

"You will come to Lord Alkupera's sanctum, where you will receive special training under His tutelage." The first clown answers the question. For some reason it feels like they're mentally connected; one person alone could do what they're splitting up on several many people.

"B-but..." It's clear what Luna is thinking about when she almost protests; she wants to stay with Rolan and the others. But to those who revere the gods, refusing this offer would be akin to heresy.

"You have friends here, huh?" The one lacking modesty in his choice of colors asks. Even though he wears a mask, one can feel the sympathy he exudes. "Unfortunately, those will not be allowed to join you. The sanctum of Lord Alkupera is a place only the chosen may enter."

But despite his sympathetic tone, his words are ruthless. It makes sense that they won't invite the families and friends if it's like an internship, as Senka put it.

"I see." Under these circumstances, the half-elf can't gather more courage to request for more time to make her decision. After all, she enrolled in the academy at the same time as I did, and was favored above even the masters that look like they have been studying here for decades.

She steps away from the center of the stage and is

guided to one corner, where she's made to watch those that follow her. Within moments, I feel eyes on me again, while other mages are called up on stage and refused one after the other.

Eventually, another person, a man a few years older than me, is interviewed. He introduces himself as Halthor Blom, speaking in a deep voice that possesses a thunderous intensity. Even though his audience consists of his superiors, just like Luna, he doesn't lower himself in humility. Maybe that's what caught their eyes.

Then he demonstrates his magic, cast through a gauntlet rather than a wand or staff. However, against everybody's expectations, it's not earth magic. He raises a hand to the sky as if grasping for something there rather than the ground.

To everybody's surprise, a lightning bolt comes down and shoots into his body. His eyes and opened mouth light up as he roars at the top of his lungs. The students standing near the front stumble back in fear, as he balls his fist and dispels the magic. Sparks play around his body, as he turns around and looks up at the stands.

Was that really magic? I don't think he spoke an incantation.

Some of the men and women in leather coats have jumped up from their seats and are staring at Halthor with round eyes. It's clear that he's what they're looking for, even if their expressions look more alarmed than interested.

"I assume you want him." One of the Curiosity Collectors say with a shrug, and it seems to be spot on. The perceived leader of the white-coats looks at the man's mentor with a very telling gaze, and the latter quickly guides him towards where Luna is waiting.

When he turns around, I find that his expression is stoic, like he has been waiting for this opportunity for a long time, and had no doubt in his success.

Judging by the reaction of the envoys, I have to wonder if every single one of them is a powerful mage. They surely know what Maou-mama is, and if they're somehow able to find out what I am, there's no way I'm getting out of here.

"Miss Marcott." Thorvald personally calls out to me after three more are denied. Since I don't have a direct mentor like the other high-level students, he's the one who announces me. A murmur runs through the crowd, and every single envoy of the gods stares at me, as I make my way up.

Mithra is among them, and this time I can be sure he's looking at me. Nothing about him tells me whether or not he knows who I am, but this would be the time to expose me if he were really working with the enemy.

Just to be sure, I stop at the bottom of the steps and close my eyes, acting like I'm nervous. In reality, I'm running a check on my body, to make sure I didn't accidentally leave any non-human signs on me. I left the survival kit that Rewera gave me in my room, as I made a habit of storing it inside my unfathomable belly for passively training myself.

Everything is fine now, I'm entirely human down to the very genetics, even though that should be realistically impossible. But so is summoning flames with an incantation and saying a single word to heal wounds; therefore, I won't question how this body of mine works.

"Miss Marcott possesses every magic affinity, including light, dark and space." The principal introduces me, and all the envoys jump up from their seats - except for the Fata and her followers, who watch in silence. Mithra stays still, but because of those bandages, I can't tell what his expression is like right now.

"Please demonstrate your abilities." One of the three

under the Fata asks of me. It's the first time that any of them reacted, let alone spoke, so I must have garnered their interest.

But I haven't learned any multi-elemental magic that I could show off to the same effect as Luna. Then again, I don't really want to impress them, or they'll take me away from here. On the one hand, failing miserably could lead to them losing interest; on the other hand, the professors would know that it's a lie because they've seen my abilities in class.

Good thing I never learned any magic during my training with Maou-mama; and even if I had, I wouldn't be so dumb as to show it off in front of humans, much less in front of a potentially traitorous court magician that could expose me right now.

"Circoluceo." I chant, and an orb of light appears above my head. It's the least powerful light spell I know because I want to hide my actual abilities in this affinity at least. So far, the staff and students haven't seen me use anything other than Sano.

But seeing me cast any light magic at all is already an eye-opener for most people present. The envoys take it with far less awe compared to the students and teachers, and Mithra still doesn't move a muscle.

Thus, I go through each element I know any spells of, but stop at dark and space. The academy taught me neither, most likely because they don't want me to learn dark magic as a demon, and I suppose no professor has the affinity for space magic.

"That is impressive." One of Alkupera's envoys comments after my demonstration is over. "Do you not have any magic of your own?"

"I'm still only a beginner." I say in the most natural manner of tone. A murmur runs through the students behind me because I didn't address him with a title, and my speech lacks any hint of respect. I really don't have the presence of mind to think of such things, when it feels like I'm being stared down by Mithra.

"I see." Another of the colorful group comments while tilting his head. "Then-"

"Lady Framtith desires you." The Fata interrupts him without a care in the world. Her voice sounds almost ethereal and echoes unnaturally as if she used magic to enhance the effect of her delivery.

Framtith is also known as the Guide of Tomorrow, the goddess of creativity, visions and fortune telling. I didn't expect that the Fata was an envoy of hers rather than of Taivass.

"Apologies." I lower my head, making sure I choose the right words to decline this offer that normally can't be refused. "I'm a demon, so I shouldn't be allowed to study under a goddess."

Once again, a murmur runs through the crowd and this time it stays. I don't know what the students are more shocked about; the fact that I openly confirmed the rumor that I'm a demon, or that I would refuse this chance that may come around only once in a generation.

From the corner of my eyes, I spot Svanhild among them, who stares at me with her mouth hanging open. It's not a very ladylike expression, but I can't fault her for it. After all this time, she learns that the person she tried to bully was a demon.

Even now, Mithra doesn't make a move, and the suspense is killing me. There was no point in hiding the fact that I'm a demon because I'm absolutely certain that the envoys were told about me before they came.

"Do you understand what you are saying?" The Fata's follower who asked me to demonstrate my magic proficiency speaks in a low and menacing tone, while she narrows her eyes.

"Yes, I understand." I look up and stare into them fearlessly, to signal that this is a decision I thought through properly. The truth is, I don't want to be taken to some god's place, where they'll surely find out what I really am eventually.

And I would never leave behind Kamii, Daica, and Hestia. Even Maou-mama's deadline is secondary to those three; I don't need the demon throne if I'm not with them.

"I will ask you one more time, Chloe Marcott: Will you take the offer of tutelage under Lady Framtith, the Guide of Tomorrow?" It seems that this is my last chance to change my mind, as the Fata stands up from her seat and asks with a downward gaze. Those eyes suggest that I won't be given a third.

"I have decided." Shaking my head, I turn away - but glance at Mithra from the corner of my eyes - before walking towards the other side of the stage. On the way, I pass by the previous two chosen candidates and find that Luna is staring at me with her mouth open, while Halthor is giving me a judgmental gaze.

"Such strong will." The most flamboyant Curiosity Collector raises his voice in unmistakable praise. "Lord Alkupera would love to welcome you to his sanctum."

"Do not attempt to persuade her any further." One of the white-jackets warns the clowns as well as Framtith's followers. "She has made her decision. Any more would be an insult to her resolve."

That's an unexpectedly nice thing to come from one of the guys I thought were completely full of themselves.

Without stopping to see the expressions of the professors or the principal, I leave the stage and walk away towards the main building. The students are obviously all staring at my back, left utterly speechless by my decision. That was a cool departure, if may I say so myself.

My heart is pounding out of my chest though, thinking whether or not Mithra will rat me out now.

Chapter 44

Space Files

"You just walked away like that?" Hestia makes round eyes when I tell her what happened during the selection of champions after I return to our dorm room.

"Yes, somehow I did." Scratching the back of my head, I take some time to consider what I've really done. "And I got away with it."

"Are you sure that was Mithra?" Senka asks the more important question. Neither Kamii nor Hestia knows who he is, so when I mentioned him in my story, they didn't react.

"Yes. I would never mistake that appearance."

"Couldn't it have been somebody else in disguise?"

"I'd rather think it was really him than be overly optimistic."

"Who is this Mithra? Do you know him?" Tilting her head questioningly, Hestia joins the conversation again.

"He's... an acquaintance. But his presence here is worrying." I try to stay vague because I fear somebody might be eavesdropping on us right now. "Let's not talk about that."

"In either case, do you think that was the right decision? Did you not consider that they might come to secretly take you away by force?" The doll girl understands my thoughts perfectly and helps by returning the topic on track.

"I will not let that happen." Hestia answers with a determined expression, and I glance at her with an eyebrow raised. I'm happy that she doesn't hesitate to stand on my side even when the enemies are envoys of the gods, but I fear she might overestimate herself.

"Same." Kamii raises her cursed arm. While she doesn't sound even half as enthusiastic as the fallen angel, I know that she will be just as fervent in helping me in my time of need. That she doesn't show it as openly is just part of her personality.

"So, what will you do now?" Senka drives our conversation forward, but then she adds something telepathically by speaking through our mental link - the one she established back when she bit off my index finger in the academy basement. "*About Mithra, that is*."

"I have a few thoughts." I reply out loud and continue in thought. "*I need to find a way to inform my mother of this*."

Good thing I found the transportation circle below the so-called storage area in the basement of the academy building. If I hadn't back then I wouldn't know what to do right now. Still, I need to learn how to activate it. And the only place where I can find information on that is the library. I haven't been there in a long time, so I hope it won't cause suspicion that I'm going there right after I practically made myself an enemy of the gods, to learn how to use space magic.

Then again, I wasn't found out when I discovered the circle, so nobody should know that I'm aware of its existence. And I can make the excuse that today I was reminded of my inadequacies in the space affinity, so going to read books on it in the library would be only natural.

"But first comes lunch." I say and sling my bag over my shoulder.

The library is as impressive as ever. I've come here a few times shortly after enrolling but didn't go anywhere especially deep. But to find the information I need, I'll have to search in places I haven't been before.

As always, there are quite a few people in the designated reading areas, and many more can be found standing or sitting in the aisles between the shelves. Some of them were present during the morning gathering, so they know what I did. The moment they notice me, they begin to stare - some in fear, others in awe.

The nature elements are accessible to everybody, while dark magic can only be found in a restricted area on the third floor, which require permits from certain professors. I search for any books on space magic but only find those that explain what it is and its supposed effects. Others mention figures in history that were capable of using it, but they're written like fairytales. None teach me spells or knowledge about the transportation network.

Among all those, I learn that space magic includes something akin to telekinesis, with which one can move objects from afar. I can understand why the spiritual elements - and especially the space affinity - are so rare; they effortlessly do what nature elements try their best to mimic.

Wind magic can achieve a similar effect to telekinesis, but it remains an imitation and is easily detectable because of the breeze it creates. Same for water magic used for healing, which only manipulates the fluids inside the target's body to speed up natural regeneration - at the cost of energy expenditure from the benefactor. In contrast, light magic seems to just mend wounds without any drawbacks.

While reading through the principles behind space magic and the various applications of it, I notice that Kamii has fallen asleep and is resting her head in my lap. She seems to have tried reading one of the books I already put aside and lost interest quickly. Glancing at Hestia, who stretches her wings on the couch across from me while reading a book on cooking, I smile at the sight. Then I return my attention to the book in my hands.

The main applications of space magic are transportation, manipulation and time. While the first one is what I need to read about the most right now, I can't help but flip to the section about the last one. If time magic means what I associate with it, then whoever can use it could be a god.

Reading through its description, I'm thoroughly disappointed; it's the ability of timekeeping which Senka told me about a while back. But doesn't that mean there are quite a lot more people with the space affinity than what Arcelia told me? After all, even the bard seems to have the timekeeping ability.

In either case, I return to what I came here to do after this utter letdown. This particular book doesn't go into any detail regarding how teleportation spells are cast, but it says that one can only teleport when within one of the ancient transportation network's circles dotted around the world.

Then what did Mithra do? He teleported Maou-mama and me around the Dominion without any circles. Maybe human magic is far behind that of demons?

Picking up a different book, I skim through it quickly. This one gives details on the telepathy part of space magic, so it's not very useful for me at the moment. Another one is about the discovery and analysis of the transportation network. However, not only does it lack a map marking locations of the circles, but it also has nothing on how to use them.

I wake Kamii up and get off the couch to make another round in the sufficiently small space magic section - it covers only a single shelf. Going over the spines of the books, I realize that none of them specifically address the usage of the teleportation circles.

In the end, I make up my mind and go to the receptionist. I ask in a roundabout manner to avoid any suspicions but am told that the in-depth space magic books are in a further restricted area within the restricted area, which only Thorvald can grant access to.

Does that mean humans do have knowledge about the circles but don't want to share them even with their own elites? Well, I assume mages are their elites because traditional soldiers could never hold their own against some of the demons I've seen that are being trained to join the army, such as the Petsobek under Nilotec.

After what I did this morning, I sure as hell won't be able to get permission from the principal to search for magic that could allow me to escape this place. Which means I'll have to sneak in at night like I've done a few times before. Surely, if the transportation circle in the basement has no countermeasures, then the restricted section won't have any either.

It's not like the magic of this world can make books grow faces and screech loudly as a kind of alarm, right?

We leave the library around the same time as the last person. Usually, this place has no closing hours, but people generally don't stay through the night unless it's exam weeks.

In the end, I spent most of my time learning the history

of the transportation network circles. All of them were discovered rather than built, suggesting that they were created by a long lost civilization with highly advanced magic - or maybe science? Whichever is the case, the humans today don't really know how to use them, and only the gods are said to be able to activate them.

So are Maou-mama and Mithra on the level of the gods? While they do seem to possess powerful magic, they didn't seem to be that awe-inspiring. Or my image of the gods is just skewed, and they aren't really as godlike as their titles suggest.

"Miss Marcott, you're really something." Ninlil's voice stops me when we come in through the door of our dorm. She's lying stretched out on one of the small couches in the entrance area, lazing about like a cat. It's clear that she's talking about my actions this morning. "Do you know how dangerous your position is right now?"

"I have an idea..." I mutter, remembering the attack from the assassins even before I corrupted Hestia. Before, only those who knew I was a demon would hire people to attack me, but now students from wealthy families who revere Fatas will start doing it, too.

"Be careful when you leave the citadel. There are children of powerful nobles from the empire in this academy, too." She warns me, implying that she thinks the same thing I just did.

I pity the fool that attacks me in a dark alleyway far from other people; it will only be a repetition of the massacre from that time we visited Daica's store in the slum district.

"I understand. Thank you for the warning." I shouldn't let anybody know that I think I'm up to the challenge. That way, they'll underestimate me when they do come for me.

"If you have any troubles, you can come to speak with

me." Ninlil sighs and offers with a smile. I have to hold myself back from trying to pet her hair. "You two, too."

She tilts her head to address Kamii and Hestia behind me, who both nod in different degrees of bashfulness.

"Now head off to sleep, it's late at night, and you have lessons tomorrow." Jumping up from the couch nimbly, the dorm mother shoos us upstairs.

Once we reach our room, I immediately slip out of my clothes and throw them onto the chair by the desk.

"H-huh?" Hestia stares at me in surprise, but then she blushes and begins to squirm while fiddling with her shirt. "I-I have not prepared my heart for this right now, Chloe."

"That's not what I have in mind." I turn to Senka lying on my bed, but from the corners of my eyes, I see a disheartened expression from the angel girl.

"Huh? Me?" She sits up with a worried expression. Apparently, she's getting the wrong impression.

"Yeah. Time for a mission."

This time, Senka is traveling inside my body from the start. When I was almost caught in the underground storage leading into the transportation circle room, I found out that she seems to be immune to the effects of being surrounded by my corrupted matter. She did complain that it feels gross, but she didn't become sick from it. Come to think of it, she also wasn't afraid of seeing my real face, so there must be something special about her.

I make my way along the tree line that separates the back of the dorms from the citadel wall and quickly move towards the library building in the form of a small vularen. Even though I can run quickly as a human, a wolf-like being on four legs is still quite a bit faster.

Peeking inside the library through a window, I see that all the lights are off. The librarian left shortly after we did, and there's only darkness now. I round the building and move towards the back entrance, where I let out Senka.

"Ugh, I really hate this mode of transportation..." She mutters with a disgusted expression the second her feet touch the ground. Then, without having to be told, she puts her hand on the lock and opens it with her strange cheat-like ability.

"Thanks." I pick her up, squeeze her to me and rub my face against hers. She only looks annoyed and doesn't say a word.

My destination is obviously the restricted area within the restricted area. I only know that it's on the third floor, but I don't know where exactly it is since I couldn't just go and scout it out.

The interior of the library is completely dark, but my night vision allows me to see like it's almost daylight. I was here earlier, but it looks different when illuminated by lamp crystals. Everything is perfectly visible, which reduces the chance of surprises, but also the coziness I felt earlier.

Climbing the circular metal stairs to the third floor, I use vularen paw pad to soften my step as I always do on my nightly exploration trips. Once again, I'm really grateful for Maou-mama's mess-up which sent me on that short trip to the Dark Continent; I remember being mad at her back then, but now I can't thank her enough in my mind since I gained such a useful template.

As I walk through the main aisle in search of the restricted area - which isn't explicitly pointed out with a sign - a person suddenly walks out from between two shelves, and we collide.

Crap, someone was here! I immediately drop Senka, press my palm on the other's mouth and push them against the shelf. But their form crumbles away under my grip, leaving only dust and hair in my grasp.

Staring at the remains in my hands, I blink my eyes in

bafflement.

"Chloe?" A familiar voice asks from behind me, and I spin around. Vitalis is standing before me in her slime form, her usually drowsy-looking purple eyes opened wide in surprise. "What are you doing here?"

"That should be my line. Why are you at the library at such an advanced hour?" I quickly counter with a question of my own, employing a reprimanding tone so that she's pressed into explaining first.

"I was thinking of making myself into a tasty jelly." As expected of the resident airhead, she says something really strange. I look at the section sign and find that it's one on potions. Is she for real?

"Are you for real?" My thoughts slip out, and I ask in a flabbergasted tone.

"Yes, I had jelly for lunch, and it was really tasty." Tilting her head and wiggling her naked liquid body, she replies with a self-assured smile.

"You're a very special one, aren't you?" To think she would sneak into the library at night for such a reason.

"Ehehe."

"That wasn't a compliment!"

"Now it's your turn: What are you doing here?" Ignoring my rebuttal, she asks me again.

"It's a hobby of mine to sneak around the academy at night, trying to avoid being detected by any of the professors." It's the truth, just not all of it in this particular case.

"That's a strange hobby." Tilting her head the other way, she silently judges me.

"You're the last person I want to hear that from!" I shout but slap my hands in front of my mouth. Damn, I'm getting pulled along into her pace. "In either case, I'm busy right now, so-"

"Who's that?" Vitalis interrupts me and asks, tilting her

whole upper body to peer around me; she's pointing at Senka lying on the ground unmoving like a doll. I realize that in all this time we've been friends, she hasn't been to our dorm room once.

"That's just a doll." Not letting anything show on my face, I turn around and pick her up. "Isn't she cute?"

"Ehh?" As expected, the slime girl's reaction is skeptical, as she eyes Senka's stitched face. "She looks hurt."

"That's alright, she's just a doll." I repeat myself, squeezing her to my chest. "Anyway, good luck in your search."

With these words, I turn around and leave, but hear splotching footsteps behind me. Swiveling my head around, I see that Vitalis is following me.

"Yes?" Looking up at me with an empty-headed smile, Vitalis makes it clear that she wants to follow me. She's known to be easily distracted even during combat class, and coming along with me seems to be the more interesting thing right now.

"Didn't you want to turn yourself into a delicious jelly?" I point at the potions section, but she doesn't even turn around to look at it.

"You're here now, so I'll come with you." Now her smile turns radiant, and I feel a twinge in my heart. That's not a face I can say no to, but I can't have her follow me around when I try to break into the restricted area.

"Okay, but you'll have to do it this way." I carry Senka with one hand and grab the slime girl by the back of her head. Even though she looks like she's made of water, the texture is more like the sweet jelly she wants to turn herself into.

"Wah, what are we going to do-" She doesn't sound especially surprised.

"No, don't say it!" I interrupt her and open up the front

of my body. Her eyes go wide at the sight, but I quickly envelop her and pull her into my depths.

This puts me on a clock since I don't know how her body will hold up inside me; she has no heartbeat, and there's no sensation of struggling. While I can keep something alive for a while, that only applies to solid living beings. For all I know, she could be dissolving right now, even though I put her in an area that doesn't digest its contents.

Without wasting any time, I begin to scour the entire third floor, until I reach a door with an opaque glass window. The runes on it read Forbidden Archives. If that isn't the name for a restricted area, I don't know what is.

"That was a bad move." Senka says while getting to work on the door.

"Huh, what do you mean?" I ask, but don't get an answer, as the lock clicks audibly. While I expected that this place would have the same level of security as the vault door to the storage room, it is only the general restricted area. I'm sure my target, which is deeper inside here and only Thorvald can grant access to, will have better safety measures.

The inside of the room is the same as the outside and looks just like a continuation of the library. But even from the entrance, I can tell that the books here are different; not only are many of them really old looking, but there's a shelf filled with ones that have black spines, and most likely black covers, too. Those must be books on dark magic, which aren't available to the general populace for obvious reasons.

Straight through the central aisle, I spot another door. It lacks a window but is steel-studded just like the vault door leading into the storage room. I hope it doesn't have an alarm either.

I walk ahead just in case there's a trap or something,

while Senka follows closely behind me on her own feet. Judging by the names on the spines of the books around me, I can tell that they describe some dangerous magic and high-level spells.

Once again, the doll girl shows off her ability to unlock anything with a simple touch. The sound of the mechanism echoes through the silent library just like the complicated lock of the underground vault door, before slightly swinging outward on its own. This one is layered as well, but not nearly as thick.

Thorvald's restricted area is just a small room with shelves lining the walls. Unfortunately, they aren't categorized, so I have to read the individual spines of the books to find what I need. As with those outside, there are many books without any labels. Every second counts, as I can feel Vitalis body inside mine, so I get to work quickly.

"I'll help." Senka offers and begins to look at those on her eye level.

I quickly narrow down the shelf on which the books on space magic are grouped together, but it's still going to be a piece of work to find one on the transportation network.

"Here." The doll girl suddenly speaks up and pulls out a book. It says 'Transportation Network Locations' on the spine, and I quickly take it from her extended hand.

"Thanks." I smile at her and begin to flip through the pages. The paper smells old, but the whole book looks quite new; considering the number of space magic users among the humans, that's only to be expected.

There's an incomplete world map included, which shows more than two dozen locations of the transportation circles. There's only a single one marked on Ceogath, so I flip to the page that describes its position. Maybe I'm lucky, and it's the one in the demon castle.

And I really am lucky. Not only does the book say that it's in Arkaim, but it also shows a sketch of the circle with all the runes on it. I didn't really expect this level of detail, but it's worrying that the humans have so much knowledge about a remote entry point to the castle itself.

Still, this book doesn't explain how teleportation through the circles can be achieved, so I'll need to keep searching.

"Where did you find this one? There should be-" I look down at Senka, but she pulls out another book from the shelf.

"This should be it." She says and hands it to me. The title, Array of the Gods, is quite vague, but if she thinks this is the right one, I'll give it a try.

After flipping through the first few pages, I can tell that it is. The book itself is even older than the previous one, and it seems to have been read a lot. The pages are dry and crumbling, so I have to be careful while handling it.

The gist of utilizing the transportation network is that it doesn't require an incantation but a clear picture of one's target location - or one's body will get ripped apart and scattered across the world. Maou-mama teleported me without the right coordinates, so I ended up with a nice little trauma.

As expected, this one also says that one needs to be anywhere within the circle, and specifies that one should never leave part of one's body outside of it when it activates. Whatever isn't in the circle is cut off cleanly.

In other words, one absolutely requires a transportation circle to be able to teleport. I think back to Mithra again and wonder, but maybe this is just outdated knowledge. In either case, I'll take this over not being able to teleport any day.

I open the other book that shows the locations of the circles again and search for the one in Kongenssoevn. It's also described in there, along with a sketch of its shape.

Comparing it to the one in Arkaim, I find that the runes making it up are entirely different, even if the overall circle is the same.

I copy both onto pieces of paper and label them appropriately. Due to the location of the network entry point under the academy, I can't take either Kamii or Hestia with me, unless they come along inside my body. And if something goes wrong, that could be really dangerous. So on my first journey, I'll do it alone and verify that it works as intended.

"Time to get out of here." I hand Senka the books, and she puts them back into their previous spots, while I gather my notes and put them in a paper folder. Pulling them inside my body, I check my surroundings to make sure I don't leave anything behind, before returning to the door.

The doll girl uses her not-magic magical ability to lock with a touch of her palm, and I pick her up before sprinting out of the restricted area. I have her do the same with the much simpler door while she's in my arms this time, and when she's finished, I jump over the handrails of the atrium. Lowering myself down into the main hall by turning my arm into a rope, I silently reach the bottom.

Since I finished my business, I want to get out of here as fast as possible. Vaulting across the desks and couches of the reading area, I quickly reach the back door. I kept it unlocked before, risking a patrol discovering it, but it was so that I can escape faster. Once again, I have Senka lock the door when we exit it.

The moment she's done, I pull her inside my body, into an area separate from Vitalis. The slime girl must be scared out of her wits inside me, so she doesn't need the shock of a cursed doll being dropped into the space with her.

I take in the cold night air for a moment to calm my

nerves. Unlike in the underground storage vault, nobody came and suddenly made it into an almost impossible mission this time. For some reason, I feel a little disappointed, but I'm actually grateful for that. I couldn't sleep for the whole night after my close brush with those professors I thought were the most dangerous at this academy - and still consider as such.

When I'm done, I transform into a small vularen and make my way back to the dorm room.

Chapter 45

Untimely Return

"Welcome back, Chloe." Hestia greets me when I open the balcony door and enter the dark room silently. Neither she nor Kamii are asleep, and they look like they've been anxiously awaiting my return. "How did it go?"

"Got what I needed. I think tonight is the best time to continue this." I insert a hand into my stomach and pull Senka out from it under the wondrous gazes of the two girls. "But first, I need to take care of this little problem here..."

I try to pull Vitalis out of my body the same way, but instead of a jelly-like mass, liquid bursts out and splatters onto the floor to form a bluish puddle. The slime girl is more than half-dissolved, and I see a melted face in the center.

The expression can only be described as ecstasy.

"Huh?" I turn to the others, but they only stare at the remains of the slime girl blankly.

"Congratulations, you just had sex with her." Senka comments in a deadpan tone, and Hestia twitches.

"What do you mean?" I only swallowed her, and I

didn't touch her once while she was inside me.

"Slimes are essentially hermaphrodites. As giving birth is a strenuous activity in the wild, when it comes to reproduction, they fight over who has to bear the children. The winner swallows the body of the loser and plants their seed in them." The doll girl explains in a perfect documentary narrator voice. "And the process is incredibly pleasurable for them."

"You could go pro with that... now wait a second!" No matter how hard I try, I can't go without a rebuttal to her joke. "I'm not a slime, and I didn't plant my seed in her."

"That doesn't matter to her. She was fully enveloped by you, and her body reacted accordingly." Shrugging, she denies my attempt to save myself from this situation.

"What is the meaning of this, Chloe?" Hestia steps forward, and I finally notice that she's wearing an almost see-through white nightgown. It's a sight to behold, but this isn't the time to stare at it.

"It's a misunderstanding." Why do I have to justify myself here? Anyway, I need to do something about this, or Vitalis might seep through the floor and drip into the room below us.

"Bring me a mop, Kamii." Hestia's tone suddenly shifts to a deadly sweet one. "I'm going to clean this up."

"What are you going to do with her?" Well, her tone leaves no room for doubt that she's going to dump her in the toilet and also flush. She has really become a yandere, hasn't she?

"Whatever could you mean?" The smile she gives me just reeks of fake innocence. "I will throw the trash out, and then you can tell us about what you learned in the library~"

I knew it!

"Chloe..." Vitalis finally lets out a weak voice, which is barely audible through the bubbling sound accompanying it. It's like she's talking with her mouth submerged. "I'll bear you... many strong children..."

"Yes, I will take care of this right away." Taking the towel that Kamii has brought from the bathroom - in lack of a mop - the fallen angel says and looks about ready to snap.

"Stop it!" I don't think it will do her good if she gets sucked into cloth. "So, what should we do about this?"

"Like I said-" Hestia begins.

"You shut up for a moment." I show her a serious expression, and she flinches. However, she somehow looks happy at being scolded. She was a bit of a masochist before, but it seems that she doesn't worry about hiding it anymore now.

Ignoring the fact that Hestia seems to enjoy being reprimanded like that, I transform my hands into two halves of a giant spoon under the wide-eyed stare that Kamii gives me. I scoop Vitalis up, then go to the bathroom, plug up the drain of the bathtub and put her inside.

"Stay here." With these words, I leave the room and close the door behind me before she can respond. Out of sight, out of mind.

"So, are we going now?" Senka asks the moment I come out of the bathroom.

"Time?" Just to be sure that it's not close to dawn, I ask the doll girl in the most concise manner possible.

"Still plenty of it before people wake up." And she gives me an answer that's as vague as this nation's timekeeping method. But since they don't separate a day into twenty-four hours, telling me the concrete hour and minute would be useless anyway.

"Then we're going now."

Once again, I'm walking down the stairs leading to the

vault door where I almost ran into Thorvald and some of the most powerful professors at the academy back then. The path here was as easy as the first time, and I even entered through the same bathroom window, which can be opened from the outside even when I don't leave it unlocked during the daytime.

Along the way, I saw Bjorn, the earth magic professor, on patrol, and wondered why no member of the staff came to talk to me about what happened during the champion selection - other than Ninlil, who didn't do so in an official capacity. I expected to be called to the principal's office, but maybe they're holding an emergency meeting on how to deal with the repercussions of my attitude before the god envoys.

I have no illusions that there won't be any. Even if the followers of Taivass may have praised my resolve, the Fata under Framtith gave me the impression that she will hold a grudge. I know from first-hand experience that the angel-winged people are nothing like one would expect when judging them by their appearances. And Alkupera's Curiosity Collectors may very well just try to kidnap me one day when I'm out of the citadel, so there's still that possibility too.

Stopping in front of the vault door, I pull Senka out from my body. As always, she complains about the mode of transportation but immediately goes to work. Just to be sure, I expand my body to cover the entire stairwell to muffle the lock mechanism's gratuitously drawn out sound effects.

Picking Senka up and pulling the door open, I sprint inside without wasting any time. Even though nobody should know we're here, I don't know how long I'll be in the demon palace - if I reach it right away.

The doll girl unlocks the dummy wardrobe's door when we reach it, and I put her down on her feet.

"Watch over the vault door. If somebody comes..." I don't even know what she's supposed to do when our break-in is found out, and I'm not back yet.

"I'll think of something. Just know that our connection won't work over the distance that you'll be away from me, so if something's up, I won't be able to warn you in advance." Senka explains the limitations of her telepathic powers.

"Thought so." Sighing, I turn to the walled-off staircase, at the end of which the transportation network circle is located. "Make sure to stay out of trouble."

"That's my line." Even though this was the perfect opportunity for her to be snarky, she replies earnestly.

"I'll be back soon." Bending down, I kiss the doll girl on the forehead. She looks up at me with a pout, but then her gaze changes into a worried one. However, she keeps quiet and only nods.

With this, I leap down the stairs while pulling out the notes I took in the library from inside my body. If these don't work, I'll feel pretty dumb. And even if they do, so many things could go wrong. Among the worst would be if I arrived in the castle but Mithra was waiting there with an ambush.

Thinking so much won't help me here. The most important thing is clearing up the situation surrounding that court magician's presence among the god envoys. I wouldn't even mind if it was something as simple as him acting as Maou-mama's agent, but I need to know the truth.

Walking over towards the center of the circle, I transform into the demon maid named Keiza - the one who came into my room to clean it shortly after I first woke up in this world. Using my body's matter, I form the appropriate maid outfit from my skin and give it the right color scheme. It's not perfect but will fool people when they don't scrutinize it. After all, the possibility that Mithra is over there is quite high, and if I were to run into him in either my previous appearance or the one I had at the academy, he'd understand that I found out about him.

Finally, I look at the depiction of the circle in Arkaim. Burning it into my mind, I close my eyes and imagine going there. The moment I do, I hear the familiar sound of being inside an active teleportation stream. Opening my eyes, I find that I'm surrounded by light just like the one I've seen so many times while traveling to various places in the Dominion with Maou-mama and Mithra.

Then the light disappears, and I'm in the dark chamber in the basement of the demon castle. Nostalgia washes over me at the memory of how I was sent through this and arrived on Yagrath missing my two arms and the lower half of my body.

Wait, that wasn't a good memory at all!

Nobody is here, so I quickly run towards the door of the chamber; I need to get to a place where a maid won't look suspicious. Keeping my back straight and putting on a neutral expression, I turn the handle and push open the door.

I very nearly walk into somebody and quickly step back while bowing. Luckily - and strangely enough - the demon maids observe Japanese customs, so my instinctive behavior blends right in.

But when I look up, I almost scream in surprise.

"I am sorry, Master Mithra!" Apologizing in an over the top manner, I bow deeply again to avoid showing my face. Then I straighten my back again and quickly walk past him.

"Wait." His muffled voice stops me dead in my tracks. I've heard him talk before a few times, though he's the type to stay quiet unless it's absolutely necessary. That he would talk here means business. "What were you doing in that room?"

"..." I turn around on the spot at a measured speed - not too quickly and not to slowly - and think as fast as my brain allows me to under the pressure of potentially being killed if he notices that something's wrong.

Why would Mithra be in front of the teleportation room right now? The only logical explanation is that he noticed my arrival through the transportation circle and came to check it out.

"I thought I heard a sound in there and came to take a look." I report with a neutral expression, suppressing my anxiety and fear. Luckily I neither reproduced sweat glands nor a heart in this body, or my forehead would be dripping, and my heartbeat would be heard throughout the castle.

"And did you find anything?" He asks in a tone I can't interpret. I can't see his face so I can't tell what he's thinking, but I pay close attention to his staff, even though there's no visible catalyst, to see if there's a sign for when he activates magic.

"Unfortunately, I did not. Maybe it was just my imagination." The tension is killing me, and I suppress a shiver from taking over my body by bowing again. "If you would excuse me then, Master Mithra..."

He doesn't say anything, and I turn around to leave without looking back. Doing so here would signal that I'm wary of something. I maintain my composure until I round a corner where he can't see me. Then I stop for a moment to gather myself; if I were in a human body, it would have broken down from the tension just now.

The biggest problem I have is that I don't know where to find Maou-mama even though I need to talk to her in private. The worst case scenario would be that she's out right now. Judging by the sunlight coming in through the tall windows of the entrance area, it's late afternoon, but she has neither a court to attend to nor any notable routine; her day to day life looks as random as it really is.

The best option would be to ask a maid. However, I don't know Keiza's manners and relationship with the others, so if I were to talk to somebody who knows her well, they may realize that I'm not her and cause a commotion, which would most likely attract Mithra before it does Maou-mama.

Thus, I walk around in thought and pass by the slightly ajar door to the kitchen. If I weren't in my current situation, I'd sneak some food from there, but I don't have time for that right now.

There's the sound of something shattering coming from inside the room, and I stop. Even though it's most likely just a maid or other servant messing up, I can't suppress my curiosity. Pushing the door open further, I peek inside, to find a hooded figure with their back to me. They move about in a flustered manner, looking around for a broom to clean up the broken jar on the floor.

Wait, are they here to sneak some food? It's still bright outside, so that must be one bold glutton. I move silently and approach the intruder from behind. My appearance is that of a maid, so I can put on a little play and scare them.

"What are you doing here?" I speak up in the serious tone that Keiza employed when I first met her.

"Hyah!" The food thief flinches and lets out a cute female voice, before spinning around. One hand is stuck in a cookie jar, the other is holding a large piece of ham to the mouth. Even with half the face hidden under the hood, I can tell who it is.

"Mama?"

I'm back in the appearance I used to have when living in this castle, and rub the bridge of my nose with an irritated sigh. I didn't expect that Maou-mama was the one trying to steal food from the kitchen like a petty thief.

"Why do you have to sneak around to have food in your own castle?" I'm looking down on her as she kneels before me in a perfect seiza position. So this is how our long-awaited reunion goes: Me catching her with her hand literally in the cookie jar?

"B-but when I eat outside of the meals, Rewera will get angry..." Her tone is like that of a sulking kid; all the charisma and poise I've seen throughout my time with her seems like a lie. I have to wonder whether or not she's even the real Maou-mama. But then again, I do remember her being a ditz and showing moments of unexpected immaturity before.

"Why are you afraid of the maid leader? She works under you! In the first place, you're the demon queen!" My irritation grows, and she shrinks under my gaze.

"Ahhh, I knew it! Every child that returns hates me for some reason!" Maou-mama pouts and tears appear in the corners of her eyes.

"Are you a child?!" I rebut, but her expression suddenly becomes defiant. Uh oh, did I go too far? "Alright, alright. I'm not really mad. It's just that I was feeling so tense earlier, and seeing you like this seemed like a bad joke."

"Hmm? Why were you tense? You finally returned, so you should be proud." She puts a finger on her cheek and tilts her head. It's an incredibly cute gesture, but it's exactly this kind of behavior that makes me question her authority as my mother. "Though I wonder how you got into the castle without anybody running around and announcing it out loud. Everybody should be in an uproar about it."

"Argh, I almost forgot!" My mind immediately returns to serious mode. "I found a transportation circle and teleported directly into the castle, but that's not important right now."

"Oh, so you used a shortcut. That is not how I intended for you to return, you know?"

"I said that's not important right now!"

"Sowwy." The cutesy tone in which she apologizes somehow infuriates me, but I don't have the time to bother with it.

"I came here as quickly as I could to tell you that I saw Mithra in the Royal Academy of Kongenssoevn." I don't know whether she even recognizes those places, but I can't waste time explaining where that is if she does know.

"You were at the Royal Academy?" Maou-mama looks at me in surprise, before a radiant smile lights up her face. "That is impressive! How did you get in there?"

She's saying this with so much joy that all my tension just escapes me like air from a punctured lifeboat.

"I got a recommendation from a saint because I have all magic affinities... no wait, that's beside the point!" I grab her shoulders and shake her in an attempt to make her enter serious mode. "Mithra was there with the envoys of the gods."

"... with the envoys of the gods?" Her expression changes and she becomes more attentive. "I know that Mithra goes to meet his daughter at the academy from time to time."

"He has a daughter?" Now I'm the one who's changing the topic, but this really interests me.

"Yes, Flann Umratawil. Did you not make the connection when you heard such a rare family name?" Maou-mama's tension dissipates as well, as she puts a hand on her cheek like a gossiping housewife. I assume Umratawil is also Mithra's family name, but I was never told that.

"Wait, Flann is a girl?" She did look somewhat girly, but I just assumed she was a pretty boy! Is she the legendary reverse trap? Unlike me, who's just a tomboy in manners and taste, that type purposefully chooses to look like a boy, either to fool others or as a kind of lifestyle.

"Oh, so you met her. As I expected, you were unable to keep the fact that you're a demon a secret before the grand master." And now she talks about Thorvald like she knows him. Considering he must be a powerful mage of the enemy faction, it's only natural that she would keep tabs on him though.

"Anyway, we're not talking about Flann right now. Mithra was with the envoys of the gods, and they came to select a new generation of champions to start another campaign."

"In what way is Mithra involved in this?" Tilting her head, Maou-mama looks skeptical.

"He just came in like he was an envoy himself. Don't tell me he was acting in an official capacity for you." That would be a bad joke if the humans and demons drew from the same talent pool to fight their wars against each other. Considering this is a fantasy world, I can't deny such a possibility though. After all, I heard there were some bizarre customs in medieval times when it came to chivalry and war.

"No, that would be ridiculous." Waving me off with a laugh, she denies my over-thinking. My urge to bop her over the head is growing with every passing moment in which she shows a decided lack of seriousness.

"Then why was he there?" Even if he went to see how Flann was doing by hiding his identity all this time, that doesn't explain him sitting in the stands like he's representing a god in the champion selection.

"Why do we not ask Mithra directly, then?" Maou-mama says with a wink.

"Chaos is accusing you of scheming and conspiring

with the humans and gods. What say you in your defense, Mithra?" Demon Queen Pelomyx announces while sitting on her throne. She has reverted to her charismatic self right after we left the kitchen, and I begin to understand that she only acts naturally when she's alone with me.

I'm standing to her right, and Rewera is taking the spot on her left with an expressionless face. Even though I did say that Maou-mama should show more dignity as the demon queen, I can fully understand why she would fear the maid leader. Her physicality and straight-laced personality are quite overbearing, now that I see her again.

The throne room is filled with maids on both sides. I spot Amerega and Nezera among them. They're the frog and bat maid respectively - the ones who served me my food on the first morning in this world. They both stuck in my memory because of their inhuman appearances, although I met many even less human-looking maids soon after.

"What are You saying, Your Majesty? I would never dare to oppose You." Mithra, who's standing in the center of the room, speaks clearly and without a hint of unease. Of course, he won't crack under accusations lacking any proof.

"I saw you in the Royal Academy during the champion selection today. You came in with the envoys of the gods as if you were one of them." I step forward and transform into my appearance as Chloe Marcott to see his reaction.

Since every inch of his skin is covered in bandages, I can't tell what kind of face he's making, as always. But the fact that he doesn't flinch at my revelation shows that he doesn't think anything of it.

"I did wonder whether that was You or not, Your Highness." But then he replies in a somewhat reverent tone, confirming that it was really him. "That was brave of You, to deny the invitation from Framtith's principal follower Apate Moirael not once but twice."

I'm speechless. While I can't see his expression, his voice makes it sound like he's genuinely praising me for my courage. Maybe I really did jump to conclusions when I saw him there, and he was acting as Maou-mama's agent, infiltrating the side of the gods to gather information for her.

"You really did that?" She turns around to me with an amazed expression. "Impressive, Chaos-chan."

"That's not the point! Why were you acting as an envoy?" If he's really an agent, then Maou-mama should know about that.

"I was working on Her Majesty's orders. Throughout the past two decades, I have become a trusted follower of Fimbria. In the Kingdom of Lares, she is known as Urslit, the Witch of the End." Mithra explains, maintaining a neutral attitude. Even though I accused him of being a traitor, he doesn't appear to feel slighted or even angry.

So he was the sole representative of Fimbria? All I know about this goddess is that she stands for the end of things. Unlike the Liberator of Souls Avilok, who awaits at the end of life to bring peace to the dead, Fimbria is the one who will be there when time itself ceases. I have no idea why somebody as nihilistic as that would have any followers though.

"I see..." Lowering my head, I suppress the urge to apologize. Maou-mama told me that as a ruler, one has to take responsibility for one's failures, but never show humility or regret. I have to maintain my pride even when I'm in the wrong. "Then it was my misunderstanding."

But that much I have to admit.

"Do not worry. I never told you about Mithra's role, so seeing him there must have been surprising." Smiling, the demon queen reassures me that this isn't my fault.

"Let me cry into your chest, mama!" I've already

gotten over the shock of learning that I was wrong about Mithra, and am using this opportunity to leap into my mother's huge breasts.

"My, what a good child." She sounds quite happy as she spreads her arms to invite me in. I instantly take it and bury my face between her bountiful mounds. "You really are the first of my children to treat me like your mother."

Now that she mentions it, I'm reminded of the fact that I never saw any of my siblings even though she talked about them before. Were they sent to oversee other cities or castles after returning from their journey?

"I've never met any of my siblings. Where are they?" I separate from her and ask.

"They were rebellious, so I ate them." Maou-mama responds in a matter of fact tone.

"Huh?" Wait, what did she just say?

"Hm?" She looks at me with an innocent expression.

"I... I may have misheard you, mama..." Maybe I really did, so I have to ask again. "You said you-"

"I ate them." Once again, a simple statement without a single shred of malice in her expression. That makes it even scarier than if she had said it with a sinister smile. Then she seems to realize something and grins mischievously. "Not in the sexual sense, silly child."

Wait, in the kitchen earlier when I scolded her, and her expression turned defiant... was she about to eat me? And not in the sexual sense either. I suppress a shudder at the realization.

"... how many of my siblings are still alive?" I doubt they knew about this when they were sent out into the world, so those who returned with a rebellious attitude towards her were eaten. In fact, she didn't tell me about this before either.

"Not a single one. As I said, you are the first to not betray me." She replies in a matter of fact tone. That's not entirely what she said before, but I now get that she implied such. "I had my eyes keep surveillance on every single one, and some died when they picked the wrong opponents. Others came back with strange ideas in their heads."

Huh, she was watching me all this time? As in, everything I've been doing? Does that include my time with Kamii and Daica in Hovsgaerden? And that one time on the rooftop with Hestia? There are some things parents should never do to their children!

"In other words, I'm the only one left?" I remember the history lesson in which I learned that the year after my grandma was launched into space, many of her progeny appeared all over the world. Back then, I considered the possibility that they were actually Maou-mama's children. "How many did you send out?"

"Too many to remember the exact number." She replies casually as if I asked her how many steaks she consumed throughout her life. In a way, she may have eaten more living beings than grilled meat though.

I think our kind may reproduce through something similar to cell division. And if that's true, she could easily have produced thousands of children throughout her life. That not a single one besides me is still alive is both sad and terrifying.

"Why... did you eat them? Why not punish them and try to re-educate them?" Maybe she never thought of doing that before.

"Because they gave me no choice. Also, it returns the energy I spent on giving birth to them, so it was for the best." She replies with a disinterested shrug and leans back while furrowing her brows, signaling that she wants to stop talking about this.

Once again, she says something scary so easily. And the scarier part is that, from a certain angle, I can understand her reasoning.

"Speaking of eating... Maou-sama, I have heard that you were stealing food again." The maid leader suddenly speaks up and stares down on the demon queen without moving her head. Her dark red eyes look like they're burning.

"Eek!" Maou-mama lets out an undignified yelp as she jumps up from her throne under the fiery gaze and quickly hides behind me. "W-who did you hear that from?"

"That is of no importance." Rewera shuts down her attempt at finding the one who snitched on her. Now I have to admit that she's really intimidating when seen from up close like this. Her face remains expressionless, but the pressure from her words is almost tangible. "We talked about this before, Maou-sama. As your punishment, your dinner will be reduced."

"Nooo, anything but that! Dinner is the most important meal of the day!" Maou-mama sounds really pitiful as she comes forward from behind me and pleads to the maid leader.

I understand that the maid leader has the air of a strict mother, but where's your dignity as the demon queen?

"You said the same about breakfast and lunch. In either case, you have only yourself to blame, Maou-sama." Even though she maintains a respectful tone, she remains relentless even when subjected to my mother's unsightly pleading.

"Mama, stop it. It's disgraceful..." I shake my head.

"Buuut..." She looks close to crying. Where did the charisma she exuded just moments ago disappear to? It's even worse than when I caught her red-handed earlier.

"Alright, I'll bring you something good next time I come here." I sigh in mental exhaustion. Did I really have to come back in the first place? It feels more and more like a wasted trip.

"What do you mean, next time you come here?" Maou-mama suddenly regains some of her earlier composure when she hears what I said.

"I have to return to the Royal Academy as quickly as possible." The longer I'm gone, the more likely it is for somebody to find that the vault door to the transportation network circle was left open. And I obviously want to reassure Kamii and Hestia of the fact that I'm alright. Also, I have to deal with the half-dissolved Vitalis in our bathtub.

"Do you really have to leave already, Chaos-chan? You just came back." Her composure fades away again and makes way for a lonely pout. It's such a cute expression that I almost forget she's my mother.

"Yes, I have people important to me waiting anxiously for my return." I go in for a hug, and Maou-mama takes me into her arms.

"People important to you, huh? Introduce them to me one day." When we separate, she gives me a warm gaze that seeps into the depths of my heart. That's the mother in this world whom I've come to love and respect after just a few weeks with her.

"That reminds me that there's one more thing before I go." I have to get it off my chest, or it will keep nagging at the back of my head.

"Yes?" Smiling expectantly, she awaits my question.

"Are you somebody who reincarnated into this world?" I ask directly. All evidence points that way, including the casual usage of Japanese honorifics in a world where the Japanese language doesn't even exist.

"... let us leave that for another time, Chaos-chan." She puts a finger over her lips, winks, and smiles mysteriously. It's basically a confirmation. "Mithra, if you would."

"Understood, Your Majesty." The court magician in blue steps forward. "Is Your destination the transportation network circle under the Royal Academy?"

"Yes, I need to pick up somebody from there." And lock the vault door to hide all evidence of our nightly disappearance. Even if I'm caught roaming the hallways afterward, I can always say that I was just going on an adventure.

Suddenly, I feel two hands grabbing my chest from behind and fondling me with trained fingers. They're obviously Maou-mama's because nobody else here would dare to do this.

"Hyah?!" Huh, did that voice just now come out of my mouth? I free myself from her grip and bop her over the head. "Stop it!"

"So cold..." She looks up at me with a playful hurting expression while holding the top of her head with both hands. Then she breaks out into a smile filled with motherly love. "See you, Chaos-chan."

In the next moment, I'm surrounded by the familiar stream of light from Mithra's teleportation magic. Within moments, I'm back in the large circular room under the academy building, and my eyes take a second to adjust to the difference in lighting.

"Welcome back, Miss Marcott." A familiar voice greets me, and I spin around on the spot. Thorvald is standing at the edge of the transportation platform, and almost two dozen professors are surrounding me on all sides.

Among them I spot Basarab, Astrid, the water professor Eydis Vinterstrom, father and son earth professors Magni and Bjorn Svarteka, and even Madame Idunn is present. Then I see Kamii and Hestia, who are being held at stave-point by Aldebrand and three members of his clique.

"It is indeed a pleasure to see you back so soon." The principal says with a friendly smile. Then it disappears, and he grows serious, causing a chill to run down my back. "Now, please explain where you went."

Chapter 46

Checkmate

My mind is racing.

Time seems to be slowing down as I work my amorphous brain at maximum output to find a way out of this situation. I know that all the professors here are masters in their elements. Each one of them has their catalyst ready, and unlike with the thugs, they're on guard against the fact that I'm a demon and the possibility that my human appearance is not what it seems.

Even Thorvald is holding a small wand, of which the shaft is encrusted with colorful crystal dust. This is the first time I see his catalyst, and from its unusual appearance, which is a testament to his incredibly high level. While it rests in his hand loosely as if he's completely relaxed, I have no illusions about the fact that he's ready to cast magic the moment things turn sour. He's confident and understands that he has the advantage in this situation.

Still, it doesn't look like they will make the first move. While Aldebrand and the members of his faction are looking at me with obvious hostile glares, the principal's eyes harbor no anger or hatred. Maybe he's still hoping for a peaceful solution to all this, or he doesn't deem me worthy to receive such strong emotions from him.

However, the presence of Kamii and Hestia tells me that they came here with the intention to apprehend me, going as far as to use them as hostages to make sure I don't fight back. And the fact that they're here means the staff somehow knew I was the one who used the transportation network.

Maybe they saw Senka near the vault door and made the connection. Everybody should know through Ninlil that she's mine, so they instantly went to check on me in my room. With me absent at night, they immediately brought them here in preparation for my return. I wonder how long they've been here, and whether or not they considered the possibility that I could have just left forever.

Maybe Thorvald was convinced that I would return because leaving behind Kamii and Hestia wasn't an option. The fact that the vault door was kept open may be another hint to my intention since I could have closed it otherwise.

"Senka, where are you?" I think in my mind but receive no answer. Don't tell me she was incapacitated or worse? Maybe they knew she was actually alive and somehow tortured her into telling them everything? Somehow I can't see that happening to her, but anything seems to be possible in this world.

In either case, there's no point in thinking about how it came to this situation. The fact of the matter is that I'm here now, and there's no easy way out - unless I just run away on my own. Of course, I'd never do that.

I weigh my options under the current circumstances: I fought a group of mages and swordsmen before, but I doubt they can be compared to professors of the Royal Academy. Furthermore, the mages are far more numerous, so I'll never be able to defeat them with magic at my current level. Even the assassin mages were too much for me, and they only outnumbered me three to one.

The only choices I have are to either try talking things out to resolve this without bloodshed, or to show my real appearance in a preemptive attack. The former may waste precious time and could give them room to prepare spells under their breaths. The latter means going down a road of no return and marking myself as well as Kamii, Daica, and Hestia as the enemies of mankind.

I have to think about their safety, too. Leaving Daica aside, whom the academy may not consider a close associate of mine because I only went out to meet her once, the other two are right here. If I make the wrong move, they'll suffer the consequences. Unlike me, they don't have a convenient body that's seemingly invulnerable.

"My, what a surprise to see so many professors gathered here at this hour." I say with a sarcastically innocent smile while lifting my hands in a peaceful gesture, showing off my empty palms. Everybody knows that I don't need a catalyst to cast magic so they won't lower their guard. "Is something the matter?"

"Just a precaution; no need to worry. I-" Thorvald regains a hint of his earlier feigned friendly attitude.

"I'm not the one who seems worried." Interrupting him, I glance around and imply that all the professors surrounding me are tense.

"Ah, yes. That is because they were shaken from their sleep for a potential emergency." He explains, employing a tone that seems to ask for my understanding. "Is this an emergency?"

"You tell me, Grand Master Eklundstrom." These are fighting words, but I just have to say them. I'm at a disadvantage here, so I at least feel the need to get an edge verbally. Hestia's anxious expression as she voicelessly mouths for me to stop shows she doesn't appreciate that I'm needlessly aggravating the professors.

"I was notified that somebody had broken in here and used the transportation network. I would like to know how you were able to open the lock, but first I have to ask where you went." He stops beating around the bush and gets straight to the core of the matter with a sharp look in his eyes.

"You will find that I am full of surprises." I smile mischievously, ignoring his shift in tone. "As to where I went, I will have to keep that a secret."

"Why is that?" Going along with my stalling, the principal asks with an eyebrow raised.

"That will have to remain a secret, too." I wink at him. "But please, why don't we go to your office and sit down for a talk instead of standing around here?"

"Do you understand your situation, *demon*?" Aldebrand raises his voice in anger and gestures at Kamii and Hestia. He's signaling me that they're hostages in case I don't comply, just as I expected.

Thorvald gestures for him to shut up, but his words have already reached me. And I don't take kindly to that thinly veiled threat.

"If you touch them, I won't hesitate to kill every last one of you." I glare at the professors behind the two girls with a murderous expression, and some of them falter in fear. I'm sure they must be thinking that I possess some incredible powers to show such confidence under the current circumstances. They aren't entirely wrong about that.

"Are you sure you want to do this?" The principal may not sound like it, but he's still trying to defuse the situation and find a peaceful solution.

"That's up to you." I direct this at everybody in the

room. In reality, I'm not confident about getting out of here alive at all. But to prevent the professors from attacking, I need to put up a front.

"Chloe, do not worry about us, save yourse-" Hestia begins, but Aldebrand slaps her face to shut her up. He must have been acting under the impression that I was just grandstanding in that matter, as I was in everything else.

That was his mistake.

In an instant, my body bursts out into tentacles, and I take on my Crawling Chaos appearance. Without giving anybody time to react, I leap across the room and land a few steps from the fire professor, who instinctively raises his staff. Bridging the distance in a fraction of a second, I wrench it from his hand and pull him towards me. He stumbles and falls forward, but my entire front opens up and swallows him inside.

I'll make sure to give him a long and painful death and dissolve him slowly.

Eydis screams, and I see her drop her staff in terror before she scrambles to get away. One of Aldebrand's followers, who was pointing his catalyst at Kamii, has fallen to his bottom and soiled himself. Another is staring at me wide-eyed; his mind has gone blank at the sight of my true appearance.

"Boo!" I turn my real face to him and scare him with an almost comedic exclamation, but he turns on the spot, drops his short staff and runs away with his will completely broken.

But out of the nearly two dozen professors, only a handful lost their wits at seeing me in this form. The others point their catalysts at me and begin their incantations.

A shower of fireballs hit my back and explode, causing the tentacles that make up my skin to burst apart from the impacts before quickly mending themselves again. Their magic doesn't do much damage, but it does chip away at my mass. I spin around while spreading my arms into the individual tentacles that make them up; they turn into spikes which I extend explosively, one of each aiming to run through an enemy mage.

"Pilum Gradum!" Magni and Bjorn both step forward and erect stone pillars from the ground, which block my attacks. But they're unable to cover for all mages, and several of them are too late to create their own barriers. Five of them are skewered, two of them in places that kill them on the spot.

"Spiritia Sanctia, Servas Eon Circon Meas!" Madame Idunn quickly chants the familiar barrier spell and covers herself and two of the wounded, while the other one is shielded by the mage next to him.

Thorvald's expression is one of complete bewilderment, as he stares speechlessly at the havoc I wreaked within just seconds. Luckily for me, he's not moving his lips or aiming his wand to cast any magic. It seems he didn't think I would be such a powerful demon, or maybe he was just surprised to see me commence hostilities despite his attempt at resolving it peacefully. He only has Aldebrand to blame for that.

"Ventus Secaror!" I cast the wind-cutter spell. It's aimed at Bjorn who just came out from behind his cover and is now attempting to rush in my direction.

"Volantem Lapim!" Magni breaks off his pillar and shoots it to intercept my invisible air blade. Even though he couldn't see it, the elder Svarteka anticipated where I aimed, and the flying rock collides with the spell, causing it to shatter. The younger Svarteka rolls over the ground to avoid the deadly spray of shrapnel.

Hestia suddenly shouts out an incantation in her language which defies my hearing once again. Above her, a pure black spear appears. It flies off in the direction of a professor who's still in the process of speaking a long incantation for a large-scale spell.

"Kali Dhala!" Basarab jumps between the flying spear of darkness and its target, and a shield of black mist appears before him that swallows the spell.

At the same time, I create a shield using the tentacles of my arm and cover them in bone plates to block a volley of ice spears coming from the other side of the magic circle. They pierce my defenses nonetheless but stop short of my body. It doesn't hurt, but Kamii and Hestia are behind me, so if any spell comes through from that angle, they'll hit the two girls.

We need to get out of here. No matter how I think about it, we can't defeat them all. Even though I was able to reduce their numbers by almost half, the remaining ones won't go down so easily.

Bjorn suddenly appears right next to me and swings his fist in a hook to my body. Didn't he see me swallow Aldebrand just now? Why would he come into melee range against me?

But rather than his fist, it's a rock pillar that shoots out sideways from the ground that hits me first. I almost lose my form from the impact, as it sends me flying across the room and into the wall. Tumbling to the floor, I quickly gather myself and stand up again.

"Mico Ignis!" Astrid's voice echoes through the room. I brace myself with my shield, but the fire explosion occurs between my arm and my face.

My form bursts open, but quickly reconsolidates again. If this were only a suit made from a certain symbiote, the real body inside would have been not only exposed but also severely burned. Luckily, this is all me, although it did hurt.

"Mico Ignis!" Once again, Astrid's voice echoes through the room, but this time I'm prepared; splitting myself down the middle, I let the explosion occur in the free space between my halves, before gathering myself again and rushing forward, to return to Kamii and Hestia's side. The latter has created a black version of the barrier spell that I used in Rathgolim to protect against projectiles and is covering for the little dark elf.

"Mico Effero Flammis!" I chant a fire spell I learned from Astrid three months into my time at the academy. Normally in the form of Effero Flammis, a wave of flames that stick like napalm, I added the Mico modifier to make it remote but last less time. It's aimed across the transportation circle, where a group of five professors is clustered together.

"Sorca Inversiga." This is the first time I hear Thorvald chanting a spell. He seems to have gathered himself and is now joining the battle.

I brace myself because I don't know what his magic does, but then I realize that my Mico Effero Flammis didn't go off. Don't tell me that incantation allows him to cancel spells? I didn't hear anybody else cast anything, so that's the only explanation.

That's cheating!

"Ortum Terram!" The Svarteka father and son combination chant from both my sides, and I look at what they're doing. The ground in an area around me rises, but they obviously aren't done. "In Gremium Terram!"

They both throw their arms up as if they're flipping a table, and two giant slabs of stone flip up on both sides of me. Holding out my arms, I stop them with all my strength, but the force is too much.

"Confractum Murum!" I scream out desperately, and luckily the slabs are considered walls, as one of them crumbles away. Bjorn is in front of me and stares in surprise. Not letting this opportunity born from his carelessness slip by, I extend a massive spike that runs him through the stomach.

"Nooo!" Magni roars on the other side when he sees his son wounded by my attack. This may be the perfect opportunity to take him out as well.

Suddenly, another of Astrid's explosions rocks my vision. Just as my face gathers back together from the impact, a volley of ice spears pierces through my body. I pull them out quickly, in case the follow-up spell that causes them to shatter into tiny sharp shards is cast. The moment I do so, a burst of wind causes me to stumble sideways, where a pillar of flames shoots up and scorches the surface of my entire body. Just as the fire subsides, another explosion from Astrid throws me forward, where I receive a stone pillar from Magni to the face.

"Enough of this!" My body bursts open in rage, and I grow in size. I haven't used my Crawling Chaos voice because I feared that Kamii and Hestia could be affected by it, but I'm running out of options. Even if they can't kill me in one hit, they'll whittle away at me with all these spells one after the other. "You-"

"Gravico Slosito." I hear Thorvald's voice, and the world around me distorts as my weight increases. I spot the principal with his wand raised and pointed at me, so it's safe to assume that he's the one who cast it. This is clearly a gravity spell, which should fall under the domain of space magic.

He was the one human in the whole world who has the space affinity? Why is my luck so bad! And my larger size became my downfall too.

I set one foot before the other slowly, and stone spikes rise out of the ground from the back and the front. They move at normal speeds despite the increased gravity, and I can't dodge. Their sharp tips run me through and stay to hold me in place. Bjorn has his hand on the ground and is smiling triumphantly even while he's coughing up blood due to the hole in his stomach.

"Humans!!!" I roar, and several of the professors drop their staves to cover their ears. Surprisingly, the little dark elf and the fallen angel are both fine, although it may be thanks to the barrier protecting them even from sound waves.

Melting my form down and tearing myself free from the stone spikes, I point an arm at Thorvald, explosively extending it forward like a lance.

"Barita Spaco." He doesn't even seem too concerned about me focusing him now and speaks in a firm but level tone. The space in front of him seems to bend, and my limb is deflected by it, causing me to miss.

But I expected that he would have something like that, as I continue to extend my arm, then spread out the tentacles into individual spikes, with which I run through two of the mages standing behind the principal. One of them takes a spike through the throat, while another is pierced through the chest.

An air blade cuts into my upper arm near the shoulder from the side but is unable to sever it. Pulling back my arm, I swing it around in the same motion and form a blade along its entire length.

"Sarapi Baleda!" Basarab jumps forward and creates a curved blade of pure darkness, with which he meets mine. Even though it's made from a spell, it seems to be as solid as a real sword and blocks my swipe.

"Malferma Spaco de Sigelita Tempo." Thorvald waves his wand in my direction and chants another spell I don't know. Of course, I don't. He didn't tell me that he knows space magic in the first place, let alone teach me any.

Time around me seems to slow down, while the voices of the professors sound like a tape being sped up. My thoughts are still at normal speed, but my body doesn't want to move any faster. Rather than increasing gravity, this is practically time manipulation.

But when spells enter the area around me, they're slowed down as well. Astrid's fire magic ignites in front of my face in slow-motion, so I bend backward while growing bone plating on the surface of my skin in slow motion. At the same time, I notice that Magni has come around and is chanting something quickly. Then the ground around me rises to seal me inside with the explosion, which tells me that it's most likely bigger than any previous ones.

That's when the time-slowing magic ends, and I see from the corner of my eyes that Kamii has left Hestia's barrier and swung her arm at Thorvald, breaking his concentration. But the wall seals me in before I can react, and the fire spell explodes. The bone plating I was in the process of creating finishes just in time to block most of the damage.

"Confractum Murum!" I shout, and the wall around me crumbles to reveal Basarab standing right in front of me.

"You shall forget-" He speaks in a commanding tone and my mind blanks out for a moment.

When I come to, I find that I must have taken a few steps back. I can see that Thorvald has his wand at the ready, while another mage has grabbed Kamii's cursed arm with one hand while twisting her other behind her back. She has an expression of pain on her face.

"How dare you!" I swing my left arm around and turn it into a lance, aiming it at the professor holding her.

"Ventus Secaror!" The same professor who cast the wind blade to try and sever my arm earlier does it again. It hits the lance, but only leaves a deep gash rather than cut through it. However, it's enough to mess with my aim, and I miss my intended target.

"Hasta de Lumin!" As I pull it back, I try with magic again.

"Sorca Inversiga." Thorvald speaks the same incantation as he did when my Mico Effero Flammis didn't go off, and the spirit spear that appears above my head vanishes again. So it really was a counterspell. "Svinganto Forso."

Suddenly, Hestia comes at me from the side with her wings spread. Judging by her surprised expression, I can tell that this wasn't intentional. Was it the effect of the principal's short incantation just now?

"Pelanto Forso." He points his wand at us, and I quickly grab Hestia while spinning my body around to cover her. Expanding my entire side into a bone shield, I brace for whatever comes our way.

It comes in the form of a powerful pushing force that sends me flying across the room with the fallen angel in my arms. I expand my body to cushion our fall - especially for the girl in my arms - and find that we have landed on the transportation circle.

"Wha-" I turn to look at Thorvald in surprise.

"Goodbye, Miss Marcott." He states with a bitter expression and waves his wand at the edge of the circle.

"No, Kamii!!!" I explosively extend my arm in her direction, but it's cut off cleanly along with our surroundings in the familiar stream of light that accompanies teleportation magic.

Seconds later, we're back in real space. The temperature isn't much different from that in the academy, but I find that we'rc surrounded by sand dunes as far as the eyes can see. It's night, and there's a magnificent starry sky above us.

But I don't have the presence of mind to think about that at all. I look down to find that there's no transportation circle. At the same time, I can't for the life of me remember what the one in the academy looked like. And without that information, I can't teleport back even if

I have an entry point.

It's clear this is a place in a completely different climate zone, but I don't have the survival kit with the map inside my body, so I can't check our location. The one time a map of the whole world would have been useful, and I don't have it!

"Aaargh!" I roar at the top of my non-existent lungs and smash my massive fists into the sandy ground. Then I turn around to Hestia while turning into my human form again. "W-"

But before I can complete even a single word, I feel heat expanding from inside my body. In the next instant, my stomach and chest begin to bulge before my entire torso bursts open, and an explosion of fire belches outward.

From the opening, a ragged man jumps out, his clothes and skin melted in some parts and scorched in others. He's holding a red crystal in his hand and breathes hard with a deranged expression, compounded on by the fact that his face is barely more than a skull with eyes in the almost lidless sockets.

It's Aldebrand.

He falls to his knees, unable to support himself due to the damage his body has sustained and breathes with a rattling sound. His lungs must be damaged, as he's unable to even speak, glaring at my form.

But I'm in much worse shape. I peer down to find that the massive hole in my torso is blistering and bubbling in an attempt to alleviate the burns and mend the damage. It feels like the entire space inside my body is a single large burn.

This is the first time I've felt this much pain in both my lives. Not even all the times I fell and scraped my elbows and knees, all the times I sprained an ankle or dislocated a shoulder put together comes even close to a fraction of what I'm feeling right now.

If I were a human, I'd have died already... But I think I might actually be dying...

"How dare you!!!" Hestia screams, and her crimson eyes begin to glow in murderous hatred.

"Mico Coru-" The half dead professor is somehow able to press words through his damaged vocal cords to chant a spell and lift the fire catalyst in our direction.

Then his body freezes up before it begins to disintegrate in the breeze, falling apart and disappearing into the dust of the desert. Only his clothes and the red crystal he was holding remain, lying in the sand as a silent reminder of his erased existence.

"Chloe!" Hestia turns around to me, and I can see that her eyes are no longer glowing.

Was Aldebrand's disintegration caused by those eyes? A part of me wants to analyze it, just like it analyzed Kamii's cursed arm despite being engaged in an intense battle against the Graebern in Rathgolim. However, I'm in so much pain that the thought is quickly replaced by trying to think of a way to heal myself.

"Sano..." I mutter and try to raise my hand which is barely able to maintain its form due to my lapsing concentration. The spell doesn't work for such a huge wound, and under these circumstances, I can't recall any of the longer spells that I read in the book Arcelia gave me. I never bothered to practice them properly since they were never needed before.

Hestia begins to chant next to me, but once again, I can't comprehend the sound she makes; it seems to elude my mind rather than my hearing. When she finishes, a dark and murky aura surrounds my body, and the sense of pain begins to subside. I watch in surprise as my wounds close and the burnt parts revert to their natural state.

"Thank you, Hestia..." I say when the process is

finished and look down at my diminished body size. Enough matter was irrevocably destroyed, but at least not a single burn remains. Even my insides feel healed. "You... saved my life."

Then I pass out.

Afterword

Has it already been over half a year since the last book now? Time sure flies, especially when you're live-updating a web novel while working on an almost completely rewritten book version for earlier chapters.

This time, there's nothing to explain in regards to the names of the characters, so I'll explain something in regards to the names of the characters anyway:

The observant and Scandinavian among you may have already noticed this, but the Kingdom of Lares is pretty much Scandinavia as a whole - with Iceland thrown into the mix. Thus, the names are amalgamations of Old Norse and Old Germanic ones.

That's all, folks!

Yes, I won't waste your time with telling you my thoughts about things most would know at a glance and move directly to the acknowledgements.

As always, a big thank you to the artists of this volume's wonderful covers:

The amazing Whisper, who recently did the ebook cover for volume one. It was a painful process of trial and error with me once again because I'm just too indecisive or have impossible requests. Thank you for listening to my selfishness for all this time, and I hope this will boost your motivation to work on the next five volumes as well.

Just like last time, the paperback cover is an oil painting on canvas, and created by my very own mother. Without you, I wouldn't be here - in many senses - so I thank you from the depth of my soul.

Now, a big shoutout to you Patrons who have stuck with me from the start and those of you who joined along the way. Even though my new updates became sporadic once again, most of you have stayed with me through these times. Without your support, my motivation would have tanked long ago, so this goes out to all of you:

Doctor Fenderson Francis Fieldman the Fifth, ashadun, Dra
Sawyer Aubrey, Mark, Olinn, Erich D.
taichi1082, Cheshire Fish, Dante Perez, bannable, Demian Buckle, Chip Chamberlain, Cryostorm, Niawo N, amtrac
Sager ALSoqair, Elsydeon, Oracle, Deathbricks, C.S. Sturmer
and fifty-two more both current and former.

And once again, last but not forgotten, are all my readers from across the world! If you have been with me from the

very start, you will notice the mounting differences between the initial version and the books. Even if you came later, the web novel is still a legitimate story in itself, so you can give it a try. To those who picked up this book before volume one - quickly go back, you shouldn't be here yet! Alas, it's too late when you read this.
But to all of you I say: Welcome to the Chaos!

At this rate, volume three will be incredible. Look forward to it!

November 2018
J.J. Pavlov (Meakashi)

Printed in Great Britain
by Amazon

38944894R00246